J

Dear
Pen
Pal

SEP 17

aH

BY HEATHER VOGEL FREDERICK

The Mother-Daughter Book Club series

The Mother-Daughter Book Club

Much Ado About Anne

Dear Pen Pal

Pies & Prejudice

Home for the Holidays

Mother-Daughter Book Camp

The Spy Mice trilogy

Spy Mice: The Black Paw

Spy Mice: For Your Paws Only

Spy Mice: Goldwhiskers

Once Upon a Toad

The Voyage of Patience Goodspeed

The Education of Patience Goodspeed

Absolutely Truly

THE MOTHER-DAUGHTER BOOK CLUB

Dear
Pen
Pal

Heather Vogel Frederick

Simon & Schuster Books for Young Readers
New York London Toronto Sydney

For my life-long pen pal Cyn Keith

SIMON & SCHUSTER BOOKS FOR YOUNG READERS
An imprint of Simon & Schuster Children's Publishing Division
1230 Avenue of the Americas, New York, New York 10020
This book is a work of fiction. Any references to historical events, real people, or real locales are used fictitiously. Other names, characters, places, and incidents are products of the author's imagination, and any resemblance to actual events or locales or persons, living or dead, is entirely coincidental.
Copyright © 2009 by Heather Vogel Frederick
All rights reserved, including the right of reproduction in whole or in part in any form.
SIMON & SCHUSTER BOOKS FOR YOUNG READERS is a trademark of Simon & Schuster, Inc.
For information about special discounts for bulk purchases, please contact Simon & Schuster Special Sales at 1-866-506-1949 or business@simonandschuster.com.
The Simon & Schuster Speakers Bureau can bring authors to your live event. For more information or to book an event, contact the Simon & Schuster Speakers Bureau at 1-866-248-3049 or visit our website at www.simonspeakers.com.
Also available in a Simon & Schuster Books for Young Readers hardcover edition
Book design by Lucy Ruth Cummins
The text for this book is set in Chapparral Pro.
Manufactured in the United States of America
0316 OFF
First Simon & Schuster Books for Young Readers paperback edition September 2010
8 10 9 7
The Library of Congress has cataloged the hardcover edition as follows:
Frederick, Heather Vogel.
Dear pen pal / Heather Vogel Frederick.—1st ed.
p. cm. — (Mother-Daughter Book Club ; [3])
Summary: Four very different friends in Concord, Massachusetts, and their mothers continue their book club, reading Jean Webster's *Daddy-Long-Legs*, while getting to know their own pen pals from Wyoming
ISBN 978-1-4169-7430-7 (hc)
[1. Interpersonal relations—Fiction. 2. Mothers and daughters—Fiction. 3. Clubs—Fiction. 4. Pen pals—Fiction. 5. Books and reading—Fiction. 6. Ranch life—Wyoming—Fiction. 7. Wyoming—Fiction. 8. Concord (Mass.) —Fiction. 9. Webster, Jean, 1876–1916. Daddy-Long-Legs—Fiction.] I. Title.
PZ7.F87217De 2009
[Fic]—dc22
2009014982
ISBN 978-1-4424-0848-7 (pbk)
ISBN 978-1-4169-8258-6 (eBook)

AUTUMN

> "Don't you think it would be interesting if you really could read the story of your life—written perfectly truthfully by an omniscient author?"
>
> —Daddy-Long-Legs

Jess

> *"When you get accustomed to people or places or ways of living, and then have them suddenly snatched away, it does leave an awfully empty, gnawing sort of sensation."*
>
> —Daddy-Long-Legs

Dear Miss Delaney...

"What's this?" I ask, picking up the letter that's lying in the middle of my plate and scooching my chair closer to the table.

"I guess you'll have to read it and find out, won't you?" my mother replies. There's a funny tone in her voice and she's smiling across the table at my dad. One of those mysterious *we know something you don't* kind of smiles.

Frowning, I start to read:

"Dear Miss Delaney,

Congratulations! We're delighted to inform you that you have been nominated for a Colonial Academy Founder's Award. Created in honor of Harriett Witherspoon, the illustrious educator and suffragette who established our school, this award for academic excellence is offered each year to an outstanding local eighth-grade girl. It is indeed an honor to be nominated for this scholarship, and we hope you will accept it. Once again, congratulations—we look forward to welcoming you to our school!"

I toss the letter aside and start assembling my burger. "I don't want to go to Colonial Academy," I tell my parents matter-of-factly. "Pass the ketchup please, Dylan."

My little brother removes one sticky paw from the ear of corn he's busy gnawing and shoves the bottle over to me. I pick it up gingerly, trying to avoid the buttery smears where his fingers touched it. Out of the corner of my eye I see my parents exchange a glance.

"Honey, are you sure you understand?" says my mother. "They're offering you a full scholarship!"

"So?"

"Shouldn't you at least think it over?"

"I did," I reply, slapping the top of the bun onto my burger. "I don't want to go."

My mother glances over at my dad again, her brow puckering with concern.

I sigh. "Look," I tell them. "I want to stay at Walden Middle School with my friends. I don't want to go to some dumb boarding school with a bunch of snobby rich kids."

Dylan and Ryan start to snicker.

"Hush!" My mother frowns at them, then turns her attention to

Heather Vogel Frederick

me again. "Sweetheart, they're not snobby rich kids." She pauses. "Well, some of them are rich, that's true, but underneath they're just normal girls like you."

My mouth, which is open to take a bite of hamburger, gapes at her instead. *"Normal?* Mom, gimme a break! Have you been downtown and seen those kids? Some of them have *chauffeurs!* Their parents are movie stars and politicians and stuff like that."

"Moooovie stars!" chorus the twins.

"Boys!" my mother scolds again. "Jess, I think you're exaggerating just a tiny bit, don't you? There are plenty of wealthy people who are perfectly nice and normal. Just look at the Wongs. You'd never know they were—"

"Bazillionaires?" my dad suggests.

"Michael! I'm trying to make a point here, and you're not helping."

"Sorry," my dad says cheerfully.

"At any rate," my mother continues, "I think you're being too hasty about this decision, Jess. It's an amazing opportunity. Besides, you already spend part of your day away from Walden—I don't see how going to Colonial Academy would be all that different."

"True," says my father. "It's not like it's in China—it's right here in town."

Great. Now he's ganging up on me too. How can I make them understand why I don't want to leave Walden Middle School? Especially after it's taken me so long to fit in. Sure, they're right, I'll be taking math and science classes at Alcott High again this year, but that's hardly the same as being away from my friends all day every day. What would I do without Emma and Cassidy and Megan? Where would I sit at lunch? And how could I leave Half Moon Farm, the one place on earth I feel completely happy and safe? I like sleeping in my own bed, in my own room. I don't want to have to sleep in a dormitory, and share a room with some girl I don't even know.

I set my hamburger down on my plate. My stomach is starting to tie itself in knots. "I just don't want to go," I say flatly.

My parents are silent. The only sound in the room is coming from my brothers, who are chomping loudly on their corn. I look out the window and spot a familiar figure on a bike, riding past our farmstand. It's Kevin Mullins. He's been doing this all summer. He'll ride by, and if he spots me in the front yard he makes a beeline in my direction, telling me he was "just in the neighborhood." Which is a big lie, because he lives way up on Ripley Hill Road and my house isn't on the way to anything.

"This really is a once-in-a-lifetime opportunity," my father says. "Surely there must be some nice girls who go to Colonial Academy."

Nice? I think of the squadrons of students parading around downtown in their designer clothes, bragging to one another about their vacations to places like Nantucket and Palm Beach and Switzerland. The girls from Colonial Academy are like a whole fleet of Becca Chadwicks, only worse. At least Becca never called us "townies." I shake my head again.

But my mother isn't taking no for an answer. "Your father's right," she says. "You already know some of the students there. Lots of people here in town send their daughters to Colonial once they get to middle school and high school. There's Nicole Patterson, and that Bartlett boy's older sister—what's her name?"

"Lauren," I mutter.

"That's the one. And how about Ellery Watson? You used to play with her sometimes back in elementary school."

I can tell by the looks on their faces that my parents are really excited about this stupid Founder's Award, but accepting it is absolutely, positively out of the question. Goat Girl at a private school? I would so not fit in.

My mother places her hand on my father's arm. "Talk to her, Michael," she urges.

My dad reaches over and tugs on my braid. "At least think it over, okay? Colonial Academy is one of the best schools in the country."

"How'd they even get my name?" I grumble.

My mother reaches for a manila envelope on the sideboard behind her and pulls out a sheaf of pages. She riffles through them, then plucks one out. "Let's see here . . . award . . . Witherspoon . . . local eighth-grader. That's funny—there's no mention of who nominated you."

"Don't you think that's kind of creepy? It's like somebody's been spying on me."

My father laughs. "It just means that someone observed your academic abilities, honey. Your principal, probably, or maybe one of the guidance counselors. It would be pretty hard not to notice the smartest kid at Walden."

"I'm not the smartest," I reply sullenly. "Kevin Mullins is way smarter than I am." My eyes stray to the window. By the entrance to our driveway, Kevin is still riding around in circles.

"He didn't get nominated," says my mother. "Colonial Academy is a girls' school."

Which is another really good reason not to go, in my opinion. But I keep that thought to myself, because it's obvious my parents have their minds made up already.

My mother pulls out another sheet of paper. "They sent us an invitation to tour the academy and its facilities, followed by lunch with the headmistress. New student orientation starts soon, so we'll have to hop on this if we're going to make it happen."

"But I don't want to make it happen!" I tell her, starting to feel a little desperate. "What about my chores? Who's going to help look after the goats and the chickens and everything? Half Moon Farm needs me!"

"We'll work something out," says my dad. "The boys are going into the third grade—they're responsible enough to take over the morning milking. You did at their age."

I shoot my twin brothers a skeptical look. "Responsible" is not the first word that comes to mind when I think of Dylan and Ryan. They may be almost nine, but they act more like they're six most of the time.

My mother plucks a brochure from the pile of papers she's holding and slides it across the table to me. "Just look at this place, Jess! State-of-the-art science labs, a professional theater, a fabulous music department—you could take voice lessons again! There's even an equestrian center."

I glance down at the brochure. I didn't know Colonial Academy had horses.

"It would be kind of like getting an early taste of college," my father coaxes.

"College?" I leap to my feet. "I'm not even fourteen yet! Why are you trying to get rid of me?"

I storm upstairs and fling myself on my bed. Sugar and Spice, our two Shetland sheepdogs, are close on my heels. They pace around my room anxiously, whining. The dogs hate it when I'm upset. But how could I not be? I can't believe my parents are even seriously considering this. *Colonial Academy?* No way. I grab the phone off my night table and dial the Hawthornes' number. I need to talk to my best friend.

Emma picks up on the first ring. "Hey," she says.

"Hey back."

"Oh, it's you. Hi, Jess."

She sounds a little surprised, and I realize she was probably expecting Stewart Chadwick.

"Something awful happened," I blurt out, my voice quivering. "I got this letter from Colonial Academy and it turns out I've been nominated for some scholarship and my parents want me to go but I don't want to!"

"Whoa, hold on a sec. Run that by me again?"

I take a deep breath and repeat everything I just told her.

Emma is quiet for a long time. A really long time. So long, in fact, that I start to think maybe she's hung up on me.

"Are you still there?"

"Yeah," she replies. "I'm just thinking."

"What's there to think about? It's a horrible idea."

"I suppose," she says. "I mean, it would be horrible not to see you at school every day. But it's not like you'd be going to China or someplace."

My stomach lurches. Emma is sounding weirdly like my parents. She was the one person I thought I could count on to be on my side. "You mean you think I should go?"

My bedroom door opens a crack and my mother pokes her head in. I frown and point at the phone, but she tiptoes in anyway and places the Colonial Academy brochure at the foot of my bed, then sneaks out. She leaves it open to the picture of the stables. A beautiful chestnut mare stares at me from out of one of the stalls.

"You've got to admit it's an honor to be nominated for something like this," Emma continues. "Your mom and dad are right about that. I think you should at least go check it out. I mean, think about it— boarding school! That's pretty cool."

"Maybe I should call Cassidy and see what she thinks."

"She's still at her grandparents', remember?"

Heather Vogel Frederick

Cassidy's mother got married a couple of weeks ago and she and Stanley Kinkaid, Cassidy's new stepfather, are on their honeymoon. Cassidy and her older sister Courtney are staying with their grandparents at their condo in downtown Boston.

"I'll ask Megan, then."

"She went with the Chadwicks to Cape Cod."

It's Labor Day weekend, and most of the rest of the world is off someplace having a last blast of fun before school starts. Not us, of course. This time of year the Delaneys never budge from Half Moon Farm. Too much work to be done. The Hawthornes don't go away very often either. They're on kind of a tight budget, plus Emma's dad always says he hates fighting holiday traffic and who'd want to be anywhere but beautiful Concord this time of year anyway?

"Boarding school, Jess!" Emma repeats. "That's so awesome! Maybe I could come visit you sometime."

Perfect. Now Emma's sounding excited too. And even a little bit envious.

"Still," she adds quickly, "I'd really miss you."

"Don't worry," I tell her, shoving the brochure off the bed with my toe. "You won't have to miss me. There's no way on earth I'm ever going to Colonial Academy."

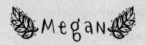

Megan

*"The school uniform reduced all to a dead level
in the matter of fashion."*
—Just Patty

It's doomsday.

I'm standing in my bedroom staring at myself in the mirror. I turn to one side, then the other. So does Mirror Megan. I push the sleeves of my polo shirt up. I pull them back down. Mirror Megan pushes her sleeves up and down too. I make a face. Mirror Megan makes one back.

"It's hopeless," I tell her. "Completely and utterly hopeless."

Absolutely nothing is going to make this hideous outfit look any better. I still can't believe that the school board voted to make us wear uniforms at Walden.

My cell phone rings. It's Becca.

"Hey," I say glumly.

"Hey," she echoes, just as glumly. "So which one did you decide to go with?"

"Polo?"

"Yeah."

"Maroon," I tell her.

"Me too. The other one is awful." Becca heaves a sigh. "Remember when picking out clothes for the first day of school used to be fun?"

"Uh-huh. This totally stinks."

"No kidding. Oops—my mom's calling. She's going to drop me off on her way to yoga. See you at school!"

"See you."

I hang up and look in the mirror again. Mirror Megan sticks out her tongue at me. Maroon is so not our color. But my only other choice—a yellow that's supposed to be gold but that's actually a revolting shade of mustard—is even worse. If they're going to make us wear uniforms, why couldn't they at least have switched our school colors to something better? Even boring old navy and white would be better than this. I close my closet door with a sigh, leaving Mirror Megan on her own to face the sea of maroon and gold and khaki that's hanging inside.

My mother, of course, thinks school uniforms are the best idea in the history of the world.

"Kids are way too fashion-conscious these days," she says. "I've been doing some research online, and all the experts agree that wearing uniforms helps students focus on their studies."

Blah blah blah. Who cares what the experts say? Everybody I know thinks school uniforms are a horrible idea. I rummage through my jewelry chest and pull out the biggest hoop earrings I can find, then add a stack of bangle bracelets and thread a rhinestone-studded belt through the loops of my khaki pants. There's no rule—yet—about accessories. I checked. For the crowning touch, I pair black-and-white-and-pink-striped socks with my new black clogs. I don't care if the colors clash with the rest of me. At least my feet will look good.

I grab my backpack and stump out of my room. Not that anyone would hear me. The floors of our house are covered with thick white carpet that muffles everything. I don't care—I stump down the hall anyway.

My parents are in the kitchen eating breakfast. My dad puts down his newspaper and smiles. "Don't you look sharp."

Sharp? Not exactly the look I'm going for here, even if it were the truth.

"Very nice, honey," agrees my mother.

I sigh. My parents totally don't get fashion. Particularly my mother. This morning she's decked out in a bright green sweatsuit that makes her look like a big peapod or something. I know she's got a yoga class later, but still. And who wears a beret unless they live in Paris, France? *Nice look, Mom,* I almost say, but the sad thing is, she'd believe me.

I sling my backpack onto the floor and slump into my seat at the table. There's something that looks suspiciously like a cinnamon roll on my plate. It smells suspiciously like a cinnamon roll too, but I poke at it cautiously with my fork, checking underneath for hidden tofu. My mother doesn't do cinnamon rolls. She doesn't believe in white sugar or flour, and

Heather Vogel Frederick

she definitely doesn't believe in frosting. Especially not for breakfast.

"What's this?" I ask.

My mother frowns and takes a bite of her oatmeal.

My dad winks at me. "A little treat for the first day of school. I was awake early, so I made a trip to the bakery."

When I was little, my father and I always used to sneak off on Saturday mornings for cinnamon rolls. They're still my favorite. "Thanks, Dad."

"Let me get you some real food," says my mother, pushing back from the table and crossing the kitchen to the refrigerator. "You need some protein to balance out all that sugar."

My father and I grin at each other.

"We've been wanting to talk to you," my mother adds, handing me a container of strawberry yogurt. Organic, of course.

I take a bite of cinnamon roll and eye her cautiously, mentally reviewing what I possibly could have done wrong now. But she's got something else on her mind besides me for once.

"We're going to be having a house guest for a while," she continues.

Uh-oh, I think. House guests are like cinnamon rolls. My mother doesn't do them. What is going on this morning?

"Who?" I ask.

"Your grandmother is coming for a visit."

I almost choke on my bite of roll. *Gigi?* My mother's mother lives in Hong Kong, and I don't think she's been to our house since I was a baby. I talk to her on the phone every few weeks or so, but the last time I saw her was when we flew over to China for a family reunion right before I started middle school.

My mother's lips are pursed as tight as a buttonhole. My father gives her a worried glance and clears his throat. "Yes, well, Gigi's getting along in years now," he says. "I feel—your mother and I feel—that she needs to be closer to family."

"Really?" I don't remember my grandmother seeming all that elderly last time I saw her, and she sure sounds fine on the phone when we talk, but maybe my parents know something I don't.

My mother starts clearing the table. She plunks the dishes into the sink with a little more oomph than usual and rattles them around noisily.

"So when's she coming?" I ask.

"Thanksgiving," my mother replies shortly. She and her mom don't get along that well. They're really different, for one thing. Actually, Gigi is different from just about every other grandmother that I've ever met.

"How long is she going to stay?"

The silverware in the sink clanks vigorously.

"Um, we're not sure," says my father, with another anxious glance at my mother's back. He takes one last sip of coffee, glances at his watch, and stands up. "If you're ready to leave, I can drop you at school on my way to work."

I'm quiet on the drive down Strawberry Hill toward town. My

Heather Vogel Frederick

dad listens to the news on the radio and I look out the window, my thoughts a mixture of dread at having to show up in front of everybody at Walden wearing what I'm wearing and curiosity as to my grandmother's upcoming visit. Mostly dread. Having to wear a uniform is almost enough to make a person want to go to Colonial Academy. Jess got out just in time. It's going to be weird, though, not having her at school with us this year. None of us thought she'd go, but her parents really wanted her to and I guess they worked out a compromise. Jess will live in the dorm during the week, and on the weekends she'll get to come home to Half Moon Farm.

We pull up by the flagpole a few minutes later and I stare gloomily out the window at the swarm of students by the school's front door. If there's one consolation, at least I won't be the only one at Walden today who looks like a complete idiot.

My dad reaches over and pats me on the leg. "Have a great day, honey, and don't sweat the uniform too much. I had to wear one to school when I was growing up, and I survived."

I shoot him a look. He laughs. "Yeah, that was back when dinosaurs roamed the earth, right?"

It takes me a while to find Becca in the crowd. When the bell rings, the two of us line up along with everyone else. Our principal, Mrs. Hanford, and vice principal, Mr. Keller, are checking us all in this morning to make sure we're wearing our uniforms.

Sure enough, some kids forgot, or didn't get the information packet the school sent out a few weeks ago, or just plain didn't want to. They get sent to the office to call their parents. Mr. Keller's eyes narrow when he sees my belt and jewelry and socks, and he scans his clipboard. There's nothing in the rules against accessories, though, which I already know, so he has to let me in. Becca is right behind me.

"Hey, guys," calls Emma, spotting us in the hallway. "Nice rhinestones, Megs. Wish I'd thought of something like that."

"There's always tomorrow," I tell her.

"And the day after that, and the day after that," adds Becca, making a face. "We're stuck with these stupid uniforms until high school. See you two at lunch."

The three of us head off in different directions. No one from our book club is in the same homeroom this year, and hardly any of us have any of the same classes except social studies and math. Lunch will be the only chance for all of us to spend time together.

Walden's hallways are awash in maroon and mustard—excuse me, "gold." The girls mostly look disgusted or embarrassed or both, and the boys—well, boys don't seem to care that much about clothes, so it's pretty much business as usual for them. They're pushing and shoving and teasing one another like they always do.

When I finally get to math class, I see that Cassidy is wearing the mustard-colored polo, which looks even worse on her than my maroon one does on me. I can't believe her mother let her out of the house in it. Cassidy's got that pale, freckled skin that lots of redheads have, and next to the shirt her face looks all yellow and sickly. It's like when Emma and I were little and used to play that game where we'd hold

Heather Vogel Frederick

dandelions under each other's chins to see if we liked butter. From the looks of Cassidy Sloane this morning, butter is her favorite food. I know better than to say anything to her though.

At lunch, I get to our table just ahead of Becca and manage to snag a seat next to Zach Norton.

"Hey, Megan," he says.

"Hey back," I reply, trying to sound casual. My heart always beats a little faster when I sit next to Zach.

He's wearing a maroon polo, just like me, only on him it looks great. Of course, Zach Norton could show up at school in a garbage bag and still look great. He's tall and blond and has gray-blue eyes that Emma once called "the color of the wind" in a poem she wrote about him, which is the perfect description. Out of the corner of my eye I see Becca heading our way with her tray, and she does not look happy. I ignore her. Becca considers Zach her private property, but from what I can tell, he's not interested in her, so she might as well let one of us sit next to him now and then and have a chance to breathe the same air that he's breathing.

Becca would never admit it, but she's pretty thrilled that being in the Mother-Daughter Book Club gives her eating rights at our table. Jess used to call our table the hybrid, because there's such a weird assortment of kids at it. Besides all of the members of our book club, there's Ashley Sanborn, who's friends with Becca and me. Jen Webster was going to sit with us, too, but she moved to St. Louis with her family over the summer, which means the Fab Three are now the Fab

Two, or Double Trouble, as Cassidy has renamed them. Zach, the most popular boy at Walden Middle School, sits at our table because he's on the baseball team with Cassidy, and his friends Ethan MacDonald and Third—Cranfield Bartlett III—sit with us because Ethan plays baseball too, and Third plays hockey with Cassidy. Cassidy is as big a jock as any guy I've ever met—bigger even, maybe. She's good at just about every sport under the sun.

I sneak a peek at Ethan and Third, who both shot up over the summer. Ethan's trimmed down a lot, too. They both look, well, good. Nowhere near Zach Norton's league, but still, not bad, either.

From the looks of it our table is going to be stuck with Kevin Mullins again this year. Kevin is Walden's resident junior genius. He grew a teeny bit over the summer, but he's still pretty short. Mostly that's because he should really be in, like, fifth grade, but he got bumped up to middle school because he's so smart. Emma says he's like a stray puppy now that Jess, his human security blanket, is at Colonial Academy, and she's right, because today he's looking even more pathetic than usual.

"Move, dwarf," Becca commands, setting her tray down next to his.

Kevin slides hastily down to make room. Emma glares at Becca, who sighs. "Just kidding, Kevin," she tells him, but he keeps his distance anyway, eyeing her warily.

Cassidy is the last to arrive. She plunks down next to Emma and opens her lunch bag.

"So what's on the menu today?" Ethan asks, leaning closer. Like me, he has a plate of Walden Middle School spaghetti, which tastes pretty much like school cafeteria spaghetti anywhere on the planet, I'm willing to bet.

Our table's big daily ritual ever since Cassidy's mom got her own cooking show on TV is to see if we can talk Cassidy into sharing her lunch with the rest of us. My mother loves packing my lunch, but I hardly ever let her do it. I'd honestly rather eat cafeteria food. There's never anything normal about a Lily Wong lunch. Brown rice is often involved, along with unpronounceable things like arugula and tahini. Could she ever just send me with a peanut-butter-and-jelly sandwich and a couple of store-bought cookies? No way.

But a Clementine Sloane lunch—oops, make that a Clementine Sloane-*Kinkaid* lunch—now that's something different. Cassidy's mother always packs leftovers from the show. Truly amazing leftovers.

Cassidy grins and makes a big show of looking into her lunch bag. "Oh, man, does that ever smell good," she says, inhaling whatever's inside.

"Dude, come on, quit playing around," whines Ethan.

"You don't have to get all worked up about it," Cassidy tells him. "It's just a ham sandwich, an apple, and some chips." She pulls out a plastic container, lifts up one of the corners, and pretends to look surprised. "Oh, and I almost forgot. A chocolate volcano cupcake."

Ethan groans. In fact, we all groan. Mrs. Sloane-Kinkaid's chocolate volcano cupcakes are *legendary*, as Emma would say.

"I especially like them after they've cooled off," Cassidy continues, obviously enjoying torturing us. "You know, when all the gooey stuff in the middle gets kind of fudgy."

The bidding for the cupcake is fast and furious, and in the end Kevin wins by offering to help Cassidy with her math homework for an entire month. Jess used to do that, and now that she's gone, Cassidy's going to need all the help she can get. So am I, for that matter. Neither of us is very good at math, and this year we're taking pre-algebra.

The rest of the day passes quickly. After the final bell, I head out to the flagpole where the buses are lined up. Mrs. Chadwick is waiting in the parking lot for Becca and Ashley, who are heading to a dance class. They invited me to take lessons with them, too, but dance just isn't my thing. Besides, I have a stack of fashion magazines waiting for me at home. I've been saving them up because I knew the first day of school was going to be a tough one, what with the uniforms and everything, and I figured I'd probably need some cheering up. Plus, there are leftover cinnamon rolls, too.

"Megan!" Emma runs up behind me, her round face flushed with excitement. "I've got a great idea—let's go surprise Jess!"

I think longingly of what's waiting at home—including the latest issue of *Flashlite*—but the chance to finally get a peek at Colonial Academy is too tempting.

"Sounds fun. Should we invite Cassidy to come too?"

Emma shakes her head. "Fall ball started today and she's at practice."

I fish my cell phone out of my backpack and call my mom to see if I can go. She says okay, and then I pass the phone to Emma, who calls her father for permission too. Mr. Hawthorne says that our plan sounds fine, and that he'll call Mrs. Delaney so she can let Jess's school know we're coming.

"Be sure and tell her to keep it a surprise," Emma says. She hangs up and passes me back my phone. "He said I should invite you and Jess to our house for dinner. He's making his famous first-day-of-school meat loaf."

Mr. Hawthorne is a writer. He works from home, and he's in charge of all the cooking at Emma's house, which is a good thing since her mom hates to cook and is almost as bad at it as my mom. My mouth starts to water just thinking about Emma's dad's meat loaf. It sure beats the heck out of the organic eggplant-and-edamame surprise that my mother is probably whipping up for our family right now, but I don't mention that when I call home again to let her know about the invitation.

When everything is settled, we head for Emma's bus, which is the only one that stops downtown. After we find a seat, I tell Emma about Gigi.

"That is so awesome, Megan!" she says, then sighs. "My grandparents live in Seattle, which isn't Hong Kong but it might as well be. They don't get to come see us very often."

A few minutes later, the bus stops by the library and the two of us get off.

"We should have gone to your house first to change," I grumble to Emma, plucking at my maroon polo shirt with its dumb Walden

Middle School logo. "I can only imagine what the Colonial Academy girls will have to say when they see these stupid uniforms."

"Too hot to walk that far," says Emma. "We'll just have to brave it."

We cross Main Street and head toward the private school's fancy iron gates. As we pass under them, I glance around curiously. Emma's been over to the campus a couple of times already to see Jess, but this is my very first visit. My mother tried to get me to take a tour back in fifth grade, and would have been thrilled if I'd wanted to go, but I said no way.

"This is the quad," Emma tells me as I follow her across a big square of green lawn surrounded by stately buildings. "And those are the dorms." She points to a row of white houses that line the far edge. "Jess lives in Witherspoon, with the other eighth graders."

It's cool and dark inside the entry hall. There are oriental rugs on the hardwood floors, and off to one side is a huge living room with a grand piano in front of a stone fireplace. On the other side of the entry hall is a small office, where a youngish woman is sitting with a baby in her lap.

"Hello, girls," she says cheerfully. "I'm Kate Crandall, the housemother here at Witherspoon. Can I help you?"

"We'd like to see Jess Delaney," Emma replies politely. "I'm Emma Hawthorne, and this is Megan Wong."

Jess's housemother smiles. "Oh, yes, of course. You've been here before, haven't you, Emma? Mrs. Delaney just called to tell me that you two would be stopping by."

Emma waggles her fingers at the baby on Mrs. Crandall's lap. "Hi, Maggie!"

Heather Vogel Frederick

Maggie gives her a toothless grin and kicks her feet happily.

"Hey, look—she matches my socks." I point at Maggie's black-and-pink-and-white-striped T-shirt and black corduroy jumper, then pull up one of my pant legs and stick out my foot.

Mrs. Crandall inspects my ankle. "You two look like you belong together."

She holds Maggie out to me and I take her carefully. I don't have much experience with babies. Maggie is heavier than she looks, and wiggly. I hold her close, worried that she might slip out of my grasp. She smells good, like shampoo and soap. "She's a really cute baby," I say, leaning down to sniff her hair. Maggie reaches up a chubby hand and tugs on one of my hoop earrings.

"Oops, I should have warned you," says Jess's housemother, quickly disentangling us and taking her back again. "Maggie has a thing for jewelry."

"She's pretty stylish, for a baby," I tell her. "I like her outfit."

"Why, thank you," says Mrs. Crandall. "I'll take that as a real compliment, coming from you. You're pretty stylish yourself."

I make a face and Mrs. Crandall laughs. "Ah yes, the controversial school uniforms. I read about them in the local paper."

Maggie bounces up and down in her mother's arms again, and watching her, I find myself suddenly itching to pull out my sketchbook. Would it be really weird if I added baby clothes to my future fashion line?

"Have fun tonight," Mrs. Crandall tells us, and Emma and I say good-bye to Maggie, who waves her plump fist at us in response.

"Mrs. Crandall is really nice," I whisper to Emma as we start up the stairs.

"I know," Emma whispers back. "Her husband is Jess's math teacher."

"Their baby is cute too."

Emma nods. "Jess babysits for them a lot."

I feel a pang of envy. I've never babysat for anybody. Not once. Nobody's ever asked me to. Maybe since I'm an only child, people figure I wouldn't know what to do with a baby. Which is probably true. Emma and Jess both babysit. They took a training class together at our local rec center, but that was back in sixth grade when the three of us weren't getting along, so I wouldn't have gone with them even if they had invited me to.

I wonder if maybe Jess would let me babysit with her sometime. I really wish I wasn't an only child, but my parents—well, my mother anyway; I've never really talked to my dad about it—only wanted one kid. My mother says the planet is overpopulated. She is really determined to help save the earth, so it will probably always just be Mirror Megan and me.

At the top of the stairs, there's a long hallway stretching in both directions. Emma turns left, and I follow her down to the last room at the very end. She flings open the door without knocking, startling Jess, who is sitting at her desk.

"Surprise!" we both cry.

Heather Vogel Frederick

Jess takes one look at our uniforms and bursts out laughing.

"Thanks a bunch," I say crossly. Even though Jess isn't dressed in anything special, just shorts and flip-flops and an old T-shirt she got when our book club went to see *Little Women* on Broadway, she looks as pretty as always. She has deep blue eyes and this amazingly thick blond hair that she's worn in a braid down her back forever. I'd love to have hair like Jess's, but then she always says that about mine. I don't know why she thinks my straight black hair is anything special, but she told me once it's as shiny as anthracite. Of course I had to ask what that was, and she explained that it's a kind of glossy black coal. I know she was trying to pay me a compliment, but *coal*? Oh well, that's Jess. She loves rocks and minerals and anything to do with science.

"This is the first time I've been happy that I'm here instead of Walden," Jess tells us with a grin. "I am so glad Colonial doesn't make us wear uniforms!"

Emma looks around the room. "Where's Savannah?"

"Downtown shopping with a friend."

"Good," says Emma, relaxing visibly. "We've come to rescue you from her clutches. Dinner is at my house tonight. It's all arranged. You just have to be back by eight for study hall."

"Awesome." Jess closes the textbook on her desk.

"What classes will be you be taking?" I ask. School hasn't started yet at Colonial Academy, but Jess has been here for a few days already for new student orientation.

"Civics—that's what they call social studies here. Plus I have Honors

English, Algebra II, Environmental Studies, Latin, and Chorus. You know, the usual stuff."

Usual for a brainiac like Jess, maybe. I'm not in honors anything, and there's no way I could do high school math and science yet, let alone Latin.

"So how's it going?" I ask, looking around the room, which seems really nice. It's a big corner room with windows on both sides, and there are two twin beds, two desks, two dressers, and two closets. You can tell which side of the room belongs to Jess, because she has posters of animals on the walls.

Jess shrugs. "It's okay. I really, really miss you guys, though."

"Have you made any new friends yet?"

"A couple."

Jess is a whole lot less shy than she used to be, but I can imagine how hard it must be for her, starting over at a new school. It would be hard for me, and I'm not shy at all. Plus, from what Emma has told us, her roommate is not exactly friend material.

"I want to hear more about Savannah Sinclair," I say. "Is her dad really a senator?"

Jess nods. "Uh-huh. From Georgia."

"So what's she like?"

"Um, she's new this year, like me," she replies, a little cautiously.

"And?" I prod. "Emma tells us she's kind of a pain, right?"

Jess nods again.

"C'mon, tell her what you heard yesterday at lunch," Emma urges.

Heather Vogel Frederick

Jess sighs. "Look, you guys, I'm really trying to make the best of this. I don't know why on earth the school decided to stick the two of us together—Savannah is . . . she's, well, she's like Becca Chadwick used to be, only worse."

"A whole lot worse," adds Emma.

"Yeah," Jess agrees unhappily. "Anyway, yesterday I heard some of the other girls talking, and apparently she got kicked out of her last school. I guess she flunked out. She's here on academic probation."

"Wow." My grades aren't fantastic, but even I've never flunked anything. Digesting this news, I cross the room to the dresser on the far side and inspect the collection of silver-framed photos displayed on it. "Is this her?" I ask, pointing to one of them.

"Yeah," says Jess.

I pick up the picture and study it for a moment. It's a black-and-white close-up that looks like a professional photographer took it. "Nice clothes, but she totally has a fivehead."

Emma stares at me, shocked, then starts to laugh. "Megan, that is *so mean!*"

I grin. "You know I'm right, though."

"What's a fivehead?" asks Jess, puzzled.

I point to the picture, which shows Savannah wearing her hair swept back off her face. "Bigger than a forehead."

Jess starts to giggle too. I pick up another picture, this one of a distinguished-looking silver-haired man and an ultra-chic blond woman. There's something scrawled across the bottom of it, and I peer at it more closely. *For our darling Savannah, from Daddy and Poppy with all our love.*

"Her parents?" I ask, and Jess nods.

Across the room, the door opens and I turn to see two girls standing there. "Don't touch my things," commands one of them in a steely Southern accent.

I quickly set the photos back down on the dresser. Savannah Sinclair is tall, almost as tall as Cassidy, with a long mane of chestnut brown hair. She's wearing designer jeans and the exact same dove gray T-shirt the model on the cover of the new *Flashlite* that's waiting for me at home is wearing, plus really expensive boots—I know, because I saw some just like them at the mall last weekend. It's a little too early in the season for boots, but something tells me I shouldn't point that out to her.

"So are these the friends you've been telling me about, Jessica?" drawls Savannah. "From your mommy-daughter *book club?*" She gives Emma and me a scornful glance. "Which one is Clementine's daughter?"

Cassidy's mother used to be a supermodel, the kind that everybody knows just by their first name.

"Uh, Cassidy didn't come," Jess replies. "She's at baseball practice. You've met Emma before, though, and this is Megan Wong."

Savannah flicks her eyes up and down my uniform. "I thought you said Megan was a fashion designer."

I feel my face flush with embarrassment.

"We came straight from school," says Emma defensively. "We didn't have time to change."

"I would die before I'd go to a school that made me wear something like *that*," says Savannah, folding her arms across her chest and leaning against the doorway. "Wouldn't you, Peyton?"

"Absolutely," agrees her friend.

The five of us stand there, glaring at one another, until Emma grabs her backpack. "Time to go," she tells Jess and me, and we grab our things and stalk out of the room behind her.

"Fivehead," I whisper, but only when we're safely out of earshot. It's hard to hurl a good comeback at someone like Savannah when you're wearing something as ridiculous as I am. "Sheesh, Jess, how can you stand her?"

"I don't have a choice," Jess says gloomily. "We're stuck with the roommate they assign us for the whole year. Some stupid school philosophy about learning to get along with others."

"With Savannah Sinclair?" I reply. "Good luck."

"Too bad Becca and Cassidy aren't here," Emma says. "They'd have cut her down to size."

We cheer up at this thought, and, laughing about what our friends might have said or done, the three of us head across town toward Lowell Road, and Mr. Hawthorne's waiting meat loaf.

CASSIDY

"Nothing so fosters facility in literary expression as letter writing."
—Daddy-Long-Legs

"So Jess, how's it going at Colonial Academy?" asks my mom.

Our whole Mother-Daughter Book Club—except for the Chadwicks, who are late—is crammed into the Hawthornes' little kitchen, getting ready for our first meeting of fall. We're having a potluck supper—potluck because Mrs. Hawthorne joked that no one would come if she offered to do the cooking. Emma's dad is away for the weekend at some football jamboree with Emma's older brother, Darcy.

Jess's eyes slide over to Emma and Megan and me. "Um, okay I guess."

Which isn't exactly true. Jess likes her classes, and she's made a couple of new friends, but she really, really doesn't like rooming with Savannah Sinclair. I haven't met her yet, but from what Emma and Megan have told me, Savannah's main goal in life seems to be to make Jess miserable. She's constantly making snarky comments about her

Heather Vogel Frederick

clothes, which—let's face it—can't compete with a senator's daughter's wardrobe, not that that should matter. It didn't help that Jess accidentally wore her barn jacket back to the dorm last Sunday night after being home over the weekend. I guess Savannah kicked up a huge fuss and complained to their housemother about how stinky Jess was and how she couldn't possibly be expected to share a room with a girl like her. Emma did a funny impression of Savannah's tantrum at our lunch table yesterday, complete with Southern accent, but even though I laughed, it still made me mad. Jess has been through enough in that department, what with the way Becca and her wannabees used to call her "Goat Girl."

"Jess is still settling in, aren't you, honey?" Mrs. Delaney says as she arranges a platter of crackers and goat cheese and fresh vegetables from their farm. "Her father and I are very proud of her, though. It takes a lot of courage to try something new—especially a new school. But of course it's a wonderful opportunity."

Mrs. Wong nods. "Wonderful," she agrees, taking some plastic wrap off a bowl of brown and green noodles. It's probably supposed to be a salad, but you can never tell with Mrs. Wong. She's always bringing weird stuff. For all I know, it's dessert. She glances over at Megan and sighs deeply. It's no secret that Mrs. Wong always wanted Megan to go to Colonial Academy.

Megan picks up a carrot stick. "Don't get any ideas, Mom," she says, reading her thoughts. "Besides, it's not like I could get in with my grades."

I grin at her. Unlike Jess, who's practically a prodigy, and Emma, who's pretty smart, too, except for math, Megan and I are probably tied for bottom place in our class. Maybe not quite the bottom, but let's just say our report cards aren't the kind that parents stick on the refrigerator.

"So," says Mrs. Hawthorne, "tells us about your roommate, Jess."

Jess fidgets with her long blond braid, letting her gaze wander around the room. She loves the Hawthornes' pink kitchen. I'm not a big fan of pink—too girly—but even I have to admit it's kind of cheerful. Emma's dad is always threatening to sneak down in the middle of the night and paint it some other color. "Something more manly," he says, arguing that he's really entitled, since he does all the cooking. But he only says it to tease Mrs. Hawthorne. This is her dream kitchen and he knows it. Mrs. Hawthorne got the idea from a house she stayed at in England when she was a college student. It had a pink kitchen, and she decided that when she had a house of her own someday, she'd paint her kitchen walls that color too.

"Jess?" says Mrs. Delaney. "Mrs. Hawthorne asked you a question."

"Sorry," Jess replies, snapping out of her daydream. Jess drifts off like that sometimes. I always figure she's solving equations or something.

Jess looks over at Emma's mother and smiles politely. "My roommate's name is Savannah Sinclair."

"Do you like her?"

"Um . . ." She hesitates, and looks over at Emma and Megan and me again.

How could she even begin to explain Savannah Sinclair? Like us, Savannah is in the eighth grade. But unlike us, Savannah comes from a Very Distinguished Family. We know this because she's told Jess so at least seventy-five times already. To hear Savannah tell it, she says, the Sinclairs not only came over on the Mayflower but actually built it, and then single-handedly founded the United States once they landed on Plymouth Rock, which they seem to have had a hand in placing conveniently near the shore too.

"Savannah's father is a senator," Mrs. Delaney tells our moms. "From Georgia."

Mrs. Wong raises her eyebrows. "Oh," she says. "*That* Sinclair. Wow. Well, I'm sure it will be very educational rooming with his daughter. You'll learn a lot."

Jess shrugs. So far, all she's learned from Savannah is that she was right about Colonial Academy. The students are a bunch of rich snobs.

"Cassidy, would you open these for me?" asks my mother, passing me a paper bag full of plastic containers. She puts the slow cooker we brought onto the counter and plugs it in.

"Mmmm," says Mrs. Hawthorne, lifting the lid and taking an appreciative sniff. "It smells fantastic, Clementine. What is it?"

"Tortilla soup," my mother replies. "We're taping the Super Bowl special this week, and I thought this would be a fun alternative for viewers to the traditional corn-dogs-and-nachos junk-food binge."

My mother has her own TV show—*Cooking with Clementine*.

It's kind of a hassle, because our house is the set, and there are always film crew people around redecorating everything, depending on what season is the focus of each episode. But the food really helps make up for it.

"It has a vegetarian base," my mother continues, going into full TV-host mode. She smiles at Mrs. Wong. "That's for you, Lily." Megan's mom doesn't eat meat, or much of anything else for that matter, and what she does eat has to be organic and natural and all that stuff. "Then I brought toppings for us to choose from. There's chicken, and shrimp, and grated cheese, and avocado, and corn, and cilantro. Oh, and tortilla strips, of course."

My stomach growls. "Can we eat soon?" I beg. "I'm starving!"

"Me too," echoes Emma. "I wish Becca and her mother would hurry up and get here."

Right on cue, the doorbell rings. Emma races down the hall to answer it. We can hear her talking to the Chadwicks, and then—

"Let the party begin!" cries Mrs. Chadwick, flinging her hands into the air and striking a pose as she makes a grand entrance.

There's a shocked silence as we all turn and stare. Becca slinks in behind her.

"Do you like it?" Mrs. Chadwick asks, twirling around. She's draped in some sort of a flowy leopard-print top over black leggings, and it swishes out as she spins. Melville, the Hawthorne's cat, runs for cover.

"Uh . . . ," my mother begins.

"It's a whole new me, right?" trills Mrs. Chadwick.

Heather Vogel Frederick

"You can say that again," I mutter under my breath, and my mother shoots me a warning look.

"I took Stewart down to New York for his first modeling gig over the weekend," Mrs. Chadwick continues. "They call photo shoots 'gigs,' you know."

My mother raises an eyebrow. "You don't say," she notes drily. She used to be a model, a really famous one, before my sister and I came along, and before Dad died and before we moved here to Concord and she got her own TV show. "How did it go?"

Stewart Chadwick is Becca's older brother, and Emma's boyfriend—well, sort of. Emma keeps saying they're just friends, but I've spotted them holding hands a few times when they don't think anybody's looking. Stewart's kind of dorky, but last spring, when we put on a fashion show to help raise money to pay the taxes on Jess's family's farm, he got "discovered," as they call it, by the editors at *Flash* magazine. Now he's working part-time as a model for their teen spin-off, *Flashlite*.

"Wolfgang said Stewart handled it like a pro," Mrs. Chadwick brags. "He was a bit overwhelmed at first, you know, but he's a Chadwick and we Chadwicks are made of stern stuff."

Very stern, I mouth to Jess, whose lips quirk up in a smile. Mrs. Chadwick is known around Concord for her sharp tongue.

"Anyway, I had a chat with Wolfgang afterward, and he gave me some fashion advice."

Wolfgang is the fashion director at *Flash*, one of the magazines my mom used to work for. My sister, Courtney, calls him "Mr. Hip."

I can only imagine what he thought of Mrs. Chadwick.

"He convinced me that I needed a new look," Mrs. Chadwick continues.

"New look" doesn't even begin to cover it. Becca's mother's blond hair used to be poufed up into one of those bouffant things that look sort of like a football helmet, one you maybe take off at night and set on the bedside table. Now it's about two inches long and spiked up all over her head. She looks like a porcupine. A really big porcupine. Mrs. Chadwick has been working out more—she's in the same yoga class now with all our moms—but she's still on the large side.

"It's very, um, fresh," says Mrs. Delaney politely.

"Fun," adds Mrs. Hawthorne.

"Quirky," offers Mrs. Wong.

"Lively," echoes my mother.

Emma elbows me in the side. Our mothers are playing the synonym game. The Hawthornes invented it—they play it at dinner all the time. Emma's family is crazy about books and words and stuff. I guess that's what happens when your mom's a librarian and your dad's a writer. Kind of like the way my mom talks about fashion and food and decorating all the time. Only I'm not crazy about that stuff at all and we haven't made up a game about it.

Mrs. Chadwick doesn't seem to notice. She laughs, a strange tinkling sound compared to her usual foghorn guffaw. "Wolfgang says I need to connect with my playful side."

She bats her pale, robin's-egg-blue eyes. Emma's father says that in addition to her temper, Mrs. Chadwick has a piercing gaze that can pin a poor unsuspecting sap to the wall at forty paces. Right now, though, that gaze is peeking out at us from behind a pair of glasses whose leopard-print pattern matches her shirt. I squint at her. And are those rhinestones sparkling in the corners of the frames?

My mom is biting her lip. I can tell she's trying not to smile. Mrs. Hawthorne and Mrs. Delaney suddenly get really busy rearranging the crackers on the platter. Becca looks like she wants to crawl under the kitchen table. It must be hard having someone like Calliope Chadwick for your mother. Especially the new and improved Calliope Chadwick.

New and improved Calliope Chadwick turns to her daughter. "Smile, Becca," she barks, sounding more like her old self.

Becca jumps, startled, then bares her teeth at us.

"You got your braces off!" exclaims Mrs. Wong.

Becca gives us a real smile this time. "Yeah."

"Congratulations!" says Mrs. Hawthorne. "I remember when Darcy got his off—it was a big deal."

I slap Becca a high five. "No more metalmouth!"

"And you've done something with your hair, too," notes my mother. She puts a finger under Becca's chin, turning her head this way and that. "Highlights?"

Becca nods.

"Flatiron?"

Becca nods again.

My mother nods back approvingly. "Very nice."

Becca looks ridiculously pleased. I guess for some people, getting a compliment from a former supermodel is a big deal. I frown, looking at Becca's hair. I honestly can't tell the difference. It looks the same as always to me. But then, I'm about as clueless about anything to do with fashion as, well, Mrs. Chadwick. Okay, maybe not *that* bad.

Mrs. Chadwick puts a big round loaf of bread on the counter. "I picked up some sourdough for us from Nashoba Brook Bakery."

My stomach growls again. "Can we eat now?" I plead.

"Cassidy Ann," warns my mother. "Manners!"

"No, no, she's right—we're all hungry," says Mrs. Hawthorne. She passes a bowl to Mrs. Chadwick. "You first, glamour-puss. We can continue our conversation in the dining room."

I get in line at the counter with Emma, who makes goggle-eyes at me behind her mother's back. "Glamour-puss?" she whispers.

I extend my fingers like claws and paw at the air, growling softly. We start to snicker.

"Shut up," snaps Becca.

We take our bowls into the dining room, where Emma has made a big WELCOME BACK TO BOOK CLUB—YEAR THREE! banner and hung it between the front windows. Once we're seated, Mrs. Hawthorne turns to the Chadwicks. "We were discussing Jess's first month at Colonial Academy," she tells them.

"Ah," says Becca's mother, flashing Jess a curious glance. "How do you like it?"

Heather Vogel Frederick

Jess stares down at her soup. "Fine," she replies softly.

"I always wanted to go to boarding school," Mrs. Hawthorne says, smiling at her. "Ever since I read *The Secret Language*—are you familiar with that book?"

Jess shakes her head. Emma nods, of course. I swear she's read every book ever written. In fact, her family probably *owns* every book ever written. They have bookshelves everywhere—even right here in the dining room.

"Oh, wow! I haven't thought of that story in years!" exclaims Mrs. Delaney. "Remember 'ick-en-spick'?

"And 'lee-bossa'?" adds Mrs. Hawthorne.

"Sounds like fun," says Mrs. Wong. "Maybe we should read it this year for book club."

"No way," says Emma. "Sorry, Mrs. Wong, but it's for, like, third graders. But it's still a great book. You can borrow it if you want, Jess."

"So are you having fun staying in the dorm?" asks Mrs. Chadwick. I guess Becca hasn't brought her up to speed yet on Savannah Sinclair.

"Well," says Jess, with a cautious glance at her mother, who is beaming proudly, "I haven't had much time for fun yet. Mostly I just go to classes and do homework."

"Tell us about your classes," Mrs. Hawthorne prods.

Jess musters a little more enthusiasm. "They're really good. I like all my teachers so far, especially Mr. Crandall, my math teacher. I'm taking Algebra II—"

"I'll bet you miss Kevin Mullins," I say, teasing her a little. "He sure misses you."

At Walden, Jess and Kevin used to take the bus up to Alcott High every day together for advanced math and science classes.

Jess turns bright red, and Emma kicks me under the table.

"What?" I demand.

Emma shakes her head at me and frowns, like I'm supposed to know what she's all worked up about. I shrug and stuff another piece of sourdough bread into my mouth.

"You were saying, Jess?" Mrs. Hawthorne says smoothly.

"Besides Algebra II, I'm taking Environmental Studies, and Civics and Honors English. Oh, and Latin and Chorus too."

Mrs. Chadwick is looking at Becca with the same wistful expression that Megan's mom had on her face a few minutes ago. It occurs to me that maybe Mrs. Chadwick wanted Becca to go to Colonial Academy too. But Becca couldn't get into Colonial Academy in a million years. School is not Becca Chadwick's number one priority. That would be boys, with clothes a close second.

"How about extracurricular activities?" asks my mother.

"I'm taking voice lessons, and they make everybody do sports of some kind." Jess wrinkles her nose.

I can't believe there are people who don't like sports—I play baseball and ice hockey and just about everything else—but there are and Jess is one of them.

"I'm learning how to ride English-style," she continues.

Heather Vogel Frederick

"The Academy has its own stable," explains Mrs. Delaney.

"Wow," says Mrs. Wong. "That's great, Jess!"

After dinner, we all go into the living room and my mother brings out an album of pictures from her honeymoon. She and Stanley Kinkaid—my new stepfather, but I'm still getting used to thinking of him as that—went on a cruise to Canada.

"I want to go to Prince Edward Island someday too," says Emma, as everyone crowds around the sofa for a look.

"Is that you and Stanley?" Jess asks my mother, pointing to one of the photos.

As if it could be anybody else. How many other six-foot-tall former models are married to short, bald accountants?

My mother nods. "It was so romantic on the ship," she says, and everybody sighs. Everybody but me, of course. I don't particularly want to think about romance when it comes to my mom and Stanley Kinkaid. Not that I don't like him—he's a good guy and everything—but I'm still not comfortable having him around all the time.

Everyone oohs and aahs at the pictures of the farmhouse that was the inspiration for Green Gables, the home of Matthew and Marilla Cuthbert and Anne Shirley in the *Anne of Green Gables* books we read last year. They were okay books, I guess. Actually, they were pretty good. But I'm still hoping we read something a little different this year. More action, and that kind of stuff.

"So, shall we get down to business?" Mrs. Hawthorne asks, after everyone has seen the album. "We got to talking after yoga class—"

Beside me, Emma groans quietly. I slouch down in my chair and pick at the scab on my knee. Our moms do not have a good track record with ideas sparked at yoga class.

"We know we promised that this year you'd get to choose the books we read, but after I heard about Jess going to Colonial Academy I told Shannon and Clementine and Lily and Calliope that we just have to read *Daddy-Long-Legs*!"

Our moms all nod in agreement.

"Now we're talking!" I exclaim, sitting up straighter. "Finally, something besides all this girl stuff. So is it about other kinds of spiders too? Or just daddy longlegs?"

On the sofa beside me, Becca shudders. "I hate spiders."

"Me too," says Megan.

Jess looks wary, and Emma starts to giggle.

"Um, actually, Cassidy, I hate to disappoint you, but the book has nothing to do with spiders," says Mrs. Hawthorne.

I slump back in my seat again. Of course it doesn't. I should have known better.

"Come on, honey, you've got to give it a chance," says my mother. "Phoebe promises we're all going to love it."

"It was one of my absolute favorites when I was your age," Mrs. Hawthorne tells us. "It's about an orphan girl who goes to college thanks to a secret benefactor—"

"Kind of like Jess, at Colonial Academy?" says Megan.

"Exactly," Mrs. Hawthorne replies. "That's what made me think

Heather Vogel Frederick

of it. The whole story unfolds through the orphan's letters to this mystery man, whom she calls 'Daddy-Long-Legs.'" She rummages in the canvas bag propped next to her chair. "We've come up with another idea too," she continues. "I got an e-mail from an old college friend over the summer, and it turns out Melanie and her daughter are also in a mother-daughter book club. I called her up and we agreed that it might be fun to team up this year and read the same books together, then write one another about what we're reading. You can all be pen pals!"

Megan gives her a blank look. "Pen pals?"

"You know," says Emma, "someone you write to and they write you back."

Megan still looks puzzled. "You mean like texting them or something?"

Her mother shakes her head. "Nope. Just good old-fashioned snail mail."

"With envelopes and stamps?" I blurt out, horrified.

"Exactly," says Mrs. Hawthorne.

I turn to my mother. "Mom!" I protest. "No way! That's like homework! I have enough to do between sports and school without having to write letters to someone I don't even know."

"We're only asking you to write each other once a month," my mother explains. "We know how busy you all are."

"Can't we just use IM or something?" Becca pleads. "Letters are lame."

"Nonsense," her mother retorts. "We talked it over and agreed. We want you girls to learn the art of writing real live pen-and-ink letters."

"But that's so old-fashioned!" wails Becca. "Nobody writes letters anymore!"

"Well, you all are going to," says Mrs. Hawthorne in her no-nonsense librarian voice that means *quit whining*. My mother has a voice like that too, only I call it her Queen Clementine voice. "Every civilized person on this planet should be able to write a real letter." She pulls a stack of envelopes out of the canvas bag on the floor by her chair. "And I have your first letters from your new pen pals right here. We'll start with you, Becca. We've paired you up with Zoe Winchester."

She passes a pink envelope to Becca, who reluctantly opens it and takes out the picture that's tucked inside. Mrs. Chadwick leans over her shoulder, peering through her leopard-print glasses at a girl with shoulder-length brown hair and a lot of lip gloss. "She's really pretty, don't you think?" she says encouragingly. "Her mother is the mayor, too."

"Mayor of what?" says Becca sullenly.

"The town where she and the other girls all live," Mrs. Hawthorne explains. "Gopher Hole, Wyoming."

I start to laugh. I laugh so hard I fall off my chair. "Gopher Hole?" I finally manage to wheeze. "Are you kidding me?"

Mrs. Wong whips out a map. Megan's mother loves maps. "See for yourself," she tells us, pointing to a minuscule black dot. "Gopher Hole—halfway between Laramie and Cheyenne."

Emma and Jess and Megan and Becca and I all stare at the dot.

Heather Vogel Frederick

"The Wild West!" says Mrs. Wong. "Won't this be fun?"

Megan flashes her mother a *you have got to be kidding me* look, which is exactly how I'm feeling.

Mrs. Hawthorne holds up another letter. "Cassidy, your pen pal is Winky Parker."

"Winky?" I frown. "What kind of a stupid name is that?"

My mother nudges me with her foot. "Manners!" she whispers.

"Apparently her real name is Wilhemina," Mrs. Hawthorne explains.

"Cute nickname," says Mrs. Delaney.

I snort. *Cute?* I guess if my name were Wilhemina, I'd want a nickname too, but what human being would want to be called Winky? It's like something you'd name a kitten, not an actual live person.

"Her parents own a dude ranch," Mrs. Hawthorne continues, passing me an envelope. "See the return address? Gopher Creek Guest Ranch."

I take the letter grudgingly. At least the envelope's not pink. The photo inside reveals a girl with short dark hair and a big grin. She's perched on a black horse with a white smudge on its nose and she's wearing jeans, a red gingham shirt, and an actual cowboy hat. I flip it over. *Winky riding Bingo* is written on the back. Great. Her horse's name is just as stupid as hers. Possibly even more stupid.

"Winky's an athlete like you, Cassidy," Mrs. Hawthorne continues. "She's a rodeo princess, and her mother tells me she's won all sorts of ribbons and prizes."

"Athlete" and "princess" are not two words that I would ever put together in the same sentence. That would be like calling me a "hockey princess." I shake my head in disgust.

Mrs. Hawthorne distributes the other letters. Jess's pen pal is Madison Daniels, the daughter of an art history professor at the University of Wyoming. Her picture shows a girl with molasses-brown skin and a round, friendly face. Her hair is braided in rows and she's playing what looks like an electric guitar.

"See, Jess?" says her mother. "You two have something in common—music."

Emma is paired up with Bailey Jacobs, the daughter of Mrs. Hawthorne's college friend. The photo shows the two of them standing in front of a bookstore. They're both wearing pony tails and identical smiles.

"Hey, Bailey's mom's bookstore is called 'Shelf Life,'" says Emma. "That's really clever!" She's the only one of us who's sounding the least bit excited about this whole pen pal thing. Figures.

Mrs. Hawthorne hands the last envelope to Megan. "Yours is from Summer Williams," she tells her. "We picked her for you because she likes to sew."

"Isn't that perfect, honey?" says Mrs. Wong. "You two will have tons to write about."

"Perfect," mutters Megan. She opens the envelope and stares glumly at the enclosed picture of a tall, sturdy girl in overalls. She has waist-length blond hair and is standing next to a quilt with a blue ribbon on it. Megan and Becca exchange a glance. The expressions on their faces echo what I'm feeling, which is not thrilled. Really, really not thrilled.

Heather Vogel Frederick

"Can we trade pen pals with someone else, Mrs. H?" asks Megan.

"Megan!" exclaims her mother, shocked. "That is incredibly rude! Summer's already written you a letter!"

"We tried our best to match you girls up with a pen pal you'd have something in common with," says Mrs. Hawthorne, looking a little disappointed that we're not all more excited about her scheme. "I know they may not be perfect matches, but let's give it a try here, okay?"

The living room is quiet as the five of us read over our letters and look at the photos of our pen pals. Emma is the only one smiling.

"What's for dessert?" I ask finally, breaking the silence.

"Kimball Farm," Mrs. Hawthorne replies. "My treat."

This announcement cheers us up a little. Ice cream at Kimball Farm is a tradition for our book club's kickoff meeting.

As we head out the door, I shove the envelope from Winky of Gopher Hole into my back pocket.

Final score? Cassidy—0. Winky Parker—0. It's totally a tie for last place.

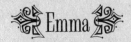

Emma

> "It's awfully hard for me not to tell everything I know. I'm a very confiding soul by nature, if I didn't have you to tell things to, I'd burst."
>
> —Daddy-Long-Legs

"Emma!"

Way off in the distance, I hear my mother's voice. It doesn't really register, though, because I'm reading. My mother always says that when I've got my nose in a book, the house could burn down around me and I wouldn't notice. She's right, mostly. My ears actually do hear her words, but my eyes and most of the rest of me stays glued to the words on the pages. I hate tearing myself away from a good story, and *Daddy-Long-Legs,* which is what I'm reading now, is definitely a good story.

"Emma! Telephone!" This time her voice gets through to me, especially when she adds, "It's Stewart!"

"Okay!" I close the book reluctantly and uncurl myself from my favorite armchair.

"It's Stewart!" mocks Darcy in a high, syrupy voice.

Heather Vogel Frederick

I aim a swat at him as I pass the sofa, but he's expecting it and holds up his history book like a shield, so I smack my hand against its hard cover instead.

"Ouch!"

"Serves you right," he says smugly.

I glare at him. Brothers can be so lame sometimes. Usually I don't mind being related to Darcy, but lately he's really been bugging me. For some reason he can't resist teasing me about Stewart, and it's useless to try and tease him back—girls have liked Darcy since he was practically in diapers, so it's no big deal to him.

I pad across the front hall to my dad's office and pick up the receiver. "Hey."

"Hey," says Stewart. There's a click as my mom hangs up the extension in the kitchen. "What's up?"

"Not much," I tell him. "I'm just reading."

"Anything good?"

"Yeah. You probably wouldn't like it, though."

"Why not?"

"Well, it's for book club, for starters."

"Oh," he says. "Another girl book?"

"Yup. It's pretty funny, though. It's called *Daddy-Long-Legs* and it's about this orphan girl named Jerusha—"

"*Jerusha?*"

"The lady who runs the orphanage picked her name off a tombstone."

"Sheesh."

"No kidding. Anyway, Jerusha changes her name to Judy when she gets to college." I explain to Stewart how one of the trustees pays for her education, in exchange for her writing to him each month. "Her letters are really funny, and she illustrates them with these hilarious drawings."

"Sounds kind of good," Stewart says.

"You can read it when I'm done, if you want."

"I might."

We talk for a while, mostly about books and school and skating. I take figure skating lessons at the same rink where Stewart practices hockey. We're both pretty terrible, but we keep trying anyway. Stewart calls us "gluttons for punishment."

"Do you want to hear my latest poem?" I ask him.

"Sure."

"It's about how I feel when I'm skating." I read it to him, and when I'm done, he's quiet. I've learned not to panic when he does that and assume that he doesn't like something. He's just thinking it over. Stewart can be really serious when something's important, which is one of the things I like about him so much, and the reason that he's one of the few people I share my poetry with these days.

"It's really good, Emma," he says finally. "I especially like that line about 'flying on frozen dreams.'"

"Yeah, that's my favorite bit too."

"Hey, I almost forgot! Congratulations on getting elected editor of

Heather Vogel Frederick

the *Walden Woodsman*. I knew you would. You're the best writer at your school by far."

"Thanks," I reply shyly. I was pretty surprised when Ms. Nielson, the faculty advisor for our middle school newspaper, made the announcement. I'd assumed it would be Becca Chadwick, because she's so popular.

"So I guess I'll see you tomorrow then." Stewart gets community service credit at Alcott High for being a student advisor for the *Woodsman*, and tomorrow's our regular weekly meeting. "Maybe we can take the bus home together."

"Okay." I feel my face getting warm, and I'm glad Darcy's not here to notice. Stewart lives just down the street from me, and when we take the after-school bus home from our meetings, he always holds my hand.

I guess Stewart is my boyfriend. He's a boy, after all, and he's my friend. But we haven't kissed or anything like that, so maybe that disqualifies us. We're both kind of shy in that department. Mostly we just talk, and sometimes we go for walks, and sometimes we go to the movies or the rink together. Everybody at school teases me about him, though, and some of the other girls are even jealous. Which is kind of hilarious, actually, since absolutely nobody liked Stewart last year at all. Except me.

Last year, Stewart was just part of the wallpaper—Becca Chadwick's dorky older brother, in his highwater pants and scratched-up glasses. But then, the ugly duckling morphed into a swan, as my mother puts it. Now that he's done some modeling for *Flashlite*, it's like Stewart's a celebrity or something. Last week two sixth graders hung around after school and waited until our editorial meeting was finished, then took pictures of him with their cell phones. Poor Stewart was mortified.

"So Becca told me tomorrow is 'Donuts with Dads,'" says Stewart.

"Uh-huh."

"I wish they had that at Alcott. I sure miss those pumpkin donuts."

Walden Middle School is big on traditions, and "Donuts with Dads" has been around forever. Every year, a couple of weeks before Halloween, we're all invited to bring our fathers to school for breakfast. In the winter we have "Granola with Grandparents"—which I never get to go to, because my dad's parents aren't alive anymore, and my mom's parents live so far away—and then in the spring there's "Muffins with Moms." They're pretty nerdy traditions, I suppose, but like Stewart, I'll probably miss them too, when I move up to high school next year.

I glance around my dad's office as Stewart and I launch into a discussion about our favorite donuts. My father is a writer—book reviews and author interviews and feature articles for newspapers and magazines, mostly. He's working on a novel of his own, though, too. I want an office like his someday, with bookshelves everywhere and a comfortable chair like the one I'm sitting in, and a desk cluttered with slips of paper with interesting things written on them like "character arc" and "put real plums in the imaginary cake" and "Zelda Malone." That last one is probably a name for a character, I'm guessing.

Heather Vogel Frederick

Right now, my office is a notebook. I carry it with me just about everywhere I go, to keep track of stuff I overhear people say, things that might make good bits of dialogue, plus interesting words I learn, descriptions of things, lines of poetry, good names for characters— that sort of thing. I'm careful not to keep my finished poems in it, though. Not after what happened in sixth grade. That's when Becca Chadwick got ahold of one of my notebooks and read a poem aloud that I'd written about Zach Norton, my former crush. She read it right in front of him, and it still makes me squirm to think about it. These days Stewart and my dad are the main ones that I let read my finished poems, along with my mom and Jess, of course.

Not that I've seen much of Jess lately. She stays really busy during the week with homework and her singing and riding lessons. She's made a couple of new friends, too—some girl from San Francisco named Adele and another one from New York named Francesca, who goes by Frankie. This is great, of course, especially since she's stuck with such a loser roommate. I'm not jealous, it's just that I miss her a lot. I didn't think it would be that big of a deal, Jess going to boarding school, especially since Colonial Academy is right here in Concord. But it is. It still feels strange not having my best friend with me at Walden. I keep looking for her in the hallways, and expecting her to sit beside me in homeroom and at lunch. School's just not as much fun without her there, even though I get to see her on the weekends and talk to her almost every weeknight. Jess's parents got her a cell phone so she can keep in touch with them and with all of us, plus Colonial Academy issues all of its students laptop computers. That almost makes me want to go there, except of course my family couldn't afford it and I doubt I'd qualify for a scholarship. So for now I'm stuck sharing the computer in the kitchen with Mom and Darcy.

Behind me, the office door opens a crack and my mom pokes her head in. "Emma, it's past bedtime," she says. "You have an early morning tomorrow with your dad. Better say good night to Stewart now."

"Okay," I reply. She closes the door again and I relay her message to Stewart.

"I'll see you tomorrow after school, then," he says, and we say good-bye and hang up.

I'm smiling as I head upstairs to my room. Talking to Stewart always makes me happy, plus there's the prospect of pumpkin donuts for breakfast and the possibility of hand-holding on the bus ride home tomorrow.

That happy feeling lasts until exactly 8:37 the next morning.

"There you are, Emma!" Mrs. Hanford, our principal, swoops down on me as I'm standing in line for my donuts and juice. She's holding one of the orange programs they handed out at the door. "I've been looking all over for you! Are you ready? We need to get started."

I stare at her blankly. "Ready for what?"

"Oh my." Mrs. Hanford looks surprised. "Didn't Ms. Nielson tell you? As our school newspaper's new editor, you're supposed to give a little welcome speech this morning."

Pure, hot terror spikes through me. *"What?!"*

Heather Vogel Frederick

My dad, who is across the buffet table drinking coffee and chatting with Mr. Wong, glances over and lifts an eyebrow.

"Uh, Rosalie?" Mrs. Hanford turns and crooks her finger at Ms. Nielson, who is deep in conversation with Becca Chadwick's father. Ms. Nielson's smile fades when she spots me.

"Oh my goodness, Emma!" she gasps. "I completely forgot!"

"This is not good." Mrs. Hanford looks from Ms. Nielson to me and back again. "Not good at all. It's already printed on the program." She flaps the piece of orange paper back and forth like a distress signal.

The two of them stand there, looking worried. Not half as worried as me, though. I feel like I'm going to cry.

"You'll just have to wing it," Mrs. Hanford says firmly. Before I can protest, she grips me by the shoulder and propels me toward the makeshift stage that's set up at the far end of the cafeteria. I throw my dad a desperate glance and point frantically at the program he's holding. He looks down at it, frowning.

Ms. Nielson trots along beside us. "You'll be fine, Emma," she whispers. "Keep it short and sweet, and just mention three things—school spirit, the importance of student involvement, and our special offer for *Woodsman* subscribers if they sign up today. It's a good fundraiser, and the dads are always happy to chip in."

Three things, I think to myself, *just three things*.

"Good morning, everyone!" The microphone Mrs. Hanford is holding squeals, and I cringe, along with everyone else in the cafeteria. Mr. Keller, who's not only our vice principal and football coach but also the one in charge of all the A/V stuff, rushes to fix the feedback.

I stare out at the crowded cafeteria as all sorts of crazy thoughts rush through my mind. Like Stewart riding in on a white horse and carrying me away. Or maybe Cassidy picking up the mental message I'm trying to send her to pull the fire alarm. I don't care how much trouble we'd be in, anything would be better than a slow, humiliating death in front of the entire school. Which is exactly what's going to happen to me in about thirty seconds. It's not that I'm shy, like Jess— although she's nowhere near as bad as she used to be—it's just that I really, really hate public speaking. I've always dreaded oral reports, and I don't like being the center of attention. I'm a writer. Writers are the quiet ones, my dad always says. The observers. We're not happy being thrust into the spotlight.

I glance over at the table where all my friends are sitting, completely oblivious to my plight. Megan and Becca and Ashley are talking and laughing, and Cassidy is busy pelting Zach and Ethan and Third with bits of donut. Third is sitting beside his dad, Cranfield Bartlett II, and for a split second I wonder whether people call him "Second." Next to Mr. Bartlett is Kevin Mullins, who's got his finger up his nose. Nice.

Except for the finger, Kevin looks exactly like his dad. They're both really pale, with dark hair worn in identical bowl cuts and big, owlish glasses. Mr. Mullins is pretty shrimpy too. Cassidy's started referring to Kevin as "the world's smallest stalker," after Jess and I explained how he's been loitering around Half Moon Farm. He developed a big

Heather Vogel Frederick

crush on Jess over the summer, and he hardly knows what to do with himself now that she's at Colonial Academy.

Mr. Keller finishes fiddling with the amplifier and gives Mrs. Hanford a nod. She taps the microphone, then lifts it to her mouth again. "Is everyone enjoying the donuts?"

The response is deafening. The boys all stamp their feet and everybody claps and cheers. Over by the buffet table, I see my dad and Mr. Wong hoist their coffee cups in a salute.

Mrs. Hanford beams. "Wonderful," she says. "I'd like to thank the PTA for organizing this year's event. It's always such a treat to spend time with our Walden families."

She blabs on for a while about the importance of parents being involved in their children's education, and what a fine school Walden is, and how the new school uniform policy has already proved a great success.

Megan catches my eye and makes a face when she hears this. I grimace back at her. Success according to the school board, maybe, but it's been a huge failure as far as we're all concerned. It still makes me mad that none of the students were asked for their input. Couldn't they have let us vote or something?

"Here to help me welcome you all this morning, and with a few announcements of her own, is the new editor of our school newspaper, Emma Hawthorne!"

Just three things. I cling desperately to Ms. Nielson's words as Mrs. Hanford passes me the microphone. The applause dies down and I take a deep breath, trying to quell the rising tide of panic that's threatening to drown me. For the life of me, I can't remember what the three things are I'm supposed to talk about. School uniforms, maybe? No, that wasn't it.

"Uh, good morning," I say, my voice sounding unnaturally loud. I wince and lower the microphone a little.

"Good morning!" everyone choruses back.

"Welcome to Walden Middle School." There's a long pause while I try to think of something else to say. "I'm Emma Hawthorne."

I'm stalling for time, and it shows. Across the room, someone snickers. I force myself to smile. "Uh . . ." My face is bright red by now, and my palms are slick with perspiration. I grip the microphone more tightly.

Then I remember! I'm supposed to say something about the paper. A few more seconds tick by as I try and remember exactly what. "I, uh, really hope you'll read our school newspaper. I'm the editor. It's called the *Walden Woodsman*."

Like they don't know its name. There's a polite patter of applause, which would be encouraging if it wasn't so pathetic. Even Kevin Mullins looks like he feels sorry for me, which is about as sad as it gets. I wish the floor would open and swallow me up.

I stand there like a lump. A lump in a ridiculously ugly school uniform—why oh why did I decide to wear the gold polo today of all days? This must be how Jerusha Abbott felt in *Daddy-Long-Legs* when she had to wear the John Grier Home's horrible blue-and-white

Heather Vogel Frederick

gingham orphanage dresses that she hated so much. There's nothing helpful about feeling ugly.

"Uh . . ." My mind is a complete and utter blank. I try to think of something else to say but I can't. I flick a glance at Mrs. Hanford. Her lips are pressed together, and her arms are folded tightly across her chest. Mr. Keller's arms are like that too, but that's his usual stance. Still, he looks a little more belligerent than usual. Even Ms. Nielson's smile looks like it's been plastered onto her face.

Squirming inside, I cast around frantically for something else to say. Did Ms. Nielson mention something about school spirit?

"Go, Walden!" I finish weakly.

Mrs. Hanford lunges for the microphone, and I hand it to her in relief. Somehow I manage to stumble back to where my dad is still standing with Mr. Wong. I can't face my friends right now.

"It's not my fault!" I whisper. "They didn't tell me I was supposed to make a speech!"

My dad puts his arm around me and gives me a squeeze. "It wasn't that bad," he whispers back, which is a complete lie.

"It was a train wreck," I moan, my eyes filling with tears.

My dad gives me another squeeze. "Okay, so you tanked. Big deal. It happens to the best of us."

I shake my head. "I'm never going to live this down."

After my dad leaves, the day spirals from bad to worse. As if it's not humiliating enough that half the school is doing imitations of my big nosedive, I get a B minus on the English paper I worked really, really hard on and thought for sure would earn an A.

At lunch, my friends can see how upset I still am, and they're nice enough not to mention my speech. Even Becca manages to resist the temptation, and Cassidy tries to cheer me up by offering me her dessert.

"It's pie week," she announces, passing me a plastic container.

Zach stares at her, incredulous. "Your mom is doing an entire show on pie?"

"Yeah," says Cassidy. "So what?"

"So what?" echoes Zach. "So what kinds of pie?"

Cassidy shrugs. "I dunno. Coconut cream, I think, and strawberry rhubarb. Apple, cherry, lemon meringue, and maybe blueberry streusel, too."

Normally I'd be drooling like crazy at a list like this, but today my stomach's so tied up in knots it doesn't even register.

Zach scoots back from the table and runs around to where Cassidy is sitting. Everybody near us stops talking and cranes to look as he gets down on one knee and reaches for her hand. Cassidy snatches it away, scowling, so Zach clasps both of his hands together instead and folds them to his chest. "Cassidy," he begs, "can I come live at your house?"

Everybody laughs except me, and as the conversation picks up again Zach goes back to his seat. I slide the container over to him without comment.

"Really?" he says, amazed at his luck.

Heather Vogel Frederick

I nod and he opens the container. "Mmm, cherry! Emma, you are the best! Thanks!"

If Zach had told me last year that I was the best, I'd have been over the moon. Today I don't even care.

At our editorial meeting after school, I can barely look Ms. Nielson in the eye. It's not that I'm mad at her, exactly—especially since she's apologized about a hundred times—it's just that every time I look at her I feel embarrassed all over again. She keeps our meeting short and sweet, just like my speech should have been, and I barely get a chance to talk to Stewart. Right as the meeting finishes Mrs. Chadwick shows up to take him to a dentist appointment, which means I won't get to ride the bus home with him like we'd planned, and it turns out he won't be at the rink later either.

"Sorry, Em," he says. "I promised Mom I'd help her and Becca get ready for tonight."

At least I have book club to look forward to. It's our first one ever at the Chadwicks'.

Becca gets a funny look on her face, and it occurs to me that she's worried her mother will embarrass her, which she probably will. I look over at Mrs. Chadwick. I'd be embarrassed too, if my mother showed up at school in a zebra-print jumpsuit.

"It'll be fine," I whisper to her. "Relax."

Becca shoots me a look. "You are so clueless sometimes, Emma," she tells me, and stomps out after Stewart and her mother.

Puzzled and hurt, I head for the school bus, which lets me off at the skating rink. My dismal day continues, because I have absolutely the worst skating lesson ever. I spend most of the time sitting on the ice, and not on purpose. Finally, when I manage to stay upright for more than ten seconds, I catch my toe and stumble, sending my glasses flying and me flying after them. As I land, I hear a crunch.

"Oh, no!" I cry. Glasses are expensive. My parents are not going to be thrilled about this.

Mrs. Bergson puts her hands on her hips and shakes her head. "This just isn't your day, is it?" she says, but not unkindly.

The tears, which I've been fighting all day, finally start to spill over.

"Oh, dear," says Mrs. Bergson. She fishes in the pocket of her fleece jacket and pulls out a hankie. A real cloth one, with flowers on it. I didn't know anybody even used that kind any more. But then, Mrs. Bergson is really old. "I'll trade you," she says, taking my broken glasses from me. "Wipe your tears, now. It's nothing to get upset about. We all have an off day every now and then."

I find myself pouring out my tale of woe to her, and when I'm done she pats me on the shoulder. "You've had enough skating for today," she says. "What you need is some cocoa."

She leads me over to the snack bar and buys me a cup of hot chocolate, and we sit side by side in the mostly empty bleachers. I slant a glance at her as she tinkers with my glasses. Mrs. Bergson has short white hair and wrinkled skin that looks tan all year long and really bright blue eyes. My dad calls her "spry," which is a good word to describe her. I remind myself to add it to my notebook later.

Free skate starts, and some hockey players start to drift in, including my brother. I spot him out on the ice and he waves his hockey stick at me. I give him a halfhearted wave back.

"Better?" asks Mrs. Bergson after I finish my cocoa.

I nod.

"Good. You take it easy now, and I'll see you next week." She passes me back my glasses, which she's managed to repair with a little duct tape.

I offer her the soggy hankie in return, but she waves it away. "Keep it," she tells me. "Maybe it will help bring you better luck."

But it doesn't.

I promised to pick Jess up at school on the way from the rink to our book club meeting, and when I get to her dorm the very first person I run into is Savannah Sinclair.

"Oh, it's you," she says, looking at me as if I was something icky she just stepped in. I'm suddenly acutely aware of my duct-taped glasses, which probably make me look even dorkier than Kevin Mullins, and the fact that my hair is all sweaty from skating and the long walk over here, and that it's stuck every which way to my head. Savannah, of course, looks like she just stepped off the front cover of some glossy magazine. "Jess isn't here," she tells me, crossing the entry hall toward the stairs. "She's finishing up down at the stable."

I retreat to Mrs. Crandall's office.

"Well, hello, Emma," she says, looking up from some forms she's filling out and smiling at me. "Nice to see you. Waiting for Jess?"

I nod. I still can't believe how young and pretty Mrs. Crandall is. Somehow I'd thought of a housemother as somebody a lot older, with gray hair up in a bun like Mrs. Lippett, the stern head of the orphanage in *Daddy-Long-Legs*. But Mrs. Crandall's hair is brown, like mine. It's curly like mine too, but she wears hers shoulder-length. Looking at it, I wonder if maybe I should grow mine out.

Jess finally shows up, and after changing out of her riding clothes into clean jeans and a sweatshirt, she walks with me over to Hubbard Street to get Cassidy and Mrs. Sloane. I mean Mrs. Sloane-Kinkaid. I'm still adjusting to her new name. Cassidy and her family live in this cool old Victorian house, and there's a light on in the turret, which probably means Cassidy is up there. It's her favorite hangout.

"Is Cassidy ready?" I ask, when Courtney answers the door.

"She'll be down in a minute," she replies. Courtney is Cassidy's older sister. She's a senior in high school this year and looks just like her mother, with the same long straight blond hair and huge blue eyes. Cassidy, on the other hand, with her red hair and gray eyes and freckles, looks like a stray that they picked up somewhere. Or an orphan. But she's not—she just takes after her dad. Her real dad, not Stanley Kinkaid.

"Hurry up, Cassidy!" Jess yells up the stairs. "It's book club time!"

"Shhhh," Courtney shushes her. "My mother's napping."

"Isn't she coming tonight?" I ask, disappointed. Book club won't be the same without Mrs. Sloane-Kinkaid.

Heather Vogel Frederick

"Yeah, but she's going to be a little late. She asked me to see if you guys would mind taking over a few of the leftover pies."

"Sure," Jess replies. "No problem."

I don't tell Courtney that with the way my luck is going today, I'll probably drop them.

We follow her down the hall to the kitchen. Mrs. Sloane—I mean Mrs. Sloane-Kinkaid; am I ever going to get that straight?—did some remodeling before her TV show started this season, and they have this big professional refrigerator now with glass doors. Jess and I peer longingly at the row of pies on the middle shelf.

"I'm starving," says Jess.

"Me too," I add, feeling hungry for the first time all day.

While Courtney packs up the pies, I browse through the stack of college catalogs that are piled on the kitchen counter. "Have you decided yet where you want to apply?"

"UCLA is my top choice," Courtney replies. "I really miss California."

The Sloanes moved out here to New England from Laguna Beach a couple of years ago, after Cassidy and Courtney's dad died. I fish the UCLA catalog out of the stack and leaf through it. They have a lot of writing classes. Maybe I'll think about going there someday.

"Cassidy will miss you if you go all the way to California," says Jess.

Courtney laughs. "I'm not so sure about that," she replies. "She'll probably be glad to get me out of her hair."

Cassidy and her sister argue a lot, but I think Jess is right. Darcy's a pretty good big brother, but if I had a big sister, I'd want her to be just like Courtney.

Cassidy finally slumps into the kitchen. She doesn't say a word in reply to our greetings, just plucks a jacket off one of the pegs in the mudroom and pulls it on. I guess she's having a bad day too.

"Tell Mrs. Chadwick that Mom will be over soon, okay?" Courtney says, loading us up with bags of pies and shooing us out the back door.

It's dark outside, and chilly now, with Halloween only a few weeks away. Normally, Cassidy's mother would have the house all decked out for the holiday, but I don't see even a single pumpkin on the steps. Weird.

The three of us walk as fast as we can without endangering our cargo, cutting over on Walden to Main Street, and from there to Monument Square. Becca and Stewart live on Lowell Road, just past the Colonial Inn. Cassidy's still really quiet, but Jess and I chatter away, and we're breathless by the time we reach the Chadwick's house.

"There you are, girls!" says Mrs. Chadwick. "We were beginning to worry that you weren't coming." She peers past us into the darkness. "Where's Clementine?"

"Mom will be over in a little while," Cassidy tells her. "She's napping."

Mrs. Chadwick frowns, then crosses to the foot of the stairs.

"Check out her earrings," Jess whispers.

"How could I miss them?" I whisper back. Dangling from Mrs.

Heather Vogel Frederick

Chadwick's ears are a pair of tiny monkeys eating peeled bananas, and every step she takes sets them swaying vigorously.

I overheard my mom and dad talking about Mrs. Chadwick recently, and my dad said something about a "midlife crisis." I don't know exactly what that entails, but I wonder if it involves jungle prints and exotic earrings.

"Rebecca!" Mrs. Chadwick bellows. She hasn't gotten the "it's a whole new me" thing down pat yet in the voice department. "Your friends are here!"

Becca clatters downstairs a moment later, followed by Stewart and Yo-Yo, the Chadwick family's big, friendly Labradoodle. Yo-Yo makes a beeline for the bags of pies we're carrying.

"Down, boy!" says Stewart, grabbing his collar. He tosses me a smile, and for the first time all day I start feeling like maybe the world isn't such a terrible place. I smile back at him.

"What's in the bags?" Becca asks.

"Pies," Jess tells her.

Mrs. Chadwick looks at us suspiciously over the top of her leopard-print glasses. "Pies?"

"Leftovers from *Cooking with Clementine,*" Cassidy explains, still sounding grumpy.

Mrs. Chadwick purses her lips. "I already have our meal planned. Pie is not on the menu."

"Oh, come on, Calliope, you can never have too much dessert," says Jess's mom, opening the front door behind us and letting herself in. Mrs. Wong and Megan are right behind her. "There's always room for pie." She gives Jess a hug and a kiss. "Hi, honey! How's your week going?"

Mrs. Chadwick still looks annoyed. "Well, put them on the counter in the kitchen out of Yo-Yo's reach. And Stewart, put Yo-Yo in the basement before he gets into something. I don't trust him around food."

"I don't trust me around food either," Jess whispers as Stewart coaxes Yo-Yo away from the grocery bags. "I can't believe how hungry horseback riding makes me."

"What's for dinner?" I ask Becca.

Becca gets the same look on her face she had earlier at our editorial meeting. Her eyes slide away from mine. "You'll see."

Uh-oh, I think. This doesn't sound promising.

Mr. Chadwick appears and builds a fire for us in the living room, then disappears again. Dads usually tend to make themselves scarce when it's book club time. "A little too much female energy," my father says. We gather around the hearth to wait for Cassidy's mother. The Chadwicks' house is kind of stuffy and formal—Mrs. Chadwick really likes antiques—but the flicker of flames in the fireplace helps make it a little cozier. A few minutes later the doorbell rings.

"Sorry I'm late," says Mrs. Sloane-Kinkaid.

Mrs. Chadwick takes her coat, then nods at Becca. "If you'll excuse Rebecca and me, we need to leave you for a few minutes," she says. "Stewart? Will you take over as host?"

As Becca and her mother vanish upstairs, Stewart leads us out of the living room and across the hall. "Welcome to the John Grier Home!" he announces, not sounding too happy about it. He slides open the pocket doors to the dining room.

We all stand there, openmouthed. The Chadwicks' formal dining room is barely recognizable. The walls have been stripped of the paintings that usually hang on them, and there's not a curtain in sight, just a big paper banner over the windows that reads JOHN GRIER HOME. The table is completely bare except for a metal cup, bowl, and spoon at each place, along with a blue gingham napkin.

"Are those Boy Scout mess kits?" asks Mrs. Wong, looking closely at the place settings.

"Mom had me borrow a bunch from my friends," Stewart replies. "She said something about them being like the tin plates they used at the orphanage in the book you're reading."

"What is your mother up to?" I whisper to him.

"She made me promise not to tell," he whispers back.

Megan and Jess exchange a worried look.

"I thought it would be fun to do a theme night," says Mrs. Chadwick from behind us. We turn around to see her standing there in a shapeless gray dress. Her hair is gray and shapeless too. She's wearing a wig, its locks piled up in a bun. She forgot about her earrings, though, and the monkeys swing mischievously with every turn of her head, undermining the stern effect. "You may call me Mrs. Lippett, and you are all my charges."

"Very clever, Calliope," says my mother, but I don't think it's clever at all, especially when I think about what the orphans at the John Grier Home actually ate.

"Rebecca!" Mrs. Chadwick trumpets once we're seated. "We're ready!"

Becca skulks in through the doorway. She's wearing a blue gingham dress and carrying a tray with a pitcher on it and a big metal bowl.

"Ah," says Mrs. Delaney. "The orphanage uniform. Of course."

Mrs. Chadwick beams proudly.

Becca moves around the table, filling our tin cups with water and ladling spoonfuls of something that looks like pale yellow oatmeal into each of our bowl.

"Dig in, everyone!" says Mrs. Chadwick. "It's cornmeal mush."

Across from me, Cassidy's mother spoons up a bite, turns pale, and excuses herself hastily. Cassidy watches her go, a peculiar expression on her face.

"Did orphans really eat this stuff?" asks Jess, prodding at the glop with her spoon.

"Well, in Jean Webster's books they did," says Mrs. Chadwick, sounding defensive. She looks over at Becca, whose face is aflame with embarrassment. Now I understand why she was so huffy at our editorial meeting this afternoon. This is almost as humiliating as my speech.

"I thought that by serving what the orphans might have eaten, you girls would gain a better understanding of those less fortunate than you are," Mrs. Chadwick continues stiffly. "It might interest you

Heather Vogel Frederick

to know that the money I would have ordinarily spent on dinner I've set aside to donate to a charitable cause."

Mrs. Wong brightens at this, naturally. "What a wonderful idea, Calliope!"

"Are there orphans in Concord?" asks Megan. "Maybe we can give them the money."

"I don't think so, although there is a family shelter I'm sure could use some help," my mother tells her. "These days there aren't many orphanages, as every effort is made to place children in need with foster families. The orphanages that do still exist are nothing at all like the grim institutions they used to be."

"Maybe we could donate some to the Concord Animal Shelter, too," Jess suggests. "That's sort of like an orphanage. I mean, people drop off kittens and puppies and hope that they'll be able to find a good home."

"That's a nice idea," Mrs. Wong says, and everyone nods, even Mrs. Chadwick.

I look at my mother hopefully. "Don't you just hate the thought of orphan animals?"

"Yes, Emma, and no, Emma, you may not have a puppy," she replies automatically.

I've been wanting a dog for as long as I can remember, and my parents have said no for just as long.

Mrs. Sloane-Kinkaid returns to the table and takes her seat while the rest of us poke dolefully at our bowls.

"Perhaps it's time for dessert," suggests Mrs. Delaney. "What do you think, Calliope?"

"I don't recall the orphans in *Daddy-Long-Legs* ever eating pie," says Mrs. Chadwick with a wounded sniff. She looks around the table at our hopeful faces. "Oh, very well, if you all feel that strongly about it," she says crossly, throwing down her gingham napkin and sounding more like her old waspish self. She excuses herself and trundles off, the monkeys and their bananas bobbing indignantly.

"How about we all sneak out for pizza later?" Mrs. Delaney whispers, when she's out of earshot. "My treat." She puts her arm around Becca's shoulders and gives her a squeeze. "No offense to your mom, of course. Her heart is in the right place."

Becca doesn't answer.

"It could be worse," Jess tells her. "You weren't at the first book club meeting at my house. My dad tried to get us to wear lilac crowns and do the dance of the maypole maidens."

The corners of Becca's mouth quirk up. "Really?"

"Really," says Jess, and we all start to laugh, remembering. We're still laughing when Mrs. Chadwick returns with the pies.

"What's so funny?" she demands suspiciously.

"Nothing," says my mother. "Just a happy memory. What do you think about dessert in front of the fire, Calliope—I mean, Mrs. Lippett? Don't our orphans deserve a little warmth?"

"And can I please take this stupid dress off now, Mom?" asks Becca.

Heather Vogel Frederick

Her mother sighs. "Oh, why not," she says. "We've abandoned everything else."

Mrs. Chadwick is still sulking as my mother passes around our monthly handouts.

Fun Facts About Jean

1) Jean Webster was born July 24, 1876, in Fredonia, New York, and christened Alice Jane Chandler Webster.

2) Her great-uncle was Mark Twain, author of *Tom Sawyer* and *Huckleberry Finn*. A big fan of cigars, Twain was "the smokiest man I'd ever met," Jean would later recall. She also told an interviewer, "I am not sure that my grand-uncle's fame as an author was really a spur to my own ambition. As a child I was always trying to write something even before I had a very clear idea of what the word 'author' meant."

3) While attending Lady Jane Grey boarding school in Binghamton, New York, Webster changed her name to Jean to avoid confusion with her roommate, who was also named Alice.

"Hey look," I point out. "Jean changed her name at school, just like Jerusha changed hers to Judy in *Daddy-Long-Legs*."

"A lot of authors get ideas for their stories from real life," says my mother.

I remember the name "Zelda Malone" on the slip of paper in my father's office, and wonder if the novel he's working on is based on any real people. He's been really secretive about his book, and it's driving my mother nuts.

Megan puts her page into her binder. "I'll bet Jean Webster knew someone like Savannah when she was at school," she says. "Don't you think she'd have to, to invent a snooty roommate like Julia Pendleton for Judy Abbott?"

"Interesting point, Megan," says my mother.

"Maybe we should start calling Savannah 'Julia,'" Megan adds, and Cassidy and Jess and I all snicker. Becca gets kind of quiet, though, and Mrs. Chadwick frowns and opens her mouth like she's going to say something, but takes a bite of pie instead.

"At least Judy had Sallie McBride, too," I note. "If I ever have a roommate I want one just like her."

We talk about the characters in the story for a while, and agree that Judy Abbott is a kindred spirit, just like Anne Shirley was last year. We talk about how much we like her, and how much we can't stand Julia Pendleton and her obsession with her superior family tree.

"I love what Judy wrote about Julia's family coming over in the ark," I say, "and her father's side dating back further than Adam."

"That's *just* like Savannah!" Jess exclaims, and Mrs. Chadwick gets a funny look on her face again.

Heather Vogel Frederick

"So what was your favorite part of the book so far, girls?" Mrs. Hawthorne asks us.

Before I can stop it, my hand shoots up.

"Emma!" everybody choruses.

I snatch my hand down again. "I can't help it," I tell them, and it's true. Our third year of book club, and I still can't break the habit.

Becca smirks at me, and I squelch a sudden urge to throw my plate of pie at her. Once a Chadwick, always a Chadwick, I think, and then I feel guilty because Stewart is a Chadwick too.

"So what was it you were going to say, sweetheart?" my mother asks.

"Oh, just that I really liked this part." I open my book and start to read: "'You can't know how I dreaded appearing in school in those miserable poor-box dresses. I was perfectly sure to be put down in class next to the girl who first owned my dress, and she would whisper and giggle and point it out to the others.'"

Jess gives me a sympathetic smile, but my mother looks puzzled. Doesn't she remember making me wear all those clothes from Nicole Patterson? The only good thing about having to wear school uniforms is that now I don't get stuck with all her hand-me-downs. My eyes flick over to Becca, who's looking a little sheepish. She should. She knows exactly what I'm talking about, because she's the one who used to tease me about wearing Nicole's cast-offs.

"So who else has some comments about the book so far?" my mother asks.

The room is quiet. I look around at my friends. Jess is fiddling with the carpet. Cassidy is suddenly very intent on her pie. And Megan and Becca are trying not to look at each other.

"Wait a minute, didn't you guys do the rest of the reading?" I say in disbelief.

"I've been really, really busy," Jess says. "You don't know how tough some of my classes are. Plus, there's Savannah to deal with. . . ." Her voice trails off.

"I tried, but I'm getting behind in math now that Jess is gone," says Cassidy. "I almost flunked the last test, even after Kevin tried to explain it to me. Plus, I had to write to my pen pal." She looks at her mother accusingly.

It's been a really long, horrible day, and thanks to Mrs. Chadwick's stupid theme night idea, I'm still hungry. "How are we supposed to have a book club if nobody does the reading?"

"Emma," my mother chides. "It's not that big a deal. Sometimes people get busy. We can all catch up next month."

"Maybe we shouldn't even have a book club!" I continue, my voice rising. "What's the point? Everybody's off doing other stuff these days anyway."

I try not to look at Jess, but I can't help it. She looks back at me, stricken. She should have been there this morning, when I crashed and burned. That's what best friends are for. And instead, she's off at her new school with Adele and Frankie and all her other new friends. I don't care if she's stuck with a Julia Pendleton clone for a roommate,

Heather Vogel Frederick

and I don't care about the stupid scholarship. It's no excuse.

"I think we'll call it a night," my mother says, hastily putting her book and papers into her bag. "Come on, Emma. Let's get you home to bed."

I don't even get to say good-bye to Stewart. *Great*, I think. *If that isn't just the nonexistent cherry on my un-sundae of a day.*

"That was really rude!" my mother scolds as we head down the sidewalk toward home.

I don't even try to muster an argument. She's right.

"I know you've had a rough day," she continues. "Your father called and told me what happened this morning. But that's no excuse!"

She goes directly upstairs when we get home, and I hear the bathwater running. My mother always retreats to the bathtub when she's feeling stressed. Either that or she makes herself a cup of tea. I think about seeing if I can squeeze some sympathy out of my father, but his office door is closed and he's hung the DO NOT DISTURB—ON DEADLINE sign over the door handle. Ever since Darcy and I were little, it's been drummed into us that when we see this sign, we don't bother him. "Not unless there's fire or blood," as my father says.

He tells me that since I'm a writer too, I'll understand. And the thing is, I do. I heave a sigh and head upstairs to my room. A meltdown is incredibly lame, but it's not an emergency.

Melville is curled up on my bed, and I sit down beside him and stroke his fur. I glance at the clock by my bed. There's no point calling my friends—they're probably still at the Chadwicks, talking about what a moron I am. Or on their way to get pizza. Darcy must still be at the rink, and I can't get ahold of Stewart without risking Becca or her mother answering the phone. There's no way I want to talk to either of them.

"I guess it's just you and me, Melville," I tell my cat. I talk to him for a while about the injustice of everything. Melville doesn't say much, but his rumbling purr sounds sympathetic.

"It's like all of a sudden everything just went haywire," I complain. "I thought eighth grade was going to be great. I'm the editor of the paper, and I have a boy who likes me. But my best friend isn't there, plus I made a complete idiot of myself in front of the whole school today and then I broke my glasses and then, to top it all off, I totally alienated everybody at book club."

Melville licks a paw and swats at his ear.

"I'm sure if you were human you'd agree with me, wouldn't you?" I murmur, scratching him under the chin. "Being a teenager is horrible."

Melville curls up and goes to sleep, which is not exactly the reaction I'm looking for. I really need to talk to someone. My gaze wanders over to my desk. The blue envelope from Bailey Jacobs is laying on it. I've read her letter a zillion times already, and looked at her picture almost as much too, but I grab the envelope anyway and take them both out.

"See, Melville?" I say, holding up her photo. "This is my new pen pal." Even though it's a school picture, Bailey looks nice. Like me, she wears glasses and her hair is brown, but hers is chin-length and tucked behind her ears, not curly and short like mine. In the photo, she's smiling a friendly smile, not one of those fake "it's school picture day!" smiles.

I open the letter and start to read aloud:

Dear Pen Pal,

My name is Bailey Jacobs and I'm in the 8th grade. My mother and your mother were friends back in college. I guess they liked the same things, because your mother is a librarian and mine owns a bookstore. It's called Shelf Life, which I think is a pretty good name for a bookstore. We live in a small town near Laramie called Gopher Hole. I know what you're thinking-stupid name, right? But it's actually a really nice place. It's not historic like Concord, where you live. No famous writers ever lived here, and there weren't any famous battles fought here like there were in Concord. We're only famous for our tumbleweeds, ha ha. It's really pretty, though. Every which way you look there are rolling plains that stretch all the way to the Medicine Bow Mountains. Our town has lots of ranchers and cowboys—real ones, not the fake ones you see in movies—and then there are the normal folks like me and my family. My dad is the manager of one of the local banks. We moved out here because he thought Laramie was too crowded. He's a real country boy, but I really love Laramie. The University is there, and there are shops and restaurants and a really great library. Gopher Hole is so small we don't even have a middle school. They just stick all of us kids into one building with two rooms—K-5 on one side, 6-8 on the other. It's practically a one-room schoolhouse. I can't wait until next year, when I'll get to take the bus to Laramie High. For now, though, I'm stuck in Gopher Hole.

Your friend,
Bailey

I smile at the little sketch she made beside her name of a girl stuck in a gopher hole. It looks just like one of the line drawings from Judy Abbott's letters in *Daddy-Long-Legs*. I like Bailey's sense of humor, and I like having her for a pen pal.

I reach over to my desk and grab some paper and the special fountain pen that Cassidy and her mother gave me for my birthday a couple of years ago, and I start to write.

Dear Pen Pal,
Did you ever have one of those days where everything goes completely, horribly wrong?

Heather Vogel Frederick

WINTER

"*Getting an education is an awfully wearing process!*"

—Daddy-Long-Legs

Jess

"It isn't the big troubles in life that require character. Anybody can rise to a crisis and face a crushing tragedy with courage, but to meet the petty hazards of the day with a laugh—I really think that requires spirit."

—Daddy-Long-Legs

Cassidy's front door swings open wide.

"Happy Thanksgiving!" cries her mother. Mr. Kinkaid has his arm around her waist, and they're both beaming.

"Happy Thanksgiving!" we chorus back, crowding into the front hall.

For once, there's no camera crew around. Nobody's going to be filming us today for *Cooking with Clementine*—it's just the turkey, the stuffing, and us. "Us" meaning everyone in our book club and their families.

"Is anyone else here yet?" I ask, looking around.

"Nope," Mrs. Sloane-Kinkaid tells me. "You're the first ones, and just what we need to get this party started."

My little brothers peel off their coats and drop them on the floor.

Ignoring my mother's protests they thunder upstairs, heading for the turret. They love Cassidy's house. Especially the turret. I know the feeling. I wouldn't trade Half Moon Farm for anything, but it doesn't have a turret.

Shaking his head wearily, my father picks up their coats and hangs them in the closet. "Boys," he says, shaking his head.

Cassidy's mom and Mr. Kinkaid look at each other and smile.

As usual, Mrs. Sloane-Kinkaid has decorated the house within an inch of its life. She loves holidays. There are carefully arranged piles of dried gourds on the lower stair steps and on the front hall table, and the banister is twined with Bittersweet vine—*Celastrus scandens* is its Latin name, which I know because of my Latin class at school. I've been practicing at home on the weekends by memorizing the scientific names for all the plants around our farm. I love the way everything in the natural world has an official-sounding Latin name—plants and animals, clouds and stars. It makes the world seem so orderly. I finger the Bittersweet vine's bright red and orange berries, which match the colors of the gourds and the autumn leaves that are artfully scattered on the front hall table.

"It looks pretty, doesn't it?" says my mother. "I should make more of an effort at our house."

Like she has time for that kind of froufrou stuff these days. Mom's had to pick up a lot of slack around the farm now that I'm not there during the week to help out, which makes me feel bad. She says it's completely worth it, though, to have me at Colonial Academy. My par-

Heather Vogel Frederick

ents are still excited that I'm going there. "I think our house always looks nice," I tell her.

"Thanks, sweetie." She smiles at me, then glances over my shoulder and lets out a yelp of surprise.

I whip around, expecting to see, I don't know, maybe a live turkey or something, but it's only the mannequins. Cassidy's mother has a quirky sense of humor, and she has these life-size mannequins she got somewhere that are always lurking around on holidays. They weren't around this Halloween, for some reason, but last year Mrs. Sloane-Kinkaid dressed them up as vampires and hid them in the bushes by the front porch. They scared the socks off Emma and me when we came over to pick up Cassidy to go trick-or-treating.

Today they're standing by the entry to the living room, dressed in Pilgrim outfits. The girl Pilgrim is holding up a sign that reads: HAPPY and the boy Pilgrim is holding up another one that reads: THANKSGIVING.

Mrs. Sloane-Kinkaid laughs. "I didn't mean to startle you, Shannon."

"No harm done," my mother replies. "You know I love your mannequins. They're always hilarious!"

"Creepy is more like it." Cassidy thuds down the stairs. She hates the mannequins.

"There you are, honey," says her mother, handing her a stack of small cards. "Would you and Jess mind doing the place cards?"

Cassidy and I head for the dining room. There are going to be a lot of us here for dinner, and all the extra leaves have been added to the table, along with a second table that sticks out a little into the hall.

"Let's put the dads out there," I suggest. "They won't mind."

Cassidy gives me half the stack and starts plunking hers down in front of each place setting. The place cards are cute, with a picture of a big turkey beside each of our names, which are written in Mrs. Sloane-Kinkaid's swooping cursive.

"Be sure to put Emma next to Stewart," I remind Cassidy.

I wait until she's at the other end of the table to put my last two place cards down: *Darcy* and *Jess*. I feel a little thrill of anticipation at the thought of sitting next to Emma's brother, and hope Cassidy doesn't notice what I've done. Not that she would—she's pretty oblivious when it comes to boy stuff.

When we're done, Cassidy heads back upstairs and I follow her. As we pass the narrow stairway on the second floor that leads up to the turret, my brothers' voices float down toward us. They're squabbling, as usual. They've invented this complicated game called "ogre in the tower" that they play every time we come over to Cassidy's. I have no idea what the rules are, but they always end up fighting. Cassidy and I go into her room and close the door. I spot a scruffy tail sticking out from under the bed.

"Hey, Murphy," I coax, kneeling down on the floor beside him. "You can come out now. The coast is clear." Murphy is not fond of my brothers.

"Leave him alone," says Cassidy, flopping down onto the bed on her stomach.

"You're grumpy today," I tell her. "Hasn't anybody ever told you

Heather Vogel Frederick

that Thanksgiving is a day for being happy and grateful?"

She shoots me a look.

"How's hockey going?" Hockey is Cassidy's favorite subject, so I figure maybe this will cheer her up.

She merely grunts in reply. I perch on the edge of the bed beside her and try another angle. "Have you heard from Winky recently?" I kind of wish I'd gotten Cassidy's pen pal. Winky Parker likes animals too, and she even has a horse. One that's meant to ride, not plow fields like Led and Zep, our big Belgian drafthorses that my dad named after Led Zeppelin, his favorite rock band. I really can't complain about them anymore, because I get to ride almost every day now. At Colonial Academy, the equestriennes are each assigned a horse to share with two or three other girls for the year, and mine is a beautiful dark gelding named Blackjack.

My pen pal, Madison Daniels, is fine and everything, and she's been really nice about sending me CDs of her music—she's in a band called "Moonrise," which I think is a really cool name for a band—but her letters are super short and I don't feel like I know her very well yet at all. The letters Emma gets from Bailey and Cassidy gets from Winky are long and chatty and full of details about life in Wyoming, which sounds like a great place to live. Winky's family's dude ranch is really interesting—kind of like Half Moon Farm, only with tourists.

Without lifting her head off the pillow, Cassidy snakes out an arm and grabs an envelope from her desk. She slaps it down beside me on the bed. I take the letter out and start to read:

Dear Pen Pal,

Don't you just love <u>Daddy-Long-Legs</u>? I don't usually like to read much, and at first I thought this whole book club idea was really stupid, but I have to admit I really love this book. And I especially love Judy Abbott. She makes college sound like so much fun. I can't wait to grow up. I love it here on our ranch, but I want to see the rest of the world too. The farthest I've ever been is Denver. I wish this letter was as funny as one of Judy's, but I'm not a very good writer and I sure can't draw. I think her little pictures are hilarious, don't you?

Our guest season ended a couple of weeks ago, and now we're getting the ranch ready for winter. The summer help is gone, so my brothers Sam and Owen and I have been pitching in to help Daddy and Pete with repairs. We've got fencing to mend and all the harnesses and saddles to clean and put away for the winter and the chicken coop to scrub and whitewash plus lots of roofs to check for leaks. Then there are all the guest cabins to sweep out and close up and stuff like that, so I'm keeping really busy after school.

I took Bingo out for a ride up to Lonesome Ridge yesterday morning early, and on the way back it

started to snow. It was snowing so hard by the time I
got home that Mom declared a ranch holiday and let
us stay home from school because they were predicting
a blizzard. She fixed us a second breakfast, and
served it up in the dining hall like we were guests.
It was awesome. Daddy built a fire in the big stone
fireplace, and we all sat around afterward talking
and then we played Sorry and I won which made my
brothers mad. Pete got out his fiddle and "strangled
the cat" as he calls it when he plays (did you know
that some violin strings are made from sheep innards
called "catgut"? Is that gross or what?!), and my
brothers and I pushed back the tables to make room
and practiced roping chairs until Mom said to quit it
and sent the three of us outside. We had a snowball
fight and Sam and Owen got me back for winning at
Sorry and then we came back in for hot chocolate and
now I'm writing to you.

I hope everything is fine in Concord. Tell me more
about hockey. I've never played.

Your friend,

Winky Parker

I fold up the letter and put it back in its envelope. "Winky's letters kind of makes me wish I lived on a ranch."

"In Gopher Hole, Wyoming?" Cassidy throws her pillow at me. "Please."

"Well, it would be better than being stuck at Colonial Academy with Savannah Sinclair."

Cassidy perks up a bit at the mention of Savannah. All my friends are weirdly fascinated with my roommate. "So what's Julia up to now?" she asks. Since our last book club meeting, we've all started calling Savannah "Julia," after Julia Pendleton in *Daddy-Long-Legs*.

"Oh, you know, the usual," I tell her. "She's made sure everyone on campus knows I'm there on a scholarship, not because my family can afford to send me, and she's always finding other things to needle me about. Like the fact that I'm stuck here in Concord over Thanksgiving weekend while she's jetting off to Aruba with her family."

"Who cares about stupid old Aruba?" says Cassidy with relish.

"Exactly. And she loves to point out that she's better at horseback riding than I am, but that's no big surprise since she's had her own pony since she could barely walk and I've spent my life riding Led and Zep, who are more like elephants than horses."

"I love Led and Zep!" Cassidy protests.

"I know, I know, I do too," I reassure her. "But for real riding, Blackjack is a lot better. Except when Savannah hides dried thistles under my saddle."

"She did that?"

I nod. "Uh-huh. Right before my last riding lesson. When I mounted him, Blackjack bucked me right off and I landed in a pile of horse apples."

Cassidy looks puzzled.

"You know," I tell her, holding my nose.

"Oh," she says. "I get it. Apples—that's funny." She grins, the first smile I've seen from her all day.

"You wouldn't think so if it had been you!"

The thing is, if it weren't for Savannah, and for the fact that I really miss my friends, especially Emma and Cassidy, Colonial Academy would actually be okay. I like all my teachers and classes, and my new friends Adele and Frankie are really nice. They're the exact same height and from the back it's hard to tell them apart, because they both have short dark hair. But Adele has bangs and Frankie doesn't, and Adele has blue eyes and Frankie's are dark. They both love to sing, just like me, and the three of us are in Chorus together. We're all thinking of trying out for MadriGals, Colonial's elite a cappella group.

Frankie and Adele have been at the school since sixth grade, and this year they're roommates. Their room is just down the hall from Savannah's and mine, and I spend most of my free time hanging out there with them. Adele has a TV, so sometimes after evening study hall we watch movies and stuff, but mostly we just talk. Frankie is hilarious, and she does a wicked Savannah imitation.

The other great thing about Colonial Academy is the equestrian program. I love riding. Blackjack is awesome, and I'm learning really fast.

My instructor says at this rate I may be able to start jumping soon.

The doorbell rings downstairs. My heart does a little somersault as I hear Mrs. Hawthorne's voice followed by Darcy's deep laugh. A few seconds later Emma comes bursting into the room, bringing the aroma of roast turkey wafting in behind her.

"Happy Thanksgiving!" she cries, giving us both a big hug. This makes me really happy, because after her meltdown at our last book club meeting things were a little awkward for a few days. I guess I hadn't realized how much my switching schools had bothered her, especially since she'd seemed all in favor of it and everything. I was so worried about myself, and how I was going to fit in, that it honestly never occurred to me to worry about Emma being lonely. I figured she had Stewart and the book club, so it really surprised me when I found out she was feeling a little jealous of my new friends. Anyway, we talked it all out and now we're over it. We'll be best friends forever, Emma and me, no matter what.

"How can you two stand being stuffed away up here when it smells so good down there?" Emma closes her eyes and inhales deeply. "Mmm mmm."

Cassidy sits up. "You're right," she says. "I'm starving! Let's go get something to eat."

My stomach flutters again as we enter the kitchen, but not because I'm hungry. Darcy is sitting on a stool at the island counter, looking at college brochures with Courtney.

He looks up and sees me. "Hey, Jess! Come check these out."

Heather Vogel Frederick

I cross the kitchen and climb up on the stool next to him. He tugs my braid, like he's always done since I was a little kid, and gives me a smile. I smile back. I'm still kind of shy around Emma's brother. Probably because I've had a crush on him since sixth grade. I keep hoping that maybe he'll notice, and feel the same way about me.

The doorbell rings again, and my brothers, who have abandoned the turret and zeroed in on the food like a pair of heat-seeking missiles, push past me to go answer it. They return a minute later trailing the Chadwicks.

"Hi, everybody!" says Becca's father, rubbing his hands together as he sniffs the air. "Happy turkey day!"

Stewart makes a beeline for Emma, and Becca heads directly for Darcy and me. Somehow she manages to squeeze in between us.

"Ooo!" she squeals. "College brochures! I can't wait to go to college, can you?"

I slide off my stool and retreat to the stove, where Cassidy is ladling up hot cider. She passes me a mug.

"Thanks."

"Becca's an idiot, by the way."

I look over at her, startled. Does Cassidy know how I feel? I hope it's not that obvious, and I start to worry that maybe Becca knows too. I would hate for Becca Chadwick to guess that I have a crush on Darcy. I still remember what she did to Emma in sixth grade when she found out Emma liked Zach Norton.

There are days when I wish Becca wasn't in our book club. She's a lot nicer than she used to be, so maybe our moms were right, maybe book club has been good for her. But Emma and I think it's possible she's a frenemy. Mrs. Hawthorne is the one who told Emma about that word. She found it in a book she was reading about teenagers—Mrs. Hawthorne is always reading books about how to understand your kids and be a better parent, even though I think she's already a really good one. Anyway, she says a frenemy is a friend who is partly an enemy, or a friend that you kind of dislike. That pretty much describes how I feel about Becca. She's like the vine on Cassidy's banister—bittersweet. Sometimes she's nice, sometimes she's not. Thinking about the vine makes me think about Latin classifications, and I smother a grin as a wicked little thought pops into my head. *Chadwickius frenemus.* The perfect name for Becca. I can't wait to tell Emma.

"We'll get started with dinner as soon as the Wongs arrive," Mrs. Sloane-Kinkaid tells us. "Lily just called to say they're on their way."

"I'll pop the sweet potatoes in the warming oven," says Mrs. Chadwick, who in honor of the holiday has traded in her jungle look for something more subdued. Well, a bit more subdued. Today she's got on a purple dress with a pattern of fall leaves on it. The only sign of "new and improved" Calliope Chadwick is the big jangly stack of purple and gold bracelets she's wearing.

"Did you make the kind with the little marshmallows on them?" Cassidy asks.

"Is there any other kind?" Mrs. Chadwick replies, and Cassidy lets out a groan.

Heather Vogel Frederick

"Have an appetizer, honey," says her mother. "That'll help tide you over." She points to the platters of cheese and crackers and stuffed mushrooms that my family brought. "Everybody, please help yourselves."

Courtney slides the cheese platter across the island counter and Cassidy grabs a cracker and spreads it with goat cheese. Just as she's about to take a bite, she recoils in alarm.

"WHAT is that awful SMELL?" she cries.

My father laughs. "That's our latest creamery creation—a brand-new cheese we're calling 'Blue Moon.'"

Cassidy makes a face. "It smells like dirty gym socks."

"Cassidy Ann!" exclaims her mother.

"Well, it does," she insists.

My brothers think this is hysterically funny, of course. "Gym sock cheese!" they shout gleefully, and chase each other around the kitchen until my dad nabs them.

"You've got a point, actually, Cassidy," he says. "Blue cheese definitely has a, uh, distinct fragrance. But for those of us who love a good blue, Shannon and I think maybe we've hit on something special here."

Mrs. Sloane-Kinkaid takes the offending cracker from Cassidy, who's still holding it at arm's length, and nibbles a corner of it. "Mmm, you're right, Michael—it's fabulous! I need to think about doing an episode on artisan cheeses."

The doorbell rings again, and my brothers wrench themselves free from my dad's grip to go do their duty again. A minute later they herd the Wongs into the kitchen. Megan is carrying a big brown paper bag.

"Uh, this is my grandmother, everybody," she announces.

"Welcome, Mrs. Chen," says Stanley Kinkaid.

"Call me Gigi," Megan's grandmother replies.

"From her favorite movie," Mr. Wong explains. "My mother-in-law is crazy about old musicals. Especially when they're set in Paris."

"My favorite city," Gigi tells us, her lips quirking up in a smile.

Megan's grandmother is nothing like what I expected, except for the fact that she's petite. Smaller than me, even, and I'm pretty short. I guess I was expecting somebody really ancient, for one thing, and she doesn't look that old at all. And since she's Mrs. Wong's mother, I guess I thought she'd be dressed like Mrs. Wong, who is wearing yoga pants today as usual, sandals and thick wool socks, and as a festive touch, a long-sleeve T-shirt with a silhouette of a turkey inside a red circle with a slash through it. Megan's grandmother, on the other hand, reminds me of Isabelle d'Azur, the stylish editor of *Flash* magazine who came to our fashion show last spring. Her wool suit is the exact shade of reddish-orange as the bittersweet berries in the hall, and it goes perfectly with her brightly patterned red and orange scarf, big gold earrings, and bright red lipstick. I glance over at Megan, surprised that she hasn't whipped out her sketchbook yet to draw her.

Gigi's dark almond-shaped eyes dart to and fro around the

Heather Vogel Frederick

kitchen like a very alert little bird. "Hello, everyone," she says, her English brushed with a soft accent. "You girls must be Megan's book club friends."

While Cassidy's mother introduces us all around, Megan's mother slips out of the kitchen. She reappears a minute later carrying a platter. On it is a pale brown glistening oval.

"I brought a Tofu Tom," she announces, placing it on the counter next to the crackers and Blue Moon cheese.

Darcy leans closer. "Are those supposed to be legs?" he asks, prodding it doubtfully.

Mrs. Wong nods. "It tastes just like the real thing, too."

Her mother shudders delicately and nods at Megan, who reaches into the paper bag she's carrying and pulls out a casserole dish. She sets it on the counter next to the Tofu Tom.

"Oh my gosh!" says Darcy, lifting the cover. Inside are a pile of fat little bundles topped with a dot of orange—chopped carrot, maybe? "These smell amazing, whatever they are."

Mrs. Sloane-Kinkaid's face lights up. "Chinese dumplings? Gigi, you didn't!"

"I certainly did," Megan's grandmother replies smugly. "You can't have a proper party without *siu maai*."

"You really shouldn't have," says Cassidy's mother.

Megan's grandmother gives the Tofu Tom a withering glance and Megan's mother presses her lips together tightly, like maybe she's trying to keep some words from popping out. A guilty look creeps across

Mr. Wong's face. He quickly puts his arm around his wife's shoulders and says, "Aren't I lucky to have two such wonderful cooks under my roof? And isn't it just like my generous Lily to make sure all the vegetarians with us here today have something to feast on as well?"

Emma looks over at me and grins. Mrs. Wong is the only vegetarian here today, as far as we know.

"The Tofu Tom looks really intriguing," says Mrs. Hawthorne tactfully. "And I'm sure it's delicious. I know I can't wait to try a piece."

"Me neither," echoes my mother, which I don't think is entirely truthful, but I know she's trying to cheer Mrs. Wong up.

Mrs. Wong's lips unclench a bit.

"Now," says Mrs. Sloane-Kinkaid briskly. "If you'll all go and find your seats, we can get dinner started."

Everybody else crowds around the tables hunting for their place cards. I walk directly to where Darcy is standing by his chair. He smiles at me.

"Hey," he says. "I was hoping I'd get a chance to talk to you today."

"Excuse me," says Becca, "but I think that's my seat." She reaches around me and plucks the place card off the table, waving it under my nose. *Becca* is written on it.

Chadwickius frenemus switched our place cards!

As I stand there, my cheeks burning with humiliation and resentment, Becca slides into what was supposed to have been my seat.

I move away blindly, blinking back angry tears, and eventually find where she put me—at the other end of the table, stuck out in the hall between Mr. Chadwick and Mr. Wong. Adding salt to my wound, Emma and Stewart are sitting across from me, holding hands under the table.

"Better get some of these before they disappear," says Mr. Wong, serving me up some of Gigi's dumplings. "They're fantastic."

"Thanks," I mutter. Right now, I'm not feeling hungry in the least.

"So, Courtney, have you decided on which colleges you're going to apply to?" asks Mr. Hawthorne.

Down the table a ways, the smile slips off Cassidy's face.

"Well, UCLA is my first choice," her sister replies. "But I'm also looking at USC and Pepperdine."

"I can't believe my baby is going to college!" says Mrs. Sloane-Kinkaid wistfully.

"It won't be long now before all our babies are in college," my mother says.

"All except for one." Mr. Kinkaid puts his arm around Cassidy's mother. "Honey? Do you want to tell them, or should I?"

Cassidy throws her mother a pleading look, and shakes her head vigorously.

Her mother sighs. "We've got to let people know sometime, sweetheart," she tells her.

"Know what, Clementine?" asks Mrs. Hawthorne.

"Stanley and I are going to have a baby!" Mrs. Sloane-Kinkaid and her new husband beam at us.

We all gape at them except Cassidy, who looks like she has her own personal thundercloud—*cumulonimbus*—over her head.

"Really, Clementine!" huffs Mrs. Chadwick, looking shocked. "At your age!"

Beside me, Mr. Chadwick squirms a little in his chair. Becca's mother has a knack for saying exactly the wrong thing sometimes.

But Cassidy's mother just laughs. "I'm hardly a fossil, Calliope."

"Oh, Clementine, congratulations!" cries my mother. She gets up and runs around the table and gives her a big hug. Mrs. Hawthorne and Mrs. Wong do the same.

"That explains the naps and nausea," says Mrs. Hawthorne. Seeing our puzzled looks, she explains, "Women who are expecting need a lot of extra sleep, and sometimes in the first few months certain foods make them feel queasy."

"Like with the cornmeal mush?" I say, remembering how Mrs. Sloane-Kinkaid bolted from the table at our last book club meeting.

Mrs. Chadwick's mouth prunes up at this.

Cassidy's mother waves her hand dismissively. "It had nothing to do with your dinner that night, Calliope—pretty much everything is making me queasy at the moment. I'm amazed I've done so well today!"

"Do you know what you're having?" Emma asks.

"They tell us it will be either a boy or a girl," Mr. Sloane-Kinkaid deadpans, and Cassidy rolls her eyes.

"Seriously, though, no," says her mother. "Stanley and I don't want to know. It's too much like opening a Christmas present ahead of time. We want to be surprised, and we'll be thrilled with whoever

Heather Vogel Frederick

is in here." She places her palms on her tummy protectively.

I try not to stare but I can't help it. Her stomach still looks completely flat to me.

"Are you going to get fat?" my brother Dylan blurts out. "Jess's goat Sundance had a baby and she got really fat."

Everybody laughs.

"Yes, honey, I'm going to get fat," Cassidy's mom assures him. "But I won't have a baby bump for another month or two. I've only just finished my first trimester."

"What fun to have a new baby to look forward to!" exclaims Mrs. Hawthorne. "We'll have to throw you another shower."

"I'm counting on it," says Mrs. Sloane-Kinkaid. "I gave away all of the girls' baby things years ago."

"Would you rather have a boy or a girl?" Megan asks her. She's been really quiet, and I wonder if she's wishing it was her mother who had made this announcement. Megan's always wanted a little brother or sister. She told me so when she helped me babysit for Maggie Crandall a couple of weekends ago.

"Either one is fine with us, honey. Really. If it's a girl, I'll just have to start another Mother-Daughter Book Club when she's old enough, and if it's a boy, Stanley will have someone to toss a football around with. Besides Cassidy, of course."

"Can we talk about something else?" says Cassidy sullenly, and her mother's smile fades.

I'm guessing Cassidy's not totally on board with this idea. I look over at Emma to see if she knows anything, but she just shakes her head at me.

"What are you reading in your book club, girls?" Megan's grandmother asks, changing the subject.

"We're almost finished with *Daddy-Long-Legs*, and then we're going to start *Just Patty*," Emma tells her politely.

"I'm not familiar with *Just Patty*, but I loved *Daddy-Long-Legs* when I was your age! It's so romantic. And funny, too—all those letters Judy writes. Does anyone still write letters these days?"

"The girls have pen pals, Mother," Mrs. Wong tells her, and explains about the book club in Wyoming.

"The more I hear about this book club, the more I like the idea," says Gigi. "I wish they'd had book clubs like this back when you were a girl, Lily. Wouldn't we have had fun?"

"Sure, Mom," says Mrs. Wong, but she doesn't sound too enthusiastic.

Down the table across from Cassidy, my brothers are busy putting black olives on their fingertips. They wave to each other, waggling their fingers like alien tentacles.

"That's enough, boys," says my dad, scooting the olive dish out of their reach.

Cassidy scoops a handful onto her plate as it goes by. She waits until nobody's looking, then sneaks them one by one under the table to Dylan and Ryan.

Heather Vogel Frederick

"You're going to make a fabulous big sister," I hear my mother whisper to her.

Cassidy scowls down at the heap of sweet potato casserole on her plate.

Trying my best to ignore the way *Chadwickius frenemus* is laughing her head off at everything Darcy is saying down at the other end of the table, I pick up my fork and start to eat. Cassidy's mother is an amazing cook, and the stuff everyone else brought is pretty fabulous too. Well, except for the Tofu Tom, which doesn't taste a bit like turkey despite what Mrs. Wong said. Gigi's dumplings are little bundles of goodness, stuffed with shrimp and ground pork and spices and topped with a spicy-sweet dipping sauce. Not the usual thing you eat at Thanksgiving, but delicious anyway.

After a while, Stanley pushes back from the table. "I can't eat another bite," he groans. "I say we go for a walk before the game starts."

Cassidy's stepfather is almost as big a sports nut as Cassidy. I, on the other hand, have no clue which football teams are even playing today.

"Great idea, honey," agrees Cassidy's mother. "We can have dessert when we get back. Just leave the dishes where they are. We'll deal with them later."

We grab our coats and pile out of the house—all except for Megan's grandmother, who opts to stretch out on the sofa and take a little nap instead. "I'm still jet-lagged," she says, waving us out the door.

We head toward downtown Concord, my little brothers racing

ahead, crunching through the crisp brown leaves that are scattered over the sidewalk like spilled cornflakes. The sky overhead is a deep, clear blue.

"A perfect November day," my mother says, putting her arm around me. I lean into her and she kisses the top of my head.

"How about we go over to Colonial Academy?" my dad suggests. "I'll bet Jess would be willing to give us a tour."

The campus is deserted, of course—everyone's gone home for the holiday weekend—but even I have to admit it looks pretty on an afternoon like this, with the white buildings and bare-limbed trees silhouetted against the bright sky.

"It's like a perfect New England college campus," sighs Cassidy's mother. "Are you sure you want to go back to the West Coast next year, Court? Don't you think it would be fun to find someplace picturesque like this, that's a little closer to all of us?"

Cassidy looks over at her sister, a hopeful expression on her face. Courtney tucks her chin into the collar of her jacket.

"I guess I'll look at a few places out here, but I really miss California."

Cassidy kicks a rock and sends it flying across the still-green lawn of the quad.

I point out my dorm and the windows to my room, and then I lead everybody down the back road to the stables and introduce them to Blackjack, who nickers softly when he sees me.

"Hey, boy," I say, pulling from my pocket the apple that I brought with me from Cassidy's house. "Miss me?"

Heather Vogel Frederick

I explain how those of us who choose riding as our sport are each assigned a horse to take care of, and how we're learning everything from basic horsemanship to dressage. "Right now I'm still doing a lot of flatwork—you know, transitions from walk to canter and stuff like that—but I hope I'll get to do some jumping soon."

Darcy holds Dylan and Ryan up so they can pat Blackjack's neck. Blackjack leans over the stall and whiffles in my hair.

"He likes you, doesn't he?" Darcy says, smiling down at me.

I smile back at him, but before I can reply, Becca appears.

"Come on, Darcy," she says, tugging at his sleeve, "there's a really cute horse over here I want you to see."

Since when does Becca Chadwick like horses? She stays glued to Darcy's side as we all start back up the road toward the quad. Emma and Stewart are glued together too, shoulders touching, although they're not holding hands. If they think they're fooling anybody, they're wrong. The grown-ups are all watching them, giving one another knowing nods and winks. Megan is talking to Cassidy and Courtney, and my brothers are whirling around like two little autumn leaves, their arms stuck out as they chase each other, pretending to be airplanes.

"Let's all share what we're grateful for," suggests Mrs. Hawthorne, tucking her hands in her pockets. "This is Thanksgiving, after all. I'll start—I'm grateful for family and friends."

"I'm grateful for fleece," shouts Dylan, whizzing by.

My mother sighs. "Honey, surely you're thankful for something besides fleece."

Cassidy watches my brothers as they kick at a pile of horse droppings. "I'm grateful that my mother isn't having twins."

Everyone laughs except Mrs. Sloane-Kinkaid, who gives Cassidy a pained look.

Mr. Chadwick is grateful for a wonderful day and a wonderful meal, Mrs. Wong is grateful that we're all happy and healthy, and Mr. Hawthorne is grateful that his novel is coming along so well.

"I'm grateful for all my beautiful girls," says Mr. Kinkaid, smiling at Cassidy and her mother and sister. Then he leans over and cups his hands around his mouth and speaks directly to Mrs. Sloane-Kinkaid's tummy. "And I'm grateful for whoever's in there!"

We all laugh at this, and at Mrs. Chadwick, too, when she twirls around dramatically in her purple cape, which matches her purple dress, and shouts, "I'm grateful for purple!"

Becca's face turns beet red and I smother a grin. *Serves you right*, I think.

"I'm grateful for friends," says Emma, looking at me and at the same time carefully not looking at Stewart. Her cheeks are pink, though, so I know she means him just as much as she does me and the rest of the book club.

"Let me guess—I'll bet Megan's grateful for school uniforms," jokes Mr. Wong.

"Da-ad!" Megan protests.

"I'm grateful our daughter has this wonderful opportunity to attend Colonial Academy," says my mother, putting her arm

Heather Vogel Frederick

around my shoulders again and giving me a squeeze.

"And I'm grateful to whoever nominated her for the award and made it possible," adds my dad.

My heart sinks. I want so much to please my parents and make them happy and proud of me, but a big part of me wishes I could still be at Walden Middle School with my friends. I know I shouldn't worry about it yet, but I have a feeling my parents are going to want me to go to Colonial Academy for high school, too, if my scholarship is extended, and all my life I've been looking forward to Alcott High. I'd be there for two whole years with Darcy before he leaves for college!

Dad keeps telling me I've got the best of both worlds right now, because it's not like I had to go away to boarding school or anything, I'm still here in Concord. Still, I really miss sitting in classes with Emma, and eating lunch at our table, and I even miss Kevin Mullins. Well, sometimes, anyway.

Lately he's gotten bolder, riding his bike around the quad and leaving notes for me with Mrs. Crandall. Incredibly stupid notes, like "Do you know the square root of pi by heart?" and "I got an A on my math test" and stuff like that. He found out that my parents got me a cell phone, and somebody—Becca, probably—must have thought it would be funny to give him my number. My phone will ring in the dorm sometimes and nobody is there, but I know it's him because I can hear him breathing, and besides, like I'm not going to know who it is when I see MULLINS on my Caller ID?

Lately I don't bother answering his calls, which is probably mean but I don't want to encourage him, plus Savannah Sinclair would have a field day if she ever got wind of the fact that a pipsqueak like Kevin has a crush on me.

Now, if it were Darcy Hawthorne leaving me notes and calling— but that doesn't look like it's going to happen anytime soon. Darcy will probably always just think of me as his little sister's friend. I glance over to where he's talking and laughing with Courtney and Becca. Darcy has the nicest smile. It really lights up his brown eyes.

Mrs. Hawthorne interrupts my daydream. "How about you, Jess, what are you grateful for?"

Right now, it would be easier to tell her what I'm *not* grateful for. I slant a glance up at my dorm room windows. Savannah Sinclair. *Chadwickius frenemus*. Switched place cards.

But it's Thanksgiving, and I sigh and muster a smile. "Dessert," I reply. "I'm grateful for dessert. Let's go back to Cassidy's."

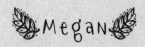

Megan

> "A woman, whether she is interested in babies or microbes
> or husbands or poetry or servants or parallelograms
> or gardens or Plato or bridge—is fundamentally
> and always interested in clothes."
>
> —Daddy-Long-Legs

The school bus drops me off at the bottom of our long driveway and I trudge up toward the house, tucking my chin into the collar of my jacket and wishing I'd worn a hat and scarf. It started to snow a little as we left Walden Middle School, and the icy January wind whips the flakes around me, stinging my cheeks.

Fingers numb, I fish my house key out of my pocket and slide it into the lock. "I'm home!" I call out, slinging my backpack onto the front hall bench.

"In here!" a voice calls back. It's my grandmother.

I follow my nose to the kitchen, which smells amazing. Gigi sure knows how to cook. We've been feasting ever since the day she arrived. My dad didn't work late a single night for the entire month of December, he was so eager to get home for supper. Last night I heard him complaining to my mother that he's gained five pounds, but he sure sounded happy about it.

My grandmother looks up from the counter where she's busy chopping onions. She pauses, wrinkling her nose. "It really is awful, isn't it?"

"The onions?"

"The uniform."

I glance down at today's outfit—khaki pants with a long-sleeve maroon polo shirt and a maroon sweater with a mustard-gold stripe around the V-neck—and grimace. "Yeah."

"We'll just have to see what we can do about that," Gigi tells me, turning back to her onions.

I plunk myself down at the kitchen table, where a glass of milk and a plate of peanut butter cookies are waiting for me. My grandmother's doing, of course. If my mother had left a snack it would have been rice cakes and carrot juice, or maybe something made out of seaweed, her latest and possibly most horrible discovery.

"A real American girl snack," says Gigi, winking at me. "Clementine gave me the recipe."

"Thanks, Gigi." I take a bite and give her a thumbs-up. Looking pleased, my grandmother returns to her chopping. I watch her, wondering if she dresses up like this when she cooks back at home in Hong Kong. As usual, my grandmother is dressed to kill—a gray wool pencil skirt that is definitely designer and probably cost as much as the stove

Heather Vogel Frederick

she just baked the cookies in, high heels, a white silk blouse accented with a double rope of pearls and a pink flowered silk scarf for a pop of color, and a gray cardigan that I'm sure is cashmere.

"Your mother's at one of her meetings this afternoon, I can't remember which one, something about landfill, maybe? She said she'd be home in time for your book club. Oh, and a letter came for you today." Gigi points her knife at a stack of magazines and mail at the far end of table. Right on top is an envelope that's covered with stickers—teapots and kittens and flowers and stuff. I don't even have to open it to know who it's from. I stare at it glumly.

"You're not happy to get a letter?"

I shrug. "It's just my book club pen pal."

"Maybe you could read it to me. Give me something to think about while I chop."

I open the envelope. Out falls a picture of a quilt. Of course. Summer must sew in her sleep. She's written me three letters so far, and each one's come with a picture of a different quilt she's just finished. I mean, quilts are fine and everything, but they're not exactly my style. It's hard to work up much excitement about a blanket.

> Dear Pen Pal,
>
> I took the copy of _Flashlite_ magazine you sent me, the one with your interview in it, to school last week and showed it to everybody. All my friends think it's incredibly cool that we're friends. Even Zoe Winchester, and she doesn't think anything is cool. I

feel sorry for Becca, getting stuck with Zoe for her pen pal. Zoe thinks that just because her mother is the mayor of Gopher Hole, that puts her in charge of everything. But I suppose that's gossip, and my mom always tells me not to gossip, so I guess I should write about other stuff instead of Zoe.

Did I tell you that my last quilt won second place in the Holiday Fair in Laramie? I gave it to my sister Ellie for Christmas to put in her bedroom in her new apartment. She and my sister Tessa go to the University of Wyoming over in Laramie, and they decided they didn't like the dorm so they found this cute little apartment to rent. My brother Andy's going to live with them next year too. The rent is pretty cheap, and they all have part-time jobs, so they figure they can afford it, which is good because my mom says she's already stretched pretty thin paying their tuition.

With Ellie and Tessa off to college now, Rose and I have the bedroom all to ourselves. It feels like we're living in a fancy hotel—I've always shared a room with all of my sisters, and for the first time in my life I actually have my own closet. Not that I have anything to put in it. Mostly I wear my big sisters' hand-me-downs.

My mother says she doesn't feel quite like the

Heather Vogel Frederick

old woman in the shoe anymore, even though there are still six of us at home sharing two bathrooms. My mom and Rose and I share one, and Andy and Peter and Danny and Tim share the other one. Guess which one is neater?

Business at the Cup and Saucer is slower now that winter's here. Wyoming winters are pretty fierce, and most folks are happy just to stay holed up at home and eat their meals in their own warm kitchens. We still get a fairly good breakfast crowd, though, especially people commuting to Laramie. I think my mom's hot coffee and fresh donuts are pretty hard to resist. It's a good thing our diner is just down the street from our house, because we've had so much snow already this winter there are some mornings it's all the boys can do to shovel a path down the sidewalk so Mom can open up.

Have you finished _Daddy-Long-Legs_? Didn't you love it? My favorite part was the ending. Did you guess what was going to happen? I don't have a boyfriend yet, do you?

Your friend,

Summer Williams

I snort. Summer always signs her letters like that, with

her full name. Like maybe I'll have forgotten it or something.

I keep reading:

> P.S. This is the new quilt I worked on over winter vacation. I think it's my best one yet, and I'm going to enter it in the State Fair next summer. My mom let me use a bunch of scraps from some old trunks up in the attic. She says there's a story behind every patch, so I'm calling it "The Story Quilt."

I fold up the letter and put it back in the envelope, feeling annoyed, which is how I always feel when Summer writes me, but also envious. Does everyone on the entire planet except me have brothers and sisters? How many does one person need anyway? I can't even keep track of how many kids there are in Summer's family.

"That wasn't so bad," says Gigi. "She sounds like a nice girl."

"I guess."

"She didn't say anything about her father. Does he help with the restaurant?"

"Her parents are divorced. He lives in Denver, I think."

"Ah. That must be difficult for Summer. May I see the picture she sent? You'll have to hold it for me because my hands are all onion-y."

I fish the picture out and Gigi leans over my shoulder to look at it. She smells good. My grandmother always smells good, thanks to the enormous bottle of expensive perfume on her dresser.

"A Victorian crazy quilt!" she cries. "How beautiful! Look how intri-

Heather Vogel Frederick

cate the stitching is. Summer is right to enter it in the fair—I'm sure she'll win a prize."

I shrug, and Gigi kisses the top of my head. "Count yourself lucky to have such nice friends, Megan. Friends are one of life's richest blessings."

This sounds like something my mother would say, but somehow it doesn't irritate me as much coming from Gigi.

"What are you making?" I ask, changing the subject.

"Dim sum," she replies. "For your book club tonight."

"Oh man! You rock, Gigi!"

She smiles. "I assume that means thank you, so you're welcome."

I love dim sum—although I'd never had it homemade before my grandmother came to visit. I'd only had the kind they serve at the restaurant in Boston my parents like to go to on the weekends sometimes. I love the way the food comes around on trolley carts in those cool little bamboo baskets, and you get to pick what you want. My mother never cooks Chinese, except for these stir-fry things she makes up involving lots of tofu and weird vegetables like kohlrabi and rutabaga and kale. But that's fake Chinese, not the real stuff.

I put my empty plate and glass in the dishwasher, then lean against the counter to watch. "It looks complicated," I tell her.

She laughs. "Dim sum just takes patience, that's all. It means 'a touch of heart'—did you know that? Perhaps because it's a labor of love." She hands me an apron. "Here, I need an assistant. Good thing my beautiful granddaughter is here to help."

That's another thing I love about my grandmother. She always says really nice things to me. My mother, on the other hand, always seems to be on the lookout for things to pick on or correct.

"Look how tall you are!" Gigi adds, tilting her head and smiling up at me. She's petite, like Jess and her mother. "I think maybe you grew while you were at school today."

I have to laugh at that. It's true, though, that I've grown a couple of inches this past year. I'm the same height as my mother now.

We work together chopping and slicing for a while, and I glance out the window over the sink. It's still snowing, Nothing major, not enough to close school, but enough to make everything look pretty, like the coconut my grandmother is busy sprinkling onto the *no mai chi* we're going to have for dessert. Snowballs with peanut filling. Perfect.

"A good night to stay inside and enjoy hot food," says my grandmother. "I like the snow, though. It's pretty. We never get winter weather like this back in Hong Kong."

Gigi always seems to know what I'm thinking. She's more like a friend than a grandmother, which I still find surprising. I know she's a surprise to my friends, too. I'm sure they were expecting one of those little wrinkled peasant ladies like they always show in magazines and movies about China, the kind who dress in those pajama out-fits. Instead, they got—well, Gigi. Who's got fewer wrinkles than I do, dresses in couture from Paris, wears pearls even when she's sleeping, and wouldn't be caught dead in a pair of yoga pants, ever.

Heather Vogel Frederick

"I have something for you when we're done," she tells me, her dark eyes sparkling.

"What?"

"You'll see," she says with a mysterious smile.

Half an hour later, the food is finished. We put everything on trays in the fridge, ready to be cooked after our friends arrive. Then we head downstairs to the guest quarters. That's what my mother calls the entire lower level of our house, which is more like an apartment than a regular guest room. It even has its own little kitchen and everything. My mom stocked it with food before Gigi arrived, but my grandmother only uses it for making tea. "Why would I want to eat down here, away from my family?" she said when she first saw it.

I spend most afternoons after school down here now, and I was here for most of winter vacation, too. Emma and Jess and Cassidy came over a lot to watch movies (Gigi has tons of DVDs of old musicals, which are corny but fun), and Cassidy says Gigi is a kindred spirit, mostly because she's really competitive when it comes to playing cards and board games. And Becca and Ashley love it when Gigi lets us go through her jewelry and clothes and try everything on. Like Summer said about her new quilt, there's a story behind nearly everything my grandmother owns, from shopping triumphs (she loves bargains) to encounters with famous designers. Gigi travels to Paris every spring for Fashion Week, and she says she wants to take me sometime too.

"Is that the surprise?" I ask, pointing to two packages on her bed.

She nods. "But first, let's see what we can do about that awful uniform." She riffles through her closet. "Here," she says, plucking an exquisite silk shirt from its hanger and handing it to me. It's a shade of maroon that the sweater I'm wearing could only hope to be in its wildest dreams, deep and rich and vibrant, like a perfectly ripe plum.

"I wish," I tell her regretfully, looking at the label, which I never ever thought I'd actually see in person, "but we can only wear polo shirts."

"Ridiculous rule." Gigi sniffs.

There's a knock on the door and my mother pokes her head in. "You two bonding over fashion again?" she says. Her smile looks a little strained. My mother could care less about clothes most of the time, and I think she's been feeling a little left out.

"We're just trying to liven up your daughter's pitiful school uniform," Gigi explains. She crosses to her dresser and rummages in her jewelry box. "Why don't you wear these tomorrow?" she says, handing me a pair of diamond earrings the size of peanuts. My mouth falls open. "The uniform may be a lost cause, but just knowing you've got something beautiful to accessorize with will make you feel a whole lot better."

"Mother!" says my mom, looking shocked. "Megan can't wear your diamond earrings to school! What if she loses them?"

Gigi waves her protest away. "Nonsense, darling, she's fourteen now—practically a grown-up. She won't lose them. Besides, I need to be able to spoil my only granddaughter once in a while."

I have two boy cousins—my mother's brother's sons. They live in Hong Kong too. I put Gigi's earrings on. They're absolutely stunning, like twin stars. I turn my head this way and that, staring at my

Heather Vogel Frederick

reflection in the mirror on my grandmother's dressing table. Mirror Megan smiles back at me, as enchanted as I am with the way the earrings sparkle.

Behind me, my mother says something angrily in Chinese. Gigi responds, and pretty soon they're having a full-blown argument. I have no clue what they're saying—I don't speak much Chinese—but I can tell from the tone of their voices that neither of them is very happy. There's been a lot of arguing in the weeks since my grandmother got here. My mother and Gigi, my mother and my father—I'm pretty much the only one not arguing these days. Just last night, I overheard my parents quarreling in the living room, after they thought I was asleep. Mom was upset because Gigi had reorganized the kitchen cupboards and drawers, and she couldn't find anything.

"Can't you just let her have fun?" my dad had said. "It's not like there's any harm done."

"Fun," my mom had replied sarcastically. "Right. Mother puts the 'fun' in 'dysfunctional.'"

The problem is, Gigi *is* fun, and my mom is so serious all the time. It's like she doesn't know how to relax. Everything is always life and death for her. Protecting the environment. Being a good steward with Dad's money by supporting every charitable cause under the sun. Bugging me to good grades so I can get into a good college and have a good career.

It's not like she's not capable of having fun—I've actually seen her do it. That time we went to New York with the book club, for instance. And last year, at our fashion show, she was really funny as the emcee.

But most of the time, forget it. She can't even eat a cinnamon roll, for heaven's sake! I wish she could be a little more like Gigi.

With one final burst of Chinese, my mother leaves the room, slamming the door behind her. Gigi sighs, shaking her head.

"Some things never seem to change," she tells me sadly. "But this is for your mother and me to straighten out, not for you to worry over." She hands me the smaller of the two packages. "Here."

Curious, I open the box and lift out the contents, which have been carefully wrapped in tissue paper. "Wow," I exclaim.

"It's a *kei pou*," says Gigi.

"It's beautiful."

It's a silk dress, tailored in the traditional Chinese fashion, long and slim through the body and finished with a high notched collar, cap sleeves, frog button closures, and a slit up one side of the hem. The turquoise brocade is richly embroidered with an intricate design in pink and gold and white.

"Plum blossoms and butterflies—for long life and beauty," Gigi tells me. "A long time ago this was mine, and then it was your mother's, and now it's yours."

I hold the dress up against me and run my hand along its soft, sleek surface.

"Try it on," coaxes my grandmother.

I don't need any encouragement. Slipping out of my khaki pants and polo shirt, I carefully undo the row of knotted buttons and pull it over my head.

Heather Vogel Frederick

"Perfect," says Gigi. "Just the right length, too. You can see where I had the hem let down for your mother years ago."

I cross to the dressing table to take a look. Mirror Megan beams back at me in approval. The color is incredibly flattering to our ivory skin and dark hair, and the form-fitting, feminine cut makes me look— well, grown-up. "I love it!"

"Your mother never liked traditional clothes," my grandmother continues. "When she left for college in Boston she left it behind. She couldn't wait to be an American girl."

"Really?" I knew that my mother went to M.I.T., because that's where she met my dad. But I didn't know about the other stuff.

"I used to love to wear that dress when I was your age," Gigi continues. "My mother gave it to me for my fourteenth birthday, and I wore it when she took me to tea at the Peninsula Hotel—very fancy."

For my fourteenth birthday, my mother gave me a membership in the Sierra Club and bought an acre of rainforest in my name. I give Gigi a sidelong glance, wondering how two such different people could be related. She and Mom are like Mom and me, only in reverse.

The intercom on the wall crackles. Our house is kind of big, so my dad installed intercoms to keep us from having to holler all the time. "Your friends are starting to arrive, Megan," my mother says, her words clipped and flat. She's obviously still mad.

"Okay, Mom!" I tell her. "I'll be up in a minute."

Gigi hands me the other parcel. I open this one to find three bolts of fabric, all of them richly embroidered Chinese silk brocade just like my new dress, only in different colors and patterns—emerald green with dragonflies, fire-engine red with bamboo leaves and cherry blossoms, and a deep midnight blue covered with peonies.

"Oh my gosh, Gigi, is this all really for me?"

She nods, her little bird's face beaming. "It's vintage, too, just like the *kei pou*. I'd forgotten I had it—it must have been my mother's. I found it when I was cleaning out my apartment to come here. My fashion designer granddaughter needs proper materials to work with."

I give her a hug, squeezing her tight. "Thank you," I whisper.

She squeezes me back. "You're welcome." She places her palms on my cheeks, framing my face. "Those earrings are the perfect accessory," she tells me, turning my head slightly from one side to the other. "But I think you need a splash of perfume."

She douses me with scent, then shoos me out the door. "Now go upstairs and wow your friends. I'd better start cooking the dim sum."

I sprint up to my bedroom clutching my new bolts of fabric, which I slide under my bed for now. I want to keep them a secret until I decide what to make with them.

Becca and Emma are in the living room, waiting for me.

"Oh my gosh, Megs, you look amazing," says Emma, her eyes widening.

I twirl around. "Gigi gave it to me. It used to be hers when she was my age."

"Doesn't that make it a little out of style?" says Becca.

Heather Vogel Frederick

"Nope, it means it's vintage, and vintage never goes out of style," I explain. "Stars wear vintage designer clothes to the Oscars and stuff all the time."

"Those aren't real, are they?" she asks, peering at my earrings.

I nod, smiling. "They're just on loan, though."

Becca gets really quiet, and I realize that she's envious. Her grandmother is nice too, but she's no Gigi.

The doorbell rings and Cassidy barges in, her hair still all sweaty from hockey practice. At least she changed out of her uniform. She collapses onto the sofa.

"How's your mom?" I ask her.

"Still barfing."

"Eeewwwww," says Becca.

Emma wrinkles her brow. "I thought morning sickness was only supposed to last the first few months?"

"Don't look at me," snaps Cassidy. "I'm not the expert."

"I think it's cool she's expecting," I tell her. Now I'm the envious one. "A little sister or brother—lucky you!"

"Can we not talk about it, please?"

Cassidy's still really touchy about the baby.

Jess is the last to arrive. "You look just like a princess in a snow globe," she tells me, pointing to the window behind me. I look over my shoulder to see that someone—Gigi, I guess—turned on the spotlights in the backyard, illuminating the birch trees and the falling snow.

It does kind of look like a snow globe. I fling my arms wide and twirl around again. I'm too old to be twirling, but I don't care. In this dress I really do feel like a princess.

"What's new with Julia?" Becca asks Jess. Like all of us, Becca is completely fascinated with Savannah Sinclair. Savannah, or "Julia" as we mostly call her, is one of our favorite topics of conversation whenever we get together.

"Ugh," says Jess. "Don't ask."

"C'mon," Becca coaxes.

Jess sighs. "Oh, okay."

We all crowd around her so we won't miss a word.

"All she can talk about these days is her ski trip to Switzerland next month," Jess tells us. "She's taking Peyton with her, and they keep asking me where I'm going for our break."

"I thought you just had a vacation?" Cassidy looks puzzled.

"Private schools are on a different schedule than public schools," Jess explains. "We had the same break over the holidays that Walden does, but at Colonial Academy there's a week in February, too, so everyone can go skiing. And another week in the spring, so everybody can go to the Caribbean and work on their tans, I guess."

"Sheesh," says Cassidy. "Lucky you."

"It's not like I'm going anywhere," Jess retorts. "I'll be stuck here in Concord, just like you."

"Trust Savannah to be going skiing someplace exotic, instead of somewhere normal like New Hampshire or Vermont," gripes Emma.

Heather Vogel Frederick

The kitchen door swings open and our moms appear.

"Oh my goodness, Megan, what a gorgeous dress," says Mrs. Sloane-Kinkaid, who is looking pretty stunning herself in jeans and a chic peach-colored tunic sweater with a big cowl neck. They must be maternity jeans, because she's starting to show now. She's got brown leather boots on and a big slouchy hobo bag to match. I can tell I'm going to have to go back downstairs for my sketchbook.

Cassidy's mother crosses to where I'm standing and traces the embroidery with a well-manicured fingertip. "That fabric is absolutely stunning."

"It's vintage," I tell her.

"Oh, wow—that makes it even more special."

My mother makes a face at Gigi. "Mother, you didn't give Megan that old thing, did you? I remember when you tried to foist it off on me."

"You just don't appreciate beautiful workmanship," my grandmother replies.

"Hmmph," says my mother. "Sweatshop labor is more likely."

"Your grandmother had it made at the finest dress shop in Hong Kong!" Gigi replies indignantly. "Their staff were never underpaid!"

My mother doesn't look convinced. Gigi marches back off to the kitchen in a huff and I sit down on the sofa next to Cassidy, who eyes my *kei pou*.

"I like the dragonflies," she says grudgingly.

We all turn and stare at her.

She glares back at us. "What?"

"Uh, nothing," I reply. "It's just—you don't usually care about clothes."

Cassidy lifts a shoulder. "Dude, I didn't say I wanted to marry it or anything, I just said I liked the pattern on the fabric. It's cool."

Mrs. Sloane-Kinkaid chuckles. "So, I am raising a girl after all," she says, arching an eyebrow at the other moms. Cassidy scowls and scooches up the leg of her sweat pants, then busies herself checking out the bruises on her shins.

Gigi appears, bearing a tray. "I hope everyone is hungry," she says, setting it on the coffee table.

"Dim sum? Gigi, you didn't!" says Mrs. Hawthorne.

"I certainly did," my grandmother replies. "With Megan's help, that is." She glances over at me, her dark almond eyes crinkling at the corners, then starts lifting the lids of the bamboo baskets. "This one is *Har gau*—steamed shrimp dumplings in rice flour wrappers—and this is *Caa siu baau*—steamed barbecued pork buns—and we also have *Cheun gyun*, fried spring rolls, and *Wu gok*, yam puffs."

"Don't forget the *No mai chi*," I add, hoping I'm pronouncing it correctly. "They look like snowballs. For dessert."

"Oh my word, you're spoiling us!" cries Mrs. Delaney.

"I don't recall Judy Abbott and her friends eating Chinese food," says Mrs. Chadwick, whom I'd barely noticed until now. She's dressed from head to toe in white tonight and blends in with our living room rug and furniture. She sounds kind of snippy, which means she's probably still mad about cornmeal mush night.

Heather Vogel Frederick

"I'm sure they would have if they'd had someone like Gigi around to cook it for them," says Mrs. Sloane-Kinkaid, loading up her plate.

"I made ginger sesame seaweed salad, too," my mother says in the tight voice I've been hearing a lot of lately. She puts a dish of slimy-looking green stuff down on the coffee table next to Gigi's feast. "It's high in vitamins and nutriments like iodine. Very good for you."

Nobody touches it except her, of course. The dim sum is just so much better.

"Not gonna barf again, are you, Mom?" says Cassidy, watching as her mother wolfs down a pork bun.

"Not on your life," Mrs. Sloane-Kinkaid replies, licking her fingers. "In fact, I think dim sum just might be this baby's favorite food." She pats her tummy contentedly.

"So, shall we get started?" says Mrs. Hawthorne finally.

I leap to my feet. "Wait! I need my sketchbook!" I race down the hall to my room and grab it, then race back and settle on the floor by the sofa.

"So, how did everyone like the book?" Mrs. Hawthorne asks.

Eyes shining, Emma leans forward. "I couldn't believe it when Judy's mysterious benefactor turned out to be—"

Becca claps her hands over her ears. "Don't tell me!" she shrieks. "I haven't finished yet!"

"Rebecca!" her mother chides. "You told me you were done."

"Busted," whispers Cassidy with a grin.

Becca glares at her. "I can't help it, I had math homework."

"There's no harm done, Becca," Mrs. Hawthorne assures her. "And I promise we won't spoil the surprise, will we, girls?"

"What are some of your favorite parts of the book *besides* the ending?" Mrs. Delaney says.

"I loved Judy's little drawings," I reply, my pen swiftly outlining Mrs. Sloane-Kinkaid's purse.

"I loved it when she made a window seat out of a bureau with a pillow on top," says Jess. "I wish I could do that in my dorm room."

"Maybe you could do it at home instead," her mother suggests. "Your dresser is old anyway. We could work on it over your break next month."

I look up from my sketch and find myself wishing my mother was a little more like the other mothers. Well, except for Mrs. Chadwick. I love Becca and everything, but I would so not want Mrs. Chadwick for my mother. Mrs. Delaney and Mrs. Hawthorne and Mrs. Sloane-Kinkaid, though, they all know how to have fun.

"I loved Judy's descriptions of Lock Willow Farm," says Emma dreamily. "She made it sound like such a perfect spot for a writer. I'd like to have a place like that to go to in the summer so I could work on a book too."

Emma's determined to be a writer when she grows up. She's even started looking at colleges that have good writing programs. Things have quieted down for me since the *Flashlite* article last year, but I'm still pretty sure I want to be a fashion designer, so I keep sketching and sewing. I dropped by the library last week and Mrs. Hawthorne helped me do some research about design schools. It's still kind of far away to think

Heather Vogel Frederick

seriously about, but my mother always says it's good to have a goal.

I draw Mrs. Sloane-Kinkaid's baby bump. It's hard to believe there's an actual little person growing inside there. I give my mother's flat stomach a wistful glance, then flip to the sketch I did of Maggie Crandall a few weeks ago when I went over to Colonial Academy again to help Jess babysit. Should I add maternity wear and baby clothes to my future fashion line? I think about this for a moment, then sigh. I have babies on the brain these days. I close my sketchbook and shove it under the sofa.

"I like the part when Julia's Uncle Jervis comes to visit, and they ditch Julia and go out for tea and Julia gets mad," Cassidy says.

"Yeah," Becca agrees. "And how he turned out to be so nice and nobody could believe he was an actual Pendleton."

"Maybe Savannah has a nice uncle somewhere to redeem the Sinclair name," says Emma.

"One that's called something besides stupid *Jervis*," adds Cassidy. "Sheesh."

I notice Mrs. Chadwick and Becca exchange a glance, but before I have time to wonder about it, Mrs. Hawthorne reaches into her canvas bag for this month's handouts.

FUN FACTS ABOUT JEAN

1) While an undergraduate at Vassar College, Jean Webster made a name for herself as a "shark at English." She wrote plays, published stories in the *Vassar Miscellany*, edited and

illustrated her yearbook, and earned $3 a week for a newsy column about college life that she wrote for the local paper, the *Poughkeepsie Sunday Courier*, at a time when 35 cents would buy a lobster dinner at a local restaurant.

2) Jean was independent, witty, cheerful, optimistic, modest, and beloved by her friends and family. She was determined to earn her living as a writer, and did exactly that, graduating from college in 1901 and publishing her first novel, *When Patty Went to College*, in 1903. It was based on some of her experiences at Vassar, and a few years later she went on to write a prequel, *Just Patty*, based on her exploits at the Lady Jane Grey boarding school.

3) Jean loved to travel, and spent a semester abroad visiting France, Italy, and England. In 1906 she toured Asia, including such exotic destinations as Cairo, Bombay, Burma, Java, Ceylon, Singapore, Saigon, Hong Kong, and Japan.

4) A successful journalist, novelist, and playwright, Jean would eventually write a total of eight novels and numerous unpublished stories and plays. The books that became bestsellers in her day and that have endured to ours are her stories about girls at school and college.

Heather Vogel Frederick

5) In 1912, *Daddy-Long-Legs* began its record-breaking career first as a serialized story in *Ladies' Home Journal*, then as a hugely popular book which reviewers called "a package of condensed sunshine" and "an effervescent little love story." A sequel, *Dear Enemy*, was also a best seller.

6) *Daddy-Long-Legs* was adapted for the stage by Jean and toured nationwide. In Washington, D.C., it was viewed by none other than President Woodrow Wilson, who "fell out of his chair laughing," Jean wrote to a friend at the time. Her play went on to become a smash hit on Broadway and in London.

"What does 'effervescent' mean?" asks Cassidy.

Her mother holds up a glass of sparkling cider. "Bubbly."

"That's a good description of the book," says Jess. "It's definitely bubbly."

"Frothy," adds Emma.

"Vivacious," says her mother.

"Lively," suggests Mrs. Chadwick.

"Exuberant," says Mrs. Delaney.

I look over at my mother, who is frowning at the untouched bowl of seaweed salad. "Fun," I whisper to myself sadly.

"So Jean Webster visited Hong Kong?" says Gigi, sounding pleased. "I never knew that."

"And enjoyed it very much," Mrs. Hawthorne reports, consulting her notes.

"See, Mrs. Chadwick?" says Cassidy, reaching for the last coconut ball. "Judy and Sallie and their friends might never have had dim sum, but I'll bet the author did."

Her mother sits bolt upright. "That gives me a wonderful idea!" she exclaims. "How about a dim sum episode on my TV show? Would you be willing, Gigi?"

"Why not?" my grandmother replies. "Sounds like fun."

My eyes slide over to my mom, who has a distant expression on her face. *"Mother puts the 'fun' in 'dysfunctional'"*—wasn't that what she told my father? Last year, Cassidy's mom promised to do a vegetarian episode and let my mom be in charge, but that hasn't happened yet. My mother gets up and silently clears away our dishes.

Gigi watches her as she heads for the kitchen. There's a worried pleat between her eyebrows, and I remember what she said earlier downstairs, about things never changing between my mom and her. I turn and look outside again, where the snow is still falling in the birches. I'm not feeling like a princess in a snow globe any more. I'm feeling more like the princess caught in the middle. If I wear Gigi's dress and her earrings, and happen to like her cooking better than my mother's, does that make me disloyal? If I like to have fun, am I a bad daughter? Do I really have to choose sides?

Why is life always so complicated?

Heather Vogel Frederick

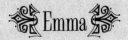 Emma

"Should you mind, just for a little while, pretending you are my grandmother?"
—*Daddy-Long-Legs*

"Trust Nutmeg to pick the coldest day of the year to have her kittens," I grumble, my words puffing out in frosty clouds as I trot behind Jess toward her barn.

"You won't mind once you see them," she calls back over her shoulder at me, laughing. "They're so cute!"

Shivering, I follow her up the ladder to the hayloft and the old storage room that Mr. Delaney let us have for a hangout. We don't come up here much in the winter. There's no heat and we'd freeze to death, especially on a day like today when February is giving us the cold shoulder.

That's pretty good, I think, and pause for a second to pull out the little notebook that I keep tucked in my pocket for when inspiration strikes. I jot down *February—cold shoulder*. This is an old writer's trick that my dad taught me. Ideas are like stray cats, he says. They show up at your doorstep at inconvenient times, and they'll slip away again unless you take care of them.

He's right, too. If I don't write things down the minute they come to me, I always forget them later, even when I'm sure I won't.

"Quit dawdling, Emma!" Jess calls from the other side of the storage room.

I put the notebook away and cross to where she's kneeling by a pile of old horse blankets in the corner. For some reason, the Delaneys' barn cats all think this is the best place on Half Moon Farm to have their kittens. Probably because it's right above Led and Zep, and some of the warmth from their stalls seeps through the gaps in the floorboards.

Jess lifts a corner of one of the blankets, revealing a pile of furry bodies nestled deep in its folds. "See?" she whispers proudly, as if she'd produced the kittens herself. Jess loves animals of every sort, but especially baby animals. And between the goats and the chickens and the barn cats, there are always plenty of those at Half Moon Farm.

"It's okay, Nutmeg," she reassures the mother cat. "We just want to look at your babies."

Nutmeg blinks up at us and purrs. I count five little fuzzballs cuddled up next to her, sound asleep. Jess is right, they are incredibly cute. Taking off one of my mittens, I reach out a finger and gently stroke the nearest tiny pink belly.

"Maybe your parents will let you have one," says Jess, who has been trying to console me ever since the holidays.

I've had "puppy" at the top of my Christmas list for the past five

Heather Vogel Frederick

years. Birthday list too. But so far my parents keep saying no. My dad says Melville rules the roost at our house, and it wouldn't be fair to spring a puppy on him in his dotage. "Dotage" means old age—Melville is thirteen, same as me, but in cat-years that's ancient. I think this is just a convenient excuse, though. My dad isn't a big fan of dogs.

We watch the kittens until we get too cold, then head back down to the barn to the creamery where Jess's dad is making cheese. Mr. Delaney spends a lot of time in the creamery these days, because Half Moon Farm's line of organic goat cheeses has really taken off this year. Jess tells me that loads of restaurants are ordering it directly, some from as far away as New York, and a bunch of organic grocery stores are stocking it now too. Blue Moon is the farm's second most popular brand, right after the original plain kind, Half Moon.

"How are my two best apprentice cheesemakers today?" says Mr. Delaney.

Jess gives him a halfhearted smile. I know she feels guilty not being able to help out more, now that she's at Colonial Academy. "Your best ones? We're your only ones, Dad."

Her father gives her braid a tug. "You're still the best, though." Turning to me he says, "Jess tells me you took Eva Bergson to 'Granola with Grandparents' last week."

I nod.

"What a great idea! Her husband coached my hockey team when I was the twins' age, and she was there at every practice and every game. She's a terrific lady."

Mom was the one who encouraged me to invite her, after Gran and Paw-Paw told me they'd rather come visit in the summer when the weather is nice. Flying to the East Coast from Seattle in early February is too iffy, they said, what with snowstorms always threatening to shut down the airport.

I was nervous about asking Mrs. Bergson. I really like her and everything—she's a great skating teacher, which is only natural since she skated in the Olympics about a hundred years ago. But it's not like I really know her, so I was kind of surprised when Mom suggested it. I went ahead and invited her, though, and we actually had a lot of fun. Everybody in town knows her, because she's been teaching skating at the rink here in Concord forever, so there was this big cluster of people around her practically the entire time we were at school. I had no idea she'd taught so many people I know, including Ms. Nielson and a bunch of the other teachers. Even Mrs. Hanson, our principal, took skating lessons from her once.

I'd been worried about having to make conversation, but Megan brought Gigi, of course, and she and Mrs. Bergson really hit it off. It turns out Gigi is a big fan of figure skating, and loves to watch all the competitions on TV, so the two of them had tons to talk about. Plus Cassidy's grandmother was there too, and thanks to Cassidy she knows a lot about hockey now, so there were never any lulls for me to have to try and fill in.

As a thank-you for inviting her, Mrs. Bergson asked me to her house for tea. "Now that we've broken the ice," as she put it, smiling at

Heather Vogel Frederick

her own lame joke. I'm supposed to go there later today, after we help Jess's dad with the cheese.

Jess and I roll up our sleeves and get to work cleaning and washing all the equipment. Everything has to be kept spotless and sterilized in the creamery, and that's a large part of our job as "apprentice cheese-makers." We wear rubber gloves so we can use really hot water to rinse everything before we load up the industrial-size dishwashers, and we even have to put our hair up in those net things like the lunch ladies in the school cafeteria. We're used to them now, but the first few times we put them on we both just cracked up.

A while later the barn phone rings and Mr. Delaney answers it.

"Okay, hon," he says. "We'll be right in." He hangs up and turns back to us. "That was your mother, Jess. Lunch is ready."

After lunch—tuna sandwiches and Mrs. Delaney's homemade carrot soup—Jess and I head up to her room.

"Has Madison written to you lately?" I ask.

"Just one letter since that Christmas card I got back in December." She rummages in her desk drawer and holds up a CD. "She sent me another recording of her band."

"Moonrise?"

"Yeah."

"I still think that's a totally cool name for a band."

"Yeah, me too. Want to hear it? They're pretty good."

I nod and Jess pops it in her CD player and we listen for a while.

She's right—the music is pretty good, especially Madison's guitar. A person could actually dance to this stuff.

"So what did she say in her letter?" I ask, curious.

Jess rummages in her drawer again and pulls out an envelope, which she hands to me. I open it and start to read.

> Dear Pen Pal,
>
> My mom and dad and little brother and I went to Chicago to visit my grandparents for Christmas. It was fun. We drove down Miracle Mile to look at all the lights and shop displays, and we went to the movies with our cousins a couple of times and on New Year's Eve we all went to the Navy Pier on Lake Michigan to watch the fireworks. They were awesome. I got the new guitar I asked for, and some CDs and clothes and stuff.
>
> Happy New Year from your friend,
> Madison Daniels

"Kind of short, huh?" I say.

"Yeah."

"She seems nice, though, and it was really sweet of her to send you some more music."

"I know, but I still don't feel like I know her very well yet. Not like you and Bailey."

My pen pal and I are like two peas in a pod. Bailey and I write each

Heather Vogel Frederick

other at least once a week, but I keep telling Jess not to worry, she's still my best friend. I also point out that if anyone should be feeling worried, it's me, since she has Frankie and Adele now, who are real live flesh-and-blood friends, not just pen pals.

I tell Jess that it's only because she's at Colonial Academy and isn't around as much to talk to that I write so often to Bailey. And that she shouldn't worry too much about Madison not writing to her all that often. Some people just aren't big letter-writers.

"So what's Julia been up to lately?" I ask, moving on to our pet topic. Savannah Sinclair is endlessly fascinating.

"Oh, just more of the usual," Jess replies, flopping onto her bed. She leans back on her pillow, crossing her arms behind her head and staring up at the ceiling. "I'm still hearing all the details about her stupid ski trip. Her family's going someplace called St. Moritz. I guess it's pretty fancy. All she and Peyton can talk about is how amazing it's going to be and how sorry they are for me because I'll be stuck here over the break in pokey old Concord."

"What's wrong with pokey old Concord?" I ask. "You'll have fun. I know I'll be in school, but I've already asked my mom and she's promised we can have a sleepover at my house over the weekend before you have to go back. And who cares what Miss La-di-da Sinclair thinks anyway?"

Jess sighs. "I guess you're right."

At three, Darcy shows up to get me. My parents won't let me ride my bike to Jess's in the winter—the roads are too slippery this time of year and it gets dark too early—and since Darcy has his license now, he's going to drop me off at Mrs. Bergson's before going to the movies with his friend Kyle. Afterward, Stewart's going to meet me and walk me home. He doesn't have his license yet.

"I haven't seen much of Jess this year," says Darcy as I get into the car.

"I know," I reply. Jess is standing on the steps to her back porch, waving, and I wave back. So does Darcy.

"I kind of miss having her around," my brother continues, backing out of the driveway. "She's a nice kid."

I give him a sidelong glance. Is he dropping a hint? "Well, she's kind of busy at her new school," I reply cautiously.

"Does she like Colonial Academy? Those girls always seem kind of stuck-up to me."

"Some of them are," I agree. "But some of them are really nice, too. And Jess loves her classes. You know how smart she is. Plus, she's learning how to ride."

"Cool." Darcy pulls out onto the main road. "Belknap Street, right?"

I nod, wondering if I should say anything to him about Jess. Does he know that she likes him? Darcy doesn't have a regular girlfriend, although there are a few girls he hangs out with now and then. I have no idea how he feels about Jess, but he must have noticed how pretty she is. She's spent enough time at our house over the years. Megan and Becca and Ashley are always telling her that she should wear makeup and stuff, but Jess can't be bothered and she doesn't need it anyway.

Heather Vogel Frederick

She's perfect just the way she is, as far as I'm concerned.

Before I can decide whether or not to say anything to him, though, we pull up in front of a big yellow Colonial house.

"This is it," my brother says. "Have a good time, and say hi to Mrs. Bergson for me." My brother plays hockey for the Alcott Avengers, and spends more time at the rink than I do.

I get out of the car and head up the walkway to the front door. There are four doorbells—Mrs. Bergson told me that the house is divided into four condominiums—and I push the one marked "Bergson." The intercom crackles.

"Is that you, Emma?"

"Yes."

"Come on up. I'm the left-hand door at the top of the stairs."

The front door buzzes, and I push it open and go inside. Upstairs, Mrs. Bergson's door is ajar.

"Hang your coat in the closet!" she calls. "I'll be there in a minute. I'm just finishing up here in the kitchen."

She appears a minute later, wiping her hands on a dish towel. "Welcome," she says warmly, giving me a hug. "Would you like a tour?"

"Sure."

Mrs. Bergson's condo is small, but really nice. All the rooms have high ceilings and there are three fireplaces, one in the living room, one in the dining room, and one in her bedroom. "These rooms were all bedrooms once upon a time," she tells me. "Old-fashioned houses can't be beat for fireplaces."

There's a fire in the living room, or "sitting room," as she calls it, and a tea table has been set up in front of the hearth between two comfortable armchairs. I take a seat, suddenly feeling a little shy. I glance surreptitiously at Mrs. Bergson as she pours our tea. She's medium height, like my mother, and very fit. Her face is weathered and tan and covered with wrinkles, but they're more like what Mrs. Sloane-Kinkaid calls "happiness lines" than wrinkles, because she's always smiling. Her bright blue eyes look out at the world from beneath a tidy cap of white hair, and she doesn't wear a speck of makeup. I guess when you're that old, you figure why bother?

I take the teacup she passes me and look around the room. There are framed photographs everywhere, some on the piano, others on the mantel, and still others on the bookshelves flanking the fireplace.

"My late husband and me," she says, pointing to a portrait on the mantel of a slim blond couple. They're on a mountaintop somewhere, laughing. "Wasn't he handsome?"

I nod and she passes me a plate of cookies. I take one and bite into it. It's thin and crispy and delicious. "Yum," I say, and Mrs. Bergson smiles.

"Yum for sure. They're *Pepparkakor*—Swedish gingersnaps. My husband's grandmother's recipe. Nils was from Sweden, you know. A speed skater. We met at the Squaw Valley Olympics a very long time ago."

"Do you have any kids?" I ask her, and she shakes her head.

"No," she replies, a trifle sadly. "They just never came along." She

Heather Vogel Frederick

brightens. "But of course I have had many, many children in my life over the years through my teaching. And perhaps, since I got to pretend to be your grandmother last week, you wouldn't mind pretending to be my granddaughter once in a while."

"Okay," I reply, feeling shy again.

She smiles and pours me another cup of tea and I start to relax.

The sitting room is cozy, with the fire crackling and the cheery floral slipcovers on the sofa and chairs and February banished outside. A last few rays of feeble winter sun slant in through the big windows, lighting up the bookshelves. Curious to see what kinds of books Mrs. Bergson likes to read, I set my teacup down and wander over to look at some of the titles. Poetry and biographies and mysteries, apparently—especially Agatha Christie and somebody named Dorothy Sayers—and she has a lot of my favorites, too, including *Little Women* and the *Anne of Green Gables* series. She even has some of Jean Webster's books.

"We just read *Daddy-Long-Legs* for our Mother-Daughter Book Club," I tell her, taking it off the shelf.

"You did? Oh, good—I'm so glad to hear that girls are still reading that wonderful book. It was one of my favorites when I was your age. So amusing and clever! And of course you know what they say, if you have books, you have friends."

She takes another sip of tea, and I put the book back and sit down again. It occurs to me that maybe Eva Bergson is a little bit lonely. Maybe that's why Mom suggested I invite her to Granola with

Grandparents. I look around for a cat or a hamster or something, but from what I can tell she doesn't seem to have a pet.

"Mrs. Bergson," I say slowly, as an idea dawns on me, "why don't you join our Mother-Daughter Book Club?"

She looks surprised. "Me? But I'm not a mother, and I don't have a daughter."

"No, but you like the same kinds of books that we do, and you're sort of my adopted grandmother now. Megan Wong's grandmother comes to our meetings."

"Really? Well, now, that would be fun, wouldn't it?" She smiles at me. "It's very kind of you to think of inviting me, Emma, but I think perhaps you'd better check with your mother and your friends first, to see how they feel about it."

I promise her that I will, and we eat a few more cookies and drink some more tea and then she brings out her photo albums from when she was in the Olympics, and from all the years she's spent coaching and teaching. She even lets me hold her Olympic medal. It sits solidly in my palm, cool to the touch, and I'm surprised at how heavy it is.

"Is it real gold?" I ask, tracing the design on it with my finger.

Mrs. Bergson shakes her head. "They were until 1912, but after that they started making them out of silver, with a gold coating."

"Wow."

"Here, why don't you try it on to see how it feels."

Mrs. Bergson slips the loop of ribbon over my head.

Heather Vogel Frederick

"This is probably as close as I'll ever get to being in the Olympics," I tell her with a grin.

"You've come a long way since your first lesson, Emma," she replies, smiling back at me. "I won't lie to you, it's true you probably won't be making the Olympic team anytime soon, but there's more to life than just competition. There's also the joy of doing something just for the sheer love of it."

Our conversation turns to school, and I tell her about Jess going away to Colonial Academy this year, and how hard that's been, and about working on the school newspaper, and about Walden's stupid school uniform policy.

"I still can't believe we have to wear them," I finish. "And I really wish they'd asked the students what we thought before springing the decision on us."

Mrs. Bergson sips her tea and regards me thoughtfully. "Didn't you just tell me that you're the editor of your school newspaper this year?"

I nod.

"Well, for goodness sake, Emma, the pen is far mightier than the sword and always has been." Mrs. Bergson puts down her teacup and leans forward in her chair. "I should think a smart girl like you would be able to do something about the uniforms, if you set your mind to it."

"Me?" I stare at her. "What can I do?"

"You're a writer—write!"

"But I already ran an article reporting on the whole thing right after school started."

"There's a difference between reporting and editorializing," Mrs. Bergson tells me. "To change minds, you'll need to write a persuasive opinion piece, perhaps, or do some investigative reporting. Maybe you could look into the effect of school uniforms on grades at Walden, and see if there's really been a change. Or how about family budgets? Surely it's an extra expense for many families to have to buy uniforms."

I look at her, astonished. Mrs. Bergson is way different than I thought she'd be. She's much more than just a skating teacher, for one thing. She's smart and she's funny and she likes to read the same kinds of things I do—she's a kindred spirit, like Anne Shirley and Judy Abbott and Jo March.

And she's right about the family budget angle. We're not poor or anything, but my dad doesn't make much money as an aspiring novelist and my family relies mostly on my mother's librarian salary. My parents weren't too thrilled to have to buy me a whole new wardrobe this year, even if it was mostly just khakis and polos. I hear their conversations when they think I'm not listening, and I know how expensive it is to live in Concord. I know about the high property taxes, and I know about the leak in the attic roof and the dry rot in the basement and the engine trouble in our beat-up station wagon that's almost as old as Melville. And I know they're trying to save for college for me and my brother on top of everything else. My parents worry a lot about money. I guess all parents do, except for maybe the Wongs. School uniforms would have been hard on the Delaneys, too, if Jess hadn't gotten a scholarship to Colonial Academy. Her family's always joking around about how they live on "Ramshackle Farm."

I whip out my notebook and jot down a few ideas about this possible new story idea. Across the tea table from me, Mrs. Bergson smiles to herself.

I'm completely taken by surprise when the clock on the mantel chimes five. I had no idea two hours could fly by so fast.

"My friend Stewart will be here any minute to pick me up," I tell Mrs. Bergson.

"Stewart?"

"Chadwick. You've probably seen him at the rink. He's tall and skinny and has dark hair and sometimes wears glasses. He plays hockey on the rec team."

"Ah. That Stewart." Mrs. Bergson gives me an impish look, and we both start to giggle. Stewart is *terrible* at hockey. He admits it too. The thing is, though, he really likes to play. So he just keeps on trying. "You've got to admire his spirit," says Mrs. Bergson, as if she'd read my thoughts. I nod, and we giggle again.

The doorbell rings and Mrs. Bergson gets up to buzz Stewart in. He looks surprised when I greet him at the door with the Olympic medal around my neck.

"Is that—?"

"Yup," I tell him.

"I'll trade you," Mrs. Bergson says to me, holding out my coat and nodding at the medal.

Stewart grins. "I don't know, Emma," he says. "Maybe you should just let her keep the coat."

Mrs. Bergson laughs. I hand her back her medal and she lets Stewart try it on while I'm getting my things, and then she gives us some cookies to take home with us.

"I'll let you know what the rest of the book club thinks about my idea," I tell her as we head out the door.

"Thank you, Emma."

"What idea?" Stewart asks once we're outside.

I explain about having Mrs. Bergson join our book club, and then I tell him what she said about the pen being mightier than the sword and all the ideas she had for the school newspaper.

"Good point," says Stewart. He takes my hand. We're both wearing mittens but it still feels nice. We walk fast, because it's cold. Passing the entrance gates to Colonial Academy on the way to Keyes Road and the shortcut home, I spot Adele and Frankie on the quad. I call out to them and wave.

They hurry over, glancing curiously at Stewart.

I wonder what Jess has told them about me—and about Stewart. He's not looking much like male model material tonight. For one thing, he's got his old glasses on, because he's just come from hockey practice at the rink and he always wears them to play in since he doesn't care if something happens to them. For another, his hockey stick is sticking

Heather Vogel Frederick

up out of his backpack and he's wearing this goofy hat with earflaps that looks like maybe it used to belong to Elmer Fudd.

"Uh, Stewart, this is Adele Bixby and Frankie—Francesca—Norris," I say politely, introducing him to Jess's friends. "Adele and Frankie, this is Stewart Chadwick."

They both get really giggly all of a sudden, which is totally not like them, and that tells me that Jess must have explained about Stewart. She probably showed them one of his pictures, too, in *Flashlite*. I sigh. I suppose I should be used to this reaction from other girls by now, but mostly I just find it annoying. Sure, Stewart is cute and everything—even his dorky glasses and hockey stick and hat can't hide that fact completely—but he's still just Stewart.

We stand there chatting for a while, and then I hear boots scuffing on the snowy sidewalk behind me and turn to see Savannah Sinclair and her friend Peyton Winslow approaching. They stop talking when they spot us.

"You're Jess's friend, right?" Savannah says, but it's a statement more than a question.

I nod.

"The one she makes cheese with every weekend?" Savannah looks over at Peyton and smirks when she says the word "cheese."

"Uh, yeah."

"My, what exciting lives you two lead." She glances at Adele and Frankie. "Sure makes you wish you were a townie, right, girls?"

"Um, I should probably get going," says Adele, inching away. She clearly doesn't want to tangle with Savannah. Not that I blame her.

"Me too," adds Frankie. "Later, guys."

As Jess's friends retreat back to safety beyond the academy's iron gates, Savannah turns her attention to Stewart. "So who's this?" she asks rudely.

"Stewart Chadwick," I tell her reluctantly. "Stewart, this is Savannah Sinclair."

"Do you make cheese too?" Savannah asks him.

Stewart shakes his head, setting his earflaps flapping. "Alas, that is not one of my talents, although I do enjoy consuming it now and then."

I cringe slightly inside. Stewart always gets really formal and ultra-dorky when he's nervous, and I can tell Savannah is making him nervous.

Savannah's eyes narrow. "Wait a minute, aren't you that guy Jess told me about? The *Flashlite* guy?"

Thanks, Jess, I think to myself.

"Uh," says Stewart.

Savannah purses her lips as she looks him up and down, then smirks at Peyton again. "They must really be scraping the bottom of the barrel at *Flashlite* these days."

"Funny," I retort, glaring at her, "I was just saying the same thing to Stewart about Colonial Academy. It's amazing the kinds of students who manage to get admitted."

Savannah's face turns an ugly shade of red, and I grab Stewart and pull him down the sidewalk before she can fire back. As I hustle him around the corner of Keyes Road he looks over at me admiringly. "The kitten has claws!" he says. "Go, Emma! Way to stick up for your man!"

Now I'm the one blushing. Is that how Stewart thinks of himself? As my man? We don't talk much about that kind of stuff when we're together. Embarrassed but happy, I break into a jog and we run, laughing, the rest of the way to my house.

We're breathless by the time we get there.

"I can't see a thing," I complain. "My glasses are all fogged up."

"Mine, too," Stewart replies. "It's the blind leading the blind."

Reaching over his shoulder and grabbing his hockey stick out of his backpack, he starts tapping it back and forth in the driveway. I giggle as he leads me to the back door.

The porch light must have burned out, because it's dark by the steps. I hear my dad rattling around inside in the kitchen, getting dinner ready. Stewart usually gives me a hug good-bye, but tonight it lasts longer than usual.

"Thanks for being my hero back there," he whispers.

I can feel his heart thudding against my jacket and my heart starts to beat a little faster, too. Is this it? Is he finally going to kiss me? With a sudden flash of panic, I wish I'd had time to brush my teeth after having tea with Mrs. Bergson. I wish I knew what to do, too. A first kiss isn't like the Olympics or anything—it's not like you can train for it.

And then suddenly we're standing in a spotlight, or what feels like a spotlight. I raise up on tiptoe and peer over Stewart's shoulder to see our station wagon pulling into the driveway. Darcy's home from the movies. He starts honking wildly, and Stewart drops his arms and steps away from me.

"What is your *problem?!*" I holler at my brother, furious.

He pokes his head out the window. "Just giving the lovebirds a little encouragement!" he calls back, and then he and Kyle both start laughing like maniacs.

I stand there feeling foolish, and so embarrassed I want to cry.

Stewart gives my hand a squeeze. "I'll see you at the editorial meeting after school tomorrow, okay?"

"Okay."

He jogs off toward home. Disappointed, humiliated, and boiling mad, I rush inside, slamming the door behind me.

"What on earth is the matter?" asks my dad, blinking in surprise.

"Nothing!"

"Did you have a nice time with Mrs. Bergson?"

"Yes!"

"Emma, what's going on?"

"I don't want to talk about it!" I reply, then blurt out, "Darcy is a moron!"

Sometimes my brother can be completely clueless. How can Jess possibly like him? Feeling my father's puzzled gaze on my back, I stomp out of the kitchen and upstairs to my room.

Heather Vogel Frederick

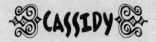

CASSIDY

"I am going to pretend that all life is just a game which I must play as skillfully and fairly as I can. If I lose, I am going to shrug my shoulders and laugh —also if I win."

—*Daddy-Long-Legs*

One minute left in the third period, the score is tied, and the Minutemen are out for blood. We've snatched the championship away from them the last two years in a row, and they're breathing fire trying to turn this semifinal game around. If they beat us today, they advance to the final round. If we beat them, we have another shot at the championship and it's *good-bye Minutemen, see you next year.*

I'm voting for *good-bye and see you next year.*

Up in the stands, Mom and Courtney and Stanley are on their feet screaming their heads off. So is the rest of the Mother-Daughter Book Club. Even Mrs. Chadwick, who is wearing a huge fake fur coat and matching hat, is jumping up and down like some sort of deranged wombat.

"CASS-I-DY! CASS-I-DY!" The Concord Comet fans are chanting my name. I wave my hockey stick and they cheer.

"It's all yours, Sloane," says Coach Danner with a grin. He slaps me on the back. "Go get 'em, girl."

I take one final drink of water and sprint out onto the ice.

"Over here!" I shout to Third, who shoots me the puck. I take it and fly down the ice toward the goal. This is my moment and I know it. I rocket past the Minutemen defense like they don't even exist, the cheering of the crowd fueling my skates. I have the net in my sights and I'm racing for it, my hockey stick thudding its relentless rhythm against the ice as I drive the puck forward. Closer, closer. There's fear in the goalie's eye. He knows he doesn't stand a chance against—

A Minuteman wingman whips in past my blind spot. He cuts in front of me, his hockey stick snaking out to scoop away the puck. He steals it!

I scramble for position, trying to steal it back, but he's got the momentum now and he streaks past me as I stare after him in disbelief. This can't be happening!

But it is, and the wingman whips the puck back down the ice to his teammate, who takes a shot just as the buzzer goes off. Heart racing, I look up at the scoreboard. It confirms what I already know in my gut: We just lost the game.

The Minutemen and their fans go berserk, screaming and shouting and pounding each other on the back. Out on the ice, the players start dogpiling on their goalie. I skate slowly back toward our bench, furious. *I can't believe we just lost!* Worse, it was all my fault. I got too

Heather Vogel Frederick

cocky. I should have been more alert. I shouldn't have let this happen!

My eyes fill with angry tears. I blink them back. No way am I going to cry. Team captains don't cry. Especially when they're the only girl on the team. It takes every ounce of willpower I have not to, though. I really, really hate to lose.

"Circle up, Comets!" says Coach Danner, pulling us into a huddle. None of my teammates will look me in the eye, but Coach doesn't say a word about my botched job out there. He just gives us the old standard "it's not about whether you win or lose, it's how you play the game" speech. This doesn't help a bit, of course. It stinks to have the rug pulled out from under us at the last minute, and it especially stinks to be the one responsible.

After he's done, we slump off to the showers, my teammates peeling off toward the boys' locker room, while I have to skate back across the ice to the girls'. It's a long, lonely stretch this afternoon, especially since I have to go right past the Minutemen.

"Hey, princess, looks like you lost your magic wand!" one of them jeers.

"Shut up, jerkazoid!" Zach Norton vaults over the railing onto the ice beside me and glares at him.

"Settle down now, boys," says the Minutemen's coach.

Ignoring them all, I continue on down the rink. Zach slip-slides after me, finally catching up by the entrance to the girls' locker room.

"Tough luck out there, huh, Sloane?" he says.

"Luck had nothing to do with it," I retort. "I blew it."

"Yeah, well, you win some, you lose some." He gives me a rueful smile.

I can't muster one in return. "It's so not fair," I tell him hotly. "I *had* that shot."

He nods. "I know. It really stinks."

Zach and I play Little League together, and he feels the same way about losing that I do, so I know he understands exactly what I'm going through. Zach is a good guy. He comes to all our hockey games to support Third, who is one of his best friends. And I guess he comes to see me play too.

"Oh, Zach, there you are!"

It's Becca, who obviously doesn't know when to take no for an answer. Zach is so not into her—not that I really notice that kind of stuff, but even I can tell it's true. It doesn't seem to matter with Becca, though. She still keeps sniffing around. I honestly don't get why all the girls are so crazy about Zach Norton. Mr. Blond Hair and Blue Eyes—oooo! Big deal.

"We're going downtown for pizza," Becca says, leaning her forearms on the railing. Her blond hair falls forward, hiding her face. Behind her, Ashley giggles. "Want to come?"

Zach glances over at me. "How about it?" he says. "Maybe a little pizza will make you feel better."

Becca doesn't look thrilled with this idea, but it doesn't matter because I'm not going anyway. I shake my head. "I doubt it," I tell him. "I'm gonna go home and lick my wounds."

He grins. "Right."

"Plus, I've got math homework to finish before book club."

"Okay, see you at school on Monday, then."

He slaps me on the back of my sweaty head and I leave him to deal with Double Trouble and head off to the locker room to shower and change. I'm still grumpy in the car on the way home. My mom and Courtney know to leave me alone when I get this way, and even Stanley has learned by now that I'm not in the mood for a pep talk when I lose a game. Especially a crucial game like this. I still can't believe I lost us a shot at the championship!

Once we're home, I go directly inside and up to the turret without speaking to anyone. No one tries to follow me. I stay up there for a long time, staring out the windows and replaying the game over and over again in my head. What an idiot! I should have seen that wingman coming! A few tears leak out, finally, and I let them, glad that nobody's around to see. After a while, I start to feel a little more normal. The turret always has that effect on me. So I head back down to my room to tackle my math homework. I promised my mother I'd try and finish it before book club.

I'm totally not in the mood for a book club meeting, but tonight is kind of special. For one thing, it's our first meeting with Eva Bergson. Emma suggested we invite her to join us, and we all took a vote and agreed. She promised Emma she'd bring her Olympic medal to show us, and I don't want to miss seeing that. Who knows when I'd ever get another chance?

Plus, on top of that, we're meeting at Colonial Academy. Tomorrow is the start of their winter vacation, so Mrs. Crandall was able to get special permission for us to have a sleepover at Witherspoon, Jess's dorm. Today is Maggie's first birthday, and since Jess and Megan are Maggie's favorite babysitters, they didn't want to miss out on the party.

"Look at that moon on the snow," says my mother while later, as we're driving over to meet our friends. "Could it be any prettier?"

I grunt in reply, and my mother sighs. "Come on, honey, I know it's been a tough day, but you've got a fun evening with good friends to look forward to, so cheer up."

"I'll try," I mumble.

"That's my girl." We get out of the car, and she puts her arm around my shoulders as we walk up the path to the dorm.

"Come in, come in!" says Jess's housemother, who is waiting in the hallway to greet us. Maggie is in her arms, and she has one of those little paper birthday hats perched on her head. "Nice to see you again, Cassidy. And you must be Mrs. Sloane-Kinkaid. It's a pleasure to meet you."

"Please, call me Clementine," says my mother.

"Only if you call me Kate."

"Kate it is." My mother looks over at Maggie and her face lights up. She goes nuts over every baby she sees these days. "And is this your daughter? She's adorable!"

Mrs. Crandall passes her to my mom. "I hear you're going to be having a little one of your own before long."

My mother grins and pats her stomach. "You just can't keep anything secret these days, can you?"

Not that it's a secret anymore at all. My mother is six months along now, and her stomach is really sticking out. You'd think a former supermodel wouldn't want to get fat, but she is totally thrilled about her belly. She's always trying to get me to feel it when the baby is kicking, but I get the creeps just thinking about it. It's like having some weird pet in the house, or a real-live version of that spooky movie about aliens. It totally grosses me out.

"Here, Cassidy, would you like to hold her?"

Before I can say no, which I was definitely going to, my mother thrusts Maggie into my arms. I grip her awkwardly under the armpits. We stare at each other. She gives me a big grin, revealing two little front teeth, and wriggles happily. Just when I'm starting to think she's kind of cute, she sticks her fist in her mouth and sucks on it, then pulls it out and slimes my face with it.

"Mo-om!" I shriek.

My mother and Mrs. Crandall just laugh.

"I can see we have some work to do to get you up to speed in the baby department," says my mother, taking Maggie back from me. I scrub at my cheek with my sleeve.

"You girls are going to be in Witherspoon's living room tonight," says Mrs. Crandall, pointing down the hall. "Why don't you put your sleeping bag and things in there, Cassidy, then come join us in the kitchen. We're just going to have a quick little party, since it's nearly Maggie's bedtime."

The Crandall's apartment is filled to overflowing with book club members, Jess's dormmates, and relatives of the Crandalls. I spot a tall girl standing by Mrs. Chadwick and Becca, and recognize Savannah Sinclair from her picture. The few times I've been over here to visit Jess, I've managed to miss meeting her. I drift over, curious to see the notorious Julia up close. She's trying not to stare at my mother, but I can tell she's impressed. Sometimes it's useful to have a famous parent.

Maggie is perched in her high chair across from us, busily ripping open presents. She gets a stuffed toy from Jess—a chicken—which she grabs and starts waving in the air, making excited baby noises.

"Maggie loves to go for stroller rides over to Half Moon Farm and help hunt for eggs," Jess explains to the gathered crowd.

Beside me, Savannah Sinclair whispers something to the girl who's with her, and they start to laugh.

"Shut up," I whisper.

Savannah turns and sizes me up. "You must be Cassidy," she drawls. "Y'all don't look anything like your mother, do you? Pity."

I glare at her.

The next box is light blue, and tied with a cream-colored ribbon.

"Ooo, fancy store," says Gigi. "Lucky baby."

Maggie and her mom open it. Inside is a silver cup engraved with Maggie's name. Mrs. Crandall pulls out the enclosed card. "Compliments of Senator Sinclair and family," she reads. "Why, thank you, Savannah."

Heather Vogel Frederick

"Nice personal touch," I whisper to Savannah. "Babies go crazy for those silver cups, I hear."

Now it's her turn to glare.

Maggie gets a bunch more toys from the dorm students, a plastic play kitchen from her grandparents, and a crate of organic baby food from Mrs. Wong. The last present is from Megan.

"How beautiful!" cries Mrs. Crandall, whisking some sort of little overall thing out of Maggie's sticky grasp. It reminds me of something, and then I remember the Chinese dress Megan wore at our book club meeting at her house a few months ago. Maggie's new outfit is made of the same kind of stuff, only red instead of turquoise.

"Gorgeous fabric, Megs," says my mom. "And I love the buttons! Where did you find them? They're perfect!"

Mrs. Crandall looks over at Megan, stunned. "You *made* these overalls?"

Megan nods modestly.

"Oh my goodness. They're amazing. You should be a fashion designer."

"That's the plan," says Gigi, giving Megan a wink. I see Mrs. Wong watching the two of them. She has a funny look on her face.

While Maggie plays with the wrapping paper, shredding it and flinging it all over the kitchen, Mrs. Crandall serves up cake and ice cream.

"Have fun with your stupid club," Savannah says as she passes by me, holding her paper plate. Her voice is poisonously sweet. "Jess tells us y'all are going to have a taffy pull. I can't imagine anything more exciting for a Friday night, can you, Peyton? It's almost as thrilling as making cheese!"

Giving her an equally fake smile, I stick my foot out. Savannah trips over it, spilling ice cream and cake all down the front of her shirt. "Oops," I tell her. "Sorry. Didn't mean to spoil your grand exit."

"Stay out of my way, you little snot," she warns.

I cross my arms defiantly. "Make me."

My mother swoops in between us with a wet dish towel. Apologizing profusely, she dabs at the chocolate ice cream dripping down Savannah's shirt and shoots me the evil witch mother eye of death. I move hastily out of range, but I'm feeling a whole lot better than I have been all day. Score one for Cassidy Sloane.

A few minutes later, the kitchen has cleared out and all the guests are gone. Mr. Crandall carts Maggie off to bed, still clutching her stuffed chicken, which is already covered in frosting.

"Jess tells me you're reading Jean Webster this year," Mrs. Crandall says. "I loved *Daddy-Long-Legs* when I was a teenager, and now I'm reading *Just Patty*, too, since Jess is enjoying it so much. There's a lot about St. Ursula's School that reminds me of Colonial Academy."

"You'll have to start a book club with Maggie when she's old enough," Mrs. Delaney tells her.

"Definitely."

"Thank you for letting us use your kitchen, Kate," says my mother. "We'll be sure and leave it clean."

Heather Vogel Frederick

"No problem. I'll be next door in our living room, so just let me know if you need anything."

It turns out molasses taffy is a nightmare to make. It's a really involved process, what with boiling the sugar and butter and molasses mixture to just the right temperature, and it's incredibly sticky. Mrs. Bergson finally comes to our rescue.

"I made this with my mother when I was a girl," she says. "The first thing you have to do is butter your hands."

"Eeew," says Becca, and I agree, but we all submit to the greasefest.

Mrs. Bergson pairs us up with our moms and gives us each a wad of candy. "Use your fingertips," she tells us, demonstrating with Gigi how to pull the taffy into long ropes, then double it over and pull again. We all pull and pull and pull until Mrs. Bergson decides the candy looks like the right color and temperature, and then we lay it on the counter and cut it into bite-size pieces.

When we're finished and butter-free and the kitchen is clean again, we leave a plate of candy on the counter for the Crandalls, then head down to Witherspoon's giant living room. Mrs. Delaney sets our taffy on the coffee table in front of the fireplace, and we help ourselves, flopping into the comfortable leather armchairs and sofas surrounding the hearth.

"Thith thtuff ith thticky," I mumble, laboriously chewing on a piece.

"Tathtes good, though," Emma adds.

"I gueth we thould finith our taffy before we dithcuth *Jutht Patty*," says Mrs. Hawthorne, and we all start to giggle.

"Yeth," says Mrs. Chadwick. "Abtholutely."

"Since discussion is out of the question, perhaps now is a good time for handouts," says Mrs. Wong crisply. She isn't eating any taffy, of course.

Mrs. Hawthorne nods, licks her fingers, and pulls a file folder from her bag. Chewing vigorously, we look over the sheets she gives us.

FUN FACTS ABOUT JEAN

1) Jean Webster was petite, just five feet two inches, and athletic. She loved horseback riding, tennis, and hiking, among other activities.

2) She was an avid letter writer, and illustrated her letters to friends and family with little line drawings, just like Judy Abbott did in *Daddy-Long-Legs*.

3) Jean kept notebooks filled with story ideas, as well as with the best things she found while reading—bits of dialogue, phrases, description, and so on. She took the names for many of her characters in *Daddy-Long-Legs* from tombstones. In a funny anecdote she once recalled, "I sincerely believed that I had chosen names so long dead that not one of them could rise up to smite me. The book, however, had not been on sale a week before I learned that one of my names was that

of a person very much alive—as well as the name of one dead for many years—and that the alive person was highly indignant. I am very sorry."

4) Jean was fervently in favor of women's suffrage, and never passed up an opportunity to march in parades in support of votes for women, often with her fellow Vassar alumnae. Her grandmother, Pamela Clemens Moffet (Mark Twain's sister), was a political activist who served as a delegate to the National Convention for Suffragists in Washington, D.C.

"Wait a minute," I say when I get to this last one. "Back then women couldn't vote?"

"Duh," says Becca, "even I knew that. Don't you pay attention in social studies?"

"Women didn't win the right to vote until 1920," says Mrs. Hawthorne. "It required an amendment to the U. S. Constitution."

"The nineteenth," adds Emma.

I shoot her a look. Emma can be such a know-it-all sometimes.

"Women weren't considered citizens," Mrs. Hawthorne continues. "Remember in *Daddy-Long-Legs*, when Judy wrote to her benefactor about repaying his kindness by becoming a 'Very Useful Citizen,' and then she corrects herself and changes it to 'Very Useful Person' because women couldn't be citizens?"

"That's terrible!" I exclaim.

"And in *Just Patty*, their Latin teacher Miss Lord supports women's suffrage and makes the students go to lectures on Friday afternoons about women's rights," says Becca triumphantly. She looks over at me as if to say, *See? I'm smarter than you think.*

I shrug and reach for another piece of taffy.

"Actually, Wyoming granted women the right to vote in 1869," says Emma. "Fifty years before the rest of the country. Bailey told me that in her last letter."

"Really?" I reply. "That's it, I'm moving to Gopher Hole. I just can't believe that everybody else was so stupid until 1920. It's so unfair!"

"Jean Webster obviously agreed," says Mrs. Hawthorne.

"So did Harriet Witherspoon, the founder of this school, and the one for whom this dorm is named," says Mrs. Chadwick, gesturing at the wood-paneled room we're sitting in. "She was a famous suffragette."

Becca's mother is actually looking like her own normal drab self again tonight. Well, mostly. She's dressed in a plain black sweater and matching pants, and only her shoes—shiny gold boots whose tips are peeking out from underneath her pants—hint at the "whole new me."

"That's right!" says Mrs. Delaney. "Remember, Jess? It was in the school brochure. She was jailed for protesting in front of the White House."

"Harriett Witherspoon obviously understood that a worthy cause is a cause worth fighting for," says Mrs. Wong approvingly.

Heather Vogel Frederick

"Were you a suffragette, Mrs. Bergson?" asks Emma.

Startled, Mrs. Bergson starts to laugh. She laughs so hard she begins to cough. Gigi passes her a glass of water and thumps her on the back, smiling broadly.

"I'm not quite that old, Emma," Mrs. Bergson croaks, and Emma turns beet red.

"Me neither," adds Gigi, her eyes twinkling. "Just in case you were wondering."

"Sorry," mumbles Emma.

Mrs. Bergson waves her hand dismissively. "No, no, my dear, I know you didn't mean it as an insult. And actually, I'm flattered that you think me so feisty. I hope I would have been brave enough to be a suffragette like Miss Witherspoon. It takes a lot of courage to stand up for the things you believe in." She gives Emma a significant glance, and Emma looks down at the floor and smiles.

We talk for a while about the characters in *Just Patty*. Everybody thinks I'm just like Kid McCoy, the tomboy from Texas, and that Mae Mertelle Van Arsdale could be Julia Pendleton's twin.

We all agree that one of our favorite parts was when Patty Wyatt and her friends Priscilla and Constance plotted to get rid of Mae and the other roommates they didn't like.

"And didn't you love the way they named their hall 'Paradise Alley?'" says Emma. "You should come up with a name for your hall, Jess."

"How about 'The Torture Chamber'?" I suggest, and everybody laughs. Everybody but Mrs. Chadwick, who winces. What is her problem?

"Oh, I almost forgot," says Mrs. Hawthorne. "I brought something else to show you girls tonight." She pulls another file folder out of her bag. "While I was researching this month's 'Fun Facts,' I discovered that Jean Webster's papers and manuscripts were bequeathed to Vassar College. I called the Special Collections librarian and he sent me photocopies of some pictures of her."

We crowd around the coffee table as Mrs. Hawthorne spreads out a stack of pages.

"She's so pretty!" says Jess.

"And look at her clothes," adds my mother. "Aren't they stylish?"

Gigi nods. "Very elegant. Probably French." She gives Mrs. Wong a meaningful glance.

"Don't start, Mother," Mrs. Wong warns.

"Start what?" Gigi replies, her eyes wide with innocence.

"The Paris thing. Megan is too young for those high-octane fashion shows."

"Nonsense," says Gigi. "It would be educational."

Megan's grandmother wants to take Megan to Paris this spring, but Mrs. Wong won't let her go. Megan's not happy about this at all. I guess I wouldn't be either, even though I could care less about some dumb fashion show. A trip to Paris would be awesome.

"Here's one of Jean with a dog," says Emma, plucking a photograph out of the pile. "See, Mom? Every writer needs a dog."

"No dog, Emma," says her mother firmly.

Emma sighs, and puts the picture back.

Heather Vogel Frederick

Mrs. Delaney looks at her watch. "I hate to say it, but I'd better get going here. Mornings come early on the farm."

"I'd like to thank you all so much for including me," says Mrs. Bergson. "I don't know when I've had a more enjoyable evening." She holds up a finger reprovingly. "And don't forget to vote!"

We all laugh.

After we wash the sticky taffy residue off our hands, our moms help us move the furniture out of the way and spread out our sleeping bags and pillows.

"Now, you girls behave yourselves tonight," says Mrs. Hawthorne. "It was very kind of Mrs. Crandall to bend the rules a bit and let you have a sleepover."

"And try and keep it down," adds my mother. "Some of the girls upstairs have to catch early flights tomorrow."

Our mothers all kiss us good night, and promise to be back after breakfast to pick us up. After they leave, we change into our pajamas and follow Jess upstairs to the bathroom on her hall. It's almost as big as a locker room, but a lot fancier. This is Colonial Academy, after all.

I'm brushing my teeth when I look in the mirror and spot Savannah Sinclair sauntering in behind me.

"Well, if it isn't the book club girls. Did y'all have fun?"

"Put a sock in it, would you?" I tell her.

She crosses her arms over her chest. "That's not very polite. You Yankees need to learn better manners."

"Who's calling who a Yankee?" I ask her. "We're Red Sox fans."

Savannah's mouth drops open, then she starts to laugh. "You're as dumb as you are ugly, aren't you? I wasn't talking about baseball."

I feel my face flush with anger and I take a step toward her. Emma puts her hand on my shoulder. Across the room, Peyton tugs on Savannah's arm.

"Don't start anything tonight," she says. "We've got to finish packing. The limo's picking us up at six."

I put my hand on my hip, striking a pose. "The limo's picking us up at six!" I echo, mincing around the bathroom as if wearing high heels.

Savannah shoots me a look of pure spite as Peyton tows her out the door.

"Please tell me I was never like that," says Becca, watching her go.

"She's worse than you ever were," Emma assures her.

"Much worse," adds Jess.

"Yeah, she's like Becca 2.0 or something," I say.

From the look on her face, I don't think we're making Becca feel all that much better. But she's the one who asked.

As Jess leads us back downstairs, we pass Savannah heading back up. She flutters her fingers at us. "Sweet dreams, girls!"

"She's up to something," Jess mutters when she's out of range, and we race to the living room. Everything looks normal, but we circle the room anyway, scouring it for anything suspicious. My eyes wander to one of the walls, where there are framed photographs of Colonial Academy students over the decades. Some of them are in graduation gowns, some in regular clothes, some in sports uniforms.

A picture of a field hockey team catches my eye and I look more closely at it.

"Hey, is that you, Becca?" I ask in surprise.

"Huh?" she replies.

"It sure looks like you."

Everybody crowds around the photo, which shows a group of girls in kilts holding wooden sticks. I point to one of the players in the back row.

"Wow, you're right, Cassidy—she could be Becca's twin sister," says Emma.

"She's not, though." Megan points to the date on the frame. "Check it out."

Beside me, Becca shifts uncomfortably. "Actually," she tells us, "it's my mother."

"What?!" says Jess. "How come you never told us she went here?"

Becca shrugs. "Mom doesn't talk about it much. I think she's really disappointed that I didn't want to go."

Couldn't get in is more like it, I think.

Becca tosses her head. "Not that I care," she adds. "Anyway, can you picture me at an all-girls' school? No way."

I'm the first one into my sleeping bag. It's been a long day and I'm beat. As Jess goes to turn out the light, I flop back onto my pillow with a sigh, then start to turn over. My hair doesn't turn with me. It's stuck. I give it a yank and nearly pull a handful out. With a shriek, I sit up. The pillow comes with me.

"Don't lie down!" I holler, and everybody freezes. "The pillows are booby-trapped!"

Jess turns on the light and my friends all examine their pillowcases.

"Taffy," Megan says in disgust. "Savannah smeared them with taffy."

Sure enough, the taffy plate is empty, and all of our pillowcases have been hit.

Emma crawls over and inspects the back of my head. "Uh, I don't know how we're going to get you unstuck."

"You'll have to cut me out," I snap. "Find some scissors."

Becca rummages through the drawer of a nearby desk. "Got 'em!" she says triumphantly, waving them in the air.

"Bring them over here and get this thing off me," I order.

Becca pauses, hand poised over my head. She smiles. "Are you sure you trust me?"

What is Jess's new nickname for Becca? Chad-wicky something? "Yeah," I tell her. "Because you know what I'll do to you if you mess up."

The smile vanishes. "Hold still," she barks, sounding like her mother.

Becca starts to snip. And snip, and snip, and snip. "It's the best I could do," she tells me, when I'm finally unstuck.

I turn and look at my pillowcase, which is covered with long strands of red hair and taffy. I reach up and feel the back of my head.

Heather Vogel Frederick

There's a giant bald spot right in the middle. I groan. "My mother is going to kill me."

"Not if we cut the rest of it to match," says Megan. She takes the scissors from Becca's hand and steers me over to the coffee table.

"Since when are you a hairdresser?" I ask, perching on the edge.

"I'm a fashion designer," she replies. "I'm good with scissors. That has to count for something."

And actually, it does.

"You look cute, Cassidy," Jess tells me when Megan is done. There's a mirror behind the piano, and she steers me over to it. "See for yourself."

I inspect myself, turning this way and that. My hair, which had grown back out to shoulder-length after I got it cut in New York a couple of years ago, is cropped close against my head now, a lot like Emma's but not curly, of course. Jess is right. It's not bad at all. It doesn't look like her twin brothers did it and it actually has a sort of style. Not that I care much about that, of course.

"This is going to be even better for sports," I say, running my fingers through it. "Thanks, Megan." I would have cut my hair off a long time ago, actually, but my mother always talks me out of it. She keeps saying some part of me has to look like a girl.

"You know, if you spike it up with some gel, you'd look kind of like Mrs. Chadwick," says Emma, grinning at me.

"Shut up, Emma," snaps Becca.

"C'mon, Bec, you have to admit it's true," Megan tells her,

laughing. "What is it with your mom these days, anyway?"

Becca gives us a rueful smile and shrugs. "I don't know. My dad says it's just a phase she's going through. He says a lot of people try to reinvent themselves when they get to be her age. She's been talking about going back to school, and maybe getting a master's degree or something. I guess she just wants a change." She looks over at Jess. "You know, kind of like your mom back when we were in sixth grade."

Jess nods sympathetically.

"Well, at least neither of your moms decided to go and have a baby!" I tell them. "Talk about a midlife crisis!"

Laughing, we get busy cleaning up the mess. After we're done, we huddle up in a circle on our sleeping bags.

"So what's the plan?" I demand. "We've got to get Savannah back."

"I could go tell Mrs. Crandall," suggests Jess. "I'm sure she'd talk to her or something."

"Forget it," I say. "Nobody's going to do anything to a senator's daughter. And besides, she's leaving in the morning, remember?" I pitch my voice high, like Becca's when she's talking to Zach. "Six o'clock limo to catch."

"We could short-sheet her bed," says Emma.

"Gimme a break," I tell her. "What are you, ten? She deserves something a whole lot worse. This calls for something drastic. I want to make her life miserable. So miserable, in fact," I say, looking over at Jess as an inspiration dawns, "that she's going to beg for a new roommate."

Heather Vogel Frederick

"Like in *Just Patty,* when Patty and Constance and Priscilla plotted to get rid of Irene and Keren and Mae Mertelle Van Arsdale?" she replies, catching my drift.

"Exactly. We're talking Operation New Roommate here."

"How about we cut her hair while she's sleeping?" says Megan, holding up the scissors.

"That's more like it," I reply. "Other ideas?"

We brainstorm for a while. Stuff horse apples in her riding boots. Take all her underwear and hang it up in Monument Square. Put blue food coloring in her shampoo bottle. I stare out the window, thinking. The full moon stares back at me. All of a sudden I sit bolt upright. "I've got it!"

"Got what?" says Emma.

I point out the window. "The moon!"

My friends stare at me, puzzled.

"I'm thinking maybe we should give Savannah a present to take along with her to Switzerland," I continue. "You know, like maybe that extra-stinky cheese Jess's mom and dad invented?"

"Blue Moon?" Jess replies.

"That's the one."

"You mean put it in her *suitcase*?" asks Megan, and I nod.

My friends get real quiet, and then they all start to giggle. Pretty soon we're rolling on the floor, stuffing our pillows—now without their sticky pillowcases—over our faces to keep from waking everybody in the dorm.

"That—is—just—PERFECT!" hiccups Becca, who is laughing so hard that tears are rolling down her cheeks.

"I'm not sure it's such a good idea, though, even if it's funny," Emma cautions. "Remember what happened last time—with Carson Dawson, I mean."

Last year's *Hello Boston!* TV show disaster is something we still don't dare talk about when our mothers are around. We were in trouble for weeks.

"Dude, quit being such a wuss," I tell her. "This is different. We have to stick up for ourselves. We can't let Savannah walk all over us. It's time somebody taught her a lesson."

"But she's going to know it's us!" Emma protests. "It's not exactly subtle."

"Subtle is not what we're aiming for here," I tell her. "We're trying to send a message loud and clear that she can't push Jess or any of the rest of us around. Besides, we can just say it was a present for her family—who wouldn't like to get some nice homemade cheese from New England? And if it happens to be a particularly stinky kind of cheese, well, maybe we just forgot about that little detail."

"I'm in," says Jess.

"Me too," says Megan.

"Me three," says Becca.

Emma sighs. "So how are we going to get the cheese?"

"Leave that to me," I reply. "You and Megan and Becca stay here and cover for Jess and me. Savannah's going to be sneaking down

Heather Vogel Frederick

soon to check on the results of her prank, I promise you."

Jess and I pull our clothes on over our pajamas, and then we stuff our pillows into our sleeping bags to make it look like someone's in them.

"We'll be back as soon as we can," I whisper to the others. "Leave the back door unlocked."

Jess and I slip outside. The full moon is shining on the snow, so we stick to the shadows as we make our way out toward Main Street.

"The gates are locked!" I say in dismay.

"Never mind," says Jess. "There's another way." She leads me down the back road to the stables, and we cut across a field to the street, our boots crunching in the snow.

"Let's jog," I tell her.

It's over a mile to Jess's farm, and the streets are completely deserted. The air is cold in my lungs, skating-rink cold. I'm used to it, but Jess is huffing and puffing by the time we get within spitting distance of her front yard. I grin at her. "Guess the track team isn't in your future, huh?"

She shakes her head. "No way."

We make a wide circle around her house, careful not to wake Sugar and Spice, and creep into the barn through the back door. Jess grabs a flashlight off the shelf and motions to me to stay quiet. "If the chickens hear us, we're done for," she whispers.

I follow her into the creamery. She crosses to the big stainless steel fridge and opens it, then plucks a log of goat cheese from the shelf marked BLUE MOON. I give it a sniff to make sure.

"P-U, that's *nasty!* I can smell it through the wrapper." I grin at her. "It's perfect."

We close the barn up tight, and giving the Delaney's house a wide berth once again we make our way back out to the street. The return jog to Colonial Academy seems to take a lot longer. I glance at my watch as we finally pass the stables. Nearly two a.m.

"Savannah came down to check on us, just like you said," whispers Emma once we're safely back in Witherspoon's living room. "We played possum until she left."

"Good work. Where are those scissors, Megan?" I ask, and she hands them to me.

"Here, we found this in the desk, too," says Becca, holding up a length of ribbon. "To make it look like a real present."

I tie the ribbon around the log of goat cheese, then use the scissors to poke a hole in one end of the plastic wrapping. Just a small one, to make it look like something might have accidentally punctured it in the suitcase. Instantly, the odor of blue cheese leaks out. Gagging, I make a face and hand it to Jess, who squeezes it until it oozes a tiny bit of cheese.

Stifling our giggles, Jess and I creep upstairs, freezing in place when one of the treads emits a squawk as loud as a chicken. Nobody stirs, though, and we tiptoe on to the top, then down the hallway to her bedroom. I crack open the door. Savannah is sound asleep, her breathing deep and even. Her luggage is stacked by the door for morn-

Heather Vogel Frederick

ing. I can see by the moonlight that it all matches, of course. It even has her monogram on it. I shake my head in disgust. What a princess.

Motioning to Jess to keep an eye on Savannah, I carefully move the smaller suitcases aside and open the largest one, wincing at the scrape of the zipper. Savannah stirs, and I pause, holding my breath. After a moment she rolls over and starts snoring lightly. Shaking with silent laughter, Jess hands me the goat cheese and I shove it down beneath the clothes at the bottom of Savannah's suitcase, tucking some socks and underwear around it to hold it in place. Then I zip the bag up again and pile the smaller ones on top, just like they were before.

With one last look around the room to make sure we didn't leave anything that might look suspicious, we tiptoe back downstairs to our waiting friends.

"Mission accomplished," I whisper. "Operation New Roommate is officially launched! She is so going to regret messing with the Mother-Daughter Book Club."

I climb back into my sleeping bag, and for the first time since book club started this year, I'm glad I have a pen pal. I can't wait to write to Winky Parker and tell her about this prank. I'm still laughing as I drift off to sleep. Tonight almost makes up for losing the hockey game earlier today.

Final score: Cassidy, Jess, Emma, Megan, and Becca: a gazillion. Savannah Sinclair: a big fat zero.

SPRING

"*Character is a plant of slow growth, and the seeds must be planted early.*"

—When Patty Went to College

CASSIDY

"I seem to have a genius for discovering enemies!"
—*Dear Enemy*

I can't believe I'm back in Dr. Weisman's office again.

Senator Sinclair called my mother. From Switzerland. He was furious—I guess the Blue Moon cheese did its job big-time. They ended up having to throw away Savannah's suitcase, it stunk so bad. And it completely ruined all of her clothes, too.

I told my mother Savannah deserved it, considering what she did to my hair, on top of everything she's done to Jess, but she was in no mood to listen. Especially not after Senator Sinclair's call. I could only hear the conversation from our end, but I could tell he was really worked up because my mom kept wincing and holding the phone away from her ear. He must have threatened to sue or call in the FBI or something, because my mother finally pulled out her Queen Clementine voice.

"Lawsuit?" she said icily. "You want to talk lawsuits?" And then she told him that despite what his precious daughter might have told him, she was the one who had started it, and the stunt Savannah had pulled with the molasses taffy had cost me my hair in the process. "And I have the before-and-after pictures to prove it," she added triumphantly. "One foolish prank was compounded by another, Senator Sinclair, and that's hardly worth calling in the Feds about." And then she told him that she'd take care of it, and that she expected him to do the same, and she hung up.

The conversation that took place afterward between the two of us wasn't pretty. My mother hauled Stanley into the argument and of course he took her side, so I was outnumbered. Stanley kept going on about how disappointed they were with me, and how selfish it was of me to get my mother all upset, especially in her condition. Like having this baby was my idea! Then the two of them marched me down here to our family therapist's office so fast I hardly had time to catch my breath.

They went in to see Dr. Weisman first. Even though the door was closed, I could still hear my mother crying. That made me feel pretty low. I honestly never mean to get into trouble and worry her, this kind of stuff just seems to happen. Like at recess a couple of weeks ago, when I thought it would be fun to try that experiment I'd heard about, the one with the bottle of diet soda and a roll of mints. How was I supposed to know it would erupt all over Mr. Keller? While I'm brooding about the injustice of everything, my mother and Stanley reappear and it's my turn.

"So," says Dr. Weisman cheerfully, as I take a seat across from him, "do you want to talk about it?"

Heather Vogel Frederick

One thing about Dr. Weisman, he's pretty cool. Nothing much rattles him, not even stinky blue cheese in a suitcase shipped to Switzerland.

"Not really," I reply, just as cheerfully.

He nods toward the closed door, and the waiting room beyond where my mother and Stanley are now sitting. "Well, perhaps we'd better at least go through the motions," he suggests, lowering his voice. "We wouldn't want to derail your trip to D.C., after all."

Queen Clementine has decreed that unless I shape up, I won't be going along on the class trip to Washington.

I heave a sigh. Social studies is not my favorite subject—that would be PE—but still, I would hate to miss the eighth grade field trip. "There's this girl," I begin reluctantly. "My friend Jess's roommate at Colonial Academy."

He consults his notebook. "Savannah Sinclair?"

"Yeah, only we call her Julia Pendleton."

Dr. Weisman's brow puckers.

"Because she's just like this character in *Daddy-Long-Legs*. A book we read for book club."

"Ah, yes." He nods thoughtfully. "Jean Webster. My wife loves her. So tell me more about this Savannah girl."

I pick at a hangnail. "What's to tell? She's a stuck-up, spoiled rich girl who's mean to Jess and all the rest of us too. She sabotaged our sleepover party and messed up my hair, so we decided to get even."

Dr. Weisman consults his notes again. "Which you did with Half Moon Farm's 'Blue Moon' cheese?"

"Uh-huh."

"I take it Senator Sinclair is not fond of that particular brand of cheese." Dr. Weisman's face is serious, but behind his glasses his eyes are twinkling just a tiny bit.

I perk up at this. Maybe there's hope for the D.C. trip after all. "Who is?" I scoff. "Have you ever smelled the stuff?"

Dr. Weisman smiles. "Indeed I have. Blue cheese is one of my favorites. But not, perhaps, in a suitcase."

I drop my gaze. Dr. Weisman is quiet for a while. He's really good at being quiet. I guess that's part of his job. And the thing is, I trust him. He's known me for two years now, and even though I hate to admit it, he's really helped me a lot.

So I start to talk. I tell him about Operation New Roommate, and how I feel about the baby coming, and how it still feels weird to have Stanley living in the house with us even though I like him and everything, and how I know I'm supposed to be happy that Courtney got accepted to UCLA, which was her top choice college, but how I wish she didn't have to go away. I tell him about Jess, and how it bugs me when people pick on my friends. Eventually, I admit that maybe the blue cheese thing wasn't such a good idea, even though Savannah definitely deserved it. Dr. Weisman just listens, and occasionally asks me a question, and takes notes. When I'm done, he taps his pencil on the desk, then swivels around in his chair and stares out the window.

Heather Vogel Frederick

"Okay, Cassidy, I'm going to need to talk to your mother and stepfather alone one more time," he says finally, turning around to face me again.

He stands up and walks me to the door, then beckons to my mom and Stanley. I take a seat in the waiting room and this time Dr. Weisman's secretary forgets to close the door all the way so I can hear the low murmur of their voices. "Nothing terribly wrong ... a lot of change right now ... confusing time ... not an easy adjustment ... don't blame yourself" and stuff like that, and then my mom cries some more, and then it's my turn to go back in.

"Cassidy, are you familiar with Gilbert and Sullivan?" Dr. Weisman asks me as I sit down.

I glance over at my mother and Stanley, worried that this is a trick question. "Do they play hockey?" I reply cautiously.

Dr. Weisman laughs. "Heavens, no—not by a long shot. Gilbert and Sullivan were a famous musical duo. Arthur Sullivan was a composer and William Gilbert was a librettist, a writer. The two of them teamed up on some of the most sublime comic operas in history, including *H. M. S. Pinafore*, *The Pirates of Penzance*, and my all-time favorite, *The Mikado*. Are you familiar with it?"

I shake my head, wishing Jess were here. She'd have heard of these guys for sure.

"Well, in *The Mikado* there's a character called the Lord High Executioner."

I'm not liking the sound of this one bit, but I nod and Dr. Weisman continues, "There's a wonderful scene in which he sings, '*My object all sublime / I shall achieve in time / To let the punishment fit the crime / the punishment fit the crime.*'"

Dr. Weisman pauses and looks at me. "Do you understand why I'm bringing this up, Cassidy?"

Uh-oh, I think. *Here it comes.*

"You mentioned when we were talking that perhaps you acted a bit rashly in this incident, and that you might have thought the consequences of your actions through a bit more thoroughly."

I lift a shoulder. "Yeah, I guess."

"Well, that's the main thing I was looking for in talking with you today. One's own conscience always punishes one more thoroughly than any outward agent."

I look at him hopefully. Does this mean I'm off the hook?

"However, your mother insists that there be consequences, and that is what reminded me of Gilbert and Sullivan. Barring you from your class field trip is a punishment that doesn't fit the crime. It's too extreme, we agreed, given the fact that your actions were provoked. However, I think we've come up with a suitable consequence for your actions. First of all, you will need to write letters of apology to Savannah and to her parents—your mother has the Senator's address—and I'd also like you to start writing letters to the baby. At least two a week. Then I want you to come back and see me next month."

I gape at him. "You want me to write to the *baby*? Why? It didn't have anything to do with the blue cheese!"

Heather Vogel Frederick

"Cassidy," warns my mother.

"Mom! I'm not being rude, honest!" I protest. "It's just that I don't understand how writing to the baby is supposed to help. It can't even read! Plus, I've already got a pen pal."

"That's your punishment, take it or leave it," Dr. Weisman says calmly.

I glance over at Stanley and my mother again. My mother lifts an eyebrow. Very regal. Very Queen Clementine. Obviously I don't have a choice.

I sigh. "Okay, okay, I'll do it. But what am I supposed to write about?"

Dr. Weisman shrugs. "Anything at all. Hockey, school, your book club, boyfriends, whatever."

I snort. *Boyfriends? As if.*

My mother makes me sign a contract again, the same way she did two years ago when she wanted me to be more ladylike, and then we head home.

"Can you pull over for a minute?" she asks Stanley as we turn down Main Street. "Right there, in front of the bookstore."

Stanley pulls over and my mother gets out of the car and disappears inside. We sit at the curb in silence for a few minutes, then Stanley turns around and rests his arm on the top of the driver's seat. The corners of his eyes are crinkled up and he's trying to squelch a smile.

"Okay, so don't you dare ever tell your mother I told you this, because she will absolutely kill me, but the blue cheese?"

"Yeah?"

"Brilliant. Stupid, but brilliant. That little weasel deserved it too, after what she did to your beautiful hair." He reaches out a forefinger and strokes my bangs softly. "Remember, though, you never heard it from me, okay?" He turns around again and flips on the radio.

I stare at the back of his head, too astonished to reply. Obviously I still have a lot to learn about my new stepfather.

A minute later my mother reappears. "Here you go," she says, climbing back in the car and thrusting a paper bag over the back of the seat at me. I open it and look inside. Great. Stationery with little bunnies on it. Like the baby's going to notice. My mother gives me a smile, though, and I figure that's a good sign, so I force myself to smile back.

Stanley pulls into the driveway a couple of minutes later, and I hop out of the car and go inside straight up to my room. I lie on my bed for a while, thinking about everything, and then there's a tap on my door and Courtney pokes her head in.

"Can I come in?"

I shrug.

"I'll take that as a yes," she says, closing the door behind her. "So how'd it go with Dr. Weisman?"

I shrug again. "Okay, I guess."

"Are you going to get to go to D.C.?"

I roll over and stare at my hockey posters. I'll bet Cammi Granato and Henrik Lundqvist and the Boston Bruins never had to go to a shrink. "Yeah, as long as I do my homework for Dr. Weisman."

Heather Vogel Frederick

"Huh?"

"He wants me to write a bunch of letters," I explain bitterly. "As if I don't have enough letter-writing to do these days with my pen pal in Wyoming. I have to apologize to Savannah and her parents, and then he wants me to write letters to the baby. How stupid is that?"

Courtney thinks it over. "Actually, it's a pretty cool idea," she says finally. "It's kind of like keeping a diary or something. I mean, someday, when our little brother or sister is your age, he or she will be able to read the letters and know about you and the things you did and how you felt and everything."

I shrug, unconvinced. My sister walks over to my desk and picks up the picture that's propped against the lamp. "Is this your book club pen pal?"

I nod.

"What's her name again?"

"Winky."

"She's really cute. Haven't you had fun writing to her?"

Fun? I think about it. For me, writing letters is a chore. I'm not like Emma—she lives for this stuff. And I'm not some big animal freak like Jess, either, but I guess it's been interesting, hearing about life on a ranch. I know it's hard work, because I've watched the Delaneys with their farm, but Winky makes it sound exciting. Really different from tame Concord, that's for sure. Winky and her brothers get to go camping and fishing all the time, and she knows how to shoot a rifle—there are bears and mountain lions near their ranch—and how to train horses and rope a calf. I'll bet Dad would have really liked her, and I'll bet he would have loved Wyoming.

"Yeah, sort of," I finally admit.

"See? The baby is going to have just as much fun reading your letters to him or her."

"In about a decade when it can read," I grumble.

Courtney sits down on the bed beside me. "So are you going to come visit me at college next year?"

I shoot her a look. "Like Mom's going to let me."

"Why wouldn't she? I'd take really good care of you. You could fly out for spring break, maybe, and we could drive down to Laguna Beach."

That's where our family used to live, back before Dad died and we moved here to Concord and Mom married Stanley Kinkaid.

"We could visit all your favorite places," Courtney continues. "Go boogie boarding at Brooks Street beach, drive up to Crystal Cove and watch for dolphins—"

"And get burgers at the Shake Shack?"

"Definitely."

We smile at each other, remembering. It suddenly strikes me how weird this is, the two of us talking and getting along and everything. We used to fight all the time—Courtney really knows how to get on my nerves, especially when she and Mom gang up on me about clothes and stuff. But something's different this year. It's like both of us know that things are about to change forever. It's never going to be

Heather Vogel Frederick

the same again, all of us living here in the same house, doing the same things we've always done. She's going away, and next year I'll be in high school and after that I'll go away too. And then there's the baby.

"I still wish you didn't have to go," I tell her.

Courtney leans over and gives me a hug. "Don't worry so much, Cass. It's going to be fine. Maybe we can talk Mom and Stanley into getting you another cell phone—that way we can call and text each other."

The last cell phone they got me accidentally fell out of my pocket at the rink and somebody mistook it for a hockey puck. "That would be cool," I tell her.

"And you're going to like having a little brother or sister around, wait and see."

"How do you know?"

"Because I like having *you* around, you dork," Courtney says, punching me on the arm. "I wouldn't trade having a little sister for anything."

Suddenly my eyes feel hot. I roll over quickly onto my stomach so she won't see the tears. "Thanks," I mumble.

"You're welcome."

After she leaves I think about what she said, and then I reach over the side of my bed and pick up the paper bag from where I tossed it on the floor. I pull out the bunny stationery and grab a pen.

Dear Baby, I write. *I'm really, really going to miss Courtney next year. . . .*

❦ Jess ❦

"She believes that if you are a Pendleton, that fact alone admits you to heaven without any further examination. Julia and I were born to be enemies."

—*Daddy-Long-Legs*

Humming to myself, I skip down the front steps of the music building and head toward the dining hall. Chorus was especially fun today, but now I'm starving, and good lunch smells are wafting from the kitchen. Here and there purply-blue patches of early spring crocus—*Crocus vernus*—are poking cheerily through the garden beds that line the campus paths, reaching for the sun. I reach my face toward it too, savoring its warmth. But spring hasn't completely arrived yet and I wrap my jacket closer around me as the wind whips across the quad.

"Hey, Jess! Wait up!"

I turn to see Adele running toward me.

"What is it?"

"Mr. McNamara just posted the list!" she tells me excitedly, pushing her wind-blown bangs out of her face.

My heart skips a beat. "Really? Did you—"

"Yup. And so did you!"

"I did? We're MadriGals?"

She nods, her eyes shining. Most of the members of Colonial Academy's elite a cappella group are high schoolers, but every year a handful of eighth graders are chosen to audition, and a few get in. I was sure I wouldn't make the cut. I reach into the pocket of my jacket for my cell phone, to call my mom and tell her.

"Frankie didn't get in," Adele adds sadly.

I'd completely forgotten about Frankie! I look around the quad but she's nowhere in sight. "Where is she?"

"Back at the dorm. I think she wanted to be by herself for a while."

This takes a little of the shine off the news. It's hard to be completely happy about something when one of your good friends' hopes just got crushed.

"Oh, and there's something else," says Adele.

"What?"

"Savannah's name is on the list too."

I sigh. Of course. Things with Savannah Sinclair have been really awkward ever since Operation New Roommate backfired big-time. When the administration found out about our prank war, the two of us got hauled into the headmistress's office. My parents were there, too, along with Mrs. Crandall, and Savannah's parents joined us on speakerphone.

Senator Sinclair started blustering right away. "I demand that my daughter be moved to a different room!" he'd said. "I will not tolerate her being subjected to this kind of ill-bred behavior."

Savannah had pressed her lips together, trying to hide a smile. I could tell she was used to her father running interference when she got in trouble. My dad, however, didn't look too happy with the Senator's choice of words.

"Ill-bred?" he'd repeated, leaning forward in his chair like he was going to make a grab for the speakerphone. "Now, see here—"

My mother put her hand on his arm. "Michael," she warned, "let Mrs. Duffy handle this."

Mrs. Duffy didn't seem at all phased by the Senator's blustering. I guess when you're in charge of a school like Colonial Academy, you get used to dealing with big-shot parents who like to throw their weight around.

"I can assure you, Senator," she'd said calmly, "that we have conducted a full investigation into this incident, and it's quite clear that the blame rests squarely on both parties. In fact, from what I understand, it was your daughter who was responsible for the initial provocation."

Savannah's father started to argue with her, but Mrs. Duffy cut him off. "And furthermore I don't need to remind you, sir, of the conditions for your daughter's continued tenure here at our school."

This got his attention, and the speakerphone fell silent. I glanced over at Savannah, who wasn't looking quite so confident all of a

Heather Vogel Frederick

sudden. I'd forgotten she was put on academic probation.

"Colonial Academy has a philosophy about roommates," the headmistress continued. "Sometimes what initially seems like a mismatch can, in the end, prove most fruitful in the forging of character. When compromises have to be made, and there's give-and-take on both sides, valuable lessons in patience, tolerance, and diplomacy are learned. Sometimes, lasting friendships are even formed. Surely you know the truth of that, Poppy."

Over the speakerphone, I heard Mrs. Sinclair sigh. "You're right, Betsy."

Mrs. Crandall saw the puzzled look on my face, and she leaned over to me and whispered, "Savannah's mother was a student here once."

So *that* explained how Savannah got accepted! I couldn't wait to tell the book club.

In the end, Savannah and I had to apologize to each other, and promise to make more of an effort to get along. Mrs. Duffy assigned us to meet with Mrs. Crandall once a week and let her know how things were going, and asked us to be sure and enlist her help in sorting out any future differences, instead of taking matters into our own hands.

"And Savannah, one of the reasons we paired you with Jessica is because she's such a strong student," the headmistress had added. "It might behoove you to let bygones be bygones and ask for her help now and then."

"Race you to the dining hall!" says Adele, pulling me out of my daydream. I shove all thoughts of Savannah aside and take off across the quad after my friend.

After lunch, the two of us head back to our dorm. There aren't any classes this afternoon, since we've got a long weekend coming up. Our spring midterm exams start next week, and most of the girls are using the time to go home for a visit and a study break. I've promised to babysit Maggie for the afternoon before my mom comes to get me.

Mrs. Crandall is waiting for me in her office.

"Hello girls," she says. "Adele, your dad called—the airport van will be here in about an hour to pick you up. He wanted to make sure you're packed and ready to go, okay?"

Adele nods and starts for the stairs. Mrs. Crandall turns to me. "I just put Maggie down for a nap. She usually sleeps until about three, so you'll have a couple of hours to get some study time in before she's up and around again."

"Thanks, Mrs. Crandall."

She cocks her head. "Is everything okay? You look a little, I don't know, less sparkly than usual."

I manage a halfhearted smile. "I'm fine," I tell her. "I got into MadriGals."

Mrs. Crandall's eyes widen. "Wow, Jess, that's fabulous!" She gives me a hug. "It's a real honor, too—hardly any eighth graders get chosen."

I nod glumly, and her brow puckers. "So why the long face?"

"Savannah got in too."

Heather Vogel Frederick

"Oh, I see." Mrs. Crandall sets her purse on the table and takes a seat on the sofa. She pats the cushion next to her. "Want to talk about it?"

"I guess." I plop down beside her. I'm really glad I have Mrs. Crandall for my housemother. Even though I see my own mother every weekend, and can call her any time I want, it still helps to have someone here at school to talk to. "It's just that Savannah and I—well, I just don't see how we're supposed to ever be friends. She doesn't like me! I try to be nice to her, honest, and I help her with her homework like Mrs. Duffy asked, but she still keeps bugging me all the time. Plus, there's nowhere I can go to get away from her. We room together, eat together, take riding lessons together, we're both in the chorus together, and now, with MadriGals—"

"A little too much togetherness?" suggests Mrs. Crandall.

"Exactly!"

Mrs. Crandall nods sympathetically. "I understand your feelings, Jess. I've known a lot of girls like Savannah in the time I've been here at Colonial. But there's a side of her that I don't think she's let you— or anyone else—see yet, for whatever reason. So try and be patient a little while longer, okay? I think you could be a really positive influence on her."

Great, I think. Why do I always have to be the positive influence? Why can't somebody else take a turn for a change?

"Okay," I tell her, without enthusiasm.

My housemother laughs. "Now I have another assignment for you. I want you to go to the kitchen and help yourself to some of the mocha almond ice cream that's in the freezer. You need to celebrate getting into MadriGals!"

She leaves and I dish up a bowl of ice cream and settle in to study for my Latin exam. That's the only one I'm really worried about. Everything else feels like it's under control. I get a head start on my English paper too, because I want some time to relax and enjoy myself this weekend.

When Maggie wakes up I change her diaper and bundle her up and stick her in the stroller, and then I take her down to the barn to see the horses. Maggie loves animals almost as much as I do. I hold her up so she can pat Blackjack's nose, and she squeals and laughs.

I hear boots on the wooden floor behind me and turn to see Savannah coming in, dressed in her riding clothes.

"Hey," I say in surprise. "I thought you were flying to Washington this weekend."

"Change of plans," she says shortly. She disappears into the tack room and emerges a moment later carrying a saddle and bridle.

"Taking Cairo out for a spin?"

"What business is it of yours?"

"Sheesh, I was just making conversation."

"Well, make it with Maggie, okay? Just leave me alone."

"Gladly," I retort, putting Maggie back in her stroller and wheeling it swiftly out of the barn, and myself out of range of Savannah's sharp tongue.

Unfortunately, later that night at the dinner table I make the

Heather Vogel Frederick

mistake of telling my family about this latest run-in.

"Hold on, did you say Savannah is stuck on campus all weekend?" my mother asks when I'm done.

"Yeah, I guess so."

She pushes back from the table and goes into the kitchen. A minute later I hear her on the phone. "Kate?" she says.

I frown. Is my mother calling Mrs. Crandall?

"I understand that Savannah Sinclair didn't end up going home for the weekend. Uh-huh. I see. Well, do you think you could get permission from her parents for her to come here to Half Moon Farm?"

My fork clatters to my plate. I turn to my dad in horror. "What is she doing?"

He shrugs. "Beats me. You know your mother."

"Dad! She can't come here! Not Savannah!"

A moment later my mother reappears.

"Please don't tell me you just invited Savannah Sinclair to our house for the weekend!" I beg.

"It's the perfect opportunity for you to make amends," she replies calmly.

"But I've already been doing that at school!"

"This will help prove to the Sinclairs that you really meant it when you apologized. Besides, I can't stand the thought of that poor girl being stuck on campus when everyone else gets to go home."

No amount of protesting on my part has any effect, which

is usually the case when my mother makes her mind up about something. She may be petite, like me, but she's no pushover.

"She'll be here first thing in the morning," my mother tells me. "And I don't want to hear another word about it. It's the right thing to do, period."

I hardly sleep a wink all night. The worst thing is, there's nobody around for me to call on for moral support. Everybody's out of town for the long weekend. Emma's gone with her mother to a library conference in Connecticut, Cassidy is in Boston with her grandparents, Megan and her family are taking Gigi out to see the Berkshires, and Becca's in New York with her mother and Stewart, who has another *Flashlite* modeling gig.

I'm completely on my own.

The next morning after breakfast, my mother and I are doing the dishes when there's a knock at the front door.

"That must be Savannah," says my mother. "Promise me you'll be a good hostess."

"I promise," I reply sullenly. Forcing myself to smile, I follow her to the front hall.

"Hello," says Savannah coolly, as my mother shows her in. Her hands are shoved into the pockets of her navy pea jacket, and her long chestnut hair is pulled back in a ponytail.

"Hi."

Briggs, her chauffeur, comes in behind her, carrying her suitcase. Her new one, since the Blue Moon cheese wrecked the old one.

Heather Vogel Frederick

He stands there, looking a little uncertain. Mostly because there's a chicken pecking at his left shoe.

"Oh, for heaven's sake, Loretta," says my mother, scooping her up and thrusting her into my arms. "Put her back outside, would you, Jess?" She looks over at Savannah and the chauffeur, shaking her head in mock despair. "I don't know what it is with these chickens of ours, but they're just determined to be house pets. Every time one of us forgets to close the back door, they sneak inside."

The chauffeur laughs politely, but I can tell he thinks we're weird. And I don't even have to look at Savannah to know what she's thinking. I doubt many senators have chickens wandering around their backyards, let alone inside their houses.

Just then, my little brothers come dashing down from their room. They're wearing underpants on their heads, and their faces are peeking out of the leg holes.

"We're deep-sea divers!" Dylan announces.

"Watch!" adds Ryan. He pulls a straw out of his pocket and sticks it in his mouth like a snorkel, then breathes through it noisily.

"I see," says my mother calmly, as if it's completely normal for third-grade boys to run around with underpants on their heads. Which in our house is pretty much the case. "Why don't you two go search for sunken treasure in the cookie jar, then take your game outside?"

We're a freak show, I think, my face ablaze with embarrassment. Clutching the protesting chicken in my arms, I herd the twins toward the kitchen. As I put the boys and the straying poultry outside, it occurs to me that maybe a freak show is a good thing. Maybe our family will seem so incredibly weird to her that Savannah will get creeped out and leave. I return to the front hall feeling hopeful, but the only one who leaves is her chauffeur.

"Why don't you help Savannah get settled?" my mother suggests. "I'm going to start lunch. Your father's probably starving—he's been up since before dawn with Sundance and Matilda." She heads down the hall to the kitchen, leaving us standing awkwardly by the stairs.

"Was your mother really on *HeartBeats*?" asks Savannah, watching her go.

"Yup." I know exactly what she's thinking. It's hard to believe that someone who looks so ordinary was ever the star of a TV soap opera. Today my mother is dressed in her usual early spring uniform of jeans, T-shirt, and flannel overshirt. She rarely bothers with makeup on days she's not planning to leave the farm, and with two goats in labor, none of us are going anywhere today, that's for sure.

"My mother never wears jeans," Savannah informs me loftily.

"Your mother doesn't live on a farm," I snap, grabbing her suitcase and hauling it upstairs. It weighs a ton. What the heck did she bring, her entire wardrobe?

When we get to my room I heave her suitcase on the bed closest to the wall. With any luck, it will rain. Sometimes when it really pours, the roof leaks on that side of the room. That will send her flying back to Colonial Academy. On her broomstick.

Heather Vogel Frederick

I take a scrapbook from one of my shelves and toss it casually onto her bedspread. Inside are photographs I collected from fan magazines the year my mother lived in New York. She's glammed up to the hilt as Larissa LaRue in all of them.

Savannah flips through it. I can tell she's impressed, but of course she doesn't admit it.

"So how come you didn't go away this weekend like you were supposed to?" I ask.

"My parents had to fly to Brussels at the last minute," she replies. "Some NATO thing."

Savannah's father is on the Senate Foreign Relations committee. The only reason I know this is because Savannah told me. Many times, in fact. I guess it's a big deal—at least in Washington. It's not like anybody I know gives a hoot.

Thinking about Washington makes me wish I was back at Walden Middle School. Their field trip is coming up soon, and I'm really sad to be missing it. The D.C. trip has always been the best thing about eighth grade at Walden, and Colonial Academy takes their students in the sixth grade, so I missed that chance too. On the other hand, Mrs. Chadwick and Mrs. Wong are going along as chaperones, so it's possible the trip won't be quite as much fun as I think.

Savannah makes no move to unpack, but instead starts prowling around my room. She pauses by the window and looks out over the porch roof to the pastures and the barn. "Do you have horses?" she asks.

I nod.

"Maybe we can go riding later."

I smother a laugh. "You're welcome to try." Led and Zep are great behind a plow, but they're not exactly what Savannah is used to. They tolerate it when my brothers and I hop on their backs, but it's kind of like sitting on a tank, and lumbering around on a Belgian is hardly like learning dressage at Colonial Academy. I don't try to explain, though. She'll see for herself soon enough.

Savannah gives me a funny look, then continues her inspection of my room. She scans the shelf of science fair prizes and moves on to the framed photograph of me as Belle in our sixth grade production of *Beauty and the Beast*.

"Who's the cute guy?" she asks, gazing at my costar.

"Zach Norton."

"Is he your boyfriend?"

I hesitate, wondering if I should tell a white lie. I know Zach wouldn't mind—he's a good sport. I could probably even get him to play along if we ever ran into him downtown. "Actually—"

"Didn't think so," Savannah says dismissively, returning the photograph to its place. "Besides, I forgot, it's that kid Kevin something you've got a thing for, right? The little twerp who keeps leaving notes for you with Mrs. Crandall?"

Stung, I sit down on the edge of my bed. How did Savannah find out about Kevin Mullins? I can only imagine how many people she's told, too. I should have sat Kevin down a long time ago and told him

Heather Vogel Frederick

to cut it out, but I didn't want to hurt his feelings. Life is tough enough on Kevin as it is. Still, now I'm feeling really stupid that I didn't have a talk with him earlier.

Savannah continues circling my room, ignoring the holes I'm drilling in her back with my eyes. I can't believe my mother thought it was a good idea to invite her over. The least she could have done was put her in the guest room, instead of in here with me. Aren't we forced to spend enough time together at school?

Next up on the Jessica Delaney Room Tour is my bookshelf. Savannah runs a well-manicured forefinger over the titles, and my books suddenly seem incredibly dorky. Not that Savannah is much of a reader—she likes magazines, mostly, and all that gossipy stuff about bubble-headed celebrities. The only real books I've ever seen her read are the ones assigned to us for English class, and most of the time she just reads the CheatNotes versions. She even did that with *To Kill a Mockingbird*, which is the best book I've ever read in my life.

Most of my books are about science and nature, except for the ones we've read for book club. Savannah's finger, which has been moving steadily across titles like *Birds of New England* and *Teach Yourself Astronomy*, pauses at *Little Women*, then stops completely at *Anne of Green Gables*. She glances at me over her shoulder and smirks.

"Book club, right?"

I'm tempted to throw something at her. How dare she paw through my stuff and pass judgment? Before I can say or do anything, though, she spots more photos on one of the lower bookshelves. She leans down and picks two of them up. The first one is in a nice frame. My dad took it last summer, right before our book club went on the hike Mrs. Wong planned as a bachelorette party for Cassidy's mother. We're lined up with the White Mountains behind us, wearing backpacks and smiles. The other one is the picture Madison Daniels sent me with her first letter last fall.

"Who's this?" Savannah asks.

"My pen pal," I reply grudgingly. No way am I explaining about the mother-daughter book club in Wyoming.

"Y'all have a *pen pal*?" Savannah sounds incredulous. "How lame is that?" She puts the photos back, then spies an envelope that's on the shelf beside them. "Is this from her, or is it a note from your little boyfriend?"

I spring to my feet. "That's private property," I tell her, my voice rising.

Savannah holds it up in the air out of my reach. Short of jumping for it, which I'm not about to do and which wouldn't work anyway since she's so much taller than me, there's not much I can do. I cross my arms and glare at her. Grinning, she plucks the letter out of the envelope and starts to read:

> Dear Pen Pal,
> Thanks for your letter. I'm glad to hear that your parents are going to let you keep one of the kittens. Since your dad's into rock music, I think

Heather Vogel Frederick

you should name him either Jimi Hendrix or Elvis.
Maybe Elvis would be better with that
Nashville theme your mom's got going with all her
country-music-star chickens.

   Nothing much new to report here. It's still
snowing; spring takes forever to get to Gopher Hole.
Since I'm stuck indoors so much I've been practicing
a ton. The guitar I got for Christmas rocks, and I
know a whole bunch of new songs now.

   Your friend,

   Madison

   P.S. I don't care what anybody says, your
snotty roommate totally got what she deserved.

Savannah's voice trails off.

Serves you right, I think, but aloud I just say smugly, "I told you it was private property."

She tosses the letter and its envelope back on the shelf. "I'm glad I'm not in a stupid book club."

"I doubt there's one that would have you," I retort, the words flying out of my mouth before I can stop them. So much for being a good hostess.

We glare at each other, but before either of us can say anything else, my mother calls.

"Girls! Lunchtime!"

I stalk out of the room, not caring if Savannah follows. Downstairs in the kitchen, my mother takes one look at my face and points to the cellar door. "I need a jar of pickles," she says, giving me a little shove. Then she turns to Savannah. "And would you mind setting the table for us, honey?"

A moment later my mother is in the basement with me. "What is going on?" she whispers.

"She's impossible, mom!" I whisper back. "She's going through all my stuff and making fun of everything—I can't believe I have to spend the entire weekend with her! Can't we send her back?"

My mother puts her hands on her hips. "Let me remind you that you're the reason she's here in the first place," she says. "She's a guest in our home, Jess, and as such I'm expecting you to treat her kindly. Is that too much to ask?"

We go back upstairs to find Savannah standing where we left her, looking flustered.

"What's the matter?" my mother asks.

"Um, I'm not exactly sure what to do, Mrs. Delaney."

"Oh, you know, just put out plates, napkins, silverware—the usual. I left everything right there on the counter for you." She points to the counter.

Savannah picks up the stack of plates, then hesitates.

"Oh, my," says my mother. "You've never set a table before, have you?"

Her face flushed with embarrassment, Savannah says softly, "Back

Heather Vogel Frederick

home, our housekeeper always takes care of that." She shoots me a look, one that says *Don't you dare say a word*.

A snicker slips out before I can stop myself.

"Jess," warns my mother, frowning at me, then adds gently, "Savannah sweetheart, there's no shame in that, but here at Half Moon Farm life is a little different. We all pitch in to do the housekeeping, and pretty much everything else. While you're staying with us I consider you one of the family, so if it's okay with you, you're going to learn some new skills this weekend. Setting a table is a snap—Jess will show you how."

Wordlessly, I pick up the napkins and silverware. Savannah follows me into the dining room with the plates she's still holding. Using exaggerated gestures, like the kind you'd use to demonstrate something for a complete idiot or a space alien, I set a sample place at the table. Savannah watches me, her lips pressed together in a tight line. We set the rest of the table in silence. I try not to gloat but I can't help it. I can't wait to tell my friends about this.

The back door slams and I hear my father's voice. "Shannon, can lunch wait a bit? There's something I want the girls to see."

"Sure," my mother replies. "I haven't started the grilled cheese yet."

Curious, I head back to the kitchen. Savannah follows at a distance.

My father, who is scrubbing his hands at the sink, looks over at me and smiles. "You're a godmother, Jess," he says. "Our herd has new recruits as of about ten minutes ago."

I let out a squeal of excitement. There is nothing I love better than baby goats. They're even cuter than kittens.

"How about you?" my dad asks Savannah, who is standing in the doorway beside me. "Would you like to see our newborns?"

"Okay," she replies politely, flashing me an *I'm a Sinclair and I'm too sophisticated for squealing* look.

We follow my dad back outside, and Sugar and Spice come running around the edge of the barn. Savannah's face suddenly lights up.

"Shelties!" she says. "I didn't know y'all had Shelties!" She squats down to pat them. Sugar and Spice wriggle with excitement and leap up to lick her face. "They're so cute! My grandmother has one too. His name is Beau."

"This is Sugar, and this is Spice," says my father. "How about you, Savannah? Do you have any pets?"

She shakes her head, tousling her long chestnut-brown hair. "My parents are gone so much of the time, they say it wouldn't be fair to an animal. I'd love to have one, though."

"Well, you'll get your fill of them this weekend," my dad replies. "Dogs, cats, horses, chickens, goats—you name it, we've got it."

Savannah gives Sugar and Spice one last pat, then follows my father and me to the barn.

"Oh, my gosh, look how sweet you are!" I exclaim softly, kneeling down in the hay next to Sundance and her new little one. "You look just like your mommy, don't you?"

Sundance looks up at me and blinks proudly. I lean over and

Heather Vogel Frederick

give her a kiss on her forehead. "Good job," I whisper.

"She's a doe," says my father, glancing over at Savannah. "That's what girl goats are called."

Sundance's baby has the same soft brown coat and black streak down her nose as her mother does. She gives a tiny bleat as Sundance nudges her.

"Is this the goat you're always talking to Frankie and Adele about?" asks Savannah, her forearms leaning on the pen enclosure as she watches us.

I nod. "Uh-huh. She's a Nubian. I raised her for a 4-H project."

"She's pretty."

I look up, surprised, but Savannah's attention is on the goats and there doesn't seem to be a trace of sarcasm in her voice.

"I'm going to name you Sunbeam," I say, turning my attention back to the newborn.

"Come over here and check this out, girls," says my father, motioning to us.

We move to the second stall where Matilda, one of our creamy white Saanens, is lying contentedly in the straw. Next to her is a pair of small white forms.

"Twins!" I gasp. "You didn't say anything about twins!"

My father grins at me and puts his finger to his lips. "I wanted to surprise you. Keep it down, though. New mothers don't need a lot of excitement." He opens the stall and Savannah and I both tiptoe in. Matilda flicks her ear at us.

"It's just me, girl," I assure her. "And this is Savannah." We kneel in the straw.

"Can I pat one?" Savannah asks, gazing at the newborns.

I nod, and she reaches out cautiously, keeping an eye on Matilda. "The mother won't bite or anything, will she?"

"No, she's all bark," jokes my dad. "Seriously, we're family to her. She just thinks of us as a bunch of big goats."

"Feel how soft its little coat is!" Savannah's cheeks are flushed again, but with excitement this time, not embarrassment.

My father leans over the side of the pen and scoops up one of the babies. "How'd you like to hold one?" he asks, placing it gently on Savannah's lap.

"Oh!" she says, breathless. "He's adorable!"

She looks up and our eyes meet. She smiles at me—the first real smile I've ever received from Savannah Sinclair. Before I can even think about it, I smile back.

"It's a doe, actually," I tell her. "This other one's a boy. They're called bucks."

My father shoos us out of the pen after a few minutes so Matilda and her newborns can get some rest. I take Savannah around and introduce her to the rest of the herd.

"I can teach you how to milk one later this afternoon, if you want," I offer, keeping my voice casual. Somehow I can't picture a Sinclair wanting anything to do with the business end of a goat. But Savannah surprises me.

Heather Vogel Frederick

"Okay," she replies, sounding genuinely enthusiastic.

When I take her to meet our Belgians, though, her face falls.

"I know," I reply ruefully. "Led and Zep aren't exactly Blackjack and Cairo. But they're sweet and they work hard and we love them."

We stroke their noses and feed them apples and carrots, and then I take her to see the chickens. My brothers materialize at this point, intent on showing off.

"Call 1-800-Egg-Finders!" Dylan cries, dashing from nest box to nest box and then trotting over to Savannah with a trio of eggs.

"This one's from Patsy Cline and this one's from Dolly Parton and this one's from Loretta Lynn," he tells her proudly.

"You met Loretta earlier, in the hall," I explain sheepishly. "My mother has a thing for country music."

Savannah laughs. "So does my daddy. He'll get a big kick out of this when I tell him."

Dylan hands her an egg. "Eeeew," she says in surprise, recoiling slightly. "It's warm!"

The twins look at her like she has two heads.

"Well, duh," says Ryan. "It's fresh out of a chicken's hind end." He tucks his hands into his armpits and squats down, wiggling his bottom and squawking, then pretends to lay an egg. Dylan, of course, thinks this is the funniest thing he's ever seen and starts laughing hysterically.

My dad emerges from the creamery. "All right, you two, settle down," he says. "Go give those eggs to your mother." He turns to

Savannah. "So would you like to see how we make goat cheese?"

There's a long silence. Savannah's face turns bright red. So does mine.

"Ah," says my father, suddenly remembering the reason that Savannah's here in the first place. He clears his throat. "Maybe not, then." He gives Savannah a sly look. "Guess offering you a taste of Blue Moon is out of the question too, huh?"

Savannah's eyes widen in shock, then a smile tugs at the corner of her mouth.

My dad grins. "Aha!" he says triumphantly. "I knew there was a sense of humor in there!"

Savannah starts to snicker, and my father joins in and in a minute they're both laughing as wildly as my brothers were a minute ago. I stare at the two of them in disbelief. *Who are you and what have you done with Savannah Sinclair?* I want to ask this stranger who looks like my roommate.

After a tour of the creamery, the twins reappear to let us know that lunch is ready. We follow them outside, where we're ambushed by a small black creature. He pounces on my sneakers and gives my shoelace a fierce swat.

"Is this your new kitten?" Savannah asks as I bend down to pick him up.

I nod.

"He's so cute! What did y'all end up naming him?"

"Elvis," I tell her, rubbing his nose with my cheek. He bats at the tip of my braid. "My pen pal was right about the Nashville connection. It's perfect."

There's a bit of an awkward silence, as we both recall what else Madison had to say in her letter. I hold Elvis out to Savannah as a kind of furry peace offering. "Here," I tell her. "He's a little wild—he's a barn cat—but most of the time he's happy to snuggle."

She takes him from me and we continue back to the house. My mother looks out the window over the sink and spots us.

"The cat stays outside, girls," she calls. "You know the rules, Jess."

I look over at Savannah. "Sorry," I tell her. "No barn cats in the house."

"No chickens, either, right?" Savannah says lightly. She smiles at me and sets Elvis down on the back porch. "You stay here and be good, and we'll come play with you later, okay?"

Over lunch, my parents pepper Savannah with questions. It doesn't come across like they're prying or anything, though, just interested. I find out more about Savannah in one conversation than I have this entire year so far at school.

"So what's life like with a senator for a dad?" my mother asks.

Savannah shrugs. "Fine, I guess," she replies politely.

"Do you like living in Washington?" My father passes her the platter of grilled cheese sandwiches, and she takes one.

"Actually, when I'm not at school, I spend most of my time with my mother at our house in Atlanta."

It turns out the Sinclairs have three homes. One in Atlanta, one in Washington—well, Georgetown, which is some swanky neighborhood in D.C. I've never heard of but my parents have—and a summer cottage someplace off the Georgia coast called Sea Island. Although I hardly think a house that can sleep twenty counts as a "cottage."

Like Megan, Savannah is an only child. Well, almost. She has a stepbrother who's a whole lot older, like thirty or something. Her father was married before, I guess. She's traveled a ton, and she had nannies when she was little and has always gone to private school and her parents send her to fancy tennis and equestrian camps every summer. To me, it sounds like she's bragging, but my mom and dad don't seem to notice.

"Do you have any pictures of your family with you?" my mother asks.

"Yes ma'am—there's one in my purse," says Savannah, excusing herself to run upstairs. She returns a minute later with a small photo and hands it to my parents.

I crane to see it too. It's a smaller version of one that Savannah has on her dresser back in our dorm room. In it, Savannah is a couple of years younger, and she's standing between her father, who has silver hair and is wearing a suit and looks very senatorial, and her mother, who's one of those glossy blondes that so many politicians seem to marry. Savannah looks more like her dad, I think.

"So are you going anyplace interesting for summer vacation this year?" my dad asks her.

"Camp again, then Europe," she replies.

Heather Vogel Frederick

"Cool!" I try and make my voice all chirpy and enthusiastic, like Becca when she's talking to boys.

My mother shoots me a look. "That sounds wonderful, dear."

"Not really," Savannah replies, toying with her sandwich. "Especially Europe. It's pretty boring. One city's mostly like another. Plus, my father's always in some sort of meetings all day, and my mother mostly just wants to shop. It's okay, I guess, but I'd rather stay home."

My parents exchange a glance across the table. Savannah turns to me. "How about you, Jess?" she asks, making an effort to be polite. "Are you going anywhere fun?"

Does the barn count as fun, I wonder? Summer is our busiest season, and everytime it rolls around I can count on being right here on Half Moon Farm. I shake my head.

After lunch, Savannah and I go back outside and I teach her how to milk a goat. She's squeamish at first, but she eventually gets the hang of it. My brothers watch us, hanging on her every word and practicing their "y'all"s and "yes, ma'am"s. It's like they have a crush on her or something.

Dinner is a repeat of lunch, with my parents managing to extract even more information out of Savannah. She tells them about MadriGals, and it turns out she loves opera (how was I supposed to know when she's always got her headphones on?), and that she's been to the Met a bunch of times. My mom has too, and the two of them start talking excitedly about New York.

"I was just down there a couple of weekends ago," Savannah says.

"My mom helped me pick out a dress for the Founder's Day Dance."

"This is the first I've heard of any dance," says my dad, looking over at me. "How come you didn't tell us about it, Jess?"

I lift a shoulder. "I guess I forgot."

"Peyton says they have it every year," Savannah explains. "Most of the girls ask guys from The Essex School."

The Essex School is like the guy version of Colonial Academy. We've had a couple of dances with them this year, but I've missed them all because they're on the weekends. Not that I'd want to go anyway.

My mother glances across the table at me. "Who are you going to ask to the dance, honey?"

I turn beet red. I've been trying to muster my courage for weeks now to ask Darcy Hawthorne.

"How about Zach Norton?" she suggests.

"The cute Beast guy in that picture in your room?" says Savannah.

"That's him," my mother tells her. "He's such a nice young man— I'm sure he'd go with you, Jess."

I mumble something and change the subject.

After supper, my dad takes us to the video store and lets Savannah pick out a movie. My mother makes popcorn and we all cram into the keeping room, the little room off the kitchen that serves as our family room, to watch. My brothers snuggle up next to Savannah on the sofa like a pair of bookends. I watch the movie but I watch her, too, out of the corner of my eye. I'm still not sure quite what to make of this unfamiliar person.

Heather Vogel Frederick

Later that night, after we're in bed, I slip downstairs to get a glass of water. My parents are in the kitchen talking in low voices, and I pause in the shadow of the doorway. I don't mean to eavesdrop, but I can't help it.

"Poor kid," murmurs my mother. "She tries so hard to make her life sound glamorous, but you can tell how lonely she is. Nannies, boarding school, fancy summer camps—it sounds to me like her parents are too busy being important to care much about spending time with their daughter."

"Sometimes, all money can buy you is a whole lot of misery," my dad agrees.

I peek through the crack in the door. My parents are sitting at the kitchen table, holding hands. They smile at each other over their coffee mugs. I tiptoe back up to my room. Right now, I wouldn't trade my family, and life at Half Moon Farm, for all the ski vacations or summer cottages in the world.

"Your parents are really nice," Savannah whispers as I slip back into bed.

I'm too surprised at first to reply. This weekend is turning out a whole lot different than I expected. "Yeah," I say finally. "I know."

On the way home from church the next morning, my mother turns around in the truck and smiles at us. "Mrs. Crandall said something about a community service project you're involved with, Savannah?"

Savannah nods, slanting me a glance. "I volunteer at the Concord Animal Hospital every Sunday afternoon."

I just about fall off the seat when I hear this. Savannah's never said a word about volunteering anywhere. Of course, I'm never around Colonial Academy on the weekends, but still, you'd think she would have mentioned something.

"Maybe you can take Jess with you," says my mother. "It's such a nice day—you girls could ride bikes there. You can borrow mine, Savannah."

An hour later we've eaten and changed and my dad has raised the seat on Mom's bike for Savannah and we're whizzing down Old Bedford Road toward town. My mother is right—it is a beautiful day. We still need our fleece jackets, because it's a little chilly, but there are daffodils bursting into bloom everywhere, and overhead, a herd of clouds frisks through the bright blue sky like playful goats. Twenty minutes later we arrive at the shelter, pink-cheeked and breathless.

If the people at the shelter know that Savannah is the daughter of a United States senator, they don't make a big deal about it. It's obvious she's glad to see them, and they're equally glad to see her. Savannah even has her own locker. She exchanges her fleece jacket for the light blue lab coat that's hanging in it, and takes me to the front desk to sign in.

"Welcome, Jess," the supervisor says, as I sign the clipboard. "I'm Ms. Mitchell. We're always happy to have more volunteers."

She scrounges up another lab coat for me and puts us to work. Savannah Sinclair may not know how to set a table, but she knows how to clean out a cage, that's for sure. I keep sneaking glances at her, more impressed than I'd like to admit. Maybe it's all an act, but Savannah is turning out to be more like a real person than I've ever thought she could be. The spoiled Southern belle I know from Colonial Academy is nothing like this girl beside me who's scrubbing away without complaint. And who would ever have guessed that Savannah was almost as big an animal lover as me? This explains why she was so good with our dogs, and with Elvis and our goats.

The best part of the afternoon comes when we get to take some dogs outside to the fenced yard for exercise. There's a black standard poodle named Herman who's gorgeous; Kiva, an elderly malamute; a couple of energetic mutts named Tick and Tock; and Pip, a plump little golden Labrador puppy.

"We've managed to find homes for everyone but him," Ms. Mitchell tells us, coming out to check on us.

"But I thought y'all had a family lined up for him," Savannah replies, looking worried.

Her supervisor pats her on the arm. "These things happen, dear. Something came up and they had to back out."

There's a rising note of panic in Savannah's voice. "Can't you find somebody else to take him?"

"It's slow this time of year, kiddo. Things are busy around the holidays and they always pick up later in the spring, but during mud season in New England, nobody's thinking about puppies, I can assure you. Too much mess."

Savannah looks like she's going to cry.

"What's wrong?" I ask as Ms. Mitchell heads back inside.

"Pip was a holiday reject," Savannah explains. "Somebody thought he'd look cute in a Christmas stocking, but they hadn't counted on the responsibility that goes along with a six-week-old puppy. They dropped him off on New Year's Day and he's been here ever since."

"So?"

"So his time is almost up! Shelters can only take care of animals for a couple of months at most. They've extended his deadline once already."

My brow wrinkles. "Deadline? What kind of deadline?"

Savannah looks at me sadly.

I gasp. "No!"

Savannah nods.

I can hardly stand to think about it. "It's like some horrible nightmare orphanage!" I protest. "It's worse than the John Grier Home!"

"The John Grier what?" says Savannah, mystified.

"Never mind," I tell her. For a moment I actually forgot that she isn't in our book club. "We have to do something!"

"Like what?"

"Like save him!" I bend down and call to Pip and he comes running. He flings himself into my arms, pressing his warm little body against mine and panting happily. He's easily one of the cutest dogs I've ever seen. "I can't believe there isn't somebody out there who would want him." A thought crosses my mind and I

Heather Vogel Frederick

stand up, still clutching Pip. "You know what," I say slowly, "he'd make the perfect birthday present for Emma."

"That girl with the purple glasses who's always coming over to visit you?"

"Yeah. She's my best friend. Like you and Peyton."

Savannah gives me a funny look.

"Emma's been wanting a puppy forever," I continue. "Oh my gosh, she would just *love* Pip!"

"When's her birthday?"

"June."

"It's the middle of April," says Savannah. "That's two months from now. It'll be too late for Pip."

"But what if we could take him now—you and me, I mean. We could hide him somewhere—"

"What? Are you crazy?"

"Think about it. I'm sure I could get my friends to help us. There's a room up in the hayloft that my dad lets us use for a hangout. We could hide him there part of the time. And between all of us, I'm sure we can find plenty of places to stash him."

"There's a trunk room in the attic of Witherspoon," says Savannah, beginning to sound excited. "That could work. And I'll bet we could find a spot down in the stables, too."

"It's just for a few weeks," I add. "I know we can do this."

"We're going to need permission from an adult to adopt him," Savannah points out.

"Don't worry, I'll handle that." I hold out my hand. "Can I borrow your cell? I left mine at home." Savannah fishes it out of her pocket and passes it to me. "I'll be right back."

I sprint inside, grabbing one of the shelter's brochures as I pass through the lobby. Ducking into the ladies' room, I take a deep breath and dial the number on the brochure's cover.

The receptionist answers, and I close my eyes and try and pitch my voice lower, like my mom did when she was playing Larissa LaRue. "This is Mrs. Delaney," I say. I feel a twinge of guilt—I hate telling lies— but this one's for a very good cause. Doesn't that make it a white lie? "My daughter just called to tell me that you have a golden lab puppy looking for a home."

"That's right."

"We've been looking for a puppy for Jess, and he sounds perfect. Would it be all right if she brought him home with her today? I'd drive over to pick them up but I'm leaving for Boston shortly for an important appointment, and I won't be home until after you close."

"Let me talk to my supervisor," says the receptionist. She puts the phone down, and I can hear her and Ms. Mitchell talking in the background. I cross my fingers. I cross all my fingers. Thumbs, too.

Savannah's supervisor gets on the line. "Mrs. Delaney?"

"Yes?"

"This is Janet Mitchell, supervisor at Concord Animal Shelter. What you're requesting is a little unorthodox, but I don't see why we can't accommodate you, as long as your daughter fills out the paper-work and pays the fee."

Uh-oh, I think. *There's money involved?* Ignoring this possible setback, I continue, "Of course, Ms. Mitchell. And thank you so much. This will make one little girl very happy."

That part isn't a lie, at least. Emma's going to be ecstatic.

"No, no, thank *you*, Mrs. Delaney. I can assure you that this makes us very happy too. I'm so glad your daughter came in with Savannah this afternoon. Pip is one lucky dog."

I hang up and race back outside, using the other door so I don't have to go through the lobby.

"Well?" says Savannah.

"Almost home free," I tell her. "I pretended to be my mom, and it worked like a charm. Except it costs money to spring a puppy from here."

Savannah smiles. "That's where I come in," she says. "Daddy gave me a credit card."

Half an hour later, we walk out of the animal shelter with Pip on a leash. We're both giddy with excitement.

"I can't believe we just did that!" I crow.

Savannah slaps me a high five. "Way to go, Jess!"

We smile at each other, which still feels incredibly strange. Then I tuck our secret puppy into my fleece jacket, zipping it tightly so he stays secure, and climb carefully onto my bicycle. Pip wriggles a bit, but he settles down once he manages to poke his head out so he can see where we're going.

Back at my house, we pedal directly to the barn. The coast is clear, fortunately, and I scoot right up the hayloft ladder with Savannah on my heels. "Wait here with Pip," I tell her, and head for the house.

My mother is in the kitchen. "How was your volunteer shift?"

"Great!" I tell her, not even having to fake enthusiasm. "Hey, Mom, Savannah and I were wondering, since it's kind of warm this weekend, could we camp out tonight in the barn?"

Mom looks surprised. "Really? Savannah is up for that? She doesn't seem the camping type."

I shrug.

"Well, it's okay with me if it's okay with your father. You can ask him when he gets back—he's out getting pizza for supper." She smiles at me. "I'm so glad you two are getting along. I knew this weekend would be a good idea!"

I kiss her on the cheek, feeling another little prickle of guilt. "Thanks, Mom."

Racing upstairs I round up two pillows, a hot water bottle, a fuzzy bathmat, an extra blanket, a pair of flashlights, and my alarm clock. The sleeping bags and air mattresses are stored in the barn, and so are Sugar and Spice's old crates. I can snag some dog food later.

"She said yes!" I tell Savannah jubilantly, pulling the hayloft ladder up behind me just in case my little brothers are lurking around. They love to spy on me and my friends.

Savannah nods at Pip, who is blissfully asleep in her arms. "Isn't he adorable?"

I kiss the tip of his nose. "Absolutely. We did the right thing for sure. We couldn't have let anything happen to Pip."

We spend the evening setting up our sleeping area, making a nest for Pip in his crate with the bathmat and hot water bottle and blanket, and laying down newspapers in the far corner for him to do his business. We eat pizza, and work on a chart for keeping our secret puppy circulating among my friends. Every once in a while I look over at Savannah and feel like pinching myself. I still can't believe the two of us are actually having fun.

We decide that Pip will spend the weekends at Half Moon Farm, then come back with me to Colonial Academy on Sunday nights.

"On Monday night he can stay with Cassidy, Tuesday with Megan, Wednesday with Becca and Stewart, and Thursday with Zach," I say, putting a check by each name on my clipboard. "Then Friday afternoon I'll bring him home with me again."

"You really think you can hide him two nights in a row?" Savannah looks worried.

"No problem. With all the animals we have around here, even if he makes a little noise I doubt anybody will notice."

Between farm chores and frequent trips up to the hayloft to check on Pip, Monday whizzes by. I leave messages for all my friends and tell them to call my cell phone when they get home, and one by one, they call to see what's up. The minute they hear about Pip, they beg to come over.

"Just be sure not to let anything slip to Emma," I warn them.

"Jess must have told you about our new baby goats," my mother says a little while later, when Megan and Cassidy and Becca all show up.

"Uh-huh," Cassidy replies, her eyes wide with innocence, which isn't a lie because I did.

"Just try and keep it down out there, okay? New mothers need their rest."

I promise my mother we won't overwhelm Sundance and Matilda, and we don't because we barely stop to look into their pens before we climb up to the hayloft.

"Oh, my gosh, he's sooooo cute!" squeals Becca when she catches sight of Pip.

"Shhhh!" I whisper. "My dad's downstairs in the creamery!"

We take turns passing him around, and I see them watching Savannah, curious about the sudden transformation I told them about. After we hear my dad leaving the barn, we play with Pip until he falls in a contented heap at my feet.

"I guess I'd better get going," says Megan reluctantly. "My mother will be here any minute to pick me up."

"Mine too," says Becca.

"Uh-oh," says Savannah, looking at her watch.

"What?" I reply.

"I completely forgot about Briggs. He'll be here soon to get me, too."

"Who the heck is Briggs?" asks Becca.

"My chauffeur," Savannah replies, and Becca's mouth drops open. I guess she didn't believe me when I told her about Briggs.

Savannah and I look at each other in dismay. No way can we hide a puppy from her chauffeur.

"I have an idea," says Cassidy. "Gimme your cell phone, Megan."

Megan passes her the phone and she starts to dial.

"Who are you calling?" I ask.

"Darcy Hawthorne," Cassidy replies, and my heart skips a beat. "My sister's at the movies with her friends, and he's the only one I know with a car. Besides, I bet he'll help us."

"Maybe that's not such a good idea," says Becca. "What if Emma answers?"

Cassidy shrugs. "I'll think of something."

Fortunately, Darcy answers. Cassidy puts him on speakerphone, and at the sound of his familiar deep voice my heart does another little somersault.

"Hey, Darcy, it's Cassidy Sloane." She tells him the whole story, and then explains the fix we're in. "Could you make up some sort of excuse and come over here right away? Somebody needs to drive Jess and Savannah back to Colonial Academy instead of Savannah's chauffeur."

There's a pause. "Savannah has a *chauffeur*? Sheesh, Emma never told me that."

Savannah's face turns pink. "What's the big deal about Briggs?" she whispers.

"Can't your sister drive them?" Darcy continues.

"She's at the movies," Cassidy tells him. "Please? We really need your help."

"I don't know, Cassidy," Darcy says cautiously. "My parents really, really don't want a dog. Plus, remember what happened last time you asked me to keep something secret?"

How could we forget? Back in sixth grade, Emma and I helped Cassidy disguise herself so she could try out for the boys' hockey team. We ended up letting Darcy in on the secret because Cassidy forgot her helmet at the last minute and had to borrow his. The four of us got in tons of trouble, and Mrs. Sloane-Kinkaid almost pulled Cassidy out of our book club.

"I know, but this is different," Cassidy pleads. "It's life or death."

Darcy sighs. "I'll see what I can do."

Cassidy gives Megan her cell phone back and my friends say good-bye to Savannah and me. We put Pip in his crate and head back to the house to get packed.

"Just act natural," I tell Savannah a few minutes later as the Hawthorne's old station wagon pulls into the driveway. "I'll do the talking."

"Hi, Mrs. Delaney!" says Darcy, knocking on the door to our back porch.

"Darcy!" my mother replies, surprised. "Well, hello! What are you doing here?"

"I'm on my way to Kyle's and stopped by with something for Jess."

"That's *Emma's* brother?" Savannah whispers to me as he comes into the kitchen.

I nod.

"Emma with the purple glasses?"

I nod again.

Heather Vogel Frederick

"Hey, Jess," Darcy says, holding out a stuffed monkey with GO BANANAS FOR BOOKS! emblazoned on its little yellow T-shirt. "This is from Emma. She absolutely, positively wanted you to have this tonight so you could take it back to the dorm with you."

My mother's forehead wrinkles. "Really? Well, that was nice of you to bring it over."

"Mom," I say, trying to sound nonchalant. "Do you think maybe Darcy could drop Savannah and me at Colonial Academy? It's practically right on his way to the Andersons'. We want to go back a little early so we can make cookies for our dorm tonight."

"Sure, I can do that," says Darcy.

"I'm sure Briggs won't mind having the evening off," adds Savannah.

My mother considers the idea. "I don't see why not," she says. "I'll go ahead and cancel the pickup."

A few minutes later, as we're loading my backpack and Savannah's suitcase into the back of the station wagon, I turn to Darcy. "Where did you get that awful monkey?"

He grins. "Emma brought him home for me from the library conference. You'd better act surprised when she gives you yours."

After checking to be sure the coast is clear, the three of us head for the hayloft. Pip is still curled up in his crate. I open it and he stumbles out, yawning a big puppy yawn.

I glance up at Darcy, feeling shy all of a sudden. "Isn't he cute?"

"Definitely," says Darcy, and for a split second I think maybe he's looking at me instead of Pip. Then he reaches for Pip and so do I and we both grab him at the same time, our fingers intertwining. Darcy doesn't pull his hands away.

"Um," I say, taking a deep breath. It's now or never.

"Darcy," drawls Savannah from behind us.

"Yes?" he replies, looking over his shoulder.

"I'm wondering if perhaps y'all would be interested in going to the Founder's Day Dance with me at Colonial Academy?"

My mouth drops open.

"I know you don't know me but you'd be doing me a huge favor," she continues. "My friend Peyton lined up a blind date for me, but he backed out. After I bought my dress and everything!" She puts her hand on my shoulder. "And of course Jess here already has a date."

Darcy looks back at me, and for a fraction of a second I think I see a flicker of disappointment in his warm brown eyes. He lets go of my fingers. "Oh," he says.

No! I want to scream. *It's not true!*

Darcy shrugs. "Sure, why not," he says, smiling up at Savannah. "I've never been to a dance at Colonial Academy."

Savannah smiles back at him. The familiar Sinclair smirk I've come to know and hate. "You are a true gentleman."

I clutch Pip to my chest, blinking back angry tears. I can't believe Savannah just asked Darcy to the dance! And what's worse, that he said yes! Couldn't he see what she was doing? Couldn't he tell that I was just about to ask him the same thing? And that lie about me already having a date!

Heather Vogel Frederick

So much for feeling sorry for Savannah Sinclair, I think to myself bitterly. I don't care how sad and pathetic her poor little rich girl life is, and I don't care that she helped rescue Pip. There's no way we can ever be friends now.

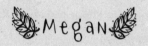

Megan

> *"I'm a foreigner in the world and I don't understand the language."*
> —*Daddy-Long-Legs*

"Ninety-nine bottles of pop on the wall, ninety-nine bottles of pop!"

I jam my pillow over my ears, trying to shut out the noise from the back of the bus, and from Becca, who's leaning on my shoulder, snoring. We left Walden Middle School at the crack of dawn this morning heading for Washington, D.C., and I'm feeling grumpy for two reasons: lack of sleep, and the fact that I'm here and not in Paris.

My parents and I took Gigi to the airport last night, and right up until the minute she got on the plane I kept hoping they'd change their minds and let me go with her. I should have known better.

I glare at the back of my mother's head, which is propped against the window of the seat in front of me. She's asleep too, and so is Mrs. Chadwick, who's sitting next to her. I can only imagine how fun this trip will be, what with the two of them as chaperones.

I yawn, and Becca stirs. "Somebody should tell those guys to shut up," she mumbles.

Heather Vogel Frederick

A minute later, somebody does. The singing has woken Mr. Keller, who stomps down the aisle and starts throwing his weight around. After he sorts the boys out, I finally manage to go back to sleep, and I sleep all the way to Connecticut. It's light outside by the time we reach our first stop and everybody piles off the buses. I stretch, then head for the restaurant along with the rest of my classmates.

Breakfast cheers everyone up, except my mother. She doesn't do fast food, so she just orders coffee, but then she has to go and grill the poor guy behind the counter about whether it's shade-grown and fair-trade certified, and of course he doesn't have a clue so she holds up the line while he goes to find the manager. I try to pretend like we're not together, but that's pointless because ever since last year, when she handcuffed herself to a tree at Jess's house and her picture ended up in the *Walden Woodsman*, everybody at school knows exactly who my mother is.

After breakfast, we pile back onto the bus and Emma breaks out a deck of cards. She and Cassidy and Becca and I start a game of rummy, which Gigi taught us how to play, and we invite Kevin, who is sitting across the aisle with his dad, to join us.

"No, thanks," he says in a low voice. I notice that he's looking pale and slightly greenish, which is not a good sign, and sure enough, a little while later, just as we're getting onto the New Jersey Turnpike, he throws up.

Becca shrieks, because some of it splatters across the aisle onto her sneaker, and pretty soon we're all shrieking and holding our noses.

Mr. Keller hollers at us to pipe down and the bus driver pulls over at the next rest stop and we all pile out again while he cleans up the mess. Kevin stands off to the side, crying, while his dad pats him on the back and tells him not to worry, it's okay, it could happen to anybody. But it's not okay, because for the rest of his life he's going to be known as "that kid who threw up on the eighth-grade field trip." Just like my mom is going to be known as "Handcuffs Wong."

The bus smells a lot better when we get back on, fortunately, and it's a warm day so we crack open the windows, which helps too. Just in case, though, the driver makes Kevin and his dad move to seats in the very front.

"How about we start finalizing our itinerary," says Mrs. Chadwick, whipping out her clipboard. Becca's mother loves being in charge.

All of us students have been divided up into "pods" of six and assigned to a pair of chaperones. Our pod includes me, Becca, Emma, Cassidy, Ashley—who got stuck sitting on one of the other buses because she was late—and Kevin Mullins, whom nobody else wanted. Most of the time all the pods will be together, like when we go to see the Declaration of Independence and tour the Supreme Court and the U.S. Capitol and get our picture taken on its front steps. We were all supposed to tour the White House, too, but our school couldn't get tickets this year. I guess it's been extra busy this spring, for some reason.

Each pod has some free choice time too, though, and Mr. Romero and Ms. Flanagan, our social studies teachers, sent home packets of information on suggested destinations a few weeks ago for us to look over. There are tons of museums to choose from, which sounded incredibly boring to me at first, but then Gigi told me that the Smithsonian has an exhibit of some of the inaugural ball gowns and other dresses worn by the First Ladies over the years. I definitely want to see that.

The best part of the trip, and the only other thing I'm really looking forward to besides seeing the First Ladies exhibit, is that on our last night we're going on a cruise on the Potomac River. We get to dress up and have dinner on the boat and everything.

Oh, and the other good thing about this trip? We don't have to wear our school uniforms at all for the next three days. I am so glad, because as far as I'm concerned I never want to wear maroon or gold again my entire life.

"Okay, so let's see, after we check in at the hotel, there's nothing planned until we all meet for dinner. I thought perhaps we'd head straight for the National Gallery," says Mrs. Chadwick, who's obviously feeling patriotic because she's dressed in jeans, a white T-shirt, and a red denim jacket. "Lots of important paintings there that I don't want you girls to miss."

Becca shoots me a look, then takes the clipboard from her mother and scans the list. "How about the National Mall instead?" she counters. "I'll bet they have good shopping there."

Behind us, Emma giggles.

"What's so funny?" Becca snaps.

Cassidy breaks the bad news to her. "The National Mall isn't a shopping center," she explains. "Don't you remember that PowerPoint presentation we watched in social studies? It's like a big park in the middle of the city. That's where the Vietnam Memorial is, and the Washington Monument and stuff."

"Oh." Becca looks disappointed and kind of embarrassed. She hates it when Cassidy knows something she doesn't.

Emma wants to go to the Library of Congress instead—she would, naturally—and Cassidy votes for the Smithsonian's Air and Space Museum. I stare out the window of the bus. I could be in Paris, France, right now, and instead I'm either going to have to look at a bunch of old paintings, a bunch of old books, or a bunch of old airplanes.

"I know Megan would like to see the 'First Ladies at the Smithsonian' exhibit at the American History Museum," my mother says.

I look over at her, surprised. Gigi must have told her. My mother carefully avoids my gaze, and it occurs to me that this might be her way of trying to make up for the fact that I didn't get to go to Paris. She knows how disappointed I am, especially since I've hardly spoken a word to her since we left Logan Airport last night.

Everybody likes this idea except Kevin and Cassidy. My mother manages to win them over by explaining that there are plenty of other interesting things to see, too, like antique cars and the original Star-Spangled Banner and George Washington's sword and even the ruby slippers that Judy Garland wore when she played Dorothy in the *Wizard of Oz* movie. "Too bad your mother isn't

Heather Vogel Frederick

with us, Cassidy—they have Julia Child's kitchen, too!"

Cassidy's forehead wrinkles. "Who's Julia Child?"

"Only the most famous TV chef ever," Emma tells her.

I wish Mrs. Sloane-Kinkaid could have come on the trip too, but her baby is due in a little over a month, and she decided the long bus ride would be too tiring.

In the end, after a lot of discussion, we decide that our free choice destinations for the other days we're here will be the Air and Space Museum, since that's the only thing Cassidy really wants to see, the Library of Congress, because Emma is desperate to see it and Mrs. Hawthorne made my mom and Mrs. Chadwick promise we'd make sure she gets there, and the Museum of Natural History, which we throw in because it has plenty of bugs and stuff for Kevin but also the Hope Diamond for the rest of us. If we have any extra time, we'll also go to the National Gallery to keep Becca's mom happy, and maybe the Botanic Garden, which is my mother's idea of fun, of course.

After another stop for lunch and a few more hours on the bus—barf-free, fortunately—we finally arrive at our hotel in Washington. It's one of those huge high-rises with an elegant lobby, the kind my dad always books for our family when we travel. It's no big deal to me, but my friends are all excited about it, and they mill around talking and laughing while our teachers and parents sort out the room assignments. All of us girls are going to be together on one floor, while all the boys will be stashed a couple of floors below us.

"Now remember, you are representing Walden Middle School, and

I will not tolerate any monkey business!" Mr. Keller tells us sternly, when we gather a few minutes later in one of the conference rooms for a group meeting. I guess he didn't get the memo about the school uniforms, because he's wearing his. The short sleeves of his maroon polo are way too small for the bulging muscles in his upper arms. A tailor could fix that, but maybe Mr. Keller likes it that way. He probably thinks it makes him look like a superhero.

Of course his comment unleashes a whole lot of chimp noises from the back of the room, and I turn around to see Zach and Ethan and Third and some of the other boys scratching themselves and generally acting like third graders. It's totally stupid but I can't help it, I laugh anyway. So does everybody else.

"I have an announcement too!" says Mr. Romero. "I just found out that, thanks to a Walden parent who wishes to remain anonymous, we're going to get to tour the White House after all!"

A huge cheer goes up, and I turn to my mother. "Did Dad buy them for us or something?" I whisper.

She shakes her head. "You can't buy tickets; they're free. It must be somebody who has a connection here in Washington."

Eventually, after a few more announcements and dire threats from Mr. Keller, we're released to our chaperones. We dump our suitcases upstairs in our rooms and then our pod heads for the nearest Metro station. Becca spots Zach and Ethan and Third and their pod and makes a beeline to where they're standing.

"Where are you guys going for free choice?" she asks.

Heather Vogel Frederick

"The Spy Museum," he replies.

"Cool!" Becca turns to her mother. "Can I go with them, Mom?"

The one thing that bugs me about Becca is that she will drop me like a hot potato if there's a chance she can do something with a boy instead, especially Zach Norton. And here I thought she was as excited as I was to see the First Ladies' gowns. Emma flashes me a sympathetic glance. She understands my mixed feelings about Becca.

"Me too, Mrs. Chadwick!" echoes Ashley, who is standing close to Third. Really close. I look at them, wondering if there's something going on that I don't know about. I haven't seen Ashley all that much lately. I was supposed to go to her birthday party last weekend but I ended up in Boston at this stupid green-living convention with my mother instead. My dad's been after me to make sure I spend as much time with her as I do with Gigi. Things are still kind of rocky between my mom and my grandmother.

Mrs. Chadwick frowns. "Absolutely not, girls," she replies. "Remember we talked about this already? We stick to our pod, and we stick to our plan."

"Maybe we can join forces for something else later, like the Air and Space Museum," suggests Mr. Mullins, who probably wants to make sure Kevin gets to spend time around other boys. Kevin gets stuck doing stuff with girls a lot of the time, because we're a little nicer to him.

Mrs. Chadwick pulls out her clipboard, and the parents all compare notes and decide that this would be okay, if everybody's in favor of it.

Becca's smile reappears, and I find myself smiling too. There might be something going on between Ashley and Third, but Becca definitely doesn't have dibs on Zach Norton and I'm definitely in favor of spending an afternoon with him.

It's a short ride on the Metro to the Smithsonian, and when we finally get to the First Ladies exhibit, it's even better than I thought it would be.

"Oh, wow," I say, when we enter the long room lined with glass cases.

Besides the ball gowns and other dresses, there's White House china and portraits and other things belonging to the first ladies too. Looking at everything keeps our group content for a while, but I'm barely getting started by the time the rest of them are ready to move on.

"Can't I stay here, Mom?" I beg. "I haven't even sketched anything yet."

"I suppose that will be all right," she replies, ignoring Mrs. Chadwick's frown. "Just keep your cell phone on in case I want to get in touch with you."

After they leave, I wander around the room slowly, taking my time as I examine the details on each of the dresses. They're couture, of course, one-of-a-kind designs, and most of them are vintage. Really, really vintage! This one gown of Martha Washington's is amazing, with hand-painted flowers, butterflies, and insects on the pink fabric. I didn't know they had stuff like that back in the 1780s. I sketch it,

Heather Vogel Frederick

along with the very first inaugural gown ever donated to the museum. President Taft's wife, Helen, donated it in 1912. I admire the white-silk chiffon, and then get busy trying to capture the flowers embroidered in metallic thread, and the rhinestone and bead trim.

I wish Gigi were here. She would totally love this! It's fine being with my mother and everything, but I just wish she got fashion the way my grandmother does.

I circle the room, dazzled and happy and completely puzzled as to why my mother doesn't find this stuff as awesome as I do. I stare dreamily at a flapper-style dress from the 1920s that Mrs. Harding wore. It has pearlized sequins and gold beads—a lot of the first ladies liked beads and shimmery stuff, including my favorite dress, one that belonged to Jackie Kennedy. It's a pale yellow silk single-shoulder design, really simple and elegant, with just the right amount of scattered crystal beads on the bodice to give it pizzazz. It's perfect.

I find a bench and start drawing. After a while my cell phone buzzes in my pocket. It's my mother.

"The museum will be closing before too long, honey," she says. "Don't you want to see any of the other exhibits?"

"Nope," I tell her, concentrating on getting the folds of Mrs. Kennedy's dress just right. "Maybe another time."

"We're in the gift shop when you finish up, okay?"

A few minutes later my cell phone buzzes again. This time it's a text from Becca: HURRY UP!

I sigh and shove my phone back in my pocket and close my

sketchbook. Downstairs, I find my mother and my friends, who are picking out postcards to send to our Wyoming pen pals. I find one of a Pocahontas quilt for Summer, and I see Cassidy holding one of the TV chef's kitchen.

"For your mom?" I ask her, and she nods.

"What are you going to send to Winky?"

Cassidy holds up another one of a lunchbox that shows a pioneer guy and a bear in front of a log cabin. "She'll think this is funny."

"They have historic lunchboxes here?" I ask, kind of sorry to have missed out on that.

"Yeah, and Kermit the Frog, too." She passes me a third postcard. "I got one of him for the baby."

After the Blue Moon cheese disaster, Cassidy had to promise to write letters to her new sister or brother so she could come on this trip. Well, that plus apologize to Savannah and her parents too, like all of us had to. She thinks the letter-writing is a total waste of time, but I don't know, I think it's kind of a fun idea. It's sort of like scrapbooking, which Becca and Ashley and I do together with Mrs. Chadwick sometimes. Mrs. Chadwick doesn't seem like the scrapbooking type, but sometimes people surprise you.

I rip a page out of my sketchbook and hand it to Cassidy. "Here," I tell her, handing her the sketch of Martha Washington's dress. "This was one of my favorites. Can you believe it's over two hundred years old? You can put it with the postcard for the baby, if you want. If it's a girl, I mean."

Heather Vogel Frederick

"Thanks, Megs."

"That was nice of you, honey," my mother says to me later, as we're leaving the museum. She puts her arm around my shoulder and gives me a squeeze.

I start to pull away, but then I remember that she was the one who spoke up and made sure I got to see the dresses in the first place, so I stop myself. I'm still really, really disappointed that I didn't get to go to Paris, but honestly, I'm tired of being mad at my mother. Even if I'm not quite ready to forgive her yet, I guess I can call a truce while we're here.

The next two days pass by in a blur. It turns out Washington is a pretty amazing place. The city was actually designed, just like a dress, but by an artist, not a fashion designer. Some guy named Pierre L'Enfant from France, which maybe explains a lot. Those French sure have a lot of style. The streets are really wide and straight, and there are all these big stately white buildings everywhere, and the view along the mall, the long, rectangular park in the middle of everything, is incredible.

I've never thought of myself as super patriotic or anything, even though I live in Concord which is, like, the most patriotic town ever, especially since the American Revolution practically started there. Still, there's something about the way everything looks here in Washington that makes me really proud, and I take a ton of pictures to show Dad and Gigi when we get home.

We end up having a great time at the Air and Space Museum, too.

The airplanes and space capsules and stuff are pretty cool, and I even get Mr. Mullins to take a picture with my cell phone of me and Zach standing inside the nose of a jumbo jet. Kevin's in it too, unfortunately, but I can always crop him out later.

Staying at the hotel with my friends is just as much fun as touring the city. Becca and Ashley and I are sharing a room, and right next to us, through a connecting door, is Emma and Cassidy's room. We just leave the door open and it's like we're all together. Mrs. Chadwick and my mother are across the hall.

"Now remember what Mr. Keller said," warned Mrs. Chadwick the first night she and my mom came over to tell us good night. "No monkey business."

Behind them, Cassidy scratched at her armpits and pretended to eat a banana. We had to stifle our giggles until they were gone. For weeks, Cassidy had been planning pranks for us to play on Zach and the other guys, but when we tried to sneak out and raid their rooms, it turned out Mr. Keller and some of the other dads were taking turns patrolling the halls. We had to pretend that we got lost looking for the soda machine, and slink back upstairs in defeat to watch movies on TV and eat microwave popcorn instead. That wasn't so bad, though, especially when we figured out that we could at least make a few prank calls to them instead.

Next to the First Ladies' exhibit, the White House tour is my favorite. Whoever got us the tickets got us the best kind, the ones that come with a guide. Some of the other tours are self-guided, which

Heather Vogel Frederick

means people get stuck wandering around by themselves. We follow our guide through all these rooms with names like the East Room and the Blue Room and the Red Room, and she tells us about the furniture and china and stuff. Mrs. Chadwick almost has a cow when she sees everything. She loves antiques.

My mother asks about the organic vegetable garden that she heard the First Lady was planting, and Kevin Mullins's father wants to know if we're going to get to see the Oval Office.

"I'm afraid that's off-limits to the public," our guide replies, and everybody groans.

I keep looking around hoping to see the president, but I guess he's off-limits too. Or at least too busy to hang out with tourists.

By the end of the tour we've learned that the White House has five full-time chefs, 132 rooms, thirty-five bathrooms, twenty-eight fire-places, and three elevators. Oh, and that it takes 570 gallons of paint to cover the outside. Our guide is really nice, but she's kind of obsessed with numbers.

Cassidy perks up when she hears that the White House has its own jogging track, swimming pool, and basketball court. She raises her hand.

"Does the president play hockey?" she asks. "He should totally put in a skating rink."

The guide shakes her head. "He loves movies, though—the White House has its own movie theater."

"Hey," Becca says to me later that night, back at the hotel. She's whispering because Ashley's fallen asleep already. "That was awesome today, wasn't it?"

"Yeah," I agree. "I'd love to live at the White House."

"You practically do! I mean, your house isn't that big, but it's white—on the inside, anyway."

I laugh quietly. "I guess you're right. And hey, we might not have five chefs, but we have Gigi."

"Have you heard anything from Jess?" Becca asks, changing the subject. "I wonder how Pip is doing without all of us there to help take care of him."

I sit bolt upright in bed. We've been so busy I completely forgot to check! I grab my cell phone off the bedside table and quickly send a text. A minute later my cell phone lights up, and I flip it open and whisper Jess's reply aloud to Becca: "Pip with Stewart 2nite, with us again 2morrow. All fine."

"Good," says Becca, and rolls over to go to sleep.

My cell phone lights up again—it's another text from Jess. R U HAVING FUN?

I lean back against my pillow and text her back. NOT PARIS, BUT YEAH. WISH U WERE HERE. I look back down at my cell phone and attach the picture of me and Zach and Kevin at the Air and Space Museum and press send.

Jess would have loved everything, even when Mrs. Chadwick got all dramatic and struck a pose right in the middle of the National Archives and started to recite the Declaration of Independence. I

Heather Vogel Frederick

thought Becca was going to die. Still, it was pretty cool to see all the original signatures at the bottom, people like John Adams and John Hancock and Thomas Jefferson and Benjamin Franklin and the others we've been learning about all year. Third got really excited when he saw Josiah Bartlett's name. I guess he's some ancient relative of his.

The light on my cell phone blinks. U 2 LOOK GOOD 2GETHER, Jess's text reads. B NICE 2 KEVIN, K?

K! I text back, and put my phone away. I don't know why she's so protective of that little pest.

The next evening, after a full day going to more museums, we're in our hotel room getting dressed for the river cruise.

"Hurry up!" Emma calls through the open connecting door. "We're supposed to be downstairs in the lobby in five minutes!"

Of course she and Cassidy are ready—they could care less about clothes. At least Emma made an effort. I might not have chosen the sandals she's wearing, but her lavender T-shirt looks nice with the black cotton cardigan sweater she put with it, and plays up her purple glasses. Dressy casual is a good look for Emma. Cassidy, though—well, if her mother were here, I'm sure she'd make her change, but she's not and I know my mom won't notice and probably Mrs. Chadwick won't say anything either. And there's no way I'm going to pick that fight. At least she's changed out of the baseball warm-up pants she was wearing earlier today.

"Megs, do you have something that will go with this?" Becca pleads. Like Ashley and me, she's changed about half a dozen times already.

I give her outfit the once-over. Cute capris and strappy sandals, and the gathered scoop-neck top she has on is the perfect shade of aqua to set off her eyes. "How about these hoop earrings?" I ask, fishing them out of my jewelry bag and holding them up.

"Perfect! Thanks!" She grabs them from me, and we both give ourselves one last look in the mirror and tell Ashley that red is definitely her color and finally it's time to go.

Down in the lobby, the boys are already milling around in a big group. "Dressing up" for them means mostly that they've traded their jeans for khaki pants—I guess they don't hate our school uniforms as much as we do—and white shirts or polos. I see Zach and wave, and he waves back, which makes me ridiculously happy. Maybe I can figure out a way to sit next to him at dinner. Feeling a little self-conscious all of a sudden, I smooth the hem of my short white skirt and wonder if the ruffle I added at the bottom is too much, or if the shell pink swiss-dot cotton I chose for my shirt is as pretty as I thought it was at the fabric store.

The elevator doors ding behind us and out walk Mrs. Chadwick and my mother. Mrs. Chadwick is looking pretty conservative, considering all the wild outfits she's been through this year. This evening she's wearing a cream-colored pantsuit with a spring green blouse, and she must have put her contact lenses in because there are no glasses, leopard-print or otherwise, in sight. My mother has ditched the tracksuit and trail shoes she wore around the city today for normal-looking black pants, black ballet flats, and a maroon short-sleeve silk shirt that I recognize as the ultra-chic designer one that Gigi had wanted me to wear to school instead of my ugly polo. My grand-mother must have loaned it to her. She's even got pearl earrings on, which is a shock, because my mother almost never accessorizes.

We have to wait a couple minutes more for Kevin and his dad, who finally appear wearing identical suits.

"Wow! A perfect ten on the Dork-o-Meter," Becca mutters to me under her breath. "He's worse than Stewart."

If I thought Washington was cool during the day, it's *gorgeous* at night. Our boat drifts down the Potomac River past buildings and monuments lit with spotlights, including the Lincoln Memorial, which looks amazing.

Dinner is really good too, some kind of pasta salad and chicken, and there's a toffee crunch cake for dessert. Since there are other people on board besides just our school group, Mr. Keller and Mr. Romero and Ms. Flanagan are on patrol to make sure everybody behaves themselves and we do, mostly, although I spot a short food fight two tables over, which is quickly squashed.

Since it's a warm night, we all go upstairs onto the deck afterward and line the rails to watch the scenery in the distance.

Some music comes over the loudspeakers, and here and there a few people pair off and start to dance, grown-ups who aren't with our group, mostly, because the music isn't like anything we'd ever want to dance to. A little ways down the rail, Ashley and Third are holding hands.

"What's up with that?" I ask Becca, who is standing beside me with her back to the view of the Washington Monument. She's more interested in watching the boys instead. "Ashley never said anything to me about liking Third."

Becca gives me a sidelong glance. "You weren't at her birthday party," she replies. "It kind of started then."

I look over at my friends again. They make a nice couple, actually. Ashley is from Guatemala—she's adopted—and her warm brown skin and glossy black hair practically glow beside Third, who's almost as pale as I am. In another month or so, he'll be bright red—he's on the baseball team, and he's got that kind of freckly skin that sunburns easily, like Cassidy's. Third used to be a whole lot shorter, but he really shot up this year. He's changed.

Everything's changing, I think. Watching Ashley and Third gives me a funny feeling, like maybe there's a race underway and I'm behind or something. Emma has Stewart now, and it looks like Ashley has a boyfriend too. I'm glad for them all and everything, but what if I never have a boyfriend? What if nobody ever likes me that way? I look around for Zach, wondering what he's up to, but he's nowhere to be seen. Probably trying to keep away from Becca, who has been making a pest of herself this entire trip.

"Hey, Megan," chirps a small voice, and I look down to see Kevin, who comes up to about my armpit. He's looking up at me through his big glasses, very serious in his tiny suit.

"Hey, Kevin," I reply.

"Nice view, huh?" he squeaks.

"Uh-huh."

"Do you want to dance?"

"Nope."

"Okay." Kevin's shoulders droop and he starts to walk away.

I sigh, remembering my promise to Jess. "Hey, Kev—it's just that my feet are really tired from walking around all day." Which is the truth, although they'd probably perk right up if Zach suddenly appeared and asked me the same question. "Try Emma. I'll bet she'll dance with you."

Kevin brightens at this. "Good idea," he says, and trots away.

Becca looks over at me and we both start to laugh.

"That kid is so *annoying*!" she says.

"C'mon, he's not that bad," I reply. "Don't forget he's only eleven."

The two of us scope out the boys for a while. A bunch of them are standing around mimicking the adults on the dance floor. Mr. Keller spots them and tells them to cut it out. Ethan, who's looking pretty good tonight in a black polo and khakis, is on the other side of the deck talking to Cassidy. She keeps reaching up and patting his face, and at first I wonder if something's going on between them but then I realize she's making fun of his whiskers. Some of the guys in our class, including Ethan, are already starting to shave, but I guess they're not used to it yet because they mostly forget to do it.

Zach finally appears, and beside me Becca goes on full alert. She slides her lip gloss furtively out of her purse and gives her mouth a swipe. *Like that's going to do anything*, I want to tell her, but I don't. I don't want to pick a fight and ruin things. Not tonight, when we're having such a good time. Zach sees Ethan and Cassidy and breezes past Becca and me without so much as a glance in our direction.

"I might as well be invisible," Becca grumbles.

"Join the club," I tell her, and she looks over at me, startled, then laughs. "Let's go get some soda.".

Later, as the boat's heading back to the dock, my mother breaks away from the group of teachers and chaperones she's been talking to and comes over to me. She leans against the deck rail, her shoulder pressing against mine. "Having a good time, honey?"

I nod.

"I'm glad." She gives me a squeeze. "Look at this amazing city! Paris couldn't hold a candle to it."

I stiffen slightly, wishing she hadn't brought up Paris. Even though I probably would have regretted not coming on this trip—you only get one eighth-grade field trip per lifetime, after all, and Gigi promised me that Paris would always be there—still, I don't really want to be reminded of what I'm missing.

And I don't want to ruin my last night here either, so I shove Paris out of my mind, where it stays until two days later, when we're back in Concord again and my mom and I drive into Boston to pick Gigi up.

Logan Airport is jammed, and by the time we find a parking place and make our way inside the international terminal, my grandmother's flight has already landed.

"She said she'd meet us by the baggage claim," my mother tells me as we thread our way through the crowd.

Heather Vogel Frederick

"There she is!" I cry, dodging past a young couple with backpacks.

Gigi's face lights up when she sees me, and she gives me a big hug. My mother kisses her on the cheek, then turns and stares at huge pile of luggage beside her. My grandmother came home with a whole lot more stuff than she took with her. Clothes, I'm guessing.

Turns out I'm right.

"Since Megan couldn't go to Paris, Paris has come to Megan," she says, gesturing at the pile of bags with a flourish.

My mother sighs. I know she thinks Gigi spends way too much money on clothes—money that could go to good charitable causes—but I for one can't wait to see what my grandmother brought back.

It takes two luggage carts to haul all of the stuff back to our car. The suitcases barely fit in our little hybrid, and I'm wedged in the backseat between the bags there's no room for in the trunk.

"So what did I miss?" says Gigi, fastening her seat belt. "Tell me all about your trip."

"Washington?" I reply. "It was fun. I took a bunch of pictures to show you. But we want to hear about Paris! Who did you see?"

Gigi rattles off a long list of famous designers and movie stars, and spends the next half hour chattering happily about fashion trends and gossip she picked up at the runway shows. Hemlines are down, necklines are up, ruffles are out, feminine silhouettes are in, the Pacific Rim is hot, animal prints have cooled off, pink is the new black, coats are bigger and bolder, and handbags are shrinking. I grab my sketchbook out of my purse and start taking notes so I don't miss anything.

We're almost home when my grandmother drops her bombshell.

"I almost forgot!" she says. "I sold one of Megan's designs."

Our car nearly swerves off the road. "You did *what*?" my mother exclaims.

"I sold one of Megan's designs," repeats Gigi, beaming at us.

"Which one?" I ask, my mind racing as I try to picture all the things I've designed so far. "Was it one of the ones from last summer's *Flashlite* spread? Who bought it?"

"Bébé Soleil," Gigi tells me proudly.

I frown, trying to recall who they are. Someone important, I'm sure, if they were at Paris Fashion Week.

"Baby Sunshine?" says my mother, who took French in high school.

I've never heard of them, but that doesn't mean anything. New fashion designers are cropping up all the time.

Gigi nods. "I called up Kate Crandall before I left and borrowed that little pair of overalls you made for Maggie for her birthday," she explains. "The designers at Bébé Soleil went crazy for them."

My heart sinks. *Baby clothes?* My grandmother picks one of my designs to take to Paris, the fashion capitol of the entire universe, and it's *baby clothes?* So much for fame and glory.

"You're not happy about this?" Gigi looks worried. "It's just a first step—a way to get your toe in the door. Besides, I couldn't pass up the opportunity. I had a good feeling about those overalls the minute I saw them. With all the interest in the Pacific Rim this season, the timing was perfect."

Heather Vogel Frederick

My mother pulls into the driveway and shuts off the engine. She turns to Gigi. "Mother, why would you do this without asking? You're always interfering."

Gigi looks hurt. "I thought you'd be pleased." She pulls an envelope out of her purse and hands it to my mother. "Maybe this will make you feel better."

My mother opens the envelope and pulls out a check. She gasps. I crane my neck over the backseat to take a look. I gasp too. There's a number on the check with a whole lot of zeroes after it.

"I'm a tough negotiator," Gigi tells us proudly. "The contract is in there too. You'll need to sign it and get it back to Bébé Soleil, Megan."

My mother shakes her head. "Well, I suppose there's nothing we can do about it now," she says. "This will go into your college account, Megan."

"Remember what I used to tell you when you were growing up, Lily? That a woman should always have a little money of her own to do with as she pleases?" My grandmother extends a finger and places it under my chin. "Surely Megan can have a little bit to celebrate with."

I'm thinking maybe I'll buy a digital camera. Becca says I should start a fashion blog, and post pictures of my designs and stuff.

"May I have a word with you in private, Mother?" my mom says, in that super-polite voice she uses when she's really, really angry.

They disappear into the house and I haul all the suitcases inside, then head to the kitchen for a snack. Hearing voices, I realize that someone left the intercom on. I know I should probably turn it off, but

I can't help myself; I stand there and listen to every word. My mom and Gigi are downstairs in Gigi's room, and they're speaking a mishmash of Chinese and English. I only catch every few words or so, but it's easy enough to figure out what they're talking about. My mom keeps saying stuff like "interfering" and "you're treating me like a child" and Gigi says stuff like "ridiculous fuss" and "nonsense," and then my mom says, "I feel like you're driving a wedge between Megan and me," and she bursts into tears.

I flip the intercom off, feeling guilty. I can't ever remember hearing my mother cry.

I think I'm beginning to figure this all out. It's not so much the fashion thing—my mother has pretty much already given up on me ever becoming an engineer or environmental lawyer or the kind of citizen she thinks is useful. She knows how much I love clothes and design, even though it doesn't thrill her, and I'm sure she gets it that this is something my grandmother and I have in common. I think the problem is that my mother feels like she and Gigi are competing for me, and she's losing.

How can I make my mother understand that just because Gigi and I speak the same language, it doesn't mean that I don't love her, too. Haven't I been careful to make time to do things with her, the way Dad said? Didn't I go with her to that stupid green-living expo, instead of to Ashley's birthday party? And didn't we spend lots of time together while we were in Washington?

Things are still pretty frosty between my mother and Gigi by

Heather Vogel Frederick

the time our next book club meeting rolls around. This month it's at Emma's house, and the two of them barely speak on the drive over. As usual, my mom hasn't bothered dressing up, but is wearing loose cotton pants and a T-shirt with THINK GLOBAL, BUY LOCAL on it. My grandmother, on the other hand, looks like she's going to Buckingham Palace for tea. She's all decked out in one of the couture outfits she brought back from Paris, a sleek little lemon-colored sheath dress in raw silk. She's wearing heels, of course, plus her diamond earrings, a matching bracelet, and a strand of pearls.

You'd never know it to look at Gigi now, but my mother didn't grow up rich. Her family was pretty average from what I've heard, just like Dad's. It was only after Mom was out of college that things changed. When my grandfather passed away, Gigi took the money from his life insurance policy and bought an apartment building in an up-and-coming section of Hong Kong. I guess it was a really good investment, and a few years later she sold it and used the profit to buy two more. Kind of like Monopoly or something. Dad says Gigi's a shrewd businesswoman and deserves every speck of the success she's had. Mom says Gigi is irresponsible and throws her money away instead of saving for the future or making a difference in the world. Gigi says she is making a difference, she's making a lot of fashion designers happy and what's the point of working hard anyway if you can't enjoy life?

"You're always so serious, Lily," she keeps scolding. "You always have been. You need to kick up your heels once in a while. It's okay to spend a little money on yourself now and then. Get a facial; have a massage; wear something besides those ridiculous yoga pants."

Are all mothers and daughters as opposite as Mom and Gigi are, and Mom and I am, or is it only my mixed-up family?

I'm still wondering about this when we pull into the Hawthorne's driveway. Everybody else is here already except for the Chadwicks, and they arrive right on our heels.

"Spring has sprung!" yodels Mrs. Chadwick, bounding into the living room dragging Becca behind her. Becca looks mortified. It's been a really tough year for her. Her mother was pretty toned down in Washington last week, and we all thought maybe she was finally over the "it's a whole new me" thing, but unfortunately she flew to New York a couple of days ago, and every time she goes down there with Stewart for a photo shoot at *Flashlite*, Wolfgang gets ahold of her and refuels her enthusiasm. I overheard Mrs. Sloane-Kinkaid talking to my mother and Gigi last week, and she's beginning to suspect that Wolfgang is making a game out of talking Mrs. Chadwick into wearing outrageous stuff. She said she was going to call and have a word with him.

Tonight, Mrs. Chadwick is camouflaged from head to toe in blossoms. The fabric of her belted jumpsuit isn't that bad, just kind of loud, a jumble of red and yellow and orange flowers that would be fine by themselves, but the problem is, when you put them with orange shoes that have three-dimensional leather flowers stitched to the top of the toes, and add huge dangly daisy earrings and spring green glasses, the effect is definitely over-the-top.

Heather Vogel Frederick

"My eyes hurt," Cassidy whispers to Jess and me, and the three of us have to stifle our giggles.

Nobody else quite knows what to say, but that's okay because Mrs. Chadwick has plenty, and for the next five minutes she keeps up a steady stream of chatter about the latest gossip at *Flash* magazine. Emma disappears to the kitchen, returning with a pitcher of lemonade and a plate of Congo Bars.

"Those look great," says Mrs. Sloane-Kinkaid, taking one.

"Here, have another," says Mrs. Bergson. "One for you, one for the baby."

Cassidy's mother laughs. She's getting really big. She has gorgeous maternity clothes, though, including the cute black-and-white polka-dot shirt she's wearing tonight. It's loose and flowy but it doesn't look like a tent, and it's perfect with her black leggings.

After everybody helps themselves to snacks, Mrs. Hawthorne steers our discussion toward Jean Webster and *Dear Enemy*.

"Are you finding it a satisfying sequel to *Daddy-Long-Legs*?" she asks.

Jess shakes her head. "It's good so far, and I like the grown-up Sallie McBride a lot, but I really missed Judy. I wish we could read her letters too, and not just Sallie's."

"I miss her too," I agree.

"She's still a character," Emma points out. "It's just that she's offstage."

"Kind of like me, at Colonial Academy," says Jess, a bit wistfully.

"Yeah, and we miss you, too," I tell her. She smiles at that.

"I like the McGurk," says Cassidy. "She's awesome."

"The doctor's crotchety housekeeper?" her mother replies.

"You would," says Becca, sounding kind of crotchety herself.

"*Chadwickius frenemus,*" I hear Jess whisper to Emma. Becca doesn't know about their secret nickname for her, but I do and I have to say it's pretty much right on target.

We talk a bit about orphan reform, and how Judy's former roommate Sallie is rising to the challenge of transforming the John Grier Home from a grim institution into a true home for the children who are living there.

"Did you know that when *Daddy-Long-Legs* became a best seller and a smash hit on Broadway, it had a huge impact on how this nation perceived orphans and orphanages?" says Mrs. Hawthorne. "Adoption rates shot up, and orphan asylums began to be inspected and regulated—it was really quite remarkable."

"The pen is always mightier than the sword," says Mrs. Bergson, shooting a glance at Emma and helping herself to another Congo Bar.

"Indeed," agrees Mrs. Hawthorne. "Jean's publisher even made dolls to sell—boys and girls in blue gingham—and donated the proceeds toward helping place orphans in families. Her books really paved the way for some substantive social reform."

Mrs. Bergson reaches into the bag that's sitting by her chair. "When I heard what we'd be discussing tonight, I thought you girls might be interested in seeing this," she says, pulling out a girl doll dressed in blue gingham.

"Don't tell me you actually have a *Daddy-Long-Legs* doll!" cries Mrs. Delaney.

Mrs. Bergson nods.

"I told you she was a hundred," Cassidy whispers to Jess and me.

"It was my *mother's*," emphasizes Mrs. Bergson, who's got really good hearing. She smiles, though, as she passes the doll to Cassidy.

Cassidy gives her a sheepish grin in return. She looks the doll over and then passes it to my grandmother, who instantly lifts the hem of the dress to look at the needlework, which is exactly what I do when it's my turn. The blue gingham is faded, and the doll is a bit worn, but it's like holding a little piece of history. The feeling reminds me of seeing the First Ladies exhibit at the Smithsonian, and I set it carefully on the coffee table when I'm done.

"Girls," says Emma's mother, fishing in her bag and pulling out a folder, "before I pass our handouts around, I have to explain that I've relabeled them for this month."

I look down at the sheet that she passes to me and notice that the word "fun" is missing.

"You'll understand why once you read them," she adds, looking kind of somber.

FACTS ABOUT JEAN

1) In addition to voting rights for women, Jean Webster was passionately interested in many other social reform

movements of her era, including orphans and orphan asylum reform, and prison reform.

2) On September 7, 1915, at the height of the success of the *Daddy-Long-Legs* stage play and just as *Dear Enemy* was published, Jean married Glenn Ford McKinney, the son of the president of Standard Oil Company.

3) The newlyweds embarked on a happy life at Tymor Farm in Dutchess County, New York.

4) On June 10, 1916, at 10:30 p.m., Jean gave birth to a much-longed-for baby daughter, Jean Webster McKinney.

5) At 7:30 a.m. the following morning, on June 11, Jean Webster died of complications from childbirth. The next day's edition of the *New York Sun* listed a daughter of Glenn Ford McKinney among the birth announcements, and his wife Jean among the obituaries.

We all gasp as we read the last fact.

"*What?!*" cries Emma. "That can't be true!"

"Afraid so, honey," her mother says sadly.

"But it's so unfair!" wails Jess. "It's so, so—*tragic*."

Becca and I both nod, and Cassidy crumples her handout in her fist.

"We moms had a long discussion about this," says Mrs. Delaney. "We could have left that last piece of information out, but we decided that you girls should know what happened to Jean."

"You've spent a lot of time with her this year, and you deserve to know how her story ended, even if it wasn't a happy ending," agrees my mother.

Mrs. Hawthorne pulls one more sheet of paper out of her bag. It's a photocopy of another picture, this one of a man in a garden with a little girl. "I thought you might like to see this," she says softly, laying it on the coffee table. "This is Jean's husband, Glenn, with their daughter. He adored her, and she lived a long and happy life."

"And Jean's books have never been forgotten," says Mrs. Sloane-Kinkaid.

We sit there in glum silence until we're interrupted by a knock at the door. I turn and look out the living room window. There's a black limousine in the driveway, and Savannah Sinclair is standing on the Hawthorne's front steps.

"Uh-oh," I mutter to Becca, and poke Cassidy and Jess with my toe. "Julia alert!"

The doorbell rings and Emma gets up to answer it. Jess follows her out of the room. Cassidy and Becca and I are right on their heels. "Um, I need to talk to Jess," says Savannah, when Emma opens the door. She's holding something behind her back.

Emma frowns. "How'd you know she was here?"

"I, uh, called her house and her dad said she was here at your book club meeting. He gave Briggs the directions."

I flick a glance at the limo. I still can't believe Jess is rooming with someone who has a *chauffeur*.

We all stand there eyeing each other.

"It's kind of an emergency," Savannah says finally.

"So what's the problem?" Jess crosses her arms on her chest. She doesn't sound like her usual friendly self at all.

Savannah holds up the something she's been hiding behind her back. It's a sports bag. "Mrs. Crandall found out," she tells us, flicking a glance at Emma. "She saw me sneaking up to the attic and followed me. She hit the roof when she discovered what was going on, and said we had to get rid of it, tonight, or she'd call my father."

Jess cuts her eyes over to Emma. "Uh, Emma, could you give us a minute here?"

Emma turns to leave and walks straight into her mother. "Have to get rid of what, girls?" she asks.

"Nothing," says Savannah, whipping the bag behind her back again.

Mrs. Hawthorne puts her hands on her hips. "It doesn't look like nothing," which is universal mom-code for *You are so busted*.

Jess sighs. "I guess we'd better tell her."

By now, the entire Mother-Daughter Book Club is crowded into the Hawthorne's front hall. Reluctantly, Savannah hands the bag to Jess. Emma's eyes widen when she sees that it's wiggling.

Heather Vogel Frederick

Jess sets the bag carefully on the floor, then unzips it.

Pip explodes out of the bag and races down the hall, his little paws scrabbling on the hardwood floor. Emma's mouth drops open as Cassidy and Becca scramble after him.

"What is *that*?" her mother exclaims.

"Uh, it's a puppy?" says Jess, as if there could be any question.

"Whose?" Mrs. Hawthorne demands.

"Emma's," Jess replies meekly.

Emma lets out a squeal, and Jess and Cassidy and I all nod at her, grinning hugely. Savannah still looks kind of unsure of herself. Becca grabs her cell phone out of her pocket and runs toward the kitchen.

"His name is Pip," Jess tells Emma, as Cassidy scoops him up and places him into her arms.

"Pip!" she repeats softly, burying her nose in his fur. Pip laps at her face and barks happily. "It's perfect. He's perfect."

"What's going on?" says Mr. Hawthorne, coming out of his office to see what all the commotion's about.

"They gave me a puppy," Emma tells him joyfully.

Her father's eyebrows just about shoot off his forehead. "Who gave you a puppy? What are you talking about?"

"It was supposed to be a birthday present," Cassidy explains.

"Only the cat got out of the bag a little early," Jess finishes lamely. "Or the puppy, I guess."

"It's from all of us," I add.

Emma looks around at us, her eyes welling up with tears. "This is the very best present I've ever had in my entire life!"

Her father and mother exchange a glance.

"I think we'd all better go in the living room and sit down," says Mrs. Hawthorne. "You too, Savannah."

Melville takes one look at Pip and scuttles under the coffee table. Emma sits down on the sofa and we all cluster around her. Everyone's attention is focused on the puppy.

"From the beginning now," orders Mrs. Hawthorne. "Slowly."

"Well, Pip was at the animal shelter when Savannah and I went to volunteer last month," Jess begins. She turns to her mother. "Remember, Mom? That weekend she came over? Anyway, he only had a few days left before they were going to, to . . ." Her voice trails off, and she reaches out and places her hand protectively on Pip's head. "Don't you see?" she continues, her voice quivering with passion. "We just had to rescue him! He was like an orphan at the John Grier Home, only worse!"

"Jessica Delaney, don't you dare try to justify this," says her mother sternly. "This is real life, not a book!"

"But we couldn't just leave him there to die!" wails Jess.

"They'd have found a home for him," says my mother. "They always do."

"No, they don't," says Savannah in a low voice. "Not always."

Mrs. Hawthorne sighs. "So then what happened? This was a month ago, you say?"

Jess nods. "We've been taking turns keeping him hidden."

Heather Vogel Frederick

"All of you?" says Mrs. Sloane-Kinkaid, incredulous.

I look down at the carpet. So does everyone else except Becca, who's still in the kitchen. We can hear her muffled voice, talking to someone excitedly.

"He sleeps in a crate," Jess explains. "So he's really easy to take care of. I kept him up in the barn in our hangout over the weekends, and then on Sunday afternoon, when I went back to school, I put him in the duffel bag and rode him back on my bike."

"There's a luggage room in the attic of Witherspoon where they store our suitcases," Savannah adds. "We put him up there overnight."

"On Mondays I kept him in the turret," says Cassidy.

"And on Tuesdays I hid him down in Gigi's room," I confess.

My mother's head whips around to where my grandmother is sitting. "You knew about this, Mother?"

Gigi gestures at Pip. "Look at the poor little thing, Lily. Someone had to help him."

My mother closes her eyes and shakes her head wearily.

"Zach Norton took him on Wednesdays," says Jess.

"Oh, for heaven's sake," says Mrs. Delaney. "You dragged Zach into this too? Jess! What were you thinking?"

"Thank heavens my daughter wasn't involved," says Mrs. Chadwick, looking smug.

Becca, who has just come back into the room, turns bright red.

"Oh, really?" says Mrs. Hawthorne, eyeing her. "So where was Pip on Thursdays?"

Mrs. Chadwick turns and stares at Becca. "Rebecca Chadwick, you didn't!"

Becca bites her lip. "We kept him in Stewart's room."

"Shame on the both of you!" her mother scolds, the flower over her left ear quivering in outrage. "Shame on all of you, in fact!"

Emma's father and all of our mothers stare at us unhappily.

"Girls, this is a huge, huge deception!" says Mrs. Hawthorne.

"Huge!" echoes my mother.

"What I want to know is how you got the puppy from one house to another without anyone knowing," says Mr. Hawthorne. "It's pretty hard to hide something like a puppy."

"Uh," Jess hesitates. She looks down at the floor again.

"That would be me," says Darcy Hawthorne, stepping into the room from where he must have been listening in the hall. "I drove him."

"Darcy!" Mrs. Hawthorne looks shocked. "I can't *believe* that you didn't have better sense than to get involved in this harebrained scheme!"

Emma's brother spreads out his fingers. "It seemed like a good idea at the time." He looks over to where Emma is cradling Pip close to her. "I mean, look at him, Mom! He's adorable! And Emma's always wanted a puppy."

There's another knock at the door. Mr. Hawthorne goes to answer it this time, and reappears a moment later with Stewart and Zach Norton.

"What did we miss?" asks Stewart, with a worried glance at Emma.

"What you missed is that all of you are going to march down to the animal shelter right this minute and take Pip back," Mrs. Hawthorne announces, rising to her feet.

"No!" gasps Emma. "Please, Mom, I can't give him back!"

"Oh, yes you can," her mother replies.

"But—"

"But nothing." Mrs. Hawthorne turns to Emma's father. "Nick?"

"Your mother and I are in total agreement on this, Emma," he says firmly. "We've said no puppy and we mean no puppy. Melville would never forgive us."

The Hawthornes' cat is still cowering under the coffee table, his green eyes fixed on Pip and his back arched rigidly.

"Girls," says Mrs. Delaney gently, "I know you meant well, but you can't just give somebody a puppy. Especially not when their parents have said no."

"Can't we take him back to Half Moon Farm with us then?" Jess pleads. "Please, Mom? We have plenty of room there!"

For a brief second hope blooms on Emma's face, but it wilts as Mrs. Delaney shakes her head. "We just added another kitten, remember, honey? There's a limit to how many animals we can feed and look after."

I turn to my mother. "How about us? Could we take him?"

"Good idea," says Gigi. "Megan needs company. Especially since she's an only child."

My mother shakes her head. "Out of the question."

"Don't even think about it, Becca," says Mrs. Chadwick, as Becca opens her mouth to speak. "Yo-Yo is quite enough dog for one family."

"Please, Mom?" begs Emma, making one last plea.

"No, Emma," says her mother. "And that's final."

My friends and I all stare at Pip, stricken. Even Savannah has tears in her eyes, just like a real person and not the plastic mannequin she usually resembles.

Unaware of his fate, Pip is still perched happily in Emma's lap, wagging his little tail so hard his whole bottom is wiggling. I blink back tears. This has been the worst book club meeting ever. First we find out about what happened to Jean Webster, and now this!

Pip licks Emma's hand. She starts to sob. Her heart must be breaking, because I know mine is. And then a gentle voice speaks up from the back of the room. It's Eva Bergson.

"Perhaps I can help."

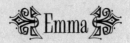 Emma

> *"They felt the thrill of the untried future, with Romance waiting around the corner."*
> —*Just Patty*

"It's going to be you for sure," says Megan.

I glance around the cafeteria, hoping no one can overhear our conversation. "You really think so?" I ask, feeling my face start to heat up.

"Dudes, do we have to talk about this again?" Cassidy throws down her fork. "You're ruining my lunch! You know how I hate all that gooshy stuff."

"What gooshy stuff?" asks Becca, setting her tray down next to Megan. Ashley is still at the salad bar—she takes forever making her "creations," as Becca calls them—and the boys who usually sit at our table haven't gotten out of PE yet.

"Kissing," Megan replies. "I just told Emma she's probably going to be the first one from our book club to get kissed."

"Too late," says Becca smugly.

"*What?!*" squeals Megan, causing everyone within earshot to turn and stare. I kick her under the table and she lowers her voice. "You never told me!" she whispers to Becca. "When did it happen? *Who?*"

Next to me, Cassidy sighs noisily. "This is so incredibly lame."

She's probably right, but like Megan, I want to hear more, even though deep down, I'm kind of envious. I guess I've been hoping that Megan's prediction would come true, especially since Stewart and I have come close a couple of times. *Does Becca really count?* I wonder. Sometimes it's still weird, thinking of her as part of our book club. Maybe I can still qualify as the first one from our *original* club to get kissed.

"It was that weekend at Ashley's birthday party," Becca tells us loftily, picking up her sandwich. "You weren't there, Megan, remember? You were in Boston with your mom at that green-living expo thing."

Megan makes a face. She told us that she promised her dad a while ago that she'd try and make an effort to spend more time with her mother. I guess Mrs. Wong's been feeling a little left out, what with Gigi here and all.

Cassidy crosses her arms and scowls. Neither of us were at the party either. But that's because we weren't invited, not because we were off having mother-daughter time. Ashley is okay and everything, but she's really more Megan and Becca's friend than ours. Not that I would have wanted to go anyway, and I'm sure Cassidy could have cared less, but still, it's not like we enjoy having our noses rubbed in not being invited.

Becca, however, is oblivious. "We were all downstairs in the Sanborn's rec room, playing Ping-Pong and listening to music and

Heather Vogel Frederick

stuff, and then somebody suggested we play spin the bottle, and Kenny Greenberg—"

"Wait a minute," interrupts Cassidy, leaning forward. "Spin the bottle? That doesn't count. It's just a stupid game. A boy has to kiss you of his own free will for it to count."

"Says who?" snaps Becca.

"Says me," Cassidy retorts.

"How come you get to make up the rules?" Becca fires back.

Before the argument can really heat up, the cafeteria doors fly open and the eighth-grade boys come swarming in. Zach Norton, Ethan, and Third are at the head of the pack. They're waving copies of the *Walden Woodsman* and chanting something.

"STRIKE! STRIKE! STRIKE!"

My stomach does a flip-flop as I realize what's going on. Even though nobody else does, the cafeteria erupts in cheers and howls of encouragement anyway. Looking worried, the lunch monitors scurry off toward the teacher's lounge for reinforcements.

Zach heads straight over to us, then bounds onto the tabletop, nearly stepping on Cassidy's leftover shrimp marinara in the process.

"Watch it, Norton," she growls, whisking her lunch to safety.

"Sorry, Sloane." Zach grins at her and holds his copy of our student newspaper over his head, then thrusts two fingers into his mouth and gives a shrill whistle. Instantly, the lunchroom falls silent.

"Hear ye! Hear ye!" he cries, and my stomach lurches again because I know what's coming.

Across the table, Becca is staring up at Zach with her mouth open. Cassidy tosses a piece of shrimp at her. "Feeding time at the zoo!"

Becca gives her a look.

"A message of great importance from the *Walden Woodsman's* esteemed editor, Ms. Emma J. Hawthorne!" Zach bows in my direction, and every eye in the room suddenly turns on me. The butterflies in my stomach turn into a herd of buffalo. I'm not used to being the center of attention.

How ironic, I think. We learned about irony when we read *To Kill a Mockingbird* earlier this year in English class, and I've been spotting it ever since. Two years ago, I would have been over the moon if Zach Norton had noticed me. And now that he does, I don't really care. I'm more nervous about what people will think of my editorial.

"Did you know he was going to do this?" whispers Cassidy. She's the only other person in the cafeteria who has a clue what's going on.

I shake my head. Zach clears his throat and starts to read. My words sound strange, coming from him.

"A Declaration of Fashion Independence," he announces, and suddenly I want to crawl under the table. Our class trip to Washington gave me the idea for spoofing the Declaration of Independence, and it seemed like a stroke of genius at the time, but now it just seems ridiculous. It's too late, though. There's nothing I can do about it at this point.

"When in the course of student events, it becomes necessary for one people to dissolve the school uniforms which have connected them with another," he begins, and I stare really hard at my peanut

Heather Vogel Frederick

butter and jelly sandwich. Every fiber of my being is fervently hoping that my friends and classmates will get what I'm trying to say. Will they understand what I mean by the importance of preserving the rights of an individual in a democracy, and that government derives its power from the consent of the governed and that if something is unfair, even something as dumb as school uniforms, we have a right to stand up and say so? Will they agree with me that clothing and fashion are a form of freedom of expression, and therefore guaranteed by our constitution?

I hold my breath as Zach gets to the last part, the part that most closely echoes Thomas Jefferson's famous words, ones that still ring in my mind from when Mrs. Chadwick recited them aloud to us at the National Archives:

"We hold these truths to be self-evident," Zach reads, "that all students are created equal, that they are endowed by their Creator with certain unalienable Rights, that among these are Life, Liberty, and the pursuit of fashion happiness."

Zach pumps his fist in the air as he reads this last line, and the cafeteria erupts again. Across the room, I see Mrs. Hanford and Mr. Keller stride through the doors. They do not look amused at all, and the buffalo in my stomach circle around for another stampede.

Mr. Keller blows his coach's whistle and starts yelling at everybody, but it takes a while for things to settle down. When they finally do, I'm hauled off with the boys to the principal's office. Naturally, Zach and Ethan and Third think this is a riot, but this is my first time in the principal's office ever and I just want to die. Especially when Mrs. Hanford calls my father.

I honestly didn't mean to start a revolution. I thought my editorial would be amusing, and thought-provoking, and that it just might catch the eye of the school board. But I can hear Mrs. Hanford having a heated conversation just outside her door with Ms. Nielson, the *Walden Woodsman*'s faculty advisor, and Mr. Keller, whose face is an unusual shade of purple, is sitting across the desk from us muttering darkly to himself about "rabble-rousers" and "suspension."

If Cassidy were here I know she'd just laugh and tell me not to listen to some moron who doesn't even have a neck, but I've never been in trouble before and I have no idea what to expect. Can they really expel someone just for writing an article in the school newspaper? I wipe my sweaty palms on my khaki pants.

A few minutes later my father arrives. Mrs. Hanford makes Zach and Ethan and Third go and wait in the outer office with the secretaries while she ushers my dad inside. He sits down in the chair beside me and gives me a reassuring smile, then takes the paper that Mr. Keller hands him. When he's finished reading my editorial, he looks up.

"What seems to be the problem?" he asks calmly.

My dad is an unassuming guy. He's medium height with curly brown hair, like Darcy and me, only his is thinning on top, and he wears glasses like me. He looks sort of like a professor. He's quiet, too, like me, and people tend to underestimate him. The thing is, my dad is really, really smart.

"What do you mean 'what seems to be the problem?'" says Mr. Keller belligerently. "Your daughter is way out of line here. She has no business making fun of the Declaration of Independence or criticizing the decisions of the administration of this school."

"What Mr. Keller means to say," says Mrs. Hanford smoothly, "is that we consider our student newspaper an integral part of the Walden Middle School community. And that as such it should reflect the views of the community as a whole, not just a single individual. Mr. Keller is right. Emma was extremely disrespectful both to our school community and to our nation."

"Interesting point of view," my father replies. "However, I thought the purpose of a newspaper—any newspaper—was to uphold our First Amendment right to freedom of speech, and that right extends to individuals as well as communities. As for disrespect, it seems to me that Emma learned a great deal while she was on her field trip to our nation's capital. After all, successful parody means first absorbing the central points of that which one is attempting to satirize, and it's obvious that Emma has done so with the Declaration of Independence. Otherwise she wouldn't have been able to articulate her views so clearly and eloquently. Frankly, I suspect Thomas Jefferson would applaud her if he were here."

Mr. Keller folds his arms tighter across his chest and scowls, but he doesn't say a word. How can you argue with Thomas Jefferson? My father looks over at me and gives me an almost imperceptible wink, and the buffalo start to subside. I was worried at first when

Mrs. Hanson called him, but now I'm really glad he's here.

"And another thing," my father continues, "Emma makes a really good point. You're educating middle school students here, not kinder-gartners. Simply to dictate policies to them doesn't necessarily serve the highest aim of education. Adolescence is a time for finding one's footing as an adult in the world, for learning to think like an adult and act like an adult. Wouldn't it have been a more valuable civics lesson if you had included your students in the planning process of the school uniform decision, and perhaps sought their feedback, thus teaching them how a true community works together?"

Mrs. Hanford seems flustered. I don't think she was expecting this. She leans forward. "This is a *school newspaper* we're talking about, Mr. Hawthorne, not the national media. The First Amendment doesn't apply."

"I beg to differ," counters my dad. "And so, perhaps, might the Supreme Court. What was it they once so famously said? That public school students 'do not shed their constitutional rights to freedom of speech or expression at the schoolhouse gate'?"

Mrs. Hanford sits back in her chair. She seems at a loss for words. Not that I blame her. I'm feeling that way myself. Where the heck does my dad come up with this stuff?

"What your daughter did was out of line," Mr. Keller repeats stubbornly. He's clutching his coach's whistle tightly in one of his meaty fists, like maybe he wants to blow it and eject us both out of the game.

"That's hardly accurate," says my father mildly. "Emma didn't say anything defamatory or inflammatory. She simply wrote an editorial—her personal opinion—and it was clearly marked as such." He holds up the paper and points to the word "EDITORIAL" in bold type that's embedded in the column of my text. That was Ms. Nielson's idea, and I'm suddenly really, really grateful she suggested it.

The vein in Mr. Keller's neck is bulging. I can tell he's not happy with the way this meeting is going. "We're going to shut this paper down!" he growls, thumping his fist on the desk. "And remove your daughter as editor!"

"I'm sure the *Boston Post* would be interested in hearing that," my father tells him. My dad writes freelance articles for the *Post*, mostly book reviews and author interviews, and he knows a lot of people in the newsroom. "It would make a great story. Especially since it's the *Walden Woodsman* we're talking about, with its obvious connections to our good friend and neighbor Henry David Thoreau. Not that my daughter's editorial was in any way an act of civil disobedience such as Thoreau engaged in—far from it—but any reporter worth his salt is bound to make that leap. Why, this might even attract national attention."

Mr. Keller and Mrs. Hanford exchange a glance.

"Perhaps Mr. Keller's remark was a little hasty," says Mrs. Hanford.

She sends my dad and me to the outer office. Zach and the others look over at us curiously. I shrug to let them know nothing's been decided yet. We can hear our principal and vice principal on the other side of the door, whispering heatedly. My dad takes my hand and squeezes it. I squeeze back. Finally, the door opens, and Mrs. Hanford beckons us inside again.

"Mr. Hawthorne, Emma," she says, "since there's only a month of school left to go, and since Emma's record at Walden up until today is completely unblemished, Mr. Keller and I have agreed that we'll be willing to overlook this matter."

Coach Keller glowers at me, and somehow I have a feeling that this was Mrs. Hanford's decision, not his. She doesn't mention anything about the uniform policy, and I don't ask. That would probably be pushing it.

My dad thanks them and shakes their hands, and once we're back out in the hall he puts his arm around my shoulders. "I'm so proud of you, Emma," he tells me, his eyes shining behind his wire-rimmed glasses. He kisses the top of my head. "That was a fantastic editorial!"

I smile up at him. "Thanks, Dad. But you were the one who was fantastic."

"My daughter the writer!" he exclaims. "Just wait until your mother hears about this. She's going to bust her buttons."

"Eva Bergson gave me the idea," I tell him. "She keeps telling me the pen is mightier than the sword."

My dad laughs. "And so it is. Another Olympic gold for Mrs. Bergson, rescuer of puppies and inspiration to writers everywhere!"

Mrs. Bergson ended up adopting Pip. She said that he's half my dog too, though, and that means I have to help take care of him. I go

Heather Vogel Frederick

over to her condo almost every day, and take him for walks when she's busy at the rink. I'm actually glad that it worked out this way. I have the puppy I've always wanted, and Mrs. Bergson has somebody to keep her company.

The rest of the day is like some kind of a dream. I've never gotten this much attention at school before in my entire life. Especially from the boys. Word of what happened in the principal's office gets around fast, and all afternoon kids I don't even know are slapping me high fives in the hallways and saying "Way to go, Hawthorne!" and "Free speech rocks!" It's like invisible me is suddenly on the radar screen. This must be how Megan felt last year, after her *Flashlite* interview. Or Cassidy when she led the Comets to their back-to-back tournament victories. Or Jess, when she's onstage singing with the MadriGals or winning a prize at the science fair. Or even Becca— well, just being Becca.

I really, really wish Jess were here to see this. I know she'd be excited for me. At least I'll get a chance to tell her all about it later. She called last night to see if she could come over today after school. She's been feeling pretty low since Saturday night, which was Colonial Academy's Founder's Day dance, and she wants to talk. I guess it was pretty much a disaster.

Jess and Cassidy and Stewart were the only other people I let read my editorial—besides Ms. Nielson, who had to approve it. My thoughts turn to Stewart, and I wonder whether maybe he'll give me a congratulatory kiss when he finds out what happened. My face gets warm as I ponder that possibility. Personally, I think Cassidy is right, and that it only counts if a boy kisses you of his own free will. So maybe I'm still in the running to be the first from our Mother-Daughter Book Club. Stewart's been gun-shy in the kissing department, though, ever since Darcy surprised us in the driveway last winter. Somehow I think it'll probably end up being Becca Chadwick after all, spin the bottle or no spin the bottle.

When I get home, there's a letter waiting for me from Bailey Jacobs, my Wyoming book club pen pal. I set it on the kitchen table, then take some butter out of the fridge to soften. I want to make something for my dad to thank him for helping me out today, and lemon bars are one of his favorites. Placing the butter on the counter, I sit down at the table and start to read:

Dear Pen Pal,

I got your postcards from Washington. I liked the one of the Library of Congress best. What a cool building! I hope I get to see it too, someday.

My mom says to thank your mom for the handouts she's been sending us. It's really interesting to learn more about an author. Jean Webster sounds like a lot of fun. Wouldn't she have been a great roommate? I couldn't believe it when I found out what happened to her. It's so sad.

Hey, maybe you and I will end up going to the same college and being roommates someday, just like Judy Abbott and Sallie McBride, and just like our moms were. Wouldn't that be amazing? You never know, right?

Spring has finally arrived here in Gopher Hole. There's still a lot of snow around, but the green grass is poking through, and there are lambs and calves in lots of the fields around town and on the road to Laramie. Winky Parker says there are three new foals out at her family's ranch too.

Remember Zoe Winchester, the mayor's daughter? The one Becca Chadwick got stuck with for a pen pal? Well, she and Summer Williams got into this big fight at school the other day. Every year we do a fundraiser for our school library, which needs all the help it can get because it's pretty pathetic, but what can you expect for a two-room schoolhouse? Anyway, Summer came up with a really great idea this year. Her plan is for each student in the school to design a quilt square that represents their favorite book, and then she'll sew them all together and display it at my mom's bookstore, where it'll get auctioned off to the highest bidder. I think Megan inspired her, when she wrote to her about the fashion show you guys had last year. I know Summer is kind of overly crazy about quilting, but I still think this is a really cool idea.

Zoe doesn't, though. She decided it was a really

stupid idea—mostly because she didn't come up with it, and Summer's going to get community service credit for organizing it and she won't—so she's been busy trying to sabotage the whole thing.

Yesterday at lunch Summer got to our table-all fifteen of us middle school kids eat at the same table—just in time to hear Zoe tell Brent Hershey and Danny Cortland that nobody quilts anymore but hicks, and that she didn't want to have to be part of some stupid hick project.

You should have seen Summer's face! Zoe's always saying snarky stuff like that, and making fun of Summer's hand-me-downs, which isn't fair because when there are eight kids in your family and your parents are divorced and your mom is trying to make ends meet by running a diner, of course you're going to wear your older sisters' hand-me-downs. Duh! Summer's usually pretty good about ignoring Zoe, but I guess getting called a "hick" practically to her face must have pushed her over the edge, because she let Zoe have it. Zoe poked her nose in the wrong wasp's nest this time, that's for sure. Or beehive, maybe. I loved that part in your last letter when you explained how you and your friends call girls like Zoe "queen bees." Where did your mom read about that again? My

Heather Vogel Frederick

mom wants to order the book for her store.

    Summer told Zoe that just because her mother is the mayor of Gopher Hole doesn't put Zoe in charge of anything at all, and it doesn't it give her the right to criticize everybody and everything either. The teachers pretty much just stood back and let Summer spill it all out. I think they're as sick of Zoe's snooty attitude as the rest of us. By the time Summer was done telling Zoe exactly what she thought of her, even the boys were laughing, and Zoe looked shocked. Shocked enough, I hope, to quit book club. Wouldn't that be nice?

    Gopher Hole may be tiny, but there's always something interesting going on, that's for sure.

    Your friend,

    Bailey

I smile, picturing the scene at school, which Bailey drew in a cartoon strip across the bottom of the page. Good for Summer.

Scrounging some paper and a pen from one of the drawers in the kitchen, I write a letter right back to Bailey, telling her all about my editorial and what happened in the cafeteria today. I enclose a copy of the *Walden Woodsman,* so she can read it for herself, then put everything in a big envelope and address it. Just as I'm taking the envelope to the front hall table to leave for my dad to mail for me, the doorbell rings.

"Jess!" I fling the door open and grab her in a big bear hug. "You'll never believe what happened at school!" I start blurting out the details before she's even inside. All of a sudden I stop. I've been thinking so much about myself that I've completely forgotten why she wanted to come over this afternoon.

"Oh, shoot, I'm sorry—I should be letting you do the talking."

"No, it's okay," she says, managing a smile. "Really, I am so proud of you, Emma! And how cool that your dad stuck up for you like that."

I nod. "I know. I'm making lemon bars for him, as a thank-you."

Jess follows me back to the kitchen and I put the kettle on because that's what my mother always does in a crisis. *A good cup of tea never hurts and usually helps* is her motto.

"So, tell me everything," I say, placing two mugs on the table.

Jess toys with her tea bag, dunking it up and down, up and down in the empty mug. "What's to tell?" she says finally. "It was horrible."

"Start at the beginning," I urge, taking a seat.

"Well, I guess that would have been at MadriGals last Friday. We were practicing 'Sumer Is Icumen In' for our spring concert, and Savannah raised her hand and told Mr. McNamara that I wasn't pronouncing the words properly."

"That's the song you were telling me about that's in Middle English, right?"

"Yeah. And I was singing it just fine. Savannah only said that to get back at me."

"Get back at you for what?"

"For telling Frankie and Adele the truth about how she lied to get Darcy to go with her. About her blind date, I mean. Peyton's friend didn't ditch her—she ditched him after she asked Darcy. Savannah didn't want anybody to know because it was a pretty lame thing to do. I guess he's one of the really popular guys at the Essex School, and she's worried she'll never get asked out by any of his friends if they hear about what she did."

"No kidding."

"So anyway Mr. McNamara made me sing all by myself, and of course I got nervous and flubbed up and then he got mad at me and told me there wasn't any room for a weak link in an a cappella group, and that I needed to be sure I was pulling my weight."

"Savannah is *such* a weasel!" I tell her. The feud between the two of them has really heated up since that weekend at Jess's house. I give my friend a sympathetic look. "So then what happened?"

She shrugs. "So then I had to go back to my room and try not to cry while Savannah and I were getting ready for the dance. I was so mad at her! She looked amazing, of course," Jess adds miserably. "The dress she and her mom picked out in New York made her look about twenty."

"Yeah, but it wasn't a Wong original," I point out. Megan doesn't know that Jess likes Darcy—Jess is worried that if we tell Megan, Becca will find out, and Becca doesn't have a great track record keeping quiet about this kind of stuff—but when I called a couple of weeks ago and told Megan that Jess needed a confidence booster for the dance, what with it being her first one at Colonial Academy and everything, Megan jumped on it. Using the dress Gigi gave her as a pattern, she made Jess her very own *kei pou*. She sewed it from this incredible embroidered silk that her grandmother brought her from Hong Kong, kind of like what she used for Maggie's overalls, only it was midnight blue instead of bright red. Jess looked beautiful in it.

The tea kettle starts to whistle and I get up and turn off the burner. "What did you do with your hair?" I ask her, pouring boiling water in her mug.

"My mother put it up into a French braid for me, and stuck flowers in it."

"What kind of flowers?"

Jess starts dunking her teabag again. "I don't know. Rosebuds, I think. And what's that stuff called? You know—*Gypsophila paniculata*?"

"Don't look at me," I say with a shrug.

"Um—oh, baby's breath."

I nod as if to say, *Of course, naturally, I should have recognized the Latin name.* "What time did Zach pick you up?"

Originally, after Savannah scooped Darcy out from under her nose like that, Jess wasn't going to go to the dance. She was too upset. But we talked it over, and I pointed out that if she didn't go, she'd be letting Savannah win. And Savannah didn't deserve to win.

I was all for leveling with Darcy, but Jess begged me not to. It would be too humiliating, she'd said. She was worried that if I told my brother that she liked him, and that there'd been a mix-up in the barn,

Heather Vogel Frederick

it would feel even worse if it turned out he didn't like her back. Besides, what if Darcy really did want to go with Savannah?

"She's pretty, after all," she'd said.

"Not half as pretty as you," I'd told her, which was true. "And nowhere near as nice."

In the end, Jess decided to go ahead and ask Zach Norton. Fortunately, he said yes, which I figured he would. Zach's always liked Jess. Not as a girlfriend—it's hard to tell who Zach likes, even though Megan keeps hoping maybe it's her—but definitely as a friend. And I told Jess that when my brother saw how fabulous she looked, and how much fun she was having with Zach, he'd be sorry he ever agreed to go with that traitor Savannah.

"So what happened when you got there?"

"The dance was in Dorchester, our dining hall," Jess told me.

"The building with all that fancy wood paneling?"

Jess nods. "Yeah, they cleared all the tables away, and the seniors decorated it really nicely, with tons of fresh flowers and one of those spangly disco ball things on the ceiling."

"Cool."

"Oh, and they put a big wreath around Harriett Witherspoon's portrait and propped it by the entrance. Zach said it looked like she'd just won a horse race or something."

I laugh. "So did Darcy see you? Did you get to dance with him?"

Jess shakes her head sadly. "No, and no. Savannah kept him as far away from me as possible all night."

We're both quiet for a minute, thinking about this. When Jess went back to the dorm the night Savannah asked Darcy to go to dance with her, they'd gotten Pip settled and then later that evening Jess had confronted Savannah.

"I was planning to ask Darcy," she'd told her roommate.

Savannah just told her that the early bird gets the worm, and how was she supposed to know, and that Jess should have been quicker. She didn't apologize or anything, and she didn't offer to uninvite Darcy either. I guess she'd already ditched her blind date by then.

I put a little sugar and milk in my tea and take a sip. "So did you actually dance?"

Jess nods. "Yeah. Zach was really nice and everything, and I tried not to let him see that I was upset. It was hard, though—every time I saw your brother I just wanted to run and hide."

I reach over and pat her arm. "Poor you! It's so not fair."

"And I haven't told you the worst part yet!"

"What happened?"

"Kevin Mullins showed up."

"What?!"

She nods again. "Just as we were all leaving. I guess he had no idea there was a dance that night, and he and his mom were coming home from a movie and he told her he needed to drop something off for me. So we all come out of Dorchester, and there he is, heading toward my dorm. Of course he spots me and comes running over with this giant encyclopedia of wildflowers he'd checked out of the library for me. I

Heather Vogel Frederick

think it was a Kevin Mullins version of a bouquet. The entire school saw him."

I wince. "Ouch. Savannah, too?"

"Of course. You should have heard her and Peyton Winslow hooting."

We're both quiet for a while. "Still," I say finally, "I'm glad you went. You would have felt worse if you'd stayed home."

"You really think so?"

"Absolutely."

Jess and I talk for a while longer, and when I can tell she's feeling a little better, I ask her if she wants to help me with the lemon bars. She agrees, and we clear our mugs away. I love baking with Jess. Before she left Walden Middle School, she'd come over at least once a week and we'd make something.

My father, who has phenomenal treat radar, wanders into the kitchen just as the first batch is coming out of the oven.

"Whatever it is smells good!" he says.

"They're for you," I tell him. "Lemon bars. A thank-you for sticking up for me at school today. It was supposed to be a surprise."

"I'm happy to stick up for my brilliant daughter any day," he tells me. "Oh, and I've got a surprise for you, too."

"You finished your novel?"

He smiles. "No, not quite. Getting closer, though. I've decided that instead of me making dinner tonight as usual, we need to go out and celebrate your literary victory."

"Really? Can Jess come too?"

My dad smiles at her. "Of course."

"And do you think maybe we can invite Mrs. Bergson to come with us?"

"Great idea," he replies.

I get to choose the restaurant, so I pick La Traviata, which has really good Italian food, and after Mom and Darcy get home we all pile into our station wagon and head over to pick up Mrs. Bergson. I make sure to scoot in up front between my mother and father so Jess can sit next to Darcy. She goes all shy like she used to, so I don't know if it helped, and it hardly makes up for not getting to go with him to the dance, but still, it's something.

Dinner is really fun. Everybody keeps making toasts—to me, to the United States constitution, to the *Walden Woodsman*, to free speech. We even make a toast to Mr. Keller, who comes in with his wife and baby daughter just as we're finishing our meal, glowers at us, and retreats to a table in the farthest corner of the room.

"Can Jess stay overnight?" I beg my mother.

"Today, anything you ask is yours," she replies, then catches Mrs. Bergson's eye. "Except a puppy," she adds, and Mrs. Bergson laughs. "How is Pip anyway?"

"Adorable as ever," Mrs. Bergson replies. "He needs a walk, by the way, girls, if you want to take him out for one after dinner."

Dad drops us off with her at her condo, and we play with Pip for a while, then we walk over to Half Moon Farm to get Jess's stuff. We're

Heather Vogel Frederick

filming the dim sum episode over at Cassidy's house tomorrow morning, so she needs the clothes she's going to wear for that. Mr. Delaney drives us back to my house in the farm truck, and Jess and I eat lemon bars and watch TV for a while until my mother tells us it's time for bed.

"You need your beauty rest for tomorrow," she tells us. "Don't stay up too late talking."

We ignore her, of course. The whole point of a sleepover is to stay up too late talking.

"So has Stewart kissed you yet?" Jess whispers to me, after I turn out the lights.

I climb back into the bottom bunk. I always let Jess have the top one when she stays over. She gets as big a kick out of it now as she did when we were in kindergarten. "No," I whisper back. "I'm pretty sure he wants to, but he just can't get up the courage."

"Why don't you kiss him?"

"I can't get up the courage either," I tell her, and we giggle.

"How about Zach? Did he try and kiss you after the dance?"

"Me? Heck, no. He was just his usual friendly self, nothing more."

Jess is quiet for a long moment, then asks, "Do you think Darcy kissed Savannah?"

That's a question I already have the answer to. "I don't think so. I overheard him talking to Kyle Anderson last Sunday when they were shooting hoops in the driveway. Kyle asked him how the dance was, and Darcy said it was okay, but that he thought Savannah was kind of fake. And he really doesn't like Peyton Winslow, either."

Jess digests this information.

"Why don't you just tell my brother that you like him?" I ask her.

"I can't!" she says, her voice rising. "Besides, he probably thinks I like Zach, anyway."

"Nope. He asked me that already and I told him you didn't."

"What?! Why didn't you tell me?"

"Because he only asked me five minutes ago, when you were brushing your teeth." I pause for a heartbeat, then grin into the darkness. "I told him you liked Kevin Mullins."

"Emma!" Jess squeals, leaning down from the top bunk to swat me with her pillow.

"Girls!" calls my mother sternly from down the hall. "Go to sleep now!"

"Did you really?" whispers Jess.

"Of course not!" I whisper back. "I was just teasing you."

"It isn't funny," she says, but I can hear her trying not to laugh.

We both start cracking up into our pillows, and it's a long time until we finally settle down enough to go to sleep.

After breakfast the next morning, my mother drives us over to Cassidy's house for the filming. Cassidy's mom and Stanley come out onto the front porch to greet us.

"Hail to Emma, the conquering hero," says Mrs. Sloane-Kinkaid, saluting me. Cassidy must have told her about what happened at school yesterday. "Or heroine, I should say."

Heather Vogel Frederick

"Thanks," I reply modestly.

I haven't seen Mrs. Sloane-Kinkaid since our last book club meeting. She's gotten really huge all of sudden. Her stomach sticks out almost as far as Mrs. Chadwick's bottom used to, before she started going to yoga class and becoming "a whole new me." I try not to stare but I can't help it. My mother notices and pokes me in the back and whispers to me not to be rude, but Cassidy's mother just laughs.

"I'm quite the walrus, aren't I?" she says, sounding pleased. "Here, girls, the baby's kicking, you have to feel this." She takes Jess's and my hands and places them against the sides of her belly, which I was expecting to feel squishy but which is really firm and springy, like one of those red rubber balls we used to use to play kickball in elementary school. I practically jump out of my skin when her tummy starts thumping against my palms.

"Amazing, isn't it?" she says, watching my expression.

Behind her back, Cassidy pretends to stick a finger down her throat and gag. Her mom's belly doesn't gross me out though. It's pretty awesome to think there's a tiny person inside.

Megan and her mother and Gigi pull into the driveway, along with the Chadwicks and Mrs. Delaney.

"Just a month left to go!" Stanley tells Gigi when she asks when the baby is due. He offers her his elbow and escorts her inside. "I hope you're going to make some more of those Chinese dumplings today. I've been dreaming about them ever since Thanksgiving."

"Looks like you've been doing more than just dreaming," Gigi teases him, nodding at his stomach. Stanley's put on a little weight too.

"You mean my sympathy belly?" he says, patting it fondly. "Since Clemmie's eating for two, I figured it was only fair that I do my part."

Everybody laughs except Cassidy, who just looks annoyed.

"Have fun today, handsome," says her mother, kissing Stanley on the cheek.

"I promise I will." He grabs his car keys from the bowl on the hall table and turns to my mom and Gigi and me. "I have to go to a charity golf tournament my company is sponsoring. Sorry I won't be here for the shoot. Say hi to everybody and save me some dim sum, okay?"

While Fred Goldberg whisks Gigi off to the kitchen to help supervise the set-up crew, Mrs. Sloane-Kinkaid takes the rest of us upstairs for a tour of the nursery.

"We haven't finished it yet," she says, "but you'll still get the idea."

The baby's going in the old guest room, right next to Cassidy. It's a tiny room, but her mother says that by the time the baby is old enough to notice, Courtney will have moved out and they can switch him or her into that room. Cassidy gets a funny look on her face when her mom mentions Courtney moving out. I guess it must be kind of hard to imagine life without your sister around. I try to imagine how I'll feel when Darcy leaves for college, but I can't.

The only thing in the room so far is a crib piled high with presents from Mrs. Sloane-Kinkaid's viewers. Cassidy says the UPS truck stops at their house just about every day now.

Heather Vogel Frederick

"It took us a while to find the right yellow," says Cassidy's mom, pointing to some streaks of paint on one of the walls. "I wanted to match the exact color of the moon in this rug I ordered." She bends over awkwardly and rolls it out for us. "See? Isn't it cute? It's a Mother Goose rug. There's the cow jumping over the moon, and the mouse running up the clock, and Little Boy Blue and Miss Muffett and Jack and Jill and Bo-Peep and Humpty Dumpty."

She waddles over to the dresser to show us some of the baby clothes people have sent, and lets out a little snort of laughter. "Actually, I think *I'm* Humpty Dumpty!"

Joyful barks from the front hall alert us to the fact that Eva Bergson and Pip have arrived. Megan and Becca and Cassidy all rush downstairs to see the not-so-secret-puppy, who is running circles around Murphy.

"Take these two wild creatures outside, would you please, girls?" asks Cassidy's mother, as the rest of us follow her down to join them.

We manage to corral the dogs and herd them into the backyard. Pip is crazy about Murphy, and fortunately Murphy is crazy about Pip, too. The two of them chase each other around, barking wildly, until they both collapse in a heap at our feet.

"So are you getting excited about the baby?" Megan asks.

Cassidy shrugs. "I guess."

"Have your mom and Stanley picked out names yet?"

"Not yet. My mom's got this long list, but Stanley keeps crossing things off it."

"I'll bet it will be fun helping out with everything—you know, feeding it and taking it for walks in the stroller and changing its diaper and stuff."

Cassidy looks at her like she's crazy. "I don't do diapers," she states flatly.

"They're not so bad," Megan tells her. "I've helped Jess babysit for Maggie a lot this year, and we had fun. Right, Jess? Bathtime's the best part. Babies are so cute at bathtime."

Cassidy doesn't look convinced.

"Since when are you so interested in babies?" I ask Megan.

She shrugs. "I don't know," she says. "I just think it's cool that she's going to have a little sister or brother, I guess. Sometimes I wish I wasn't an only child."

"Girls!" calls Mrs. Sloane-Kinkaid, sticking her head out the back door. "We're just about ready to start! Put the dogs in the garage, would you?"

Back inside, the rest of the Mother-Daughter Book Club is assembled in the kitchen. Cassidy's mother distributes aprons to everybody, which is a good thing because it hides Mrs. Chadwick's peppermint striped getup, which really shouldn't have been allowed out of the house. Megan's grandmother, who is standing in the middle of the room pointing at things with a wooden spoon like a symphony conductor, assigns us to chopping stations.

Just as we're about to start, my mother's cell phone rings.

"Oops! Sorry gang, I forgot to turn the ringer off." She steps into the hall to answer it, and when she comes back, her eyes are shining. "You'll never guess who that was!"

"Humpty Dumpty?" mutters Cassidy, and her mother shoots her a look.

"That was Jill Cunningham from the school board. It looks like Emma's editorial made an impact." My mother beams at me. "Apparently Mrs. Hanford called an emergency session today to discuss yesterday's events in the cafeteria, and Jill suggested they take Emma's plea seriously. She proposed a compromise, and the board voted and agreed to it."

"Agreed to what?" asks Mrs. Delaney.

"Free choice Fridays," my mother tells her proudly. "School uniforms won't be dropped entirely, but from now on students will be able to wear whatever they want on Fridays."

Cassidy whoops and drums on the countertop. "Way to go, Emma!"

Megan does a little victory dance. "Good-bye, khakis, hello, free choice!"

Mrs. Bergson gives me a hug. "I hate to say I told you so, but I told you so," she whispers. "Well done."

Our collective good mood carries over to the filming session, which turns out to be a lively one. Megan's grandmother is completely in her element, joking with Mrs. Sloane-Kinkaid and the crew and all of us as she demonstrates how to make the various dim sum dishes. Between takes, she flirts with Mr. Goldberg, who looks quite enchanted. Everyone looks enchanted. Gigi is irresistible. Well, to everybody except Mrs. Wong, who stays mostly on the sidelines even though Mrs. Sloane-Kinkaid and my mother and Mrs. Delaney try to draw her in. I guess she's still a little miffed that no one's asked her to do a vegetarian episode.

Gigi's food is irresistible too. By the time we're done we're all practically licking the plates, and laughing our heads off at a hilarious story she's telling us about the time she went to some fancy restaurant in Hong Kong and ordered lobster and the chef must have been new because he didn't cook it all the way and it walked right off her plate.

"I haven't had so much fun in ages," gasps Cassidy's mother, plopping down onto a chair and fanning her face with a potholder. "Gigi, you're a born TV chef! Can you believe her energy, Fred? She's worn me out."

"Mom!" says Cassidy, staring at a puddle on the floor. "Gross! You laughed so hard you wet your pants!"

Her mother looks down and her smile vanishes. "That's not—I didn't—" A look of panic spreads across her face. "Phoebe, would you call Stanley for me? Tell him my water broke."

My mother runs for the phone.

"But I thought the baby wasn't due for another month," says Jess's mother.

"It's not," says Mrs. Sloane-Kinkaid. "But it's definitely on the way now."

SUMMER

"*They were learning by the laboratory method,
the social graces that would be needed later
in the larger world.*"

—*Just Patty*

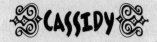

CASSIDY

*"Kid McCoy was supposed to be an irreclaimable tomboy,
but in this crucial moment the eternal feminine came
triumphantly to the fore."*

—*Just Patty*

"What the heck is taking so long?" I demand.

Mrs. Hawthorne puts her arm around my shoulders. "Try to relax, honey," she tells me. "Babies can take a while."

Pulling away, I get up from the sofa and start to pace. Our entire Mother-Daughter Book Club, plus Courtney and Gigi and Eva Bergson and Fred Goldberg, are all crammed into the waiting room at the Concord Birthing Center. It's a good thing nobody else is having a baby this afternoon because their families would have to sit on the floor.

"She's right, Cassidy," says Mrs. Delaney. "Waiting is perfectly normal. Everything's going to be fine, you'll see."

"How can you say that? How do you know?" My voice rises and cracks, and I'm practically shouting as I finish. "Sometimes everything's not all right—look at what happened to Jean Webster!" The nurse at the front counter looks over at me and frowns, but I don't care. It's not *her* mother in there having a baby.

The room falls silent. What can anybody say, though? It's true. It was right there in our last book club meeting's "Fun Facts." Excuse me, "Terrible, Awful, Horrible Facts."

Courtney gets up and comes over and gives me a hug. I lean against her, breathing hard, too wound up to hug her back. After a while she leads me back to the sofa and I sit down again. She squeezes in next to me and links her arm through mine.

The minutes tick by. I put my head against the back of the sofa and try and relax, but my knee is jouncing up and down in time to the rapid beating of my heart. Where *is* everyone? Shouldn't Stanley or the doctor come out and tell us what's going on? Shouldn't the baby be here by now? Has something gone wrong?

It's not like we didn't get here fast enough. As soon as my mother announced that the baby was on the way, everyone sprang into action. Mrs. Hawthorne called Stanley and told him to meet us at the hospital. Mrs. Wong ran upstairs to get my mother's suitcase, the one that's been ready practically since the day she found out she was pregnant. Gigi and Mrs. Delaney packed a picnic basket full of leftover dim sum to take with us. And Mrs. Chadwick—well, Mrs. Chadwick should have been a general. She started barking orders at everyone, even Fred Goldberg and the whole *Cooking with Clementine* crew. She told Mr. Goldberg to put my mom in his car, then went along with them to make sure he didn't get lost. The rest of us crammed into our

Heather Vogel Frederick

minivan and the Wong's little hybrid and followed. Courtney was too nervous to drive, so Mrs. Delaney took the wheel of our van. She must have a secret desire to be a race car driver or something, because she managed to get us here ahead of everybody.

I guess Mrs. Chadwick called the maternity ward on the way, because a team of nurses was standing by with one of those rolling beds, and they whisked my mom onto it and inside before I even managed to get out of the van. Stanley pulled into the parking lot a minute later, his bald head all pink and shiny with excitement and worry.

"Where is she?" he hollered.

We all pointed to the hospital and he sprinted through the doors and that's the last we've seen of him for nearly three hours now.

Another agonizing half hour ticks by, and then, finally, the doors at the end of the hall swing open. I sit bolt upright. A person draped in a light blue gown thing with a matching hat and face mask appears. The person pulls off the hat and I spot a bald head so I'm pretty sure it's Stanley, and then he takes off the mask and I know for sure it's Stanley. There's an expression on my stepfather's face that I've never seen before. He looks a little like the way Coach Danner did the two times our team won the New England regional hockey championship.

"It's a girl!" he announces, and bursts into tears.

To my horror and embarrassment, so do I.

Megan's grandmother looks over at me, her forehead puckered with concern. "You're not happy about a baby sister, Cassidy?"

"Is Mom okay?" I manage to stutter, as Mrs. Hawthorne hands me a tissue.

Stanley crosses the room and puts his arms around me. I hug him back, tightly. "Your mother is absolutely fine, honey," he assures me. "The doctor said it was a textbook birth, and things couldn't have gone more smoothly." He sounds so happy and calm I know he's telling the truth.

"All those prenatal yoga classes paid off," says Mrs. Wong.

"And as for your new sister, she's fine too," Stanley continues. "They're going to keep her here for a few days just to be sure, since she was so early."

"Can I go see them?" I ask, blowing my nose and feeling stupid for being such a basket case.

"You bet," Stanley replies. "The nurse will come out in a few minutes to get you. I just wanted to give you all the good news right away."

He hugs Courtney, too, then disappears again through the swinging doors. A few minutes later, as promised, a nurse pokes her head out.

"Who's here to see Mrs. Sloane-Kinkaid?" she asks, and her eyes widen as we all stand up.

"Oh, my," she says. "There are a lot of you, aren't there? Well, I suppose it won't hurt to let you take a quick peek. But then I'll have to shoo everyone out but immediate family."

We follow her back down the hall, and I push past her when we get to my mom's room. My mother looks up and sees me and her face lights up with a smile that's a mile wide. For once she's not wearing a

Heather Vogel Frederick

speck of makeup, and her hair is kind of stuck to her head like mine always is after hockey practice, but she looks prettier than I've ever seen her look before.

I'm across the room in a flash. I give her a hug and a kiss and she kisses me back and then looks down at the little bundle wrapped in white flannel that she's cradling in her arms. "Would you like to meet your new sister?" she asks me.

I look down at the baby, the one I wasn't sure I wanted, and I start to cry again. Then Mom starts to cry and so does everybody else in the room and the nurse has to go find another box of tissues.

"Babies can make you do that," says Gigi, dabbing at her eyes.

"Birth is a miracle," agrees Eva Bergson.

Everybody crowds around the bed to get a closer look, and Mom lets Courtney hold her.

"She's almost eight pounds," Stanley tells us proudly. "The doctor said it's probably a good thing she decided to put in an early appearance—she'd have been a whopper if she'd gone full-term. She's going to be an Amazon just like Clemmie." Stanley looks at my mother adoringly. For once I don't mind him using that dumb nickname. Today feels like a day to be gooshy.

"She looks like Stanley," says Courtney.

"Because she's bald, duh," I point out, and everybody laughs, even Stanley.

"So what's her name?" asks Mrs. Wong.

My mother gives her a blank look. "Um, we hadn't quite decided yet," she admits. "We thought we still had a few more weeks."

Stanley grins. "I guess Connor is out now."

"And so is Stanley Kinkaid the second," adds Courtney.

"Whatever we name her, we know we want it to start with a *C*," my mother continues, ignoring them both. "We've got a good thing going here with Clementine, Courtney, and Cassidy."

"How about Clarissa?" Becca suggests.

"Ick," I say.

"Or Kristen—you could go with a *K* name since it sounds like *C*," says Emma. "Kylie, Kelsey, Kendra, Katrina," she says, ticking them off on her fingers.

"How about Coco, like Coco Chanel?" suggests Gigi, and Megan nods vigorously.

"That's kind of cute," says my mother, gazing at the baby. "What do you think, honey?"

Stanley cocks his head to one side and frowns, thinking it over. "Coco. Hmm. I'm not so sure. It kind of sounds like something you'd name a pet poodle."

"I've got an idea!" I tell them. "How about Cammi, like Cammi Granato, the hockey player?"

"Is that short for Camilla?" Becca asks. "That's pretty."

My mother shakes her head. "Nope," she says. "No way. There was a model I had to work with once at *Flash* named Camilla. We didn't get along."

"Savannah's named after a city back in Georgia," says Jess. "Maybe

Heather Vogel Frederick

you could name the baby Concord and call her 'Connie.'"

"Dude, that is so *lame*," I tell her.

She shrugs. "It's just an idea."

"My sister's name is Caroline," suggests Fred Goldberg. "You met her once, Clementine, remember?"

My mother nods. "She's a real sweetheart."

"This is kind of like playing the synonym game, isn't it?" says Emma.

The nurse reappears, frowning. "I'm afraid I'm going to have to ask everyone but immediate family to leave now. Mother and baby need their rest."

"Not yet!" Jess pleads. "Please can't we stay just another minute or two? We're trying to pick a name for the baby."

The nurse looks over at my mother and raises an eyebrow. My mother nods, and the nurse smiles at Jess. "I guess I can give you a little more time. Make it quick, though." She closes the door behind her.

And then, out of the blue, I have it. "I know!" I cry. "Chloe!"

"Chloe," my mother repeats softly. "I like it." She looks over at my stepfather. "How about you, honey?"

Stanley nods slowly. "I like it too," he replies. "In fact, I love it. Chloe Kinkaid it is. Good work, Cassidy!"

"Her middle name can be Elaine, after your mother," my mom tells him.

I lean down and give my baby sister a kiss on the cheek. "Hi, Chloe! Welcome to the family."

The nurse comes back to clear everybody out, and our friends leave in a chorus of good-byes and congratulations. Stanley and Courtney leave too, because Courtney has to go to graduation rehearsal, but they promise to come right back afterward.

"Don't forget my cheeseburger and chocolate milk shake!" my mom calls after them. "I earned them!"

When the room is finally empty, I pull a present out of my backpack and place it on the bed next to my mother.

"What's this?" she asks.

"Something for Chloe," I tell her, feeling suddenly shy.

My mother pats the bed and I climb up and fit myself into the narrow space beside her. She passes the baby carefully to me, and at first I'm scared to hold her and worried that I'm doing it wrong, but Chloe looks up at me solemnly with big, gray-blue eyes and yawns. She's obviously not concerned.

I laugh. "That boring, am I?" I tell her softly. "Just wait until you get to know me."

"Should I open it?" my mother asks, and I nod.

Inside the box is a photo album, except there aren't any photos in it. It's filled with my letters to the baby instead. It was Dr. Weisman's idea, and Courtney helped me pick out a nice album at the Concord Bookshop. The soft green cover matches the bunny stationery, which doesn't seem nearly as stupid now as it did when my mother first bought it. The postcards of Washington are inside

Heather Vogel Frederick

too, along with Megan's sketch of Martha Washington's dress.

My mother opens it. "Oh, my goodness," she says, her eyes widening. "These are the letters Dr. Weisman had you write!"

"Uh-huh," I tell her. "I thought you might like to see them."

She turns to the first page and begins to read aloud:

> Dear Baby,
>
> I'm only writing this because I have to. If I don't, I won't get to go on the field trip to Washington, D.C. It's kind of a long story, and it involves cheese, but maybe someday I'll tell you what happened.
>
> By the time you read this I'll probably be in college. My sister Courtney—our sister Courtney—is leaving for UCLA at the end of the summer. I wish she didn't have to go. I wish things didn't have to change.
>
> The thing is, I don't like change very much. I didn't want to leave California and move to Concord after Dad died. My dad, not yours. Your dad is Stanley Kinkaid. He's a nice guy but I didn't want Mom to marry him. I didn't want a stepfather. I guess I was afraid our family wouldn't ever be the same again. I guess I'm still afraid of that happening, especially now that they're expecting you.
>
> Your new big sister,
>
> Cassidy

Looking down at Chloe now, I can't believe I actually wrote that. How could I ever have been afraid of this baby? She's absolutely beautiful. Something wells up inside me as I sit there looking at how tiny and perfect she is. Something I've never felt before. A fierce, protective kind of love. I don't want anything bad to happen to her. Ever. She yawns again, and I feel tears pricking my eyelids. It's hard to believe that this little person was inside of my mother just a few hours ago and that now she's out here, and I'm actually holding her. Mrs. Bergson is right, birth really is a miracle.

"Oh, honey," says my mother, putting the album down and looking over at me. Her eyes are filled with tears too. "I had no idea you felt this way! You don't need to be afraid—just because we're expanding our family doesn't mean you're being squeezed out. I'll never, ever stop loving you! Haven't you ever heard of 'mother love' mathematics?"

I shake my head.

"Mothers never divide, they only multiply! There's always room for more love in a mother's heart. You'll understand someday."

I gaze down at Chloe, who's drifted off to sleep, and stroke her soft little cheek with my fingertip. I think maybe I already understand.

My mother reaches out and tucks a strand of hair behind my ear. "And don't worry about Courtney going off to college, either," she says softly. "Change is the nature of life, Cassidy. Some of it's good, like new babies being born and children growing up and leaving home and all the new adventures that both of those things bring. And sometimes change is more difficult—like when your dad died. But it's nothing to

Heather Vogel Frederick

fear. Good or bad, when we rise up to meet it, change can make us stronger. It's what moves us farther along down the road ahead."

The road ahead. Sometimes I wish I could see what the future has in store for me, and for my family. But at least I know one thing. At least I know now that I'm glad Chloe will be coming along with us.

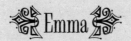

Emma

"This summer I'm going to write and write and write and begin to be a great author."
—Daddy-Long-Legs

A graveyard isn't the first place that comes to mind when you think of romance.

On a late Saturday afternoon in early June, though, with the smell of lilacs mingling with freshly-mown grass, Sleepy Hollow Cemetery isn't bad at all. Especially if you're walking hand-in-hand with Stewart Chadwick, like I am.

"So are you looking forward to school getting out?" Stewart asks.

"I guess," I reply. And I am, really. I can't believe I'm almost done with middle school, and that next year I'll be in *high school*. I get nervous already just thinking about it. The only problem with school getting out is that once it does, Stewart will be heading to Maine for the summer. He got a job as a counselor-in-training at a boys' camp. I won't see him until Labor Day.

"Hey, look!" says Stewart, pulling me off the path and onto the grass toward a nearby headstone. "Here's a good one. *Arethusa Beadle*."

Heather Vogel Frederick

I take my notebook out of my pocket and jot it down. Since I'm still too young to get a real paying job this summer—I'm going to volunteer with Jess at the Concord Animal Shelter—and with no Stewart around to hang out with, I've decided that I'm going to use the time to write my first novel. Stewart is helping me pick out names for the characters. I got the idea from *Daddy-Long-Legs*, when Mrs. Lippett found Jerusha's name on a tombstone. We've stumbled on some great ones—Ezra Nipp, Bunker Hopcott, and my favorite so far, Deliverance Severance.

I have no idea what my novel is going to be about yet, but I figure this will get me off to a good start.

We wander around for a while, and I stop by to say hello to Louisa May Alcott and Henry David Thoreau. All of Concord's famous authors are buried in Sleepy Hollow Cemetery. Maybe I will be too, someday, but when I mention this to Stewart he pokes me in the ribs.

"Quit being so morbid!" he protests, and chases me down off Author's Ridge. We tumble onto the grass at the bottom, laughing, and lie there side by side for a while. Then we get up and brush ourselves off and continue our search.

"Check this out," says Stewart a few minutes later, sounding a little nervous. He steers me onto one of the cemetery's many side paths and leads me toward a stone bench under a willow tree. Across from it is a particularly ornate gravestone carved with stone cherubs and willow branches.

"Willow was a sign of mourning back in those days," he tells me, which is one of the things I like about Stewart so much. He always knows such interesting things. Probably because he reads a lot, just like me.

"Is that why it's called 'weeping willow'?" I ask, and he nods.

We both peer at the gravestone's fading letters, trying to decipher the epitaph. "'Susannah Sugar,'" I read aloud. "'Our beloved daughter's life may have been short, but it was as sweet as her name.'"

"Oh, that's so sad!" I exclaim, reaching for my notebook again. "And poetic. Look, she was the same age as me." I copy down the name and epitaph and next to it I write "ghost?" Maybe my novel will end up being a mystery.

It's peaceful on the bench, with the willow's trailing branches screening us from view. We sit there for a while listening to the distant sound of voices from up on the ridge—probably that flock of tourists we saw earlier hunting for Ralph Waldo Emerson's grave.

I check my watch. "I should get going," I say reluctantly. "It's nearly four."

Cassidy's mom is coming home from the birthing center with Chloe tonight, and I need to be at Cassidy's house in time for the surprise party. Since the baby arrived a little early and Mrs. Sloane-Kinkaid hadn't had a chance to finish setting up the nursery, we all decided that the Mother-Daughter Book Club needed to step in. We've spent the last couple of evenings painting and sewing curtains—well, Megan did the curtains—and our moms and Gigi and Eva Bergson all chipped in for a really nice rocking chair, and we wrapped up a bunch of baby presents and piled them next to it, along with the stuff that's been coming in the mail from fans of *Cooking with Clementine*.

Stewart clears his throat. "Yeah, you should probably get going."

Neither of us makes a move to leave.

"So when are you getting your contact lenses?" he asks after a minute or so.

"Sometime this summer, I guess. I don't think my mother's made the appointment yet."

My parents promised that I could have contact lenses before I start high school next fall. Stewart got some last year when he started modeling. Sometimes he still wears his glasses—"for camouflage," he jokes—but he isn't today.

"Do you think I'll look good in them?" I ask him shyly.

"Let me see," he says, reaching over and taking off my glasses. He examines me seriously, then puts the glasses back on me. "I like you both ways."

I smile up at him. He smiles back. There's an awkward pause, and then we both start to talk at the same time.

"Emma—"

"Stewart—"

"Jinx!" I call out triumphantly, and instantly feel stupid. It wasn't a real jinx because we didn't say the same word. Stewart looks at me and smiles and keeps quiet anyway, though. That's one of the things I really, really like about him. He never tries to make me feel dumb, or pounce on something I get a little bit wrong and tease me, the way my brother might.

Now I'm wishing I hadn't said "jinx," though, because I'm dying of curiosity to know what Stewart was going to say.

I gaze down at the stone bench, tracing my finger over its surface. The cool smoothness of the marble is pocked by decades, maybe centuries, of raindrops. The wind whispers again in the willow branches. There's absolutely nobody around.

This is it, I think, my heart beating faster as I realize that Stewart planned this. That's why he sounded nervous when he brought me here. I take my glasses off and tuck them in my pocket so I'm ready.

Stewart leans toward me slightly. He smells good, like toothpaste and aftershave, or maybe it's his deodorant because I'm not sure he shaves much yet. I lean toward him, too, and then he puts his arms around me and I'm nervous and embarrassed but thrilled that it's finally happening, that he's finally going to kiss me.

I close my eyes and lift my face toward his, and the next thing I know I feel his lips—on my forehead.

My forehead?

"I'm going to miss you this summer, Emma," he whispers.

"Me too," I whisper back, trying not to sound disappointed. A forehead kiss is almost a real kiss; it almost counts. I rest my cheek on his shoulder.

We stay that way for a bit and then he clears his throat again. "I guess you'd better get going, huh?"

"Yeah."

Heather Vogel Frederick

Stewart walks me back to where we left our bicycles. "I hope you have fun at your party," he tells me. "And I guess I'll see you Tuesday afternoon."

"Uh-huh."

Tuesday is our last editorial meeting of the year—the last one for me forever at the *Walden Woodsman*. Next year we'll both be working on the Alcott High paper.

Stewart gives me another quick hug, then pedals off toward the gates to Sleepy Hollow. I follow him out onto Bedford Street and back down toward Monument Square. He gives me one final wave as he turns down Lowell Road, and I wave back and cut across the square toward downtown, and Cassidy's house.

As I ride along, I go over the last few minutes under the willow tree in my mind, wondering if I should have done something differently. Should I always wait for Stewart to make the first move, or should I just grab him and kiss him? Are there rules written down somewhere about this stuff? Probably. Maybe I should ask my mom. Or maybe not. Last time I asked her about private girl things, I wound up with a whole stack of books on my bed with embarrassing titles like *You're a Young Woman Now* and *Understanding Your Changing Body*. Darcy got ahold of them and had a field day until Dad told him to cut it out.

Bailey Jacobs and I have discussed this in our letters too, but she's as clueless as I am. Maybe even more so, since she's never had a boyfriend and I suppose that technically, Stewart is my boyfriend, kiss or no kiss. She says that with just twenty-seven kids at her school, and only a handful of boys her age, there's not a whole lot to choose from. She's hoping that next year, when she goes to high school in Laramie, things will change.

For now, I guess I'll just have to continue to be patient. It's not like Stewart doesn't want to kiss me, after all. I can tell that he does—just as much as I want to kiss him. It's just that, silly as it seems, neither of us is quite brave enough yet to make the first move.

A forehead kiss may not be the real thing, but it's a step of progress at least.

Consoled by this thought, I pedal as fast as I can down Main Street. As I turn down Walden, I almost run into Savannah Sinclair, who's crossing the street to the post office with her arms full of packages and shopping bags.

"Emma!" she yells, as I swerve past her.

Reluctantly, I brake and pull over to the sidewalk, figuring she's going to bawl me out or something.

"Hey," she says.

"Hey."

"I heard that Clementine had her baby."

I nod, wondering what she wants. She doesn't seem to be angry or anything.

"Uh, do you have time to talk?"

"I guess," I reply cautiously.

"It's about Jess."

I raise an eyebrow.

"The thing is, I had no idea she liked your brother. Before I asked him to the dance, I mean."

"Yeah, right," I mutter.

"It's the truth," she replies. "How was I supposed to know?"

"So why didn't you uninvite him when she asked you to?"

Savannah lifts a shoulder. Her eyes slide to the ground. "I don't know. I was embarrassed, I guess. I'd already, uh, uninvited the guy I was originally supposed to go with."

"The blind date Peyton set up for you?"

She nods.

"That's lame." I tell her scornfully.

Savannah sighs. "Look, I know! What I'm try to say is, I'm sorry I messed things up for her. It's just—she won't talk to me and—oh, I don't know, forget it. She wouldn't believe me anyway." She takes one of the shopping bags and thrusts it at me. "Here. I got this for Pip. I hope he's okay."

She turns and strides away, her long chestnut hair bouncing against her back. I watch her go, then hop back on my bike and pedal thoughtfully the last few blocks to Cassidy's house. Leaning my bike against the front porch, I sprint up the steps and ring the doorbell. Courtney answers it and smiles when she sees me.

"Hi, Emma," she says. "Come on in. Cassidy will be home from baseball practice any second. Your friends are all up in her room."

I hear laughter down the hall in the kitchen. Our moms are all here, and the house smells good. We decided to have a potluck for our surprise welcome home party, and Mrs. Delaney made lasagna.

Eva Bergson must be here already too, because Pip comes scampering out of the kitchen.

"Hey, boy!" I cry, squatting down and holding out my arms. Pip flings himself at me, his little body wriggling with excitement. He's always excited to see me, because usually it means he gets to go for a walk.

"Sorry, Pip, not right now," I tell him, burying my face in his fur. "Maybe after the party, okay?"

He laps at my face in response, and I laugh. At least Pip isn't shy about kissing me.

He follows me upstairs to Cassidy's room. Jess and Megan and Becca are sprawled around Cassidy's room.

"You'll never guess who I just ran into—almost literally— downtown," I say, picking Pip up and plopping him onto the bed.

My friends look over at me and shrug.

"Savannah," I tell them. I hold out the shopping bag. "She gave me this to give to you," I tell Jess. "It's for Pip."

"Really?" Jess looks puzzled, but she opens the bag. "Hey, this is really cute."

It's a pale blue collar and matching leash, with a black pawprint design running up and down the webbed material.

"So what went wrong between you two, anyway?" asks Becca.

Heather Vogel Frederick

Jess gives me a wary glance. "Uh, I don't know," she replies. "She just couldn't help being—well, Savannah. You know."

"Maybe this is a peace offering," says Megan. "She seemed pretty nice that weekend at your house."

Jess lifts a shoulder. "Maybe. It's kind of too late for that, though. School finishes tomorrow."

The other thing about private schools? They get out a whole lot earlier than public schools. We still have two full weeks of school left at Walden.

Before we can discuss this any further we hear the front door slam, followed by feet pounding up the stairs. Cassidy bursts into the room, her face a thundercloud.

"I hate Zach Norton!" she cries, flinging her baseball mitt to the floor.

"What are you talking about?" I tell her. "Since when?"

"Since two minutes ago," snarls Cassidy. "He's a world-class creep!" She bends down to untie her sneakers, then rips them off and hurls them at her closet door.

We all look at her, stunned.

"What on earth happened?" I ask her.

Cassidy starts to pace. "We were riding our bikes home from practice, right?" she says. "We always ride home together. But today, instead of him going on down Stow to his house, he turns up Hubbard with me. I figure he wants to race, so I really kick it into high gear. He chases after me and follows me into our driveway. So then I get off my bike, and we're talking like normal, and then all of a sudden he's right in my face. It was like he was stealing second or something, he just dove at me! I thought maybe I had a wasp in my hair but then he goes and grabs me and *kisses* me!"

We all stare at her as she wipes her sleeve vigorously across her lips.

"It was just so *gross!*" she finishes angrily.

Nobody says anything. Nobody knows what to say. Zach Norton kissed *Cassidy*? And then I start to laugh. I can't help it—the irony is just so completely perfect. Of all the Mother-Daughter Book Club members to get the first kiss, Cassidy Sloane is the absolute last one I would have expected.

Jess and Megan and Becca start to laugh too, but Megan and Becca's laughter sounds strained. Probably because they both like Zach and would be on cloud nine right now if he'd tried to kiss them.

"I didn't know Zach liked you!" says Jess.

"Of course he does," Cassidy scoffs. "We're teammates."

"Yeah, but you know what I mean."

Cassidy turns as red as her hair. "Why did he have to go and ruin a perfectly good friendship?" she yells. "He knows how much I hate all that gooshy stuff! How am I supposed to play baseball with him anymore? I'm never going to be able to face him again."

"So what did you tell him?" I ask.

Cassidy snorts. "I didn't tell him anything—I just threw my baseball mitt at him."

Heather Vogel Frederick

"You did *what*?" Megan looks shocked.

"I couldn't help it," Cassidy says defiantly. "He startled me. Besides, he has no right lunging at me like that." She scrambles to her feet and shoves her face close to Megan's. Megan recoils in alarm. "See? It's no fun." A little smile tugs at the corner of her lips. "I think maybe he's going to have a black eye. Serves him right."

Zach Norton likes Cassidy Sloane, I think. I mull the thought over, poking and prodding at it the way I'd poke and prod at a loose tooth. The idea doesn't hurt, so I guess I really must be completely over Zach. Megan and Becca aren't, though, I can tell just by looking at them. They're trying to hide their disappointment. Like just about all the other girls at Walden Middle School, they've been crushing on Zach since kindergarten.

I did, too, for a long time. But those feelings are long gone, thanks to Stewart. *Zach likes Cassidy*, I think to myself again. The idea is staggering. Suddenly, I can't wait to call Stewart and tell him. That's what's so great about Stewart—Zach may be blond and cute and everything, but Stewart will understand the irony.

Still grumbling, Cassidy grabs a change of clothes and heads for the shower.

"We should give her a prize," I tell the others, after she's left the room. "Something funny, to make her laugh. It will help her feel better."

Jess ducks into the nursery and grabs one of the balloons from the big bouquet we tied to the back of the rocking chair. Megan takes a pen and draws a caricature of Zach's face on it, complete with black eye. We give him really huge lips, all puckered-up and ready to go, and then Becca takes the pen and adds WORLD'S GREATEST KISSER underneath. I tie the balloon to Cassidy's baseball mitt and set it on her desk.

Cassidy spots it the second she walks back in the door. "Ha ha ha," she says. "Very funny." But she's grinning, which is a good sign, and she gives the balloon a punch as she passes it.

"This way you can relive your romantic moment anytime you feel like it," Jess tells her, and we dissolve into laughter again.

"Hey, guys!" Courtney calls up to us from the front hall. "They just turned in to the driveway!"

All thoughts of Zach Norton fly out of our heads. We rush downstairs and gather in the living room with our mothers, and a minute later the door opens and Mrs. Sloane-Kinkaid comes in. Stanley is right behind her with Chloe, who's in a car seat.

Cassidy's mom beams at us. "I suspected there might be a welcoming committee," she says happily. "Stanley's not very good at keeping secrets. His head turns pink."

As if on cue, the top of Cassidy's stepfather's bald head starts to glow. Mrs. Sloane-Kinkaid leans down—she's taller than he is—and gives it a kiss. "It's one of your most endearing qualities, sweetie," she tells him.

Behind me, Cassidy sighs. "I've had enough of this stuff for one day," she mutters. But she doesn't look too upset.

At dinner, we take turns passing Chloe around. She's really cute,

Heather Vogel Frederick

and not as squinched-up looking as she was at the hospital. Everybody takes lots of pictures, and after dessert—my dad sent over his special Pavlova, this amazing meringue thing with fruit and whipped cream and chocolate sauce that he never ever makes except for New Year's Eve—we take Mrs. Sloane-Kinkaid up to the nursery.

"Oh!" she says, her eyes shining as she surveys the room. "How beautiful!"

"It was all the girls' idea," my mother tells her. "They were inspired by *Just Patty*. Remember when the students at St. Ursula's decided to fix up the cottage for Grandma and Grandpa Flannigan? Well, they came and told us they wanted to do the same thing for you and Stanley and Chloe."

Cassidy's mother settles into the rocking chair. "How can I ever thank you?" she says. "It's really, truly perfect."

Mr. Kinkaid passes the baby to her and she smiles up at us. "I never thought I'd be going through all this again," she confesses. "Babyhood, I mean. Life is just full of surprises, isn't it?"

"And it looks like there are a few more here for you too," says Mrs. Delaney, pointing to the pile of presents.

"How about you and Courtney open them for me while I feed Chloe?" her mother says to Cassidy.

There are tons and tons of toys for the baby, and tiny little dresses and shoes and stuff, and a mobile to hang over her crib and from the Sinclairs, an engraved sterling silver rattle.

"How did they know the baby arrived?" Cassidy's mother asks.

Jess shrugs. "I guess Savannah heard me telling Adele and Frankie about it."

There's another present with the rattle, a copy of *Goodnight, Moon*, and Mrs. Sloane-Kinkaid opens the card that's taped to it. *"This was my favorite when I was little. I hope your baby likes it too. Love, Savannah."*

"How nice of Savannah," she says.

I glance over at Jess. I think about my encounter with Savannah by the post office, and it occurs to me that maybe Megan is right. Maybe this is all some sort of peace offering. But Jess avoids my gaze, and her expression is guarded.

Finally, there's just one present left—the biggest one of all. It's in an enormous box wrapped in plain brown paper and postmarked "Gopher Hole, Wyoming."

"It must be from your pen pals," says Mrs. Sloane-Kinkaid. "How sweet of them to think of us."

Cassidy rips off the wrapping and opens the box.

"It's a quilt," she says. Behind me I hear Megan whisper to Becca, "Summer Williams strikes again."

"What a lovely gift!" says Mrs. Sloane-Kinkaid. "Let me see it."

"Wait, I think there's something underneath," says Courtney, lifting the quilt out.

Cassidy dives into the box and emerges with a little rocking horse. "Cool!" she says. "It has a real leather saddle and everything."

"There's a card, too," says Courtney, plucking it from the bottom

Heather Vogel Frederick

of the box. She passes it to her sister. "You read it, Cassidy."

Cassidy opens the envelope. "Congratulations to the whole book club on your new edition," she reads, then shakes her head in disgust. "Sheesh, how corny can you get?"

"Honey!" her mother protests.

"Sorry," says Cassidy, and continues, "The Gopher Hole Gang hereby invites the newest member of the Concord, Massachusetts, Mother-Daughter Book Club to bring her big sister, her mother, and all her book club friends to spend a week at Gopher Creek Guest Ranch this summer."

Cassidy stops and looks up at us. "Hey, I think we just got invited to Wyoming!"

"Let me see that." Her mother holds out her hand, and Cassidy passes the card to her. Mrs. Sloane-Kinkaid reads it to herself. "It's true, they really want us to come," she tells us. "Winky's mother says they have plenty of room, especially toward the end of August if that works for us."

"Will that be too soon for Chloe to travel?" asks Megan's mother.

"She'll be almost three months old by then," Mrs. Sloane-Kinkaid replies. "She'll be fine." She looks around the room at the rest of us. "What do you say, girls? Do you want to meet your pen pals?"

I nod enthusiastically, but my mother presses her lips together. "We'll have to see," she replies. "It's a lovely, generous invitation but I'm not sure if this is the right time for our family."

"I know what you mean," says Mrs. Delaney. "Things are a little tight for us right now, too. Michael and I are expanding our cheese production, and we just invested in a second refrigerator."

"Nonsense," Gigi declares. "Of course we're all going! It wouldn't be the same without the whole book club. How about I supply the plane tickets? You wouldn't believe how many frequent flier miles they give you when you fly anywhere from Hong Kong. Paris, too."

"But what if you need those miles?" protests Jess's mom. "We can't use them."

"You can and you will," says Gigi, holding up her hand as my mother starts to argue with her too. "I won't hear another word about it. This book club is the most fun I've had in years, and this is the perfect ending to our year together."

I look at my mother hopefully. Am I finally going to get to meet Bailey?

She hesitates a moment longer, then gives in. "Well, okay, I guess I can't argue with that logic. Thank you, Gigi."

Mrs. Sloane-Kinkaid looks around the room and smiles. "It looks like the Mother-Daughter Book Club is heading west!"

Jess

"I've only just come and I'm not unpacked, but I can't wait to tell you how much I like the farm. This is a heavenly, heavenly, <u>heavenly</u> spot!"
—Daddy-Long-Legs

Wyoming is awesome.

My family doesn't get away from Half Moon Farm very often, but I've been a few places besides Concord. Different parts of New England, mostly—Vermont, Maine, and New Hampshire, where my aunt and uncle live. And New York City, of course. Wyoming is the farthest I've ever been from home, though. Mom says it looks like the set of a Western movie, and she's right. Looking out the bus window, I keep expecting to see a covered wagon coming toward us across the plains.

There are horses everywhere too. I've counted at least fifteen ranches so far on the drive to Gopher Hole, and all of them have horses. Even some of the plain old ordinary-looking houses have corrals in their backyards. People out here must really love to ride.

We flew in to Cheyenne this afternoon and the whole Gopher Hole Gang was there to meet us. They were just kidding when they called themselves that on the invitation they sent with Chloe's baby present, but the name has kind of stuck. They came to get us in a school bus, of all things. I guess having the mayor of your town as one of the book club moms can come in handy, because Mrs. Winchester talked the principal of the school into lending her their bus to come pick us up. It's a good thing she did, too. You should have seen everybody's faces when they saw all of our luggage. Gigi practically needed an entire bus just for hers, plus it turns out that babies need a lot of stuff when they travel. Somehow we managed to cram it all in.

Once we got out of the city—if you can call Cheyenne a city, because even though it's the capital of Wyoming it's nothing like Boston—it was like the whole world opened up. I've never seen so much sky in my entire life. Back home you can see the sky, of course, but there are hills and valleys and tons of trees that sometimes block part of the view. Out here, the view goes on forever, maybe because practically everywhere you look there are bare, windswept plains stretching out toward all those distant snow-capped peaks. The sky is endless. I know Montana is the state that gets called Big Sky country, but it might as well be Wyoming, too.

I'm sitting next to Madison in the back of the bus. Emma and Megan and Cassidy and Becca are back here too, all of us paired up with our pen pals. The Concord moms and the Gopher Hole moms are sitting up front with Gigi and Eva Bergson and Chloe and Stanley, who was allowed to come along even though he's a guy and he's not in our book club, because someone needed to help take care of the baby. Plus, from what Cassidy tells us, he got down on his knees and begged her mother, which must have been pretty hard to resist. Stanley is crazy about his new little daughter.

The adults are all laughing and talking like they've known each other forever. It's taking a little longer for the rest of us back here. Well, except for Emma and Bailey, of course. You'd think they'd lived next door to each other for their entire lives, the way they've been chattering away.

I sneak a glance around at the rest of my friends. Behind me, Winky is pointing out landmarks to Cassidy, and they seem like they're getting along okay. Across the aisle, Summer is talking Megan's ear off about quilts, and Megan looks like she's going to fall asleep but she's trying really hard to be on her best behavior because even though Summer is a little obsessed with quilting, she's also incredibly nice. "Summer's so sweet she makes my teeth hurt," Cassidy whispered to me back at the airport after we all met.

Plus, Megan's mom gave her this big lecture on the plane about minding her manners. Actually, we all got that one.

Behind them, Becca and Zoe Winchester are pretty quiet, mostly because they got into an argument at the airport about which of them has the coolest cell phone. Cassidy's already started calling Zoe "Becca West." And then there's Madison and me.

"So this is your first trip to Wyoming?" Madison asks politely.

I nod.

"Yeah, I've never been to New England before either," Madison tells me. "The farthest I've been is to Chicago, and once when I was eight we visited Disney World."

"Cool. I'd like to go there someday."

Out of the corner of my eye I watch the front of the bus, where Professor Daniels is talking to my mom. Madison's mother is tall, almost as tall as Mrs. Sloane-Kinkaid, and she has the same perfect posture that Cassidy's mother does. Her skin is as deep brown as Madison's, and she wears her hair in these loose braids that are pulled back into a ponytail. I've been trying not to stare, but it looks really pretty and I keep wondering if I could get my hair to do that. She's casually dressed in jeans and a T-shirt, but she's wearing this really interesting jewelry—big chunky orange triangle earrings and a matching bracelet. I see Megan watching her too. She's probably getting ready to pull out her sketchbook.

Professor Daniels laughs at something my mother says, a low-pitched laugh that sounds like music. When I tell this to Madison, though, she thinks it's hilarious.

"Mom can't sing for beans. Music just isn't her thing—except for listening to it." She tells me she gets her musical talent from her dad, who's an orthodontist but who likes to play piano at home in his spare time. "I get my looks from him too, I guess," she adds a little ruefully. "Dad calls it the 'Daniels' moon face' and tells me to wear it proudly."

I laugh. "I think it's a nice face," I tell her, which is the truth. I like her hair, too, which is braided in horizontal rows across her head, different than her mom's, but just as pretty.

We fall silent for a few minutes, listening to the flow of conversation around us. Becca and Zoe are finally talking to each other again,

Heather Vogel Frederick

and I can hear them discussing Beccca's favorite topic: boys.

"So have you had a good summer?" I ask Madison.

"Pretty good," she replies. "I went to guitar camp in Denver for a week, and over the Fourth of July weekend my band got to play at Laramie Jubilee Days."

"What's that?"

"They have it every year. There's music and a parade and fireworks and carnival rides and even a rodeo."

"Sounds fun."

"It is. How about you? What did you do this summer?"

I shrug. "The usual. Summertime is kind of a lot of work when you live on a farm."

"Yeah, Winky talks a lot about what it's like on her family's ranch. It sounds pretty busy. But she likes it just fine."

"Me too," I reply. "I love all our animals, and I don't mind helping out with the farm stand and the goat cheese and jam and all that stuff. Emma hangs out with me a lot. The two of us volunteered at the Concord Animal Shelter twice a week too."

Madison scans our bus-mates. "Emma's the one with the curly hair and glasses, right? Bailey's pen pal?"

"Yup. She's my best friend."

"She looks nice."

"She is. How about you? Are you good friends with anyone in particular?"

Madison purses her lips, considering. "Well, it's a little different because I live in Laramie, and mostly only see these guys once a month at our meetings."

"How did you and your mom get invited to be in the book club?" I ask, curious.

"My mom loves Mrs. Jacobs's bookstore," she explains. "They got to be friends, and she invited us to join. I'm glad, because it's been really fun, even though I wasn't so sure at first. Reading's not my favorite thing to do."

"I know what you mean."

"But the books have been pretty good, and I like Bailey a lot. Summer Williams, too, even though we're really different." She gives me a sidelong glance. "A person can only listen to so much talk about quilting, you know?"

I smother a grin. Madison is turning out to be a whole lot more fun in person than she was in her brief letters.

"Are you girls managing to break the ice back here?" says Mrs. Hawthorne, coming down the aisle toward us.

Mrs. Jacobs is right behind her with chips and sodas. "This should help tide you over until dinner," she tells us. "We've got only about another half hour to go. The Parkers have a special meal planned for us tonight, right, Winky?"

"You bet," says Winky. "Our welcome barbecue is always really good."

We pass through the outskirts of Laramie, and Madison points out the Medicine Bow Mountains in the distance, and the neighborhood near the university where they live.

"Do you want to go to University of Wyoming someday?" I ask.

She shakes her head. "Nope. I'm aiming for Juilliard."

Mr. McNamara, our MadriGals director, is always talking about Juilliard. "That's in New York, right?"

"Yeah. It's a really good music school, plus I think it would be fun to try living in a big city for a change. My mom says I have to have super-good grades to get in, though, so I'll have to work really hard in high school."

I've thought about college, but I don't have any idea yet where I want to go. Kevin Mullins has his entire future mapped out already, of course—Harvard or MIT or Cal Tech—but he'll probably end up graduating early and I want my full four years of high school, especially since two of them involve Darcy Hawthorne. If I go to Alcott High, that is. I haven't heard yet whether my scholarship at Colonial has been extended, and if it is I'm not sure I want to stay, even though this year turned out a lot better than I thought it would. Colonial Academy has a lot of things going for it—small classes with really great teachers, MadriGals, and horseback riding, for starters—but it also has two big drawbacks. No Darcy, and way too much Savannah Sinclair.

"So whatever happened with that roommate of yours?" Madison asks, as if reading my thoughts.

"Savannah? Oh, we managed to make it through to the end of the school year without killing each other," I tell her.

She laughs. "That bad, huh?"

It's been kind of tough, because the only person who knows the whole story is Emma. I haven't wanted to talk to my mom or dad or Mrs. Crandall or anyone else about Darcy, so nobody else really understands what happened between Savannah and me. I know my other book club friends think it's weird the way I went all hot and cold on her after that weekend at Half Moon Farm when she helped us rescue Pip, but then they also saw the worst side of Savannah with the taffy prank and her stuck-up attitude, so I'm hoping they're just chalking things up to that.

My mother, on the other hand, thinks I'm just being stubborn, because that last month of school she asked a couple of times if I wanted to have Savannah over again, and every time I said no. She told me I needed to continue to make an effort to be kind to her, but that was mostly because she feels sorry for Savannah, which I don't. Not after what she did.

Still, I did feel a little guilty when Savannah gave Emma that present for Pip. Especially since I shut her out completely from what was going on with him. I never asked her to come help us walk him or play with him, and I know that hurt her feelings. Maybe cutting her off like that was mean, but after the dance I just didn't want to be around her any more than I had to.

"Hey, there's the sign for Gopher Hole!" shouts Cassidy from behind us. I turn around and see a huge grin on her face. She still gets a kick out of that name.

Zoe Winchester's mother stands up in the front of the bus.

Heather Vogel Frederick

"Speaking in my official capacity as mayor, let me officially welcome you to our town!"

A cheer goes up.

"Population 2,326," Cassidy reads the sign aloud. "Man, that's like how many people go to our high school!"

Winky punches her good-naturedly on the arm. "Shut up," she says. "We may be small, but we're mighty." She points to a turnoff ahead. "There's the entrance to our ranch."

The bus slows down and turns onto a gravel road, passing underneath a big wrought-iron arch with GOPHER CREEK GUEST RANCH spelled out on it in metal letters. Behind us, Winky starts to bounce up and down in her seat.

"We're here, because we're here, because we're here, because we're here!" she sings exuberantly, and the rest of us join in, not caring if we're acting like little kids. All except for Zoe and Becca, that is, who roll their eyes at each other and start putting on lip gloss.

The bus lumbers down the long driveway. Split rail fences line either side of it, and beyond them are tall trees that Madison tells me are aspens.

"*Populus tremuloides*," she adds. "I looked it up for you, because I knew you'd want to know the Latin name."

We lurch up over a gentle rise, then a shallow valley spreads out below us. I spot the ranch in the middle. The main house is beautiful, a big log cabin with a creek running along one side of it. Dotting its banks are lots of smaller log cabins that extend partway around a big square of lawn, kind of like the dorms and classrooms do around the quad back at Colonial Academy. On the opposite side of the lawn is the barn, and beyond that, the corrals. Across the creek, open prairie stretches off toward the snowcapped peaks of the Medicine Bow Mountains.

"This is it, ladies," says Winky's mother as we pull up in front of the largest of the cabins. "Welcome to the bunkhouse!"

We tumble out of the bus. The late afternoon air smells fresh and cool, and it's sharp with an unfamiliar scent.

"Sage," Madison tells me when I ask. "I guess you don't have that back in Concord, do you?"

"Not that I know of," I reply, hefting my suitcase up the steps to the front porch.

"The bunkhouse is where we put our large groups," says Mrs. Parker, ushering us inside. "We figured you girls would want to stay together. It has its own living room where we can all gather in the evenings if we want, and your mothers will be close by in their own cabins."

The bunkhouse is awesome. The big living room has a tiny little kitchenette in the corner, and beyond that is a long bedroom lined with half a dozen bunk beds. Madison and I stake out one in a corner by a window overlooking the creek. Emma and Bailey plunk their suitcases down on the one right next to us.

"Sweet, huh?" says Bailey.

I nod. So far, I really like Gopher Creek Ranch.

"Top or bottom?" Madison asks me. "Doesn't make any difference to me."

"Top," I reply instantly, hoping she really doesn't mind. I don't know why, but I love bunk beds. I always get dibs on the top when I sleep over at Emma's. I climb up and give a little bounce on the mattress. I can't help it; I'm excited to be here. Across the room, Zoe Winchester smirks at me.

"Just ignore her," Bailey whispers. "That's what we all do."

As soon as we're unpacked we head out to explore. Our moms are getting settled in their cabins next door. My mother and Mrs. Hawthorne are sharing a cabin with Mrs. Jacobs and Professor Daniels, and Mrs. Wong and Mrs. Chadwick are paired up with Summer's mother and Mayor Winchester. Gigi and Eva Bergson have a cabin to themselves, and so do Mrs. Sloane-Kinkaid and Stanley and baby Chloe. Winky's mother is going to stay across the lawn at the ranch house.

"Gotta keep an eye on things this week," she explains. "I'm still on duty here. But you'll see plenty of me, don't worry."

She glances at her watch. "Speaking of being on duty, dinner is in half an hour. Just enough time for you to give everyone a quick tour, Winky."

"We are going to have so much fun this week," says Winky, as her mother hurries off. "We've planned some special trail rides, and my dad's going to take us fishing at Echo Lake, and Pete said he'd give everybody lasso lessons. If you're any good I can try and teach you to rope calves. The big finale is next Saturday night, when we have Ranch Idol and a square dance."

"What's 'Ranch Idol'?" Emma asks.

"Our talent show," Winky tells us. "It's really awesome. Last week this family was here from Wisconsin who could yodel."

"Imagine that," says Zoe, whipping out a tiny mirror from her pocket and checking her lip gloss again.

Emma and I exchange a glance. Zoe is shaping up to be a real pain.

"I'm so glad my mother gave her to Becca for a pen pal," Emma whispers.

"No kidding," I whisper back.

We follow Winky across the lawn—which I can't stop thinking of as the quad—to the barn. "Tomorrow morning, Pete will pair everybody up with your horses for the week, but I figured you might want to meet them all tonight," she says, her eyes bright with excitement. Winky is as bubbly in person as she is in her letters, and I like her already.

The barn smells great, just like ours does back at Half Moon Farm. I could walk into a barn anywhere in the world and feel right at home. There's something about the familiar scent of hay and old wood and harness leather mixed with the sweet smell of the livestock that I just love. Even the tang of manure doesn't bother me. I breathe it all in deeply, smiling.

My mother puts her arm around my shoulders. "Having fun?"

I nod vigorously. "I love it here!"

"Me too."

Winky introduces us to a bunch of the horses—there are over forty at the ranch—and Emma and I go nuts over their names: Tango

Heather Vogel Frederick

and Dazzle and Sheba and Jasmine, Vegas and Jitterbug and Romeo and Anthem. Bingo, too, of course. The list is endless, and really creative. Everyone agrees, though, that it's hard to beat Led and Zep.

"Your dad named your horses after *Led Zeppelin*?" crows Madison. "How come you never told me that? That is so awesome!"

She runs over and tells her mother, who laughs her deep, musical laugh.

As we're leaving the barn, an old truck putts past. The driver is wearing a cowboy hat, like just about everybody else at Gopher Creek except us. His face is deeply tanned and weather-beaten, and his hair is as white as Eva Bergson's. He waves to us and we wave back.

"That's Pete," says Winky. "He's our ranch foreman."

"There's a chicken in that truck," says Mrs. Chadwick, blinking in surprise.

We all turn and look. Sure enough, a small red-combed head is poking over the edge of the open passenger side window, watching us with bright little eyes.

"He's a rooster, actually," says Winky. "His name is Lefty and he belongs to Pete. A coyote almost got him a couple of years ago. He lost one of his wings in the fight. Pete rescued him and nursed him back to health, and he's followed him around like a little shadow ever since. You should hear the other cowboys rib Pete about him when they drive into town, but Pete doesn't care. Lefty loves to ride with him in the truck."

I grin at my mother. "Maybe we can train one of our chickens to do that."

"Don't even think about it," she retorts.

"So did the coyote get his right wing, then?" asks Emma, puzzling over Pete's rooster's name.

"Nope," Winky replies. "His left one."

We think about this for a minute, and then we all start to laugh.

"I guess cowboys understand irony too," Emma says.

Across the green, Mrs. Parker appears in the doorway of the main ranch house and clangs vigorously on a metal triangle hanging from a nearby post.

"That's the dinner bell," says Winky. "I'll have to show you the rest later."

We stop at the bunkhouse to wash up, then head for the dining hall. Mr. Kinkaid is sitting in one of the half-dozen rocking chairs spaced along the front porch, holding Chloe.

"Hi, honey!" calls Cassidy's mom. "Having fun?"

"Pure heaven," he replies, as we all cluster around him to wait with the other guests until the dining room doors open.

"Hey, Dad!" Winky calls out, leaning over the railing and waving at a tall man with salt-and-pepper hair who's standing by the huge grill. He waves his barbecue fork back at her.

"Welcome!"

Mrs. Parker flings open the doors to the dining hall. "Come and get it!" she cries, and we all file eagerly inside.

The dining hall is a big rectangular room attached at one end to the main ranch house, and there are tables for about fifty people.

Heather Vogel Frederick

Windows line both sides, and beneath them are cozy-looking cushioned benches. At the far end is a stone fireplace that's even bigger than the one in our bunkhouse living room, and there are bookshelves flanking it, along with comfortable leather armchairs and sofas to curl up in.

"Nice," I say to Madison, and she nods.

"I know. I love it when our book club gets to meet here."

We grab plates and make our way through the buffet line, then on to our reserved table, where I finally figure out the reason for Zoe Winchester's lip gloss fixation. Two reasons, actually. Owen and Sam Parker, Winky's older brothers.

"They are *seriously* cute," Megan whispers to Becca.

"No kidding!" she whispers back.

Darcy or no Darcy, I have to agree. Owen and Sam are dressed like all the other men I've seen so far here at the ranch, in jeans and boots and crisp white shirts. They both have dark hair like Winky's, sky blue eyes, sunburned faces, and big smiles.

"Boys," says Mrs. Parker. "Meet the Concord girls."

"Howdy," they reply, and Megan and Becca just about swoon.

I glance over at Bailey and Summer, who both seem a little extra giggly as well. Zoe, meanwhile, is all but drooling. Madison doesn't seem to care, and of course Cassidy doesn't either. Or is her face looking a little pinker than usual?

Owen and Sam sit with us at dinner, asking questions about life "back East," as they call it. I love the sound of that. It makes Concord seem exotic. They want to hear all about Half Moon Farm, and what it's like to raise goats and make cheese, and they pepper Mrs. Sloane-Kinkaid about *Cooking with Clementine*, which Mrs. Parker recorded for the book club when we did the dim sum episode so they could all see what we looked like.

"Those little pork things looked delicious, Mrs. Chen," Owen tells Megan's grandmother.

"Call me Gigi," she says. "And they are. Maybe I'll have to teach you how to make them this week."

The boys are impressed when they learn that Mrs. Bergson was an Olympic gold medalist, and intrigued by the fact that Cassidy plays on an all-boys hockey team. Her face gets pink again as Stanley brags about how good she is.

"She was team captain this year," he says proudly, as Cassidy stares down at her barbecued chicken and corn on the cob. "And MVP for the second time."

"There's a rink over in Laramie, but the only ice we get out here is on the creek, and that's too shallow and rocky for skating," says Sam. "But if you're that handy with a hockey stick, I'll bet you'll pick up the lasso real quick."

Cassidy gives him a sidelong smile, and I see her mother wink at Stanley.

Zoe seems to have staked out Owen as her territory, and she trails after him all evening, glaring at any other female who tries to talk to him.

Heather Vogel Frederick

"She's had a crush on Owen forever," Madison tells me as we sit in the dark around a big bonfire, looking up at the sky. I spot Cygnus, the swan, and trace its tail with my eyes up to Deneb, the brightest star in that constellation and one of the corners of the Summer Triangle. "But Winky says he thinks she's a pest."

"Sounds like Becca and Zach Norton," I murmur, hunting for Altair and Vega, the other two stars that complete the triangle. I explain to Madison about Zach, and about how he kissed Cassidy, which she thinks is hilarious, especially the black-eye part.

Bailey's mother had originally planned a book club meeting for us tonight, but by eight o'clock we're all yawning.

"I guess it's been kind of a long day for you, what with the flight and all, hasn't it?" she says, looking disappointed.

"We'll have plenty of time for book talk later in the week," Mrs. Parker consoles her. "Why don't you all get to bed now and get a good night's rest. The fun starts tomorrow."

Tomorrow? I wonder. *How could anything be more fun than today?* I climb up into my bunk and wriggle under the covers. If I lie on my side, I can look out the window at the moon, just like I can in my own bedroom back at Half Moon Farm. I close my eyes and drift off to sleep. I love it here at Gopher Creek already.

The next morning I wake up early, at dawn, well before everybody else except Winky. That's what happens when you live on a farm. The two of us get dressed quietly, so we don't wake the others, and I pull on my riding boots and follow her down to the barn to help feed the horses. Pete and her brothers are already there, along with Lefty who, sure enough, follows his rescuer around like a little feathered dog.

Owen watches me muck out one of the stalls, and nods approvingly when I'm done. "You've got grit for such a little thing," he says, giving my braid a tug just like Darcy Hawthorne always does. "I'll bet my dad would hire you on as a ranch hand in a heartbeat."

Pleased at the praise, I smile at him shyly.

"Want to go for a ride?" Winky asks. "I could take you up to Lonesome Ridge. We've still got plenty of time until breakfast."

"Sure."

We saddle up Bingo and Anthem, a buckskin mare the color of molasses taffy.

"She's beautiful," I tell Winky.

"Sweet as the music she's named for, too, and fast as the wind," she replies. "Cassidy told me in one of her letters that you've been taking riding lessons this year, and Pete and I have had her in mind for you ever since we knew you all were coming."

It's different riding Western than it is the English style I'm learning back at Colonial Academy. The saddles here at the ranch are deeper and higher than the flatter English saddles I'm used to, plus they have a knob that sticks up in the front, called a pommel. Winky shows me how to loop the reins around it once I've mounted, then she checks my riding boots to make sure they won't slip out of the stirrups.

"Fancier than cowboy boots, but they'll do," she says, nodding in approval.

Heather Vogel Frederick

Riding Anthem is a dream. She's as eager as I am to get out and explore the morning, and I have no problem keeping up with Winky and Bingo as we trot out of the corral and splash across the shallow creek and on through a stand of trees toward the open range.

"Aspens, right?" I call out, and Winky turns to me and nods.

Populus tremuloides, Madison called them, and sure enough, just as the Latin name suggests, their leaves make a soft rustling sound, trembling in the early morning breeze as we ride past. When we reach the prairie and the trees fall away behind us, Winky urges Bingo into a canter. I follow suit and Anthem surges forward. Pretty soon the two of us are whooping it up. It feels like we could ride forever out here, all the way to the mountains. Winky points to the east, though, toward a high, rocky outcropping.

"That's Lonesome Ridge!" she shouts. "Race you!"

She slaps her reins and Bingo gallops off, and Anthem needs no encouragement from me to take up the chase. Neck and neck our horses carry us up the steep slope to the top, where we rein them in to a trot and then pause, all four of us breathing hard as we take in the view.

"Listen," says Winky, closing her eyes.

I close mine, too. The wind sighs in the distant pines, sounding like the ocean. I open my eyes. "It gives me the chills. But in a good way. Is that why they call it Lonesome Ridge?"

"Yep," says Winky. "My favorite place in the world. What's yours?"

"Half Moon Farm. I don't ever want to live anywhere else."

"I know exactly what you mean. That's the way I feel about the ranch. My daddy says some places just get under your skin."

We stay for a while, listening to the wind and feeling the sun on our faces, and then we turn our horses and head back. As we approach the barn, there's a commotion overhead. I shade my eyes and look up, startled to see a helicopter appear above the trees. It hovers there for a minute, and people start running out of the cabins. My friends tumble onto the bunkhouse porch in their pajamas, and Mrs. Hawthorne and Mrs. Wong and Mrs. Chadwick emerge too, clutching their bathrobes.

"I didn't know we were expecting more guests!" Winky exclaims.

The helicopter settles onto the middle of the grassy lawn. As its propeller blades slowly whine to a stop, the door on its side opens and a tall, silver-haired man in a suit climbs out, followed by a blond woman in a white sundress.

"Oh, no!" I whisper, my heart sinking like a stone as the man turns and reaches his hand out to the chestnut-haired girl behind him. "What the heck is Savannah Sinclair doing here?"

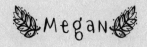

Megan

"I am beginning to feel at home in the world—
as though I really belonged in it."
—Daddy-Long-Legs

"Poppy!" shouts Mrs. Chadwick, catapulting off her cabin porch. She charges across the lawn toward the helicopter, her bathrobe flapping behind her and her arms flung wide.

"Calliope!" the blond woman in the white sundress shouts back, and they throw their arms around each other in a big bear hug.

I turn to Becca, who's standing beside me in her pajamas. "Does your mom know the Sinclairs?" I ask, astounded.

"Um," she replies, looking uncomfortable. "She made me promise not to say anything."

"What? Why?"

Becca shrugs. "I dunno. She made it sound like it had something to do with national security. Don't tell anybody, okay?"

Puzzled, I nod, and follow her back inside to get dressed.

"Poppy and I were roommates a zillion years ago at Colonial Academy," Mrs. Chadwick explains to us all a short while later at the breakfast table.

I arch an eyebrow at Becca and whisper *"national security?"* She presses her lips together and shrugs, as if to say *How was I supposed to know?*

Mrs. Chadwick and Mrs. Sinclair beam at each other. "When I found out we were coming here, I just had to give her a call," Becca's mother continues. "The Senator is an avid fisherman, and I thought it might be fun if they could join us, especially since our girls already know their lovely daughter, Savannah."

The Sinclair's lovely daughter regards us warily over her waffles.

Summer Williams leans over toward me. "Isn't she the one you guys call 'Julia'?" she murmurs, and I nod.

"We're delighted to have you here at Gopher Creek Ranch," says Mrs. Parker graciously. "And I'm sure our girls will enjoy getting to know Savannah, too."

Don't count on it, I think, looking around at my Wyoming friends.

"So you both went to Colonial Academy?" says Mrs. Hawthorne. "How come we never knew this about you, Calliope?"

Mrs. Chadwick bats her pale robin's-egg-blue eyes, which this summer are residing behind a pair of giant black glasses frames that I guess are in style but that make her look a little like Kevin Mullins. "Everyone is entitled to their secrets," she says coyly.

"Still trying to cover up your wicked past, I see," drawls Poppy Sinclair.

"We knew you went there," says Cassidy. "We saw your field hockey picture on the wall in Witherspoon."

"Is that so?" Mrs. Chadwick crunches on a piece of bacon. "Savannah's mother was on the team too."

Poppy Sinclair gives a mock shudder. "Weren't those uniforms an absolute horror?"

She and Mrs. Chadwick pick up their knives and simultaneously thump them on the table, then clank them together three times and cheer, "Goooooooo, Colonial!"

A smile creeps across Savannah's lips, and her eyes flick over to Jess. Something tells me she's heard this cheer before. The smile fades, though, when she sees that Jess is pointedly ignoring her.

Mrs. Chadwick and Mrs. Sinclair continue to reminisce throughout breakfast, laughing and joking with each other while the rest of us listen to their stories.

"And I just love what you've done to yourself," Savannah's mother tells her.

Pleased, Mrs. Chadwick runs her fingers through her prickly hair. I've actually gotten used to her new style since she got it cut last fall, and I even think it's kind of cute. Becca still doesn't, though. "It's a whole new me, right?"

"Not that there was anything wrong with the old you," Mrs. Sinclair says loyally. "But this is a bit more, I don't know—"

"Fun?" says Mrs. Chadwick, batting her eyes again.

"Exactly."

I look over at my mother. If somebody like Mrs. Chadwick can have fun, why is it so hard for her? Even my mother's breakfast plate screams *"NOT HAVING FUN!"* The food here at the Parkers' ranch is great, and there's lots of it. Which is a good thing, because all this fresh air makes a person hungry. Most people, that is. Like everybody else at our table, Gigi and I have piled our plates high with waffles and scrambled eggs and bacon and fruit salad, but all my mother took was half a banana, some yogurt, and a single slice of whole wheat toast. I sigh. I sure hope she can figure out how to cut loose a little while we're here.

"So," says Mrs. Parker, "on the docket for this morning for our group: one trail ride. Owen, Sam, you boys help Dad with the rest of the guests, okay? He's planning on taking several of the families fishing, so they'll need to be outfitted, and if one of you could help me with cowboy camp for the smaller kids this afternoon when I get back, that would be great."

Jess leans over to me. "Man, I wish my little brothers could have come," she says. "They'd have loved it here."

A familiar pang of envy stirs in me. The Delaney twins are a total pain, but I would still give anything for a little brother or two. Or a sister, I think, looking over to where Chloe is snuggled in Mr. Sloane-Kinkaid's arms.

Our pen pals all have brothers and sisters too—including Summer, who has so many I can't keep them all straight. Nobody at this table is an only child, not even my own mother! She has a brother back in Hong Kong, and my dad has two sisters. I don't understand why my parents wouldn't want me to have what they have. It's so not fair. Not

Heather Vogel Frederick

one bit. All I've got is Mirror Megan, and a mother and grandmother who can't seem to get along.

"We'll rendezvous in the barn in half an hour, okay?" Mrs. Parker continues. "Winky and Pete will get you all set up with horses, and we have plenty of extra boots and hats if you didn't bring them with you."

We clear away our dishes when we're done and scatter to get ready. Crossing the lawn—which is now minus the helicopter—I feel a tug on my sleeve. It's Summer.

"Hey, Megan, do you have a minute?"

So you can bore me to death with another quilting lecture? I think, but I don't say it out loud, of course. "Sure," I chirp, mimicking her relentlessly cheerful tone.

"I've got something for you."

I follow her to the bunkhouse's empty living room. "Wait here," she tells me, and disappears down the hall, reappearing a moment later with a large, soft package. "I made it for you," she says, handing it to me.

My heart sinks as I instantly guess what's inside. "Gee, thanks, Summer, you shouldn't have," I reply without enthusiasm.

"Open it!" she urges, hardly able to contain her excitement.

Reluctantly, I remove the wrapping paper. It's a quilt, all right, but not at all what I was expecting. "Wait a minute, is this your story quilt?"

Summer nods. "Uh-huh."

"But you can't give this away—this is your prize-winning quilt!" All Summer's talked about in her letters since the Fourth of July is how excited and thrilled she was to win first prize in the state fair's junior division, and how she got a blue ribbon and a check for a hundred dollars, which she put into her college fund.

"Sure I can. I checked with my mom and everything. We agreed that you're part of my story now, so it's perfect, don't you see? I've had so much fun writing to you this year, Megan! I'm really glad we're friends."

I stare down at Summer's unexpectedly generous gift, feeling really awful all of a sudden for the things I've thought and said about her these past months. "I don't know what to say."

"How about 'thank you'?" says Gigi, poking her head in the door. "Sorry, girls, I didn't mean to eavesdrop. I'm looking for Lily and thought maybe she was over here."

She crosses to the sofa and sits down beside me, running her small hands—practically the only part of my grandmother that's wrinkled— over the quilt. "I told Megan you deserved to win first prize when you sent her that picture last winter. It's just lovely. You did a beautiful job, Summer. Just look at that feather-stitching!"

I feel another stab of guilt. My grandmother is right. The quilt is exquisite.

"Thank you, Mrs. Chen," Summer replies modestly.

"Call me Gigi."

"Okay."

"I wish I had something to give you," I tell Summer, feeling worse by the minute. It never even crossed my mind to bring her a present.

Summer smiles at me. "You don't give a gift to get one back. You give a gift because you want to. At least that's what my mom always tells me."

Gigi nods approvingly. "Your mother sounds like a very wise woman."

Summer sits down cross-legged on the floor in front of us and launches into an explanation of the history of Victorian crazy quilts. As she shows us the different top stitches—feather, herringbone, chain, and fly—I find to my surprise that I'm actually interested, especially when she starts telling us the stories behind each piece of fabric. The green velvet is from her first holiday dress, and there's some bright yellow calico from one of her mom's old aprons, blue and white ticking stripe from a pillowcase that used to belong to her grandfather, and even some denim from her favorite overalls.

"Like a family," says Gigi, giving me a sidelong glance. "Different fabric, different people. All with different tastes and interests, but stitched together with love."

"That's exactly what my mother says!" Summer exclaims.

Gigi smiles at her. "I can see I'm going to have to get to know your mother better."

"So she doesn't mind you cutting all this stuff up?" I ask.

Summer shakes her head. "She says she can't think of a better way to preserve a memory."

I finger a piece of plaid flannel. "Who did this belong to?"

"That's from an old shirt of my dad's," she replies softly. "After he left, I found it hanging in the back of his closet, so I took it and kept it in mine. It smelled like him for the longest time."

There's sadness in my grandmother's eyes as she listens to this. I haven't thought much about how Summer feels about her parents' divorce. It must be really tough, not getting to see her dad very often. I'd really miss my father if he moved to a different city.

Summer shrugs. "That part of the story isn't such a happy one."

"How about this piece here?" Gigi asks, moving to what I hope is a cheerier square. It's a patch of faded ivory silk right in the center of the quilt.

Summer brightens. "There's an awesome story behind that one! I took it from the hem of my great-great-grandmother's wedding dress. She came to Laramie in a covered wagon."

"No kidding?" I slide my fingertip across the silk. It's cool to the touch, and just like with Mrs. Bergson's *Daddy-Long-Legs* doll, I feel like I'm touching a piece of history.

"She was heading for Utah with her parents," Summer continues, "but when the wagon train stopped here, she went into the post office to buy some stamps and fell head over heels in love with a handsome young rancher who was picking up his mail. The next morning when the wagon train left, she stayed behind and married him."

Gigi sighs. "What a romantic story!"

Summer's quilt is like some kind of a rare treasure map of her family. I push it back toward her. "You can't give this away."

She places it firmly in my lap again. "There's plenty more fabric

Heather Vogel Frederick

up in that old trunk," she tells me, then grins. "Besides, you know me. I'll have another one whipped up before your plane even touches the ground back in Boston."

My conscience prickles again. Did she guess that we made fun of her?

"Oh, there's one more thing." Summer turns the quilt over and points to the bottom right-hand corner. Something is embroidered on it. I look more closely and read: *To Megan from her pen pal, Summer. Friendship is where the best stories begin.*

"Thanks," I whisper, and this time I really mean it.

Chattering about feather stitching and wedding dresses, the three of us head down to the barn where the rest of our friends are getting ready for the trail ride. Winky steers Summer and me to a pile of cowboy boots and tells us to find some that fit. Gigi's already wearing hers—designer, of course, purchased especially for the occasion—along with impeccably tailored jodhpurs, a white silk blouse, and her diamond earrings. Pete's bushy white eyebrows shoot up appreciatively when he spots her and he quickly makes his way across the barn.

"Ma'am?" he says, offering his arm. "May I escort you to your steed?"

My grandmother doesn't miss a beat. "You bet, pardner," she replies, tucking her hand under his elbow.

Mrs. Delaney and Professor Daniels are already mounted on Tango and Dazzle, and Pete and Winky's brothers quickly get the rest of our moms settled too, including Mrs. Sloane-Kinkaid, who's practically giddy about being "off duty," as she calls it, since Stanley offered to stay behind at the ranch with Chloe today.

I've been paired with a big creamy golden mare named Siren, who Winky tells me is a Palomino. Not that I'd know the difference. I try unsuccessfully to hop up into the saddle, and finally give up to wait for a boost from Pete or one of the Parker boys.

Looking like an ad for *Equestrian Monthly* or something, Savannah Sinclair strides into the barn. She's riding Sheba this week, and she swings herself up expertly into the saddle. Jess has told us what a good rider Savannah is, and there's something about the confident way she sits on the coal-black mare's back that tells me Jess is right.

"So what's with the chicken?" Savannah asks, nodding at Lefty.

"Rooster," I correct her.

"Whatever."

From the looks of it, Lefty is not too thrilled with all the attention that Pete is paying to Gigi and Mrs. Bergson. Across the barn, he's flapping his lone wing and hopping up and down frantically, and every few seconds he makes a dive for Pete's boots.

"I think he's just being protective," I reply, briefly explaining Lefty's history.

"Like the McGurk," adds Cassidy, maneuvering Jitterbug over next to us.

"Like the what?" says Savannah.

"Never mind," I tell her. "Just somebody in a book."

Savannah grunts. "Y'all and your stupid book club." She looks over at Lefty and narrows her eyes. "A rooster's kind of a silly pet, don't you think?"

Cassidy mouths the word "Julia." I nod back. Still, I don't get it. Savannah's not even bothering to make an effort to be nice. Back when we were all taking care of Emma's puppy, she seemed almost, well, human.

Something must have happened around that time, because things between Jess and her soured again, fast. I glance across the barn to where Jess is seated on Anthem. She's been very carefully giving Savannah a wide berth since she got here, and I decide to do the same.

Trailing a still-flustered Lefty, Pete finally gets to me and gives me a boost up onto Siren's back. I must look a little nervous because he pats me on the leg. "Her name is a lot wilder than she is," he tells me with a wink. "Don't you fret, cowgirl, she'll get you there and back just fine."

"There" turns out to be plateau at the top of what feels like a mountain but I'm told is just a hill. It's about an hour and a half's ride from the ranch, and I can barely move by the time I slide out of the saddle. Rubbing my sore rear end, I limp toward one of the blankets that Pete and Winky have spread out for us in the shade. I collapse in a heap next to Becca, who it turns out is having even less fun this morning than I am.

"What is it with your mother?" mutters Zoe, staring at Mrs. Chadwick. "Was there a sale at the clown store?"

Becca's mother has really flung herself wholeheartedly into the whole Wild West theme today. She's decked out in jeans and red accessories—red cowboy boots, a red bandana, red piping and red buttons on her white Western-style shirt, and even a red cowboy hat.

"At least my mother isn't trying to suck up to some Washington bigwig," Becca retorts.

Zoe reddens. Over on the other blanket, Mrs. Winchester is busy giving Senator Sinclair a long, loud explanation of every single one of her important duties as mayor of Gopher Hole, including making sure that the flag is flying properly over the post office every day.

"Well, at least my mother—" Zoe begins.

"Girls!" calls Mrs. Hawthorne suspiciously. I swear Emma's mother has supersonic hearing. Actually, most mothers do. "What's going on over there?"

"Nothing," Zoe replies sullenly.

The ride back is uncomfortable in more ways than one.

We were supposed to have our big book club meeting this afternoon, but our mothers decide it would be rude to ditch the Sinclairs on their first day here, so instead we all end up going for a swim after lunch. Dressed in bathing suits and shorts and carrying our towels, we follow Winky along a path by the creek to a deep pool she calls the "swimming hole." The water is cold and refreshing after our hot, dusty ride, and it's actually fun until Savannah manages to catch a minnow and put it down Cassidy's bathing suit.

Cassidy calls her a "fivehead" and chases her up the creek bank, and Zoe uses the commotion to get back at Becca for her remark about her mother by plopping a handful of mud in her hair. Our mothers have to step in and separate everybody, and we all end up getting sent back to our cabins to cool off.

After dinner, our moms continue to keep a wary eye on us, and instead of playing board games back in the bunkhouse living room like we'd originally planned, they make us sit by the fire in the dining room and listen to Pete read his cowboy poetry—which is funny enough but a little goes a long way—and to Mr. Parker tell stories about the ranch's history. I fall asleep at one point, and finally excuse myself to head off to bed.

If Monday was a bust, Tuesday is even worse. Everybody seems irritated today, including our moms. We're all still sore from yesterday's trail ride, and it's all we can do to haul ourselves back onto our horses for the ride to Echo Lake.

And then of course there's the actual fishing.

"You do practice catch-and-release, don't you?" my mother asks in a worried tone.

Mr. Parker just laughs. "Now why would anyone want to go and throw good food back in the water, ma'am? This is dinner we're talking about!"

I don't think he realizes that my mother is serious.

Savannah, who complained loudly the whole way here about how much she hates to fish, goes and sulks under a tree, and Zoe gets her nose out of joint again, this time because Owen Parker and his brother are spending so much time coaching Cassidy, who's a natural at trout fishing, of course. Meanwhile Senator Sinclair, who's an even bigger windbag than Mayor Winchester, decides he knows more about fishing than either Mr. Parker or Stanley Kinkaid and gets into an argument about whether lake trout or river trout are better.

The only ones having any fun at all, it seems, are Emma and Bailey, who were smart and stayed back at the ranch. They're holed up in the bunkhouse—excuse me, "Lock Willow Farm," as they're calling it in honor of Jean Webster and Judy Abbot—writing a play together.

The third time my mother brings up catch-and-release, I throw down my fishing rod.

"Mom!" I say in disgust. "Can't you ever just relax and have fun?"

"I am having fun," she replies.

"Well, why don't you tell it to your face?" Gigi gives me a reproachful look as I stomp off, but I don't care. This whole vacation is making me grouchy.

The only good thing that happens all day is that I overhear Senator Sinclair say something to his wife about calling for their chopper. Maybe they're going to leave early.

Wednesday morning gets off to a slightly better start, with everybody making an obvious effort to get along better. Even Savannah and Zoe seem a little more subdued.

"I'll bet their mothers talked to them last night," says Jess, as she and Madison and Summer and I jog across the lawn to breakfast.

"You're probably right," Madison agrees. "I know mine did."

Jess grins. "Mine too."

Heather Vogel Frederick

I raise a hand. "Ditto."

Summer laughs. "That makes four of us."

It's cooler out today, and I zip my hoodie all the way up and stuff my hands in my pockets. The air has that crisp chill to it that says summer is on its way out and a new school year just around the corner. *Alcott High!* I hug myself, feeling a tingle of excitement. I can hardly wait.

The food here just keeps getting better. Breakfast is a yummy casserole called a Western Scramble, plus the best cinnamon rolls I've ever had in my life.

"Mom, you've got to get this recipe from Mrs. Parker," I say, reaching for another one.

My mother takes a sip of green tea and a bite of granola. "We'll see," she murmurs, which is what she always says when she has no intention of doing something.

Beside me, Gigi leans forward and looks down the long table to the far end. "Ellen?"

Mrs. Parker turns away from her conversation with Professor Daniels. "Yes?"

"I'd love to have this recipe for the cinnamon rolls. They're Megan's favorite."

"Sure! Remind me after breakfast and I'll write it down for you."

My mother shoots Gigi a look.

When we're finished eating, Mrs. Parker announces that it's free choice day. She posts a list of the available activities, and we all crowd around to see what there is to do.

A bunch of the other ranch guests decide they want to head into town and explore Laramie, and Mrs. Parker arranges for Sam to drive them in Gopher Creek's big van. Mrs. Winchester asks if she can hitch a ride as far as Gopher Hole, because she wants to check on Zoe's little sisters, who are staying with a babysitter during the day while Mr. Winchester is at the office, and also because she has an important city council meeting that she can't miss. She makes sure Senator Sinclair hears this last part, but from what I can tell he's not all that impressed. At least he doesn't say anything, except to explain the real reason he called for his helicopter, which unfortunately isn't to whisk his family back to Washington, as I'd hoped, but to take Winky's father and Stanley on a special fishing trip to some remote part of the North Platte River. As a peace offering for yesterday's "churlish behavior," as he puts it.

Great, I think. *We're stuck with Savannah.* I give Jess a rueful smile.

My mother and Mrs. Hawthorne and Professor Daniels and Mrs. Jacobs opt for a guided hike with a naturalist to learn more about the local flora and fauna—no big surprise there. Cassidy and Zoe and—big surprise here—Mrs. Chadwick, of all people, sign up for lariat lessons, although Summer points out that the only reason Zoe picked this activity is because Owen is the instructor. Emma and Bailey retreat back to "Lock Willow Farm" to work on their play some more; Madison and Becca and Eva Bergson and Summer's mother and Savannah all decide to hike to the hot springs for a soak; and Jess and Winky and Gigi and Pete head out for another trail ride.

Heather Vogel Frederick

There's no way I'm getting back on a horse so soon, so I decide to give quilting a try. Summer has offered to teach a little mini-workshop to any of us who want to learn, and Mrs. Sloane-Kinkaid signs up, along with Poppy Sinclair and Mrs. Delaney and Mrs. Parker, who has to stay behind anyway to keep an eye on things.

Even though it's still cool outside, Mrs. Parker assures us it will warm up, so we bring her sewing machine out onto the dining room porch while Summer goes to get her supplies. I still can't believe she actually brought quilting squares in her suitcase. I guess you never know when the urge to quilt will strike.

"I've always wanted to learn how to do this," says Jess's mom. "I've just never had the time, what with the farm and everything."

"I know exactly what you mean," agrees Mrs. Sinclair. "Not that I have a farm, but life in Washington is always so busy."

Quilting is a lot more fun than I expected, and so is Savannah's mother. Senator Sinclair may be what my dad calls a "stuffed shirt," but underneath all that hairspray, Mrs. Sinclair is a hoot. While we quilt she tells us hilarious stories about things that she and Mrs. Chadwick did back at school when they were roommates, including sneaking off to go skinny-dipping in Walden Pond.

"Poppy, you've given us enough ammunition for a lifetime!" says Mrs. Delaney. "Calliope's never going to hear the end of this."

"I certainly hope not," drawls Mrs. Sinclair, the corners of her mouth quirking up in a smile. "That's why I tattled on her."

By lunchtime, it still hasn't warmed up. In fact, the temperature has dropped even further, and we move our quilting bee back indoors. Mrs. Parker builds a big fire and we all help her fix lunch. Since there's only a handful of us, it's just soup and sandwiches. Cassidy and Zoe and Mrs. Chadwick and Owen Parker come in from the barn to join us, and so do Emma and Becca and "the spa girls," as Mrs. Sloane-Kinkaid dubs the group that hiked to the hot springs.

"Nothing feels better than a good soak when you're saddle-sore," says Mrs. Bergson, taking a brownie from the tray that Mrs. Parker is passing around.

"Unless it's going skinny-dipping," says Mrs. Delaney with a sly look at Becca's mom.

"Really, Shannon," Mrs. Chadwick replies pompously. "What kind of a person would ever do that?"

The quilters all start to snicker.

Cassidy's mother glances out the window and stops laughing. "Oh my goodness, look at that sky!"

Huge black clouds are gathering over the barn, and from the looks of the way the tops of the trees are starting to sway, the wind is really picking up too.

She leans down and plucks Chloe out of the baby carrier by the hearth where she's sleeping. "I hope your daddy gets back soon," she says, hugging her close. "I don't like the idea of him being out in weather like this. Especially not in a helicopter."

We drift over to the long benches that line the dining room's big windows.

Heather Vogel Frederick

"There's a storm brewing, no doubt about it," says Mrs. Parker, peering out at the sky. "I'm sure everyone's seen the signs. They're all probably heading back to the ranch right now."

"Do you think our moms are okay?" Emma asks Bailey in a low voice.

"Oh, sure," she says. "We get storms like this all the time out here. Mrs. Parker's right—they're probably on their way back already."

"How's your play coming?" I ask them.

"Great!" says Emma, and Bailey nods.

"We're thinking of performing part of it for Ranch Idol," she tells me.

"If we can get our courage up," Emma adds. "How about you, Megan? What are you going to do?"

I shrug. My talents aren't the kind you do onstage. "I'll probably just watch."

"A good audience is important too," says Madison, who's planning to play her guitar.

The phone rings in the kitchen, and Mrs. Parker goes to answer it.

"That was your mom, Zoe," she says when she returns. "She's going to stay in town until this blows over."

We look out the window again. The wind is really picking up now, and Mrs. Sloane-Kinkaid is pacing the floor, humming softly to Chloe.

"Are you going to do anything for Ranch Idol?" I ask Savannah politely. She's sitting slightly apart from us down the window seat, her long hair still wet from the hot springs.

She glances over at me. "Maybe," she says coolly. "I haven't decided yet."

Before I can say anything else, we hear the *whomp-whomp-whomp* of helicopter blades above the wind.

"Oh, thank heavens!" Mrs. Sloane-Kinkaid passes the baby to Cassidy, then runs out onto the porch as the helicopter sets down on the lawn. It releases the three fishermen, then lifts right off again to head for the safety of a nearby airport hangar.

The trees are really whipping back and forth now, and the sky is nearly black. Two minutes later, the rain starts, just a few drops at first, and then the heavens open up. Water pours from above, buckets of it streaming down the drive, clattering on the metal roof overhead with a deafening roar, overflowing the gutters, and spilling off the porch eaves.

We watch, hypnotized, and then, through the rain-streaked windows we see the faint outlines of people running across the lawn.

"It's the hikers!" says Mrs. Parker, sounding relieved.

Emma and Madison and Bailey and I all crowd around our mothers as they stumble into the dining room. Soaked to the skin and shivering, they warm themselves by the fire, thanking Mrs. Parker for the hot soup and drinks she offers them.

"I've never seen rain like this in my life!" says Mrs. Hawthorne. "It's coming down sideways out there—and it's cold, too! Isn't it still August?"

"It was last time I checked," says my mother. "You're right, Phoebe—

Heather Vogel Frederick

I've never seen anything like this either. I think Wyoming is on a different planet than Massachusetts."

Headlights flash through the windows as the ranch van lurches over the top of the rise and on down the rain-puddled driveway. It pulls to a stop in front of the dining room, and Sam Parker and the other ranch guests get out and make a run for it, but they, too, are soaked to the skin by the time they reach the shelter of the porch roof.

Mrs. Parker gets busy shuttling soup and hot drinks again as everyone mills around, talking excitedly about the storm.

"Wait a minute," says Mrs. Delaney, scanning the room. "Where's Jess?"

"And Gigi?" I add, suddenly realizing that my grandmother hasn't returned yet either.

The excited buzz dies down. Mrs. Parker circles the room, counting heads.

"Sam, go check the barn," she says to Winky's brother, who grabs a slicker from one of the hooks by the door and ducks outside again.

"Is that *snow*?" says Cassidy, gaping out the window. "No way!"

But it is. I've never seen it snow in August before, that's for sure. My mother's right—Wyoming is definitely on a different planet.

"We get all kinds of crazy weather out here," Bailey's mother tells us.

"All at the same time?" Mrs. Hawthorne replies, shouting to be heard over a loud rumble of thunder. A flash of lightning illuminates the sky.

"Oh man, thundersnow!" says Owen. "Now this we hardly ever get."

The porch door bangs shut and his brother, Sam, reappears. He looks across the room at his mother and shakes his head. She turns pale and runs for the stairs, calling for Mr. Parker. He comes down fresh from the shower and toweling his hair, which is pretty useless since he just heads outside again into the rain and snow to recheck the barn.

"No sign of them," he reports when he returns.

My friends and I all look at one another in horror. The trail riders are missing!

Another flash of lightning illuminates the lawn. In the middle of it stands a lone horse.

"It's Bingo!" Savannah cries.

Winky's horse whinnies wildly and rears up, pawing at the air. No one is in the saddle.

"Oh, my," says Mrs. Parker weakly. She turns to her husband. "John?"

Mr. Parker grabs his raincoat again and strides grimly back outside. We watch as he darts this way and that, trying to corner Bingo. But the storm has made the horse skittish, and he keeps wheeling and backing away. And then, in a flash that accompanies another clap of thunder, we see three more horses gallop across the lawn.

"Vegas, Aurora, and Anthem," Savannah says, her hands cupped around her face as she strains to see through the icy window.

"Boys!" calls Mrs. Parker, her voice tight with worry.

Heather Vogel Frederick

Sam and Owen grab their raincoats too, and charge off after their dad. All three of them are out in the storm now, struggling to corral the spooked horses. I move down the line of windows to where my mother is kneeling on one of the benches and take her hand. She grips mine back tightly.

"Is Gigi going to be okay?" I ask, pressing my lips to her ear so she can hear me above the howling of the wind.

She puts her arm around my shoulders and pulls me close to her. "If anyone can make it through something like this, it's that stubborn mother of mine," she replies, but her words are wobbly and I don't feel comforted at all.

Mr. Parker and his sons manage to rein in three of the horses and get them to the safety of the barn, but Bingo keeps whirling just out of reach. After a while they give up and come back inside. By now, the thundersnow has turned to sleet, and their hair and eyebrows are frosted with slushy ice.

"No sign of anyone," Mr. Parker reports. "And no notes in the saddle bags, either. Looks like we're going to have to form a search party."

"Did Pete say where they were going when they left this morning?" Mrs. Parker asks.

"He mentioned something about Pocket Canyon, but last I heard Winky was pushing for Lonesome Ridge. You know how she is about that place. I'm betting they're up there."

Most of the ranch's guests are what the Parkers call "tenderfeet," like me—inexperienced riders—but a few of the more able horsemen volunteer to go along on the search party with Mr. Parker and Owen and Sam. Mrs. Parker volunteers to go, too, but Mr. Parker says someone needs to stay here and man the fort. Then Savannah steps forward.

"I'd like to go," she says.

Mr. Parker shakes his head. "Absolutely not."

"But I'm an excellent rider," she insists. "Way better than Jess and almost as good as Winky. I won the Silver Spurs award last year at Colonial Academy."

"The answer is no," says Mr. Parker sternly. "It's too dangerous. Wyoming isn't some sheltered Eastern girls' school, and there's no telling what this freak storm might do next."

Senator Sinclair nods gravely. "Mr. Parker knows best, Savannah."

Mrs. Parker crosses the room to where my mother and me and Mrs. Delaney are sitting huddled together. "Try not to worry," she tells us. "Pete's lived here all his life and he knows this country like the back of his hand. He'll have found shelter for everyone."

Mr. Parker nods encouragingly. "Ellen is right, ladies," he says, but with Bingo still neighing wildly just outside the dining hall, their words have a hollow ring to them.

As Winky's father and brothers head out to round up the ranch dogs, Savannah speaks up again. "You should take Lefty along too."

Mr. Parker looks at her blankly.

"You know—Pete's rooster. We've all seen the way he follows Pete around. Maybe he can pick up his trail."

Heather Vogel Frederick

"Roosters aren't like dogs," Mr. Parker replies. "They can't follow a scent."

Savannah shrugs. "Lefty's not exactly an ordinary rooster."

"She's right about that," says Eva Bergson.

Mr. Parker sighs and runs his hand through his wet hair. "Listen, ladies, I appreciate your wanting to help, but just let us take it from here, okay?" He turns to his wife. "We're taking the two-way radio and the GPS. If you don't hear from us in an hour, call the sherriff. We may need more help."

A few minutes later we watch as the search party rides out of the barn. The thunder and lightning seem to be over for now, but the sky is still dark and it's continuing to spit a mixture of rain and snow. Over by the kitchen door, Jess's mother is wiping tears from her face as she talks on the ranch phone, probably to Mr. Delaney. The storm has knocked out the ranch's cell service. Cassidy's mother is standing next to her, patting her on the shoulder.

"There must be something we can do!" says Professor Daniels. "Just sitting here waiting is awful."

Mrs. Parker hesitates, looking at our anxious group. Then she says, "Absolutely," and holds up a hand, ticking off a list of chores on her fingers. "We need to keep the fire going, gather towels and blankets for when the search party and the trail riders return, monitor the two-way radio, keep an eye on the other radio and the TV for weather reports, man the telephone, keep the coffee going, and get dinner started. I still have hungry guests to feed."

We all leap to our feet, relieved to have something to take our minds off whatever might have happened to our friends and family. As I head for the kitchen with Summer and Emma, I look around and realize that somebody's missing. Two somebodies, in fact.

"Hey, where'd Savannah and Cassidy go?"

Mrs. Sloane-Kinkaid scans the room. "They were just here a second ago. Stanley, honey, have you seen Cassidy?"

He shakes his head.

The porch door bangs shut as Cassidy comes barreling through, her short red hair plastered to her head by the rain. She looks around at us all and grins. "I hate it when someone says you can't do something just because you're a girl, don't you? And in *Wyoming* of all places. Sheesh!"

Senator Sinclair gives her a funny look. "What are you talking about?"

"Women got the right to vote here before they did anywhere else in the country," Savannah's mother tells him. "I learned that back at that 'sheltered Eastern girls' school.'"

"Uh-oh," Emma whispers to me. "Cassidy's up to something."

Senator Sinclair must have come to the same conclusion, because his eyes narrow in suspicion. "Where's my daughter?"

Cassidy jerks her thumb toward the door.

"Cassidy Ann, you didn't!" says her mother.

Savannah's father bolts across the room. The rest of us are right on his heels. We reach the windows just in time to see Savannah riding off

Heather Vogel Frederick

on Sheba. Cassidy must have helped her scrounge some rain gear and a powerful flashlight, and there's a bulge in one of her saddlebags.

"We figured Lefty might as well go along to keep her company," says Cassidy.

Sure enough, a tiny head is peeking out from under the saddlebag's flap, only its eyes and beak visible. This might actually be funny if it weren't so serious.

"Cassidy Ann Sloane, I can't believe you helped Savannah do this, after Mr. Parker specifically said not to!" says her mother. "Don't you realize how dangerous it is out there?"

"Wait a minute," says Senator Sinclair. "Aren't you that girl who pulled the stunt with the blue cheese?"

"Don't start, Robert," says Savannah's mother, laying a hand on his arm. "What's done is done, and Savannah was right about one thing. She's an excellent rider. We'll just have to hope for the best."

"Sheba is one of the smartest horses on the ranch," says Mrs. Parker, trying to reassure them. "She won't let your daughter get into trouble."

"I hope you're right, Mrs. Parker," says Senator Sinclair. His face is red, and I can tell he's angry. Worried, too, probably. I know I am, but more about Gigi than Savannah.

Since there's nothing more to see outside, we all scatter to our assigned chores. Stanley Kinkaid and Senator Sinclair and the other remaining male guests are in charge of bringing in firewood, and Cassidy and Madison offer to help them. The kitchen is overflowing with mothers as everyone else crowds in to help Mrs. Parker. Mrs. Sloane-Kinkaid and Mrs. Delaney and most of the Wyoming moms are starting to get dinner ready, while over at the table in the far corner, Mrs. Chadwick is bossing Professor Daniels and Mrs. Bergson around as the three of them set up a command station with the radios, TV, and telephone. The remaining pen pals pair off, Summer and I to pack up the sewing machine and take it back upstairs to Mrs. Parker's sewing room, Emma and Bailey to raid the linen closet for blankets and towels, and Becca and Zoe to set the long tables in the dining room. As Summer and I pass by them, I notice that neither one is making snide remarks now. When something like this happens, who cares about who has the coolest cell phone, or who likes which boy, or whose mom is the bigger embarrassment? All any of us care about right now is getting everyone back safely—Gigi, and Jess, and Winky, and Pete.

We gather in the kitchen again when our chores are finished. It's been half an hour since the search party left and there's still no word. For some reason everybody's talking in whispers, I guess so they can hear the two-way radio and phones. I find my mother, who's keeping herself busy rearranging all the vegetables on a big platter.

"You okay?" I whisper, and she gives me a wobbly smile and nods.

"How about you?" she replies. I shake my head, because I'm not, and she puts her arms around me and pulls me close.

Ten minutes tick by, then fifteen, then twenty. Nothing. The kitchen is tense and quiet, with nothing to do anymore but wait.

Heather Vogel Frederick

Mrs. Parker looks at the clock and chews her lip. "It's been an hour," she says finally. "I guess it's time to call the sherriff."

All of a sudden the two-way radio crackles, startling us all. It's Mr. Parker.

"We found 'em!" he says, his voice jubilant. "Everybody's safe; Savannah too."

A cheer goes up in the kitchen. Mrs. Delaney bursts into tears. So does Poppy Sinclair. The senator puts his arm around her, and my mother turns to me and smiles. "See?" she says. "I told you a little storm was no match for Gigi."

The radio crackles again. "Better get that coffeepot going, because I'm bringing a herd of cold, wet, tired folks home with me," says Mr. Parker. "Oh, and we think Jess may have sprained her ankle. Other than that she's fine, though, and so is everybody else. Over and out."

By the time the search party and the rescued trail riders finally return, the storm has mostly died down, and my mother and Mrs. Delaney and I dash out to meet them. Our friends are right behind us. My mother takes one look at Gigi, who is perched behind Mr. Parker wrapped in a slicker, and starts to cry. This is only the second time I've ever known her to cry, and it gives me a funny feeling.

"I was so worried about you," she sobs, as Mr. Kinkaid helps Gigi down off the horse.

"Silly Lily!" chides Gigi. "I'm a tough old bird."

Mom laughs shakily. "I know that, but you're the only tough old bird I've got." And she hugs my grandmother tight.

Mrs. Parker herds everybody inside by the fire, and the rest of us get busy distributing blankets and towels and pouring hot soup and cocoa and coffee and tea into the riders.

"So what the heck happened out there?" asks Senator Sinclair.

"The storm caused a flash flood in Pocket Canyon," says Pete. "I managed to get everybody to high ground, but then we were stranded so I cut the horses loose. I knew they'd hightail it for home and alert you that something was wrong. After that we just hunkered down to wait it out."

"How did you find them?" Mrs. Parker asks her husband. "I thought you were heading to Lonesome Ridge."

"Well," Mr. Parker replies, "I hate to admit it, but Lefty found 'em."

Everybody starts talking at once, and eventually the story gets told several times. Each time it gets better, especially the part about Lefty.

"You should have seen him working that GPS system," brags Pete, his blue eyes twinkling under his bushy white eyebrows. "I didn't know a one-winged rooster could push buttons that fast."

Everybody laughs, and Mr. Parker turns to Savannah and Mrs. Bergson. "Even if he really used RoosterPS instead of GPS, bringing Lefty along was a good idea," he tells them. "I'm sorry I didn't take your suggestion seriously. And I'm sorry I didn't take you seriously, either, Savannah. You're a fine horsewoman, and your parents can be very proud of you."

Savannah's mother beams at her, but Senator Sinclair is still scowling.

Heather Vogel Frederick

"So what happened with you and Lefty?" Emma begs, wanting more details.

Savannah casts a sidelong glance at her father. "I just went slow and followed the trail we took on Monday. I remember Pete pointing out the cutoff to Pocket Canyon, and I was pretty sure I could find it again. Sheba knew exactly where to turn. And then, when we got closer, Lefty started squawking like crazy."

"Must have heard my sweet dulcet tones over the wind," says Pete in his raspy voice, and we all laugh again.

"We were hollering up a storm ourselves," says Winky. "I'm surprised you didn't hear us all the way back here at the ranch."

"I'm sure we would have found you eventually, once we eliminated Lonesome Ridge as a possibility," says Mr. Parker, ruffling her short dark hair. "But Lefty and Savannah saved us a lot of time. Once she got to Pete and told him we were headed for the ridge, he took off on Sheba and found us, and led us back to the others."

"Now I want you all to go and get out of those wet things," says Mrs. Parker, shooing everyone off to shower and change. "Then come right back so I can take proper care of you."

With our arms around Gigi, my mom and I head for her cabin. Ahead of us, the Sinclairs are walking with Savannah, and Mrs. Delaney and Professor Daniels are helping Jess back to the bunkhouse. She's got her arms draped over their shoulders for support as she hops along on one leg.

After I'm sure Gigi's okay I leave her in her cabin with my mom and head over to the bunkhouse to put something warmer on. I notice someone sitting in the living room and pause in the doorway. It's Jess and her mom. Jess has showered and changed, and her mother is smoothing her hair.

"I think you owe Savannah a thank-you," Mrs. Delaney says. "She took a huge risk tonight, trying to help you and the others."

Jess looks down at the floor. "I know."

"I don't know what happened between you two this spring, but maybe it's time to let bygones be bygones."

Jess lifts a shoulder and her mother sighs. "I need to go grab my sweatshirt," she says. "Wait here until I get back, okay?"

"I'm fine," Jess tells her. "My friends can help me back to the dining room."

"All right, sweetheart." Mrs. Delaney stands up. Turning, she spots me in the shadows. "Oh, look, there's Megan now. You don't mind helping Jess back to the dining hall, do you?"

"No problem," I tell her, and she leans down to give Jess a kiss, then heads back outside.

"Did you hear what she said?" Jess asks.

I nod, crossing to the sofa.

"Do you think she's right?"

"Well," I reply cautiously, "I know you must have a good reason for being mad at Savannah, and I know she's a pain in the neck, but I've been thinking—"

"And?"

Heather Vogel Frederick

"And it kind of reminds me of what happened last year at Walden Pond, with Becca. Remember when she put that picture of my mom in the school newspaper and then lied and blamed it on Emma and Cassidy? And we all almost weren't friends anymore because of it?"

"Yeah."

"Well, I had to decide whether I was going to stay mad at everybody forever, or accept Becca's apology and get over it, you know?"

Jess picks at a hangnail.

"All I'm saying is maybe you should give Savannah another chance. Remember how she helped with Pip? She does have a good side, even though she keeps it pretty well hidden most of the time. What is it that you and Emma call Becca? Maybe Savannah's a *Chadwickius frenemus* too."

"*Sinclairius frenemus?*" says Jess, giving me a half-smile.

"Exactly. The thing is, with that present she gave you for Pip and what she did today, I think she's been trying to say she's sorry, even though she hasn't actually said it, you know?"

Jess nods. "Maybe you're right."

Emma and Bailey and Madison bounce in, and we turn our attention to getting Jess off the sofa and over to the dining room.

"We'd love to have you join us tonight," Mrs. Delaney says to Savannah and her mother. "We're having a joint book club meeting, and even though I know you haven't read the book, I think you'd have fun anyway. Plus, we're going to make fudge."

"We certainly don't want to miss out on that," says Poppy Sinclair.

After dinner, Winky builds us a fire in the bunkhouse fireplace, and Mrs. Parker brings over the ingredients for the fudge, which we cook on the little kitchenette stove. While it's cooling we change into our pajamas and slippers and robes and curl up by the hearth to talk about Jean Webster and her books. Summer's mother brought some paper and stamp pads, and she shows us how to design our own stationery. I look over to see how Savannah's taking all this, but she's sitting quietly by her mother.

"Isn't it interesting," muses Mrs. Bergson, after our discussion winds to a close, "how in *Dear Enemy* the one person that Sallie McBride most disliked in the beginning turned out to be such a good friend in the end?"

Her gaze rests on Jess, who doesn't look up from her craft project.

"Yes, it is funny, isn't it?" agrees Mrs. Chadwick. "You know, Poppy Sinclair and I hated each other on first sight. It's hard to believe now, but it's true."

Mrs. Sinclair nods. "I was from this little town in Georgia, and I thought you were a big phony. Especially when you kept bragging about how your ancestors came over from England and everything." She and Mrs. Chadwick start to giggle.

Poppy Sinclair looks over at Savannah. "You know, honey, this has been really fun tonight. Maybe you and I should start a book club back in Atlanta. I know you're away at school a lot, but we could find time over the breaks and in the summer, I'll bet. We could start off with *Daddy-Long-Legs*, too. I'd forgotten that book until y'all mentioned it

Heather Vogel Frederick

tonight. It was one of my favorites when I was your age."

"Maybe," says Savannah softly.

"It's hard to believe that you're starting high school next month," her mother continues. She turns to Jess. "A lot of that is due to you, Jess. I haven't really thanked you properly for all the help you've given my daughter. Her grades have really improved."

"Not enough to make Daddy happy," mutters Savannah.

"Daddy will come around," says her mother. She looks up at us and smiles. "The senator can be kind of a tough customer."

Sounds a little like someone I know, I think, looking over at my mother.

"How about you, Jess? Will you be heading back to Colonial Academy in September?" asks Professor Daniels.

Jess gives her pen pal's mother a quick glance. "I'm not sure."

"We haven't heard anything yet from the scholarship committee," Mrs. Delaney explains.

A little smile tugs at Mrs. Chadwick's lips. She reaches into her purse, pulls out an envelope, and passes it to Jess.

"What's this?"

"You'll have to open it and see, won't you?" says Mrs. Chadwick.

Frowning, Jess opens pulls out the letter and starts to read:

> Dear Miss Delaney,
>
> Congratulations! We're delighted to inform you that your Colonial Academy Founder's Award has been extended to cover all four years of high school. You have proven

yourself to be a scholar of exceptional promise, as well as an exemplary citizen and member of our educational community. The scholarship committee unanimously agrees that you are just the kind of young woman that our founder, Harriett Witherspoon, would have been proud to have at her school. We look forward to supporting your continued growth, achievement, and success, and we hope to welcome you back to Colonial Academy this fall.

Calliope Chadwick

Scholarship Committee Chair

Jess puts the letter down and gapes at Becca's mother. "It was *you*?" she exclaims. "You're the one who recommended me?"

Mrs. Chadwick nods.

"You're Daddy-Long-Legs!" says Madison.

Mrs. Chadwick laughs. "Well, in a manner of speaking, I suppose I am," she replies. "Though it's hardly the same kind of romantic ending. I much prefer—"

"CALLIOPE!" shrieks Mrs. Sinclair, and we all jump. "Don't give it away! Savannah hasn't read the book yet."

Becca's mother mimes zipping her lips.

"Calliope Chadwick, you rascal!" says Mrs. Hawthorne. "I've been wondering for a while if maybe you had a hand in all this."

Heather Vogel Frederick

Mrs. Delaney is still shaking her head in disbelief. "So were you responsible for Jess and Savannah rooming together too?"

"Busted!" whispers Poppy Sinclair.

Mrs. Chadwick's mouth rearranges itself into a prim line. She flicks a glance at Becca. "I thought it would be good for Savannah," she admits. "It hasn't gone entirely without my notice what Jess's friendship has done for my Becca, along with that of Megan and Emma and Cassidy too, of course. I knew Savannah was having a bit of a, well, struggle with school, and when I called Poppy to suggest it, she thought it sounded like a splendid idea. It wasn't without its rocky moments, of course—"

"The Blue Moon cheese episode certainly was interesting," drawls Mrs. Sinclair.

"—but all's well that ends well."

We're all a little stunned by this round of revelations. All of a sudden I sit up straight as something else occurs to me. "Were you the one who got us those tickets to the White House?"

The prim smile reappears. "Actually, that was Poppy's doing," Mrs. Chadwick replies. "She had the senator pull a few strings."

"If you hadn't called me, though, no strings would have been pulled," says Mrs. Sinclair. "This is no time for false modesty."

"I need some fudge," says Mrs. Sloane-Kinkaid, getting up off the sofa. "This is way too much drama for me."

"And I could use a cup of tea," says Mrs. Hawthorne. "Anybody else want one?"

Talking and laughing, our mothers all head over toward the kitchenette, leaving us to ourselves. I see Savannah and Jess eyeing each other across the living room.

"So Saturday night's the square dance, right?" says Zoe, dragging the conversation back toward her favorite subject, Owen Parker.

"Yep," says Winky.

"What do people wear to a square dance?" Emma asks.

"Oh, you know, the usual stuff," Winky replies.

"Um, most of us have never been to one," I inform her. "They're not exactly big back in Concord, Massachusetts."

"Oh, right. Well, most women wear skirts, but I guess jeans are okay, too, if you didn't bring anything else."

I look over at Summer. "What are you going to wear?"

"Nothing special," she says. "I have this hand-me-down skirt of my sister's. It's better than overalls, at least." She plucks at her denim-covered leg and smiles.

Suddenly I get a flash of inspiration. I know exactly what I can do for Summer in return for the quilt she gave me. Acting really casual, I stand up and stretch, then wander off like I'm heading down the hall to the bathroom. Instead, I sneak out the back, dash across the lawn, and knock on the door to the ranch house.

"Megan!" says Mr. Parker, looking surprised to see me. "I thought you gals were at your book club meeting. Is everything all right?"

"Fine," I tell him. "Can I use your phone? I need to call my dad, and there's still no cell phone service."

"Sure."

I follow him out to the kitchen, coming to an abrupt halt in the doorway. I'd forgotten about Winky's brothers. Sam and Owen are sitting at the table in the far corner, drinking hot chocolate and playing cards. They grin when they see me in my bathrobe and slippers.

"Howdy," they chorus.

"Uh, hi," I say, feeling my face go bright red. "Just need to make a phone call." *And make a complete idiot of myself while I'm at it.*

"Don't mind us!" says Owen.

The Parkers have one of those old-fashioned wall phones with a long cord. I punch in the number for home, then stretch the cord and the receiver around the doorway into the deserted dining hall.

"Megan!" My father sounds surprised to hear my voice. "Is everything all right? Your mother called and told me what happened to Gigi."

"Everything's fine, Dad," I whisper. I want to keep my plan a secret. "But I need you to do me a huge favor." I explain what I want him to do, and he promises to get right on it first thing in the morning.

When I go to hang up the phone, I make sure to stick only my head in the kitchen this time. "Thanks, Mr. Parker."

"No problem," he replies. "See you at breakfast."

I skim back across the lawn to the bunkhouse and duck through the back door. As I pass the bathroom, I hear voices inside. It's Jess and Savannah.

"I'm really, really sorry about Darcy," Savannah is saying.

I stop in my tracks. What does Darcy Hawthorne have to do with anything?

"Honestly, if I'd known you liked him, I wouldn't have asked him to the dance," she continues.

Jess likes Emma's brother? I lean against the wall, trying to absorb this information.

"So why didn't you uninvite him, then, when I asked you to?" Jess replies warily.

There's a long pause. "My stupid pride, I guess. And stubbornness. I should have, I know, but I was worried about feeling embarrassed. I messed up, what can I say?"

It's quiet for a while again, then Savannah adds, "If it makes you feel any better, Darcy's not the least bit interested in me. He just came along out of curiosity."

Jess mumbles something I can't hear, but now everything's starting to make sense. Savannah asked Darcy to the Founder's Day dance, and that's what made Jess so mad at her. How come she never said anything about it, though, I wonder? Do Emma and Cassidy know?

"Actually, I think it's you he likes," Savannah goes on. "He kept looking over and watching you dance with that guy you brought, and he asked me a ton of questions about you."

"Really?" says Jess.

"Uh-huh."

"Why didn't you tell me before?"

Savannah lets out a whoosh of breath. "Would you have believed me?" she asks. "You were barely speaking to me. I know that's no excuse, but still. Plus, I was jealous of you. I've never had anybody like me that way. I don't even have the kind of girlfriends you do."

"What about Peyton Winslow?"

Savannah snorts, "Peyton only sticks around because it means she gets to go on trips to places like Switzerland and our summer cottage and all that stuff. She's not like your book club friends."

A few seconds tick by, then Savannah continues, "You're really lucky, Jess. People like you. You're smart, and funny, and you're always so nice to everybody all the time. Even that little twerp Kevin Mullins! Plus, you have a great family—your parents and your little brothers are awesome. That weekend I spent at your house was the most fun I had all year at Colonial Academy."

"I had fun too," Jess admits. "Well, until the end anyway."

"Look, I'm really, really sorry. I don't know what else to say. I hope you'll forgive me one of these days, and I hope that if you come back to Colonial Academy, we can be friends."

There's a burst of laughter from the bunkhouse living room, and I strain to hear Jess's reply. "Apology accepted," she says finally, the exact same words I said to Becca last year at Walden Pond.

I smile. Good for Jess.

"Pip really misses you, by the way," she adds.

"I miss him, too!" says Savannah, her voice brimming with relief and happiness. I hear the two of them coming my way and dart down the hall. I don't want to be caught eavesdropping.

The next morning dawns bright and clear. The storm has left Gopher Creek Guest Ranch freshly washed and shining in the sun, and it feels as if all the tensions that had been simmering under the surface have been washed away too. Even my mother doesn't seem wound up quite so tight, and I notice that she takes not one but two blueberry muffins from the breakfast buffet.

Today it's our group's turn to borrow the ranch van. First we head for Gopher Hole, where we stop by Mrs. Jacobs's bookstore. Bailey and her mom give us a tour, and then Mrs. Jacobs lets us each pick out a book to take home as a present. I pick one with lots of pictures of Wyoming, so I can show my dad. The mayor's office is next, where Mrs. Winchester gives us each a key to the city. "They're kind of small—I just got them at the hardware store—but we're a small town so maybe that's okay," she says.

Lunch is on Mrs. Williams at the Cup and Saucer Diner. Ellie and Tessa, Summer's older sisters, have been waitressing all summer to help earn money for school, and when they come to take our orders Mrs. Williams pretends to be a really picky customer. She mimics Senator Sinclair's Southern accent and blustery manner, which we all think is hilarious but Summer's sisters don't seem to find that funny. Maybe they think we're rubbing their noses in the fact that we're on vacation and they're not.

Our final stop is Laramie, where we get to tour the college campus with Professor Daniels and meet Madison's dad, and then we do a little shopping in town for souvenirs and stuff. Gigi buys Mom and me both genuine cowboy hats, and we get one for Dad, too, to wear when he's mowing the lawn. Our ride-on mower is probably the closest my father is ever going to get to being a cowboy.

Finally, it's time to head back to the ranch. While everyone else scatters to figure out what they're going to do for tomorrow night's talent show, I go straight to the ranch house.

"This came while you were gone," Mrs. Parker says, handing me the package I hoped would be waiting for me. "Express delivery."

I confide my plan to her, and ask if I can use her sewing machine.

"Of course you can," she says. "What a great idea!"

She sets me up in her little sewing room, and I stay holed up there all afternoon and most of the evening. On Friday morning I even skip the final trail ride. I want Summer's present to be perfect.

"Hey, Summer, do you have a minute?" I ask when she and the other riders troop into the dining room for lunch.

"Sure."

I make her close her eyes, and then I lead her upstairs to the sewing room.

"Where are we going?" she asks.

"You'll see." I turn her so she's facing her present, which is hanging on the back of the door. "Okay, you can open your eyes now."

"Oh my gosh," she says, when she spots it. "Is that for me?"

I nod.

"Megan, it's amazing! I've never seen anything like it!"

The square dance skirt is made of the emerald green silk Gigi brought me from Hong Kong. I patterned it after one of Mrs. Parker's, complete with layers of ruffles and flounces.

"Try it on," I urge.

She ducks into the bathroom and changes quickly, then waltzes back out and stares at herself in the mirror, her eyes shining almost as brightly as my grandmother's diamond earrings.

"It's the most beautiful thing I've ever owned," she says, hugging me. "Thank you!"

"You're welcome," I tell her, feeling a whole lot better about taking her story quilt home with me.

After lunch, everybody scatters to practice for Ranch Idol. Since I'm not planning on performing, I take my sketchpad and sit on the porch by the dining hall and draw the ranch instead. I want to remember it when I get back to Concord.

That night everybody comes over to the bunkhouse to watch a movie, a really terrible version of *Daddy-Long-Legs* with Fred Astaire. It has almost nothing to do with the book, and the only one who likes it is Gigi, because it's a musical and because part of it is set in France.

Saturday we hang out, talking and playing horseshoes all morning while our moms do laundry, and get started on the packing, and a few people drift off for more Ranch Idol practice, including Savannah and Jess, who have something up their sleeve all of a sudden. After lunch, we all go down to the swimming hole for a final dip.

Heather Vogel Frederick

"I love Wyoming!" Cassidy says, floating on her back and looking up at the sky.

"Me too," I echo, and it's true. This has turned out to be an amazing trip.

Dinner that night is fancy, with white tablecloths on the tables, and grilled steaks and baked potatoes and lemon meringue pie for dessert. My mother, who never eats white sugar, has a second helping of that, too.

"Go, Mom!" I tell her when I see her plate, and she grins at me.

The Parker boys clear away all the tables when we're done, and then we help them set up the chairs in rows for the Ranch Idol contest. There's a little platform in front of the fireplace, and a microphone and everything. A guest from Cincinnati kicks things off by playing a polka on his accordion, and then Stanley Kinkaid and Senator Sinclair do a really funny skit called "Who's on First?" Another ranch guest juggles, and Emma and Bailey put on a scene from the play they've been writing, which is set in a graveyard and features a ghost named Deliverance Severance.

I hadn't planned on doing anything, but then Summer runs up from the back of the room and hops onstage. "This is a Megan Wong original," she announces, showing off her new skirt.

The women in the room all crowd closer to take a look.

"What a wonderful idea, Megan," says Mrs. Bergson. "Traditional meets modern."

Summer's mother fingers the embroidery. "This fabric is gorgeous."

"It's vintage," I tell her. "Gigi brought it for me from Hong Kong."

"Pacific Rim is hot this year," says my grandmother, winking at me.

"You know, Megan, you could make a fortune selling these in Laramie and Cheyenne," Professor Daniels tells me. "Seriously—I could put you in touch with a shop or two."

"And I bet I could sell them to our ranch guests," adds Mrs. Parker.

"I'll put in an order for one right now," says the wife of the accordion player from Cincinnati.

"My granddaughter has talent coming out her fingertips," Gigi tells her.

"That's a coincidence, so does my daughter!" says my mother.

I stare at her. My mother actually made a joke! She's actually having fun!

While everybody's exclaiming over Summer's skirt, I run back to the bunkhouse and return with her crazy quilt.

"Let's talk about real talent," I say, holding it up so everyone can see. "Tell everybody the story about your great-great-grandmother's wedding dress, Summer."

She does, and a chorus of happy sighs goes up from the women in the audience when she's done.

After our unplanned act, the show continues with Cassidy and Zoe and Mrs. Chadwick showing off their new roping skills. Mrs. Chadwick and Zoe are pretty pathetic, but Cassidy's not bad at all. She even manages to lasso Sam Parker accidentally, or maybe it was on purpose. Either way, he doesn't seem to mind.

Then Jess and Savannah take the stage. I see Mrs. Chadwick and

Heather Vogel Frederick

Poppy Sinclair smile at each other, and Mrs. Delaney looks happy too.

Savannah steps forward to the microphone and explains about the singing group they're in at school called the MadriGals, and then the two of them start to sing. No instruments or anything, just their voices. I haven't heard Jess sing since sixth grade, when she was Belle in Walden Middle School's production of *Beauty and the Beast*, and she's even better now than she was then. I can't understand a word of the medieval song they've chosen but I don't need to. I just listen to the pure sound of their voices floating up to the dining room rafters, the intertwined notes swooping and swirling like the dragonflies on Summer's emerald silk skirt.

There's a hush when they're done, followed by an explosion of applause.

"How are they going to top that?" Summer whispers to me as Madison joins them onstage with her electric guitar.

But they do. Madison kicks things off with a rollicking solo, and then Jess and Savannah join in, belting out a country duet that brings the whole room to their feet, clapping and stomping to the beat.

The best part of the whole show, though, is the finale. Pete appears wearing a tuxedo and Lefty hops up on stage behind him. He's wearing a tuxedo, too. Well, sort of. It's actually one of those little fake tuxedo bib things that parents sometimes stick on their babies to be funny, only on Lefty, it really is funny.

In this totally serious voice, Pete introduces him as "Lefty the Wonder Rooster," and describes the dramatic canyon rescue, including a wildly embellished version of the GPS tale. All the time, Lefty just bobs around onstage, cocking his head and looking up at Pete as if he's hanging on his every word. When he's done with the tall tale, Pete tells Lefty to sit, which of course he doesn't, and then walks away and tells him to stay, which he doesn't either—mostly because there's a hot dog bun sticking out of Pete's back pocket. While Lefty is busy hopping up trying to snatch it, Pete pretends to get more and more worked up because he won't lie down, beg, roll over, or play dead. By this time we're all falling out of our chairs, and Senator Sinclair is laughing so hard he's crying. The most hilarious part is right at the end, when Pete runs offstage and Lefty chases him. There's nothing funnier than watching a chicken run.

Afterward, everybody gets prizes, including Pete and Lefty, who win a rubber chicken. All the guests love this, and Winky leans over to me and whispers, "They win that thing every week."

And then it's time for the square dance. The men and boys whisk all the chairs away, and Mrs. Parker brings out a bowl of punch while the band gets set up and the rest of us go back to our cabins to change.

"Wow!" says Owen Parker when I reappear in my turquoise *kei pou*. "You look really pretty!"

"Thank you," I reply.

He grins. "Beats the heck out of those pajamas you were wearing the other night. May I have the first dance?"

He takes my hand and swings me out onto the dance floor as the music starts. Over by the windowseat, Zoe Winchester glares at me and grabs for her lip gloss.

Heather Vogel Frederick

I see Pete make a beeline for Gigi. He's already got Eva Bergson on one arm, and he extends his other to my grandmother. "Looks like I've got myself the two prettiest gals in all of Wyoming," he says, as Gigi tucks her hand under his elbow and the three of them join us on the dance floor.

I figured square dancing would be kind of lame, but it actually turns out to be lot of fun. After Owen, I get asked to dance by his brother and then the son of the accordion player from Cincinnati. None of this probably counts, of course, because the boys make the rounds to all the girls eventually, even Cassidy. She's been grumbling all week about dances being stupid and that no way is she going to wear a skirt, but she's wearing one tonight and I saw her earlier dancing with Sam Parker and I didn't hear any complaints out of her then.

After a few more dances, I'm out of breath. As I go to get myself some punch, Cassidy's mom and Chloe do-si-do by me. Chloe is strapped to her mother's chest in one of those little front-pack things, and she's kicking her legs and squealing happily. For a brief flash I find myself wishing I wasn't an only child again. But then I remind myself that no family is perfect.

I look over at Jess, who's sitting with her leg propped up next to her mom. She's probably going back to boarding school this fall, mostly because she wants to make her mom and dad happy. And I look at Cassidy, who's dancing with her stepfather now but who will always miss her real father, and at Summer, radiant in her new skirt, whose real father moved away. Gigi's right, we're all like Summer's crazy quilt, our families made up of a jumble of people and places and experiences, different, maybe, but all of us stitched together by love. Maybe my quilt is different from everybody else's but there's nothing wrong with that. Maybe I won't ever have the same kind of family that my friends have, but then they won't have mine.

They won't have Gigi, that's for sure. I look over at my grandmother, who's more like a grandsister, really, and at my mom, who's finally having fun. The two of them are talking and laughing like two friends, which maybe they are, finally. At least it's a beginning, anyway.

Nope, no family is ever perfect, I think. But maybe mine is okay just the way it is.

Heather Vogel Frederick

"The world is full of happiness, and plenty to go around, if you are only willing to take the kind that comes your way."

—Daddy-Long-Legs

Mother-Daughter Book Club Questions

Thinking back to the first *Mother-Daughter Book Club* and *Much Ado About Anne*, which of the girls do you think has changed the most? Do you have the same favorite character as the first two books, or have you changed your mind?

Have you ever read *Daddy-Long-Legs*, *Dear Enemy*, or *Just Patty*? If you have, did you like them? If not, are you interested in reading them?

Do you know anyone who goes to boarding school? Do you think you would like it, or would you hate to be away from your friends and family like Jess?

Similar to *Daddy-Long-Legs*, in this book all of the girls get pen pals. Have you ever had a pen pal? What did you write to them about? Did you write snail mail letters, or send e-mails? Have you had the chance to meet your pen pal in person?

Emma is terrified of speaking in public. What fears would you like to conquer?

Savannah volunteers at the local animal shelter. Do you, or does anyone you know, volunteer? What organizations would you be interested in helping?

Megan feels like she is stuck in the middle with her mother and grandmother. Have you ever felt like you were trying to please two people at once?

Jess has a roommate at her new school. Have you ever had to share a room?

Emma, Cassidy, Megan, and Becca go on their class trip to Washington D.C., where they see several famous landmarks and museums. Have you ever been to Washington, D.C.? What would you like to see there?

Emma decides to write an editorial to protest the school uniforms. Is there anything you would like to change about your school? Do you think Emma's editorial was the best way to ask for change?

Cassidy gets a new baby sister that she didn't think she wanted, and Megan desperately wants a sibling. Do you have brothers and sisters? Are you the oldest or the youngest? The middle child? Do you get along with them?

If you are an only child, what do you like about it? What don't you like?

Do you ever babysit? Do you like babysitting? What do you like about it, and what don't you like as much? Have you ever had to change a diaper?

Do you like trying new kinds of food? What is the most exotic food you've sampled?

The girls travel to Wyoming to meet their pen pals. What is the farthest you have traveled?

Do you think Cassidy and Savannah were right to not listen to the adults and send Savannah out into the storm to look for the lost riders? What were the reasons the parents didn't want Savannah to go? If you were in a similar situation, what do you think you would have done?

Have you performed in a talent show? If so, what did you do? If you haven't, what do you think your talent would be?

Like Megan with Summer's quilt, have you ever gotten a present you didn't know how to repay? Do you think that it's important to always have a present to give in exchange for a present that you get?

Eventually Jess and Savannah become friends after not getting along. Is there someone that you have given a second chance to that turned out to be a good friend?

Author's Note

"Mothers and daughters, whether of the old school or the new . . . are recommended to read Jean Webster's delightfully sparkling and spontaneous little love story, Daddy-Long-Legs."

—Life *magazine (April 10, 1913)*

These words, written almost a hundred years ago, ring just as true today as when they were first printed. Jean Webster's *Daddy-Long-Legs* was one of those delicious discoveries I made growing up, a book I spotted on a shelf at the library, fell into head over heels, and have loved ever since. Today, one of the especially enjoyable and gratifying aspects of writing the Mother-Daughter Book Club series is getting to highlight treasures like this one, in hopes that readers will want to discover these books for themselves.

And they are! Over the past couple of years I've received a steady stream of enthusiastic e-mails and letters from fans, telling me that reading my stories has piqued their curiosity about Louisa May Alcott's *Little Women* and Lucy Maud Montgomery's *Anne of Green Gables*. Nothing could make me happier, and I hope the same will be true for *Daddy-Long-Legs* and Jean Webster's other wonderful books.

As always, I owe a great many thanks to a great many people who have helped me along the way. Last summer I had the good fortune to visit Vassar College, which was the setting for *Daddy-Long-Legs*, on a research trip. It's one of the loveliest campuses I've ever seen, and with the kind assistance of Dean Rogers in the Archives and Special Collections Library, I spent a most enjoyable day prowling through Jean's letters and scrapbooks and photos and other memorabilia. Alexandra Cooper, my intrepid editor at Simon & Schuster, gamely allowed herself to be coaxed out of the office and onto a train to Poughkeepsie to accompany me, and proved an invaluable research companion.

Thanks are also due to the Grossman family, who generously shared their mountain lake retreat with a panicked author as her deadline drew near. (In my research I was cheered to discover that Jean Webster had generous friends of her own, including ones who lent her their home in the Berkshires, where the peace and quiet enabled her to complete *Daddy-Long-Legs*.)

My agent Barry Goldblatt deserves thanks for always being available for encouragement and wise counsel, as does Helen Quigley and her family for coaching me about all things hockey. My friend Susan Hill Long's first reader advice is insightful and invaluable, and when I need a break from it all, I know I can count on Suz Blackaby and Rosanne Parry for shop talk and laughs at "Lambucks." My sisters Lisa Carper and Stefanie Milligan and soul sisters Patty Leeker, Jonatha Wey, Jane Glasser, Sarah Grossman, and Tricia McNeil never fail to astound me with their unconditional love and friendship. Above all, though, my heart overflows with love and gratitude to my husband, Steve—for everything.

What are

The Mother-Daughter Book Club

girls up to next?

Turn the page for a sneak peek!

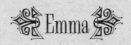 Emma

"'I often think,' said she, 'that there is nothing
so bad as parting with one's friends.
One seems so forlorn without them.'"

—*Pride and Prejudice*

Jess stares at me in disbelief. "What do you mean, you're moving to England?"

"It's just for a year."

Her blue eyes well up with tears. "Just for a year! It might as well be forever!"

I knew that breaking the news to my best friend would be hard, but I didn't know it was going to be *this* hard.

"Wouldn't you want to go, if you were me?" I ask softly.

The thing is, I really want Jess to be happy for me, the way I was for her last year when she got the scholarship to Colonial Academy. Of course I'll be sad to leave Concord, and all of my friends, especially her. But still—*England!*

I only found out about it myself an hour ago, at breakfast. My dad spilled the beans.

"Your mother and I have a surprise for you," he told my brother and me.

"Another one?" I asked. Two weeks ago, he got a call from a publisher in New York. They're going to publish his novel, the one he's been working on for years.

"Yes, another one," he replied. "Your mother and I have been talking, and we know we should probably put the money I'm getting into fixing a few things around the house, or replacing our rattletrap of a car, or beefing up your college funds."

"But ..." my mother prodded.

He smiled at her. "But," he continued, "for once in our lives, we decided to throw caution to the wind and do something a little crazy."

My brother and I exchanged a wary glance.

"It's all your mother's fault," my father said, trying to look disapproving but failing miserably. "She's wanted to go back to England ever since she was a graduate student there."

"We're going to England?" I said eagerly.

"Actually," he replied. "We're moving there."

Our complete and utter shock must have showed on our faces because my mother started to laugh. "It's just for a year," she added.

"*A year?*" my brother repeated. I was too stunned to say anything at all.

I'm still stunned, but happy, too. I try and explain this to Jess. "I know, I know," I tell her. "You should have seen us when my parents told Darcy and me this morning."

Jess, who has been staring down at the floor, looks up at the mention of my brother's name. She's had a crush on him since elementary school.

"Is he excited about going?" she asks, wiping her nose on her sleeve.

I lift a shoulder. "We're both still getting used to the idea, you know?"

Which is kind of stretching the truth. Darcy was furious.

"What am I supposed to tell the football coach?" he'd demanded. "School is starting in a couple of weeks and there's a good chance he's going to pick me to be quarterback this year."

"Tell him the truth," my dad replied. "That an amazing opportunity came up for your family, and that you'll be back in time for your senior year. You can be quarterback then."

Darcy leaned back in his chair and whooshed out his breath. I could tell that moving out of the country was definitely not part of his plan. My brother is a total sports nut. He lives, breathes, eats, and sleeps football, hockey, and baseball. Did they even have those sports in England, I wondered?

"Where are we going to live?" I asked.

"I'm working on that," said my mother. "I found a website that arranges house swaps."

My brother frowned. "What's that?"

"Exactly what it sounds like," my father told him. "You live in someone else's home while they live in yours."

"You mean other people will be using our stuff?" I didn't like the sound of this idea at all. Someone else would be sleeping in my bunk bed, and using the rolltop desk that used to be my grandfather's? Someone else would be looking at the old-fashioned wallpaper with the yellow roses that my mother and I picked out for my room after reading *Anne of Green Gables*?

My mother reached over and patted my shoulder. "Don't worry, honey," she said. "Your dad and I have it all figured out. We'll rent a storage unit for the things we don't want anybody else using while we're gone."

"What about your job?" My mother works at the Concord Public Library.

"They're letting me take a leave of absence."

"A sabbatical," my dad explained.

My mother has not just one but two master's degrees—one in library science, and the other in English literature. Her specialty? Jane Austen. She's a complete Austen nut, which is why my name is Emma and my brother's is Darcy. We're named for a couple of characters in Jane Austen's novels.

"People have been swapping homes successfully for many years," she continued, swinging into full librarian "let me give you all the information" mode. "It's a very practical and economical arrangement. The service I've been working with has found someone they think would be perfect for us."

"Who?" I muttered.

"A professor who's coming here on a teaching exchange at Harvard.

He and his family had a house lined up in Cambridge, but it fell through at the last minute."

"He's a history professor, so Concord would be the perfect spot for him," added my father. "He wants to learn about the American Revolution from our perspective."

He was right about that. Concord, Massachusetts, is practically the birthplace of the American Revolution. One of the first major battles of the war was fought here, and just about every inch of our town oozes history.

"The family's name is Berkeley," my mother told us. "Professor Phillip Berkeley and his wife Sarah. They have two boys, Simon and Tristan."

They had names. They were real people. This was really happening.

It was more than just the thought of strangers living in our house and messing with our stuff that had my head spinning, though. It was the thought of missing out on my freshman year at Alcott High, and leaving Stewart Chadwick, my sort-of boyfriend, behind. If I went to England, the two of us wouldn't be able to work together on the school newspaper the way we'd planned. Plus, there were all my other friends, too, not to mention Pip, the golden retriever puppy I co-owned with my skating teacher. And what about—

"Book club!" I blurted. "What about our mother-daughter book club?"

My mother bit her lip. "That's one piece of the puzzle I haven't figured out yet. I'm sorry, sweetheart. Maybe you can write to them, the way you do with your Wyoming pen pal."

"So this is a done deal?" said my brother. "We don't have a say in it at all?"

My parents were looking worried by now. I guess they'd been expecting us to be all thrilled about their announcement.

"Come on, kids! Where is your sense of adventure?" my father coaxed. "This is a once-in-a-lifetime opportunity! We'll be back here in Concord before you know it."

"A whole year is hardly 'before you know it,'" Darcy said icily. "I vote no." And with that he got up from the table and stalked out of the room.

I sat there feeling uncertain and confused. Was my brother right? Should I boycott the idea too?

My mother slid a piece of paper across the table to me. "The agency e-mailed me a picture of the Berkeleys' house this morning. It's called Ivy Cottage."

Reluctantly, I glanced down at the picture, then drew in my breath sharply. Ivy Cottage looked like something out of a fairy tale. It was small and snug, like our house, but it was made of stone, not wood. The front door was nearly obscured by the thick ivy that clambered up the cottage's exterior, and the windows had little diamond crisscross patterns across them. There was something else, too. "It has a *thatched roof*?"

My father grinned. "How cool is that?"

Pretty cool, I thought. Trying not to show my excitement, I asked casually, "How old is it?"

"They're not exactly sure," my mother replied. "They think it was built sometime during the reign of Queen Elizabeth the First."

"Are you serious?" said Darcy, poking his head around the corner. He must have been listening from the hall. My brother is kind of a history buff.

Sensing they were winning us over, my parents pressed the point.

"The village where the Berkeleys live is supposed to be beautiful," said my mother. "It's on the outskirts of the city of Bath."

"Jane Austen territory," added my father with a wink. "Catnip to your mother."

He took her hand across the breakfast table. My parents hold hands a lot, which isn't so bad at home but can be really embarrassing in public. My dad always says he and Mom are as crazy about each other as they are about books.

He smiled at us. "You'll get to ride a double-decker bus to school, and we plan to do a lot of exploring on the weekends. England, Scotland, maybe a bit of Europe, too."

"What about Melville?" Darcy asked, reaching down to stroke our elderly marmalade-colored cat, who had finished his breakfast long ago and was hoping for some of ours.

"The Berkeleys are willing to look after him for us if we'll look after their parrot," my mother replied.

All of this replays in my head as I'm sitting here beside Jess. I slant a glance in her direction. She's still brooding. I give her blond braid a tug. "The Berkeleys have a parrot," I tell her, hoping this will pique her interest. Jess loves animals. "And check out their house." I take the picture my mother gave me out of my pocket and pass it to her. "It's called Ivy Cottage, and it's almost four hundred years old!"

"Half Moon Farm is nearly that old," Jess grumbles. "Why don't you just move in here with us?"

I sigh. Jess is being stubborn. I hate it when she gets like this.

I know why she's so upset, of course. It's not just because I'm going away. It's because Darcy's going away too. Jess almost didn't go back to Colonial Academy this year because she was so looking forward to being at Alcott High with him. Ultimately, she decided that she might as well continue at her private school, because she'd still get to see Darcy all the time anyway. She practically lives at my house, the way I practically live at hers.

Jess takes the picture from me and stares at it. "You're really going, aren't you?"

I nod. "Uh-huh."

A tear trickles down her cheek. "What am I going to do without you for a whole year?"

"You'll still have Cassidy and Megan and, well, Becca," I remind her. Becca Chadwick is in our book club, but she's not exactly our favorite person in the whole world. "And Frankie and Adele and all your other friends at Colonial. And we can e-mail and IM each other every day."

She gives me a sidelong glance. "Promise?"

"Promise." I bump her shoulder with mine. "What are best friends for?" I look at my watch. "I've got to go. I promised my mom I'd be back in time for lunch. She says we have a ton of stuff to do to get ready. We're leaving in two weeks."

"Have you told Stewart yet?"

"Nope. You were first on the list. Remember? BFBB?"

This earns me a halfhearted smile.

Best friends before boyfriends. Jess and I made a pact this summer. I almost broke it this morning, though. I had to ride right by Stewart's house on my way over here to Half Moon Farm and I was really tempted to stop and tell him first. But I didn't. And now here I am, holding up my end of the bargain, and Jess isn't excited for me at all. Not one bit. I feel like a deflated balloon.

I try not to show my disappointment, though. I know this is hard for her.

"When are you going to tell him?"

"Right now," I reply, strapping on my bike helmet.

"How about the rest of the book club?"

I grin. "They've probably already heard. My mom was on the phone with Cassidy's mom when I left, and you know the mother-daughter book club grapevine."

I give her a quick hug good-bye and head downstairs. Pedaling down Old Bedford Road a few minutes later, though, I start to worry. What if breaking the news to Stewart is even harder than telling Jess?

When I reach his house, I prop my bike against the wrought-iron fence that surrounds his front yard and head for the front door. Becca answers my knock. "Hey, Emma," she says, not sounding too thrilled to see me. But then, she never does. "What's up?"

"Um, is Stewart around?"

It still bugs Becca a little that her brother likes me. She jerks her thumb toward the hallway leading to the kitchen. "He's out in the backyard with Yo-Yo."

"Thanks," I reply. "I'll go around."

I skim back down the front steps and trot around the edge of the house, stopping abruptly when I almost collide with Mrs. Chadwick's bottom—smaller and less alarming than it used to be, thanks to a couple of years' worth of yoga classes, but still not something you'd want to meet in a dark alley, as my father would say. The bottom in question is sticking straight up in the air at the moment because Mrs. Chadwick is bent over, weeding. She spots me and straightens up.

"Hi, Emma!" She wipes her brow, and her gardening glove leaves a broad streak of dirt on her forehead.

I squelch a smile. "Hi, Mrs. Chadwick."

"Big news, huh?"

My heart sinks. She's heard about England, then, which means she's probably told Stewart. I'd hoped to get to him first. "Um—"

"Didn't Becca tell you? I'm going back to school." I must look surprised at this, because she adds, "I'm going to become a landscape designer."

Mrs. Chadwick has been going through a bit of a midlife crisis. At least that's what my parents call it. It started last year when she got a drastic new hairdo and started wearing all these outrageous clothes. Maybe it's over now, because compared to that, a degree in landscape design seems pretty tame.

"Sounds like fun," I tell her.

She nods enthusiastically. "I decided to get a head start, before classes begin. I need the practice, and my garden needs a makeover."

I glance around at the piles of mulch and clippings and dirt mounded everywhere, wondering if this is going to be another of Mrs. Chadwick's misadventures, just like her "whole new me" was last year. It looks like a giant mole has attacked her yard. The outside of the Chadwicks' house is just as formal as the inside, what with the wrought-iron fence and tall, stiff hedges that circle the property and the carefully placed shrubs patrolling the lawn at regular intervals. Not a daffodil is ever out of place; not a rosebush dares drop a petal on the perfectly mown grass. A row of small bushes severely clipped into ornamental shapes used to march around the house's foundation. What they were supposed to be, I'm not sure. I always thought they looked like chicken nuggets. Now, though, they've been uprooted and are lying on the ground like a row of sleeping soldiers.

"Do you know where Stewart is?" I ask.

"He and Yo-Yo are back there somewhere," she replies, waving her trowel vaguely toward the shed. "Would you like some lemonade? I think I'll take a break and make some."

"Thanks," I tell her. "Maybe in a while."

As I cross the lawn, I can hear Stewart talking to his dog. I flatten myself against the shed and peer around the corner, trying to sneak up on the two of them, but the second I poke my nose out Yo-Yo spots me. With a gleeful bark, he hurls himself through the air and a second later I'm lying flat on my back in the grass with his paws planted on my shoulders. I am one of Yo-Yo's favorite people.

"Hey, boy," I say, breathless, squirming to avoid his slobbery dog kisses. "Good to see you, too."

Yo-Yo is a Labradoodle, and the sweetest dog in the entire world next to Pip. He's not very well trained, though.

"Where are your manners?" scolds Stewart. He grabs Yo-Yo's collar and pulls him off me, then reaches out a hand and helps me to my feet.

"Hi," I say, a little breathless. We stand there holding hands, beaming at each other. I suddenly remember my parents at the breakfast table this morning doing the same thing, and that reminds me why I'm here. "I, uh, have something to tell you."

"You won the Nobel Prize for literature."

"Shut up! I'm serious."

"You were named the first teenage poet laureate of the United States."

"Stewart!"

"Sorry," he replies, grinning. Stewart loves to tease me. "What's up?"

"Um, I don't really know how to say this, so I'll just say it. We're moving to England."

Stewart's smile fades. He stares at me, openmouthed. *Uh-oh*, I think. Just like Jess.

"It's only for a year," I add hastily, and explain my parents' plan.

Stewart doesn't take his eyes off me as I talk. He has beautiful eyes, deep gray with a thick fringe of dark lashes. I love to look at them. Right now, though, I'm just relieved to see that he doesn't have the same deer-in-the-headlights look that Jess did when I broke the news to her.

"A whole year, huh?" he says when I'm done talking.

I nod.

"So you won't be going to Alcott High, obviously."

I shake my head.

"And we won't be working on the school newspaper together."

I shake my head again. "Not this year."

I can tell by the way he's chewing the inside of his cheek that he's thinking things over. That's another thing I really like about Stewart. He always thinks things through.

He lets go of my hand and leans down to grab the tennis ball by his feet, then throws it—hard. It soars across the yard and Yo-Yo tears off after it. Stewart turns back to me and before I realize what's happening, he puts his arms around me. And then, just like that, as if he's done it a million times before, he kisses me.

It's a real, proper kiss this time too, not a peck on the cheek or a forehead kiss like before. Maybe it's because he didn't give me any advance warning, but I don't feel awkward at all. All I feel is thrilled.

My heart is pounding like it's trying to leap out of my chest. Stewart's is too, I can feel it. I close my eyes and kiss him back, trying to memorize every single thing about this moment. I don't ever want to forget it as long as I live. I don't want to forget the warm sunlight filtering down on us through the branches of the apple tree overhead, or the distant buzz of a neighbor's lawnmower, or the sound of Yo-Yo's happy bark as he brings the ball back and drops it at our feet. And I especially don't want to forget the way Stewart's lips feel against mine.

It's a perfect first kiss.

There's only one problem.

I'm moving to England.

Read more about girls like you!

The Mother-Daughter
Book Club
by Heather Vogel Frederick

I Wanna Be Your
Shoebox
by Cristina García

The Truth About My
Bat Mitzvah
by Nora Raleigh Baskin

The Teashop Girls
by Laura Schaefer

My So-Called Family
by Courtney Sheinmel

Published by Simon & Schuster Books for Young Readers
KIDS.SimonandSchuster.com